THE VIXEN OF A VISCOUNT

LINDA RAE SANDE

Twisted Teacup
PUBLISHING

ALSO BY LINDA RAE SANDE

The Daughters of the Aristocracy

The Kiss of a Viscount

The Grace of a Duke

The Seduction of an Earl

The Sons of the Aristocracy

Tuesday Nights

The Widowed Countess

My Fair Groom

The Sisters of the Aristocracy

The Story of a Baron

The Passion of a Marquess

The Desire of a Lady

The Brothers of the Aristocracy

The Love of a Rake

The Caress of a Commander

The Epiphany of an Explorer

The Widows of the Aristocracy

The Gossip of an Earl

The Enigma of a Widow

The Secrets of a Viscount

The Widowers of the Aristocracy

The Dream of a Duchess

The Vision of a Viscountess

The Conundrum of a Clerk

The Charity of a Viscount

The Cousins of the Aristocracy

CHAPTER 1

NEWS OF A PRODIGAL SON

A few days before Easter, 1839, Roth House, Park Lane, Mayfair

For the fourth time in the past hour, Vivian blew the strands of her wilting ringlets from the side of her face in a huff.

For the fourth time, Miss Pipkins heard the puff of air and gave her a quelling glance. "Now, Lady Vivian. It's really not ladylike to be blowing air like that," the former governess scolded.

"Oh, I wasn't aware my puffs were loud enough to be heard," Vivian replied, deciding she was in an ornery mood. She had woken up feeling peckish, and despite a cup of chocolate and a hearty breakfast, the late afternoon hour had her feeling the same as she had that morning.

Hungry. Impatient. Annoyed.

Ready to do battle.

She wondered how those who went into battle girded their loins.

Were they truly doing some sort of hardening of their nether region? Or was it a reference to the clothes they wore to cover the space at the top of their thighs? Perhaps it meant gathering up the fabric and securing it so it would allow more freedom of movement.

Her gaze went to the curved crossed swords hanging on the wall above the fireplace mantel. Father had brought them back from India, claiming they were a more civilized weapon of war.

As if war was ever civil.

Charles Wentworth, Earl of Roth, had learned too late there was nothing civil about war. His slow death due to an injury sustained fighting in Greece's war for independence was proof. That he had died much like Lord Byron had perished did not improve the situation.

Worse was the fact that Vivian's much younger brother, Hugh, had inherited the Roth earldom far sooner than he should have. Far sooner than his limited understanding of government and management skills would allow him to oversee. Why, he couldn't even sit at the carver in the dining room without some sort of box beneath his bottom.

Hugh was only six years old, after all.

At least he'd been breeched.

Imagining how she might rearrange her gown in an effort to free her legs, remove the swords from their display hooks, and prepare for battle, Vivian was prevented from completing the mental preparation when she noted her former governess' expression.

"Whatever is going through that imaginative mind of yours, make it stop," Miss Pipkins warned.

Vivian blinked, not quite ready to engage the woman who was now essentially her paid companion.

She was still mentally girding her loins.

"I was only thinking of what an embroidery of my father's swords might look like," she lied. "How I could use that silver thread that Messrs. Harding, Howell, and Company carry in their shop to fill in the blades. A bit of gold metallic thread on the hilts to enhance them," she went on, rather liking how Miss Pipkins actually turned her attention to the crossed swords, her eyes widening in wonder.

"Why that *would* make for an interesting embroidery," the governess said softly. "Yes, I can see it in my mind's eye."

That was the problem with Miss Pipkins. She could see far too much with her mind's eye. She was constantly imagining the worst, and always when it applied to her charge.

At her age of four-and-twenty, Vivian had come to realize her governess would end up spending the rest of her days in the Wentworth household—despite the fact that Vivian lived with her mother and younger brother. She had a lady's maid who could accompany her shopping or on a ride with a gentleman, but for some reason, Miss Pipkins had been kept on in her position.

Feigning indifference to the idea of the crossed swords stitchery, Vivian said, "I've changed my mind." She turned her gaze on the embroidery she'd been working on for over a week.

The never-ending stitchery, she had dubbed it, for she had removed as many stitches as she had put into the cloth in an effort to produce whatever the image was supposed to be. She had long since forgotten the inspiration behind it. She would be forgetting her manners, too, if she didn't have some sort of sustenance and soon.

As if the sustenance gods had heard her prayer, a maid wheeled the teacart into the parlor.

"Milk, sugar, a Dutch biscuit and a slice of cake," Vivian blurted, before the maid had even reached the middle of the parlor. "Sounds like a perfect tea to me," she quickly added. "I can do the honors."

"Yes, my lady," the maid replied at the same time Miss Pipkins scoffed loudly.

"Lady Vivian," she scolded. "You must wait until the tea tray is set before your hostess before you make your selections known."

"Oh, please, Miss Pipkins. It's only the two of us. I think when I am the mistress of my own household, I shall have a tea tray set up all the time. I shouldn't want any of my guests to have to wait one more minute than necessary to enjoy their tea."

"But the water will be cold," Miss Pipkins argued.

"Not in my house," Vivian countered. "I shall have hot water brought up every half-hour. Cakes added as the day goes along. More biscuits after each set of callers departs. No one shall be wanting after they leave my parlor."

The governess looked as if she was about to faint. "Oh, Lady Vivian," she said on an exaggerated sigh. "I fear you will end up a spinster given your daft ideas."

At that moment, Grace, Vivian's mother, entered the parlor, a hand going to her middle. "Oh, thank the gods. I'm starving," she announced as she hurried to the tea cart and helped herself to a lemon biscuit.

Once again, Miss Pipkins looked as if she were about to swoon.

"Vivian, you really must do the honors," Grace said from where she had settled into the upholstered chair opposite of Vivian's. "I have news and it cannot wait for dinner."

The mention of dinner had Vivian's eyes widening. "Good, because tonight I'll be having dinner at Bostwick House. Christina invited me," she said with a good deal of excitement. Dinners at Bostwick House were something she could look forward to at least once a fortnight. Different company meant different conversation. A different house meant she wasn't under Miss Pipkins' continual glare of disapproval.

"Did you let Thompkins know so he could order the coach-and-four?"

Given how long the afternoon had dragged on, Vivian could hardly remember having mentioned it to the Roth House butler. "I did. I depart at six o'clock," she said as she poured her mother a cup of tea, added a dollop of milk and a lump of sugar. She handed it to the middle-aged matron. "Please do share your news," she added as she poured another cup and handed it to Miss Pipkins. The governess didn't add anything to her tea, which only made her seem even more like a sourpuss.

"I've just seen Agnes at the bazaar," Grace said, lowering her voice as if the news wasn't to be heard by Miss Pipkins.

Agnes, Vivian knew, was Countess Weatherstone, she of the first-ball-of-the-Season fame and wife of the Earl of Weatherstone, whose gardens were the envy of every other gardener in London. They were also the breeding grounds of sorts for the aristocracy. Who knew how many heirs had been conceived between the perfectly trimmed hedgerows or in the presence of the statue of Cupid? The lack of light beyond the Japanese lanterns strung up during balls made his gardens the perfect place for illicit *affaires* and stolen kisses.

Grace inhaled and held her breath a moment before she announced, "Viscount Cougham is returning from his Grand Tour."

Vivian's teacup threatened to dislodge itself from its saucer as she looked up from the cake plate and stared at her mother.

"Bash?" she said in a hoarse whisper.

"Oh, I really don't think it's appropriate to refer to him as such any longer, darling," Grace replied. "He must be—"

"Four-and-thirty," Vivian said, settling back into her chair. She knew Sebastian Peele's age because when she'd been twelve, he'd been nearly two-and-twenty and had teased her mercilessly over her unnatural height.

Well, she couldn't help that she was taller than any other woman she knew, or that she was taller than almost all the men in London.

Thank the gods for the Grandby men—they were taller. But they were all older than she was. And they were all married.

Well, Bash was taller, too, but he had never really grown up. Now that he was returning to British shores, Vivian was quite sure he would be racing a coach-and-four at midnight. On some road outside of London. Against some unsuspecting young buck who had no idea how long Bash had held the record for the longest—and fastest—drive.

Vivian was fairly sure Bash had done such outrageous acts to prevent boredom, for right about now, driving a coach-and-four at break-neck speeds at midnight sounded rather exhilarating.

Exciting.

Fun.

How did the other young ladies of the *ton* abide the everyday boredom and strict rules that came with the unfortunate circumstance of being a young, unmarried lady? How did they continually bite their tongues when they wanted nothing more than to lash out and argue with those who saw to their upbringing?

A week ago, she wouldn't have given a second thought to Miss Pipkins' rebukes, but having spent an afternoon in the company of her good friend, Christina Bennett-Jones, on the bench of a phaeton traveling at a good clip along Rotten Row, she was beginning to wonder how she had managed to rein in her growing need to do *something*. To experience excitement. To revel in all of what life in London had to offer.

That her friend's father, George Bennett-Jones, Viscount Bostwick, had been the one to teach Christina how to drive his high-perch phaeton—and then had allowed her to do it— had Vivian wishing the viscount could be her adoptive father. She would never be allowed to drive so much as a gig if Miss Pipkins had anything to say about it.

Nor would her governess ever allow her to gamble, but Christina's father had taught his daughter how to do that, too. "For when you're married and allowed to attend the matrons' card parties," he had said as an excuse.

Christina said it was because he really just wanted someone to practice with to help him prepare for the rare evenings that he spent at his club.

Vivian shook herself from her reverie at the thought of gambling. Bash had been an inveterate gambler before his departure for the Continent. Apparently, he'd been rather good at it, taking in more than he bet and limiting his wagers to stay within his generous allowance.

Perhaps he received a larger allowance because he was an only son.

"Lord Cougham was terribly old for a Grand Tour," Grace remarked. "Why, most young men do that trip when they are newly out of university."

Vivian sipped her tea and held back what she wanted to say—that Bash had taken far longer than usual to complete university. Frequent suspensions and a habit of not attending classes helped in that regard. "Most men also only go on their tour for a year or two," Grace mused. "I believe the viscount has been gone from London for four years."

Four years, two months and twenty-three days, but Vivian wasn't counting.

"Do you suppose he's taken a European to wife?" Grace asked, her eyes rounding.

Vivian blinked, about to say, "Probably at gunpoint." On the one hand, she couldn't imagine a young lady's father allowing such a union, but what if Bash had been caught ruining the poor girl? If Bash *had* married, she wanted to know where to send the sympathy note. Not to him, of course, but to the wife. "I'm sure Lady Weatherstone would have mentioned it if he had," she said.

"Oh, you're right, of course. Agnes has been desperate for grandchildren ever since Cougham was old enough to attend balls."

About to suggest there were probably dozens of them scattered across the European continent, Vivian remembered Miss Pipkins was still in the parlor, and she instead said, "I suppose he'll be in search of a wife at his parents' ball Tuesday night."

The Weatherstone ball would be a crush. Everyone who was anyone in the aristocracy, and some who weren't, would be in attendance. Agnes Weatherstone had sent invitations to those on the fringes of the *ton*—bankers, goldsmiths, wealthy merchants and even some sea captains—as well as the usual Mayfair crowd.

By the time she had attended her fourth ball at the Weatherstone's nearby mansion, with not a suitor in sight, Vivian imagined she might draw the attention of an especially rich merchant or a goldsmith. End up married and living in the lap of luxury with a small dog at her feet and her very own modiste to make her a new wardrobe every Season.

Alas, there were no suitors from among those who had money. The only man who had shown her any interest was a stubbed-nose baron who was at least a foot shorter than her and in desperate need of a dowry to pay off his gambling debt.

Well, and Bash.

But the viscount's interest was only in teasing her. Making fun of her height and the length of her slippers—she had to have long feet in order to keep her balance. Calling her names like 'Vivian Longstocking', because, well, her stockings had to be longer than usual to be tied above her knee. 'Viv the Tall,' because, well, she was tall, but never taller than him. 'Vi of My Eye,' because...

She blinked. She wasn't quite sure *why* he called her that, or why he looked so besotted when he said it.

Perhaps he was meaning to say "sty in my eye."

For a time, she had thought he looked at her like that because he felt sorry for her. She hated him for it, though, and she huffed and puffed and blew her ringlets to oblivion when she remembered his expression.

Remembered what his eyes looked like. How they settled on her, almost as if he was trying to memorize something he could tease her about the next time they met.

"If only you were five years older," he had once said.

She'd been sixteen back then, and he'd been expelled from Cambridge for the second or third time.

"Did you hear me, darling?" Grace asked as she leaned forward.

Vivian's eyes widened when she realized her mother had obviously said something that required a response. So often, the woman could carry on a conversation all by herself. "You think he'll be on the hunt for a wife," Vivian said, pretending she had been listening all along.

Grace settled back in her chair and sighed. "There's no reason why it can't be you," she said.

Vivian stared at the biscuit on her plate and then jerked when her mother's words were finally comprehended. "Oh, I can think of several."

CHAPTER 2

THE PRODIGAL SON
RETURNS

*M*eanwhile, *at Weatherstone Manor, Park Lane, Mayfair*

Agnes Peele, Countess of Weatherstone, stared at the very tall man who was taking up most of the available space in the vestibule of Weatherstone Manor. "Sebastian? Is that you?"

The brown-haired, browned-eyed Viscount Cougham tore his attention away from the butler, his face splitting into a huge grin. "Mother," he said as he approached her.

He bowed, took both her hands to his lips and bestowed kisses on her knuckles. "You haven't changed a bit," he said in a quiet voice, keeping hold of her hands even as he stepped back.

Agnes stared at her son and then blinked. "You look... *well*," she said, as if she expected him to look as if he was on death's door.

"Thank you. I slept like the dead last night. Travel on the sea seems to agree with me," he replied. He looked beyond her to the main hall. "Is Father at home?"

Agnes' gaze swept from the tips of his booted toes to the top of his head. Sebastian's hair appeared suitably combed, and the forelock that usually bounced about on his forehead was missing. "He's in the gardens, darling. How was your

Grand Tour?"

Sebastian straightened and seemed to contemplate his answer before he said, "It was enlightening, Mother. I would recommend it to any young man in search of answers. You did get my letters, I hope?"

Agnes' eyes rounded. "Well, a few, I suppose," she replied, her facial expression suggesting someone had taken possession of her son.

Not that she wanted the original version back, necessarily. This one was very polite. Much calmer. Sedate, even.

Not the hell-bent-for-leather version that had left on his very delayed Grand Tour four years prior. The one who had raced coach-and-fours one-handed in the middle of the night and gambled at his men's club until dawn grayed the skies over London. The one who bet on horse races and was even known to ride one in a steeple chase when its jockey came down with an illness at post time.

The one who would one day be the Earl of Weatherstone, if he didn't perish in one of his many acts of derring-do.

Since there wasn't a spare heir, Sebastian Peele's death would mean his cousin would inherit. Four years ago, Agnes might have wished for such an outcome so that the Weatherstone earldom would be left in good hands.

Now she was beginning to think her son might be suited to the job.

"Are you hungry?" she asked, about to give instructions to the butler to see to a cold collation for a late luncheon.

"I'll be fine until tea time," Sebastian replied. He finally let go of her hands and added, "I'll go to the gardens and inform Father I have returned."

Watching her son make his way toward the back of the house, Agnes almost felt light-headed. Almost felt as if she might faint. Almost did, but managed to blink away the gray at the edges of her vision when Gilbert said, "Lord Cougham seems in good spirits."

Agnes turned to the butler who had been a bastion at the manor house since the turn of the century. "Lord

Cougham seems like a completely different man," she countered.

Gilbert angled his head to one side. "Perhaps he is, my lady."

*M*eanwhile, in the west gardens

"Now this looks new," Sebastian said as he approached the area where he found his aged father digging in a patch of freshly turned earth.

William, Earl of Weatherstone, looked up from where he knelt and let out a hearty guffaw. "Thought it past time I added a garden on the west side. Take advantage of the after-noon sun, when there is some." He did a double-take. "Bash?"

"The one and only, I should hope," Sebastian replied. He held out a hand and helped his father to his feet, wincing when he saw how hunched over the earl had become since he'd last seen him.

"The gossip is true, it seems," Weatherstone said. "My man of business said there hadn't been any charges from the Continent in over a month. Said you were probably on a ship bound for British shores."

Sebastian furrowed a brow. "Other than the bill for a room in Barcelona a fortnight ago, there shouldn't have been any charges from the Continent in the past *two years*," he claimed.

"Found a young widow to live with, did you?" his father asked, his brows waggling.

Once again wincing, Sebastian said, "The monks of St. Bernard are the farthest possible entities from a Merry Widow, Father."

Weatherstone stepped back and stared up at his much taller son. "Monks?" he repeated.

Sebastian nodded. "I found their monastery in the Alps—or rather their dogs found me—and I spent the past two years in their company," he explained. "It was enlightening."

Weatherstone blinked. He blinked again and looked

beyond his son a moment. "Where is Lord Cougham, and what have you done to him?"

Allowing a wan grin, Sebastian sighed. "I left him back in Greece. He was far too joyous with the Greeks. They love their independence. A bit too chuffed by all the attention he received everywhere he went."

"That would be because of all the blunt you left in your wake," Weatherstone murmured.

Sebastian nodded. "Perhaps."

"Did you take vows?" Weatherstone asked, his bushy gray brows rising in delayed astonishment at the news his son had spent two years in a monastery.

Sighing, Sebastian said, "I wanted to, but I did not. The monks understood I had to return to England and do my duty for the Weatherstone earldom," he explained. "We departed on very good terms, though, and I've been told I shall be welcomed there should I ever return."

Weatherstone stared at his son for a very long time before he said, "What happened to you?"

His son gave a start. "What do you mean?"

The earl allowed an audible sigh. "Something had to have happened to have you go to a monastery and live with monks for so long," he claimed. "Did some Italian count threaten you with a sword for having tupped his wife?"

"It was a duke, actually, but that's not the reason," Sebastian replied. "And contrary to what the gossip sheets had me doing with that Spanish opera singer, I never even met her in person."

"What about the Greek princess?"

Sebastian blinked, grimacing a moment before he finally allowed a nod. Apparently the gossip sheets on the Continent had made their way across the Channel. "I assure you, Father, she was *not* a virgin."

"Did you get a child on her?"

Sebastian's eyes rounded. "I did not. I always carried French letters with me."

"But did you use them?" Weatherstone hissed.

"Yes, Father. I might have been a randy fool when I departed for my tour, but I was not foolish whilst on it," Sebastian replied.

Weatherstone seemed to shrink back into his bent body. "So... what happened to drive you to live the life of a monk for... for two years, did you say?"

Nodding, Sebastian said, "A couple of dogs found me."

"Dogs?"

"Rather large dogs. White and brown and quite affectionate. They slobbered incessantly."

Glancing around the gardens as if he expected the dogs to be digging up his newly planted bulbs, Weatherstone arched a brow. "Where are they now?"

"Well, still at the monastery, I should hope. Ready to rescue the next wayward traveler who has underprepared for his trip and finds himself near frozen to death whilst attempting to ski."

"Ski?" Weatherstone repeated.

"It's quite exhilarating," Sebastian said with the first excitement he had shown since returning to Weatherstone Manor. "But... *dangerous* if you're not familiar with the terrain."

"So... dogs found you and...?"

"One carried a small keg of rather wonderful brandy, Father. They make it there at the monastery. Before I could even take more than a single swallow, though, the dogs dragged me by the collar to the monastery. The monks saw to defrosting me, and the rest..." He shrugged. "I am a different man, Father. A better man, I should hope."

Weatherstone stared at his son for a very long time. "No more driving horses at breakneck speeds?" he queried.

Sebastian shook his head.

"No more staying out all night, drinking and—?"

"No more, Father."

Weatherstone blinked. "Well, what will you do with yourself?" he asked in alarm.

"Learn what I must to run the earldom?" Sebastian

suggested. "Court someone? Marry? Sire an heir and a spare? It's past time I saw to doing my duty."

Taking a few steps backwards as if he was having a hard time keeping his balance, the earl stared at his son in astonishment. "Tell me, Bash. Do these monks accept donations?"

Bash grinned and dipped his head. "They do. I left all I could with them before I departed."

"Which means you'll probably need some blunt tonight," Weatherstone hinted.

"If it's all the same, I think I should like to spend this evening here at home. Catch up on my correspondence and such."

Weatherstone stared at his son in quiet contemplation before he finally nodded. "Very well," he replied.

Had anyone given him the slightest of nudges, he would have fallen to the ground in a dead faint.

CHAPTER 3

ANTICIPATING A DINNER GUEST

eanwhile, at Bostwick House, Park Lane, Mayfair
"That's not fair, Father," Christina Bennett-Jones complained when George Bennett-Jones placed his cards on the red felt card table, his hand clearly beating the one she held in that phase of play. They'd been ensconced in a game of two-handed whist since his return from Angelo's.

George smirked. "You'll catch on. And besides, you'll usually have a partner. It's easier with four players," he explained.

"I really wish Vivian's governess would allow her to play," Christina murmured. "Miss Pipkins is so strict, I feel sorry for Vivian."

"I'm sure Miss Pipkins is only doing what she thinks is best," George replied, gathering up the cards to shuffle them. "Until Lady Roth remarries—"

"Oh, I don't think she will."

"—or Lady Vivian marries—"

"That's rather unlikely."

"There's every reason to keep her under Miss Pipkin's protection," he said. He straightened, the cards forgotten, and furrowed a brow. "Why do you think it unlikely she will marry? She's an earl's daughter."

Christina angled her head to one side. "She's a very beautiful girl, and prim and perfectly proper. Has a generous dowry, I hear. She'd be perfect for any aristocrat," she said in a quiet voice.

"But?" her father prompted.

"She must be six feet tall," Christina whispered. "She practically towers over every woman in London and most of the men. I can hear people whispering behind her back," she added on a sigh.

"Oh, that," George said, one hand waving as if it was a trivial matter.

"Oh, *that?*" Christina repeated in dismay.

George cleared his throat and leaned forward. In a lowered voice, he said, "Trust me when I tell you there are men who find Lady Vivian's height a..." He was about to say something related to sexual intercourse and then thought better of it. "Benefit," he managed to say before his face took on a reddish cast. "I would tell you why, but I fear your mother would blister my ears should she find out I said anything."

Christina's eyes rounded as an expression of delight appeared. "Oh, does it having anything to do with marital rela—?"

"Here you are," Elizabeth Bennett-Jones said as she swept into the parlor, her bell skirts barely keeping up as she moved to join her husband and oldest daughter.

George was quick to stand, bestowing a kiss on his wife's cheek at the same time he wrapped an arm around her waist. "So good to see you home early," he said. The personally involved founder of the charities *Finding Work for the Wounded* and *Finding Wives for the Wounded*, Elizabeth spent most days at her office in Oxford Street reviewing applications and meeting with employers.

"So good to be home," she replied, lifting a hand to spear her fingers through his dark hair, smoothing it into place. "You must have had a spirited fencing match this afternoon," she teased.

He rolled his eyes. "With your brother, yes," he replied.

"Did he behave himself?"

George nodded. "He did. Haddon is truly a changed man," he said, referring to Christoper Carlington, Earl of Haddon and heir to the Morganfield marquessate. "If he ever gets out of hand again, I'll see to knocking him on the head."

Elizabeth gave him a quelling glance. "I expect his new wife will see to that. Juliet has Christopher wrapped around her little pinky," she claimed happily.

Juliet Comber Carlington and Elizabeth's brother had met outside of Angelo's fencing academy under unusual circumstances, a situation that had Christopher's foil nearly impaling Juliet and Christopher bumping his head when he fell in a faint to the pavement. The knock on his head cured him of a case of pomposity from which he had suffered for several years.

"Are we having another guest for dinner?" Elizabeth asked, her attention still on her husband.

"I hope so," George replied. "I invited Viscount Hartwell when I met him yesterday. I feel awful for him."

"Is he the new acquaintance you spoke of earlier?" Christina asked, curious about the newly-minted viscount from somewhere up north.

"Indeed. His father died unexpectedly only a fortnight ago, and Richard... uh, Viscount Hartwell... has been seeing to settling the estate in time to join us in Parliament on Tuesday."

"You knew his father?" Christina asked.

"I did. A widower. His wife died giving birth to his heir, and he saw to raising the boy. As far as I know, Hartwell never remarried," George explained.

"But he came to London? For Parliament, certainly?"

"Oh, he did, but only for the Season, and he never brought Richard with him," George replied. "The Hartwell viscountcy has quite a collection of Thoroughbreds, and the son is apparently quite involved in their training."

"Surely this can't be the new viscount's first time in London?" Elizabeth asked.

George allowed a shrug. "If he's been here before, I don't remember meeting him," he said. "I thought since Christina was hosting Lady Vivian for dinner, it would give him a chance to meet some young ladies he could dance with at Weatherstone's ball." His gaze darted to Christina, who lit up at hearing her father's comment.

"Oh, dear. Does Lady Weatherstone know of his arrival in London?" Elizabeth asked.

"An invitation has already been sent to Hartwell House," George assured her. "Thanks to Lord Weatherstone. He's always the first to learn of these things."

"Is Lord Hartwell married?" Christina asked, deciding she had better learn the most important information before sharing the news with Vivian Wentworth. "And most importantly, is he tall?"

George allowed a guffaw. "He is not married, and he is of what I would say is above average height."

Christina's eyes rounded. "Oh, he could be the one for Vivian," she said in a hoarse whisper.

Elizabeth scoffed. "Or for you," she countered.

Blinking, Christina stared at her mother. "Me?"

Laughing, George, said, "Why don't we all meet the young man first before we have him married off to anyone?" he suggested. "And whatever you do, don't mention that he looks exactly like..."

The sound of a throat clearing had the three of them turning to find the butler standing on the parlor threshold. "Elkins?" Elizabeth acknowledged him.

"Lady Vivian has arrived," the butler announced.

Christina's gaze shot to the mantel clock. It was already a few minutes past six. "Show her to my bedchamber," she said as she stood from the card table. "I must change for dinner," she added, turning her attention on her parents. It was only then she noticed her mother was already dressed in her favorite teal dinner gown.

"There's no need to wear anything extra special," Elizabeth said with a wink.

"Every dinner gown you own is special," George said to Christina. "I know because I paid for all of them."

Elizabeth grinned, her attention still on her oldest daughter. "If you see your sister, do mention she's to join us for dinner this evening," she said. Adeline, not quite old enough for a come-out but too old to be eating dinner with her younger brother, would probably welcome an opportunity to eat with adults on this night. "Tell her she can wear her orchid gown."

Christina scoffed. "Not white? You spoil her rotten," she complained before taking her leave of the parlor.

Elizabeth and George exchanged a quick, knowing glance. For her entire life, Christina had always believed Adeline was held in higher regard than she was, probably because she was the baby in the family and took after her mother in appearance.

"Whatever I do, who is it I must not say looks exactly like our guest?" Elizabeth asked, remembering George's interrupted warning.

George blinked. "Oh!" he replied as his eyes rounded. "Do not address him as 'Sir Randolph'," he said with a roll of his eyes. "He looks *exactly* like Reading's oldest did when he was that age," he added with a smirk, referring to the Marquess of Reading's oldest illegitimate son, Sir Randolph Roderick.

Furrowing a brow, Elizabeth said, "Well, that cannot be a bad thing. Sir Randolph is a rather handsome man."

"You needn't remind me, my sweeting," George replied, bussing her first on the forehead before kissing her quite thoroughly. When he finally came up for air, he said, "Damn, but I wish you weren't already dressed for dinner."

"Later, darling," Elizabeth murmured, a smirk replacing the look of surprise she displayed when her husband had finished kissing her. "You can dismiss your valet, and I'll see to undressing you," she added as she placed a hand on his arm. They made their way out of the parlor.

George took her hand in his and kissed the back of it. "I know exactly how I'll reward you," he whispered.

Despite her six-and-forty years, Elizabeth blushed.

CHAPTER 4

A GUEST ARRIVES FOR
DINNER

A few minutes later, in Christina's bedchamber, Bostwick House

"I hope I didn't arrive too early," Vivian said when Christina hurried into her bedchamber, breathless from the quick climb up the stairs. "I *had* to leave Roth House."

"I'm so glad you did," Christina replied as she rose up on tiptoe and kissed Vivian on the cheek. Even with her friend on tiptoe, Vivian had to lean down so her best friend could manage the greeting. "You look quite beautiful in that gown. Is it new?"

Vivian shook her head. "You're a sweetheart to say so, but it's at least a Season out of date. You seem excited about something."

"That's because I have the most wonderful news, Viv. At least, I hope it is good news."

Vivian's eyes rounded. She hadn't seen Christina so excited since her Uncle Christopher's wedding. "I would welcome any news better than what I bring," she said.

Christina frowned as her lady's maid, Perkins, undid the buttons down the back of her day gown. "What's happened?"

"I wish to hear your news first," Vivian said as she sat on the edge of the bed, not exactly sure how she felt about learning that Sebastian Peele was due back in London at any moment. He could already be in town, wreaking havoc.

"You're not our only dinner guest this evening," Christina said, barely able to rein in her enthusiasm. "Viscount Hartwell—the *new* Viscount Hartwell—will be joining us."

Her gaze darting to the gown that Perkins had spread out on the other side of the bed, Vivian seemed to think on the information before she shook her head. "I don't ever recall meeting the *old* Viscount Hartwell," she replied.

"Oh, well, he was older than my father. Widowed. Which means the gentleman who is coming for dinner may be older than us by ten years or more. We'll know for certain in only a moment..."

A knock at the door had all of them turning towards it. "That will be Elkins with the copy of *Debrett's*," Christina said. She had asked the butler to retrieve it from the library before she made her way to her bedchamber.

Given Christina's current state of undress, Vivian hurried to the door and opened it a few inches. She took the thick book from the servant, noting a pasteboard bookmark had been inserted about a third of the way into the tome.

"The page detailing the Hartwell viscountcy has been marked, my lady," Elkins said before he bowed.

"Should I ever have a household of my own, I should like very much to hire you," Vivian said with a wink.

Elkins appeared to blush, mumbled something incoherent, and hurried off.

"Oh, dear. I may have embarrassed your butler," Vivian said as she rushed to the bed and placed the book on its spine. The pages fell open to reveal the ornately printed bookmark and the details of the Hartwells.

Christina tittered. "He probably has a crush on you. Father says there are men who appreciate a taller woman."

"If only they weren't old enough to be my grandfather and weren't in service," Vivian groused. Her attention was on the book, however, and she skimmed the information before saying, "It seems the viscountcy and the family name are the same."

"Not so unusual," Christina replied, pulling the dinner gown over her head. Her maid saw to the few fastenings at the back before moving to the dressing table. Christina settled into the chair, and Perkins began redoing her hair. "This new viscount—"

"Richard," Vivian said as a finger traced the family lineage detailed in the book.

"—has apparently never been in London before."

"Born in Horncastle, Lincolnshire in 1804."

"Five-and-thirty," Christina said with a grin. "So he's not such an old fart. He's come to claim his father's seat in Parliament."

Vivian gave her friend a quelling glance. "He could be fat and bald," she warned before her brows furrowed. "His mother died in 1804. In the childbed, do you suppose?"

Christina winced. "Probably."

"No siblings... goodness, but there are no uncles, no nephews, no... no cousins," she murmured. "Oh, wait. His mother..." She squinted as she attempted to read the tiny type. "Arabella Higgins. Daughter of... ah!" Vivian said with some excitement.

"What?" Christina asked, unable to turn given Perkins had a lock of her hair rolled up in a curling iron. "Who?"

"His mother's father was Maxwell, Earl of Greenley." Her expression soured. "Oh, dear."

Christina attempted to look at Vivian by way of her reflection in the dressing table mirror. "Why do you say it like that?"

"Well, he's dead now, but if he wasn't, Greenley would be in debtors' prison. At least his heir is doing a better job of running the earldom. It's in Staffordshire," Vivian explained.

"Greenley?" Christina repeated. She was sure she didn't know any of the late earl's children—they would have been contemporaries of her mother or father. "Can you name off his children?"

Vivian flipped through a few pages and then used a long forefinger to trace the lineage. "Arabella was the oldest. Then came the heir, Maxwell, followed by Barbara, Marcus, and Beatrice." Vivian's eyes rounded. "Barbara is married to William Slater, the Earl of Bellingham."

"Aren't they Donald Slater's parents?" Christina asked with some excitement.

"Indeed. Donald is nearly as handsome as Alexander Tennison, and he's not even Greek," Vivian said with a grin.

"Isn't he about your age?" Christina hinted.

"True, but Mother would never let me marry him. He's a bastard," Vivian replied on a sigh. She turned the pages of the book back to the Hartwell viscountcy and reviewed the listing.

"But his father has recognized him as his own. Surely that counts for something," Christina argued.

"Not in Mother's book," Vivian murmured as she concentrated on the listing. "Well, Richard Hartwell is it. According to this, he's not married. If he didn't exist, the Hartwell viscountcy would have gone back to the Crown," she added in alarm.

"He'll be desperate for a wife, Viv. For an *heir*," Christina said as a huge grin split her face. "To think, you'll probably be the first young lady of the *ton* he meets!"

Vivian stared at Christina's reflection in her dressing table's mirror. "Don't you mean the second? I expect—"

"You're an earl's daughter. You'll be introduced to him before me," Christina argued.

"Bash has returned to London."

The words were said so quietly, Christina almost missed them. "Bash?" she whispered. Despite what her lady's maid was attempting to do with her hair, Christina turned to stare at Vivian. "You mean... Viscount Cougham?"

"Of course I mean *him*," Vivian replied, her manner suggesting a mix of feelings on the matter. "Mother told me during tea this afternoon."

"Oh, well," Christina whispered, slowly turning so she

once again faced the mirror. "Did you hear from him whilst he was on the Continent? Did you receive any letters from him?"

"Two. Three. Maybe more," Vivian replied, obviously dodging the real reason for the query. "But none in the past two years."

Tempted to turn around again, Christina could not when Perkins rolled up a lock of hair in the hot curling iron. "You don't owe him anything," she murmured.

"I never thought I did," Vivian replied curtly.

"But does he owe *you*?"

Vivian gave a start. "It was only a kiss, Tina," she claimed, doing her best to tamp down the excitement and resulting blush she always experienced when thinking of that night. That kiss had been far more than a kiss, and the very least of what the viscount had done to her. "He probably doesn't even remember. So, no. He owes me nothing."

Christina winced. She had always suspected there had been *something* between the Earl of Weatherstone's heir and the only daughter of the Earl of Roth. For one thing, they made excellent dance partners. Cougham didn't have to bend over nearly in half to reach Vivian. For another, they were opposites when it came to anything and everything—other than their height. Vivian's prim and proper conduct was at complete odds to Cougham's ebullient manner, and yet when he was in her company, he seemed calmer, more settled.

"Do you *want* him to owe you something?"

Vivian gave a start, but then seemed to contemplate her answer for too long before she said, "I don't know. I suppose I would have to become reacquainted with him to determine if I even like him." she said. After a slight pause, she added, "Maybe even change my ways to better match his."

Christina gasped. "What are you saying?"

Shaking her head in dismay, Vivian said, "I am tired of being Miss Prim and Proper. I am tired of doing what is expected of me instead of doing the unexpected. I am tired of spending so much time in the company of a sourpuss of a governess. And I am tired of being taller than every other woman in London."

Blinking, Christina slowly turned from the dressing table to regard her friend with an arched brow. "About damned time," she whispered. "Well, except for the being tall part, of course."

The lady's maid inhaled sharply, as did Vivian, and then all three giggled in unison.

CHAPTER 5

A NEW VISCOUNT IN LONDON

eanwhile, in front of Hartwell House

Standing at the edge of the pavement, Richard Hartwell waved and felt relief when a hansom cab changed direction and headed towards him. He'd been attempting to arrange transportation to Bostwick House for the past quarter hour, afraid he would be more than fashionably late for dinner with one of his few acquaintances in London.

From the time he had arrived in the capital two days prior —by way of a steam bus, a mail coach, and a train—Richard had felt like a duck out of water. London was far larger than he had imagined. Far dirtier. Chillier. Grayer. Not at all as he had thought it might be on the days he had spent back in Lincolnshire whilst his father was in town for the Season.

He now regretted not having made the trip at least once with Abraham Hartwell, the sixth Viscount Hartwell. Using the Hartwell horses as an excuse, Richard claimed he couldn't take the time away from their training. Colts were born during the Season, after all, and he was always determined to be present for each and every new addition to the Hartwell stables.

Thank the gods he had Godfrey looking after this year's new crop of colts. Godfrey was the only groom he trusted with keeping track of the information necessary to register the Thoroughbreds for racing and for seeing to it the newborn draft horses had a lead on them within a day of their birth.

"Where to, sir?" the hansom cab driver asked from his perch.

"Would you know Bostwick House in Mayfair?" Richard asked, wincing when he realized he had forgotten to ask George Bennett-Jones for the address of his home.

The driver gave him a quelling glance. "Of course, sir. Everyone knows where Lady Bostwick lives."

Richard blinked. *Lady Bostwick?* Whatever was she guilty of that so many people knew where she lived?

"On account of her charities, of course," the driver added, apparently noting the gentleman's look of concern.

The less-than-charitable thoughts Richard had been imagining quickly dissipated. "Take me there, please."

"Right away, sir."

Richard stepped into the cab, rather relieved it wasn't as filthy as the hackney he had ridden in earlier that day, when he needed to meet with the Leader of the House of Lords to arrange the transfer of the Hartwell viscountcy to him.

The meeting had happened so quickly—it was obvious he was one of several who had inherited during the past few months—he wasn't prepared for what to do next.

Deciding to explore the area of Westminster near Parliament, he had discovered The Three Bells, a public house which featured food as well as a number of ales and liquors. As had happened the day before, he had been addressed as 'Sir Randolph' no fewer than three times. Deciding he must bear a passing resemblance to the knight or baronet of that name, he merely nodded in response—until a luncheon he hadn't ordered appeared before him.

"Thought you'd want your usual, sir," the server said as he placed a shepherd's pie in front of him.

Richard looked up at the young man and scowled. "As it is my first time in this establishment, how could you possibly know what my 'usual' is?" he asked, irritation evident in his voice.

The servant blinked. He angled his head and blinked again. "You are not... Sir Randolph?" he countered in a quiet voice.

"Lord Hartwell, actually," he replied, wincing when he realized he had never before said his name with the honorific—he was a newly-minted viscount, after all. He turned his attention back to the pie that had been set before him. "Although I might not have ordered this, I think I shall be satisfied with it," he added, hoping the server wouldn't think him a grumpy man. Given the public house's proximity to Parliament and its clean and neat interior, he expected he would wish to return often. The place actually smelled pleasant, which was better than he could say for most of London.

"Very good, sir," the server replied. "Sir Randolph usually drinks a pint of ale with it. Would you care for the same?"

Even as it almost rankled to hear the comment, Richard found he couldn't disagree. "Yes," he replied on a sigh. Before the server could leave his table, he asked, "May I inquire how it is you're familiar with Sir Randolph?"

The server lifted a shoulder. "Why, he's Mrs. Merriweather's older brother."

"Mrs. Merriweather?" Richard prompted.

"Mr. Merriweather's wife."

Richard cleared his throat.

"Oh, Mr. Merriweather is the proprietor of this establishment, sir, and Mrs. Merriweather does the books. For The Three Bells as well as for The Queen of Hearts."

The information did little to enlighten Richard. "And this Sir Randolph?"

"Well, he's known for horses, sir."

Richard jerked at hearing this bit of information. "Randolph Roderick?" he guessed. Although Richard's primary association with horses had to do with racehorses, he did also raise draft horses. Working horses for the viscountcy's farms.

He was sure he'd seen Randolph Roderick's name on paper flyers touting draft horses for sale.

"That would be him, sir. Reading's oldest bastard."

Blinking, Richard racked his brain for a title for the Roderick name. "As in the Marquess of Reading?"

"That would be him, sir."

"And Mrs. Merriweather is the marquess'... daughter?"

The servant nodded. "She is. One of only two, poor things. All those brothers." He rolled his eyes. "The other daughter is legitimate, though," he added, leaning down to lower his voice. "And much younger than Mrs. Merriweather."

Richard considered everything the servant had said and gave him a nod. "A pint of ale," he said, before turning his attention to his pie.

Lost in thought, he had barely noticed how tasty the shepherd's pie had been.

*P*ulled from his reverie when the hansom cab stuttered to a halt, Richard glanced out the window. His gaze immediately caught the inquisitive stares of two young ladies who sat beyond one of the windows of the townhouse to his left, nearby gaslight casting their faces in a soft glow.

The brunette one looked much like any of the girls who lived in Horncastle. He was struck dumb by the auburn-haired young lady, though. An aura of delight seemed to surround her visage, her expression warm and welcoming.

Or it could have just been the way the arc of light from the gas lamp in front of the house reflected on the window pane. Richard gave a shake of his head and then nearly chuckled when he noticed how their heads turned left and right, as if they had realized they'd been caught staring and were pretending to simply watch the traffic.

The cab door opened, and Richard stepped down. "Tell me, sir. Will finding a cab later this evening be difficult?"

"In Park Lane, sir? Hardly," the driver replied as he

accepted his fare. "But if you should find it difficult, the house from where you got on board is only about a half mile north of here."

Richard's eyes rounded at hearing this bit of news. "I appreciate the information," he said, not that he would have walked to Bostwick House. A quick glance at his pocket watch had him wincing.

He was late.

CHAPTER 6

ANOTHER DINNER GUEST ARRIVES

*M*eanwhile, in Bostwick House

"He doesn't look old," Vivian murmured.

"He's not fat," Christina whispered.

"As for bald..." She waited with baited breath and then huffed when he disappeared from view.

The visitor had reached the front door of Bostwick House.

Christina giggled. "He is rather handsome," she said as she stood and shook out her skirts. "Rather conservative in his manner of dress."

Vivian did the same. The two had been on the settee at the front salon's window, perched on their knees as they waited for that night's other dinner guest to arrive. "That will change once he hires a tailor here in London," she replied. "He actually looks quite familiar."

"Indeed. He looks like Lord Reading's oldest son," Christina agreed.

"Sir Randolph," Vivian whispered in agreement.

"We should be the first to greet him," Christina suggested. "Escort him up to the parlor." Even as she said it, she could hear Elkins welcoming the viscount in the vestibule.

"Agreed," Vivian said. "Time to be bold," she whispered

just before she hurried out of the salon, Christina on her heels.

The two stood side-by-side as Elkins was about to lead the gentleman up the stairs.

"How do you do, sir?" Vivian asked, surprising Christina. "I am Lady Vivian Wentworth, and this is Miss Christina Bennett-Jones. Welcome to Bostwick House."

Viscount Hartwell immediately bowed and then watched as the two young ladies who stood before him dipped their curtsies in unison. He reached for their hands and brushed his lips over the backs of their white silk gloves. "Thank you. It's very good to meet you. I am... Hartwell," he replied, not sure if he had the introduction quite right. He'd never met two young women at the same time, nor did Lady Vivian appear old enough to be the lady of the house. She did appear to be his exact height, however, for he found he didn't need to look down to address her.

As for the shorter one—she of the auburn hair and aura of delight—he found her quite fetching. That is until recognition had her eyes rounding in wonder.

"For a moment, I thought you looked like—"

"Sir Randolph?" Richard guessed, grimacing when he realized he had interrupted her. "Apologies."

Vivian waggled a brow. "Which can never be a bad thing, since he *is* one of the most handsome men in all of London," she claimed. "All the Rodericks are, I suppose. I hope you've had a pleasant trip?" she added as she held out her hand toward the stairs. Elkins had stepped back, apparently deciding his services would no longer be required. "I understand you are new to town?"

"I am," he replied, rather startled by Vivian's words. On the one hand, he felt a sense of elation at learning he was handsome by these young lady's standards, but on the other, he was shocked at hearing the taller woman's assessment delivered so boldly.

"The parlor is upstairs," Christina said, trying hard to hide her surprise at Vivian's behavior as well as the shock she had felt at seeing just how much Lord Hartwell looked like Sir Randolph Roderick. The two could have been twins.

Understanding he was to be positioned in the middle of the two young women as they made their way up, Richard held out both arms and raised a brow when gloved hands landed on his forearms. "Although I cannot recommend travel by coach, I was quite happy with the train," he said in answer to Vivian's query.

"Travel by rail is so much more civilized than by stage-coach," Vivian agreed, even though she had never been on a train. "Why, my last trip in a coach, it was so crowded, I was practically seated on a strange man's lap."

"Have you suitable accommodations, my lord?" Christina asked, attempting to give Vivian a quelling glance without the viscount noticing. She had nearly tripped on the stairs, she was so shocked by Vivian's claim.

"Very. My father... my *late* father let a townhouse here in the capital many years ago. It's not far from here."

"We're so sorry to hear of your loss, my lord," Christina said. "My father mentioned it this afternoon when he told my mother and me you would be joining us this evening."

"Thank you, Miss Bennett-Jones," Richard replied. "His death was a bit of a surprise," he added, his attention turning once again to the younger woman. He found her appearance most pleasing and her manner more in keeping with what would be expected of a daughter of the *ton*.

"Is the Hartwell townhouse in Park Lane?" Vivian asked when they turned on the landing to climb the next set of stairs.

Richard thought the question odd, but perhaps an address in Park Lane was to be touted. "Indeed. I discovered I could have walked if I'd been unable to hail a cab."

"Had I known, I could have dispatched our coach to come for you," Christina said, deciding she rather liked the gentleman. He was as nervous as she was, and he wasn't bald.

"You are the lady of the house?" he asked.

Christina and Vivian both tittered. "Viscount Bostwick is

my father," Christina explained. "Lady Vivian is my very best friend. The lady of the house—"

"There you two are," Elizabeth said from the top of the stairs. "I see you've already met our dinner guest. Welcome, Lord Hartwell."

"Is *she*," Christina finished in a whisper as they reached the top of the stairs. "Lady Bostwick, may I present Lord Hartwell?"

Richard bowed before Elizabeth and took her hand in his. "It's a pleasure to meet you, my lady," he said before taking her hand to his lips.

Elizabeth dipped a curtsy. "And you, Lord Hartwell. You must be exhausted after your travels," she said as she took over escorting the viscount into the parlor.

"I admit the day before yesterday was a very long day," Richard replied. His eyes brightened upon seeing George, who set aside that day's issue of *The Times* before he stood to greet their guest.

"Hartwell. So good to see you again," George said as he held out a hand. He glanced behind the viscount and arched a brow when he saw Vivian and Christina standing arm-in-arm on the threshold. "I take it you were greeted properly upon your arrival?" he teased.

Richard chuckled. "I was, and I haven't been in the company of this many beautiful young ladies in my entire life," he claimed.

George grinned as he showed him to a chair. A footman hurried up with a tray of cups of coffee and a bowl of nuts. Richard helped himself to a coffee, noting the ladies were already seated with theirs, the two youngest blushing upon hearing his words.

"I take it all went well at Parliament today?" George asked.

"It did," Richard replied. "Other than the odd looks I kept receiving from people. It seems I am the long lost twin of a one Sir Randolph," he added with a roll of his eyes.

"Randolph Roderick," George agreed. "Reading's oldest. I

thought the same when I first met you," he admitted. "But it's nothing to be concerned about. Sir Randolph is an honorable man, and well known for his knowledge of horses. Comes by it honestly, with hard work in the Reading stables west of town and as a consultant at Tattersall's," he explained, referring to the auction house that specialized in selling the beasts.

"Oldest, but not the heir?" Richard countered, remembering some of what had been said downstairs.

George shook his head. "He and apparently several other half-brothers and one sister are illegitimate. Reading's marchioness has seen to bestowing him with two more sons as well as a daughter, though, so the Reading marquessate will continue unfettered."

"Unlike the Hartwell viscountcy," Richard murmured.

"Pardon?" George replied.

Richard dared a glance at the women in the room, heartened to see that they were holding their own conversation. "I am five-and-thirty," he said in a quiet voice. "Given my father has no brothers, and I have no brothers, I must find a wife and sire an heir before long."

George gave a quick shake of his head. "You have time," he said. "One only need remember Torrington didn't marry until he was six-and-forty to know that a title can be secured later in life."

"I have no intention of waiting *that* long," Richard said. "In fact, I intend to take a wife during this Season," he said, his attention going briefly to Christina.

"Well, you've come to the right place," George said, referring to London. "This next Tuesday, Lord Weatherstone's ball will feature all the new young ladies of the *ton* as well as several who are yet to accept offers." He turned his attention to Vivian. "Such as Lady Vivian. She is an earl's daughter."

Richard's gaze briefly darted to the dark-haired young woman before he frowned. "Does her father know she is *fast*?"

George blinked. "Fast?" he repeated. "Lady Vivian is

hardly fast. She is the most proper young lady in all of London."

It was Richard's turn to blink. "Most proper?" he repeated. "I hardly think so, Bostwick, unless all the other young ladies are hoydens."

Before George could respond, the butler appeared on the parlor threshold and announced dinner.

George hurried to offer his arm to his wife while Richard offered his to Vivian. Although Christina hung back—she was the lowest in rank—Richard offered his other arm.

"I shouldn't think you should go unescorted," Richard said at the same moment Adeline Bennett-Jones appeared on the threshold.

"Apologies for my tardiness," Christina's only sister said as she dipped a curtsy and joined Christina.

"It's very kind of you to offer, my lord," Christina said as Adeline hooked her arm into hers. "May I present my sister, Adeline?"

The Bostwicks paused beyond the parlor to allow the last-minute introduction as Richard passed his lips over the back of Adeline's gloved hand. Her eyes had widened, though, as if in recognition.

"Lord Hartwell is new to town. He'll be joining Father in Parliament this Season," Christina quickly explained, hoping Adeline wouldn't make a comment about his likeness to Sir Randolph.

"It's very good to meet you, Miss Adeline," Richard murmured. "And no, I have not yet met Sir Randolph although I do know of him."

Adeline giggled. "You two could play tricks on your acquaintances," she said in a hushed voice.

"Adeline," Christina scolded softly.

"Ah, but I do believe you have given me an idea," Richard replied, his eyes twinkling with delight.

"If you are in need of a co-conspirator, I shall be more than willing to help in that regard," Vivian offered, her brows waggling.

Christina blinked at hearing Vivian's comment, but before she could reply, Richard was in motion, following the Bostwicks down the stairs and to the dining room.

Footmen saw to the chairs for the younger ladies while George seated Elizabeth at one end of the table. He proceeded to the carver and surveyed the table. "If my boys were in town, we would have a more equitable arrangement."

"Are they in university?" Richard asked, settling himself into the chair opposite Vivian. Christina sat next to her, and Adeline was next to him. A quick glance in Elizabeth's direction, and he noted she was already directing footmen in the delivery of the first course and the wine.

"David is at Cambridge," George replied. "Daniel has another year at Eton."

"Or two," Vivian said with a smirk. When Richard directed a questioning glance at her, she added, "He's well known for his *naughty* behavior."

She jerked when Christina's foot hit her shin.

"Which he now knows better than to display," Elizabeth said, attempting to keep her voice sounding sweet.

Richard turned his attention on George, as if he expected him to set the record straight.

"Lady Vivian has the right of it," George said.

"George!" Elizabeth said in protest, just as bowls of soup were set in front of everyone.

"Second sons do have a tendency to test their betters," George went on.

"Apparently some first sons do as well," Richard said before tasting the soup. "I am hearing the most interesting stories whilst learning my way around Westminster."

"Oh, no doubt," George replied, curious as to which heirs the man referred. "Have you already found a favorite haunt?"

Richard considered the query a moment. "I had a luncheon and an interesting conversation with a server at The Three Bells earlier today."

"Ah, it's a popular public house," George commented.

"Owned by one Mark Merriweather. He's actually the Earl of Middleton's younger son."

"But he owns a business and... labors?" Richard asked. The idea of an earl's son employed in trade was new to him.

"Indeed. Once Middleton's heir married and started his nursery, Mark was determined to work for his living."

"Isn't that unusual?" Richard asked, his brows furrowed in wonder.

"It is for an earl's son. Given you're a horseman, you'll no doubt come across Alistair Comber. He's Aimsley's second-born. Runs Harrington's stables—he's married to Harrington's daughter—and is a consultant at Tattersall's."

"I've met him on the racing circuit," Richard commented. "His wife, as well." After a pause, he added, "Tell me, Bost-wick. Have you met this Mark Merriweather's wife?"

George exchanged a quick glance with Elizabeth. "Once, at a ball," he said. "I see her occasionally, when she is trav-eling from her office in Stafford Street to The Three Bells."

"Office?" The server at The Three Bells hadn't mentioned an office.

Elizabeth cleared her throat and said, "Rachel Merri-weather is an accountant for one of the gambling concerns in Mayfair as well as for her husband's business. She's quite accomplished." She didn't add that The Queen of Hearts was actually owned by Rachel's mother, Violet Higgins, better known throughout Mayfair as the Queen of Hearts. Unlike most, Elizabeth was fairly sure she could recognize Violet when she wasn't dressed in her huge white wig and Georgian-era style gowns.

The two Bostwick daughters inhaled softly at hearing their mother's proclamation and then quickly covered their mouths with their napkins.

Vivian leaned forward and said in a hushed voice meant for Lord Hartwell, "She's actually Lord Reading's oldest daughter. And illegitimate, like several of her brothers."

Richard struggled to suppress a wince, not at all comfort-able with Lady Vivian's obvious attempt at spreading gossip.

"A marquess, is he not?" he asked, directing his query in George's direction. "I believe I have seen him at various horse races."

"Indeed," George replied. "He has always had an impressive stables, and I happened to have met his marchioness many years before he married her."

Four pairs of female eyes turned to stare at him.

George realized how his claim sounded and quickly waved a hand. "Upon her father's death, Constance Fitzwilliam took over the care of Fair Downs in Sussex, a property adjacent to my own. Her duties included overseeing the horses, two of which had been Derby contenders. Even before her father's death, she, uh, *arranged*, rather surreptitiously, for one of my stallions and one of her mares to meet, and a winning colt was born from the union," he explained. "Mr. Tuttlebaum. A few years later, and with my permission, came Mr. Wiggins."

Elizabeth inhaled. "You never told me about that," she murmured.

Lifting a shoulder as if it was of no consequence, George said, "I was rather glad to learn someone was paying mind to my horses," he replied. "I certainly wasn't there to do so, and she saw something in Bounder that my grooms didn't, so I couldn't find fault with what she did."

"She stole your stud," Richard said in alarm.

"Hardly," George replied. "She merely borrowed him. He was returned unharmed, and I was presented with a rather generous bank draft three years later."

"He really was a winner," Christina murmured in awe.

George nodded. "As were colts from those two horses," he said proudly. "And without Miss Fitzwilliam's intervention, I never would have known."

"But did *you* profit? Other than the stud fee you were finally paid?" Richard asked, obviously concerned.

Grinning broadly, George said, "If you're asking if I had the winning bet in any races, then, yes, I did. Several times. Which meant I could bestow my lovely wife with an entire parure made from sapphires and a few additional pieces to match all her ballgowns."

The young ladies all turned their attention to Elizabeth, who blushed prettily and held out an arm to display a bracelet made entirely of sapphires and silver. "I never knew," she whispered.

"Gypsum mines are not as lucrative as coal mines, my sweeting," George said quietly. "Or I would have given you the world."

CHAPTER 7

A VISCOUNT ENGAGES IN
QUIET CONTEMPLATION

A moment later
Richard watched the interplay between his hosts and experienced the oddest of sensations. Here was a man who had been generous with his horse and had apparently kept the information of the resulting largesse to himself all these years—much to the delight of his viscountess. From the look on her face, Richard was fairly sure his host would directly benefit later that evening.

His gaze darted to Lady Vivian, whom he had already decided was far too bold in her opinions for his liking. A quick look at Miss Christina, who had finished her soup and seemed lost in thought, had him thinking he might wish to spend more time in her company. Miss Adeline, probably too young to have made her come-out, displayed a blush so bright, her orchid gown seemed to take on a pinkish cast.

"Will all of you be at the ball on Tuesday night?" Richard asked.

Affirmative nods met his query, but it was Lady Vivian who answered. "Lord Weatherstone's balls are not to be missed, my lord," she said. "And now that his son, Lord Cougham, is back from the Continent, I should think the ball will be far more festive. You will dance with all of us," she added, not making it a question.

Richard visibly swallowed. "If I can remember how," he replied with a nervous grin. "I should be happy to help fill your dance cards." He made sure his attention was on Christina when he finished the comment, heartened to see her enthusiastic nod of agreement.

He leaned back as the soup bowls were removed and the next course was set before him. "I do hope you didn't go to extra trouble on my account for this dinner," he said to Elizabeth.

"Not at all. George knows I'm always happy to host, and Vivian is a frequent guest, especially since her father's death. In fact, I should have included your mother this evening," Elizabeth said as she directed her gaze on Vivian.

"Mother has been forgoing dinners in favor of eating more cakes at tea time," Vivian said with a smirk. "And my brother isn't yet old enough to eat with us in the dining room, so I really appreciate being welcomed at your table, my lady."

Richard furrowed a brow, thinking the young woman's comment was the first instance of her showing any kind of humility. Any sort of graciousness.

Perhaps she was merely nervous around new acquaintances. Nervous enough to make inappropriate comments.

"I do have to wonder what dinner is like at the Weatherstone mansion this evening," Vivian said then. "What with Lord Cougham's return to London." She angled her head in Richard's direction. "He's such a scoundrel. Have you heard of the Four-in-Hand Club?"

Having just taken a bite of a lobster cake, Richard was forced to swallow and clear his throat before he answered. "I have, of course, although I never indulged in their reckless behavior."

"Well, Bash certainly has," Vivian remarked. "I believe he still holds the speed record. Probably still holds the record for most losses whilst gambling—"

"And yet he never lost more than he could afford," George quickly put in.

Vivian inhaled softly and returned her attention to her lobster cake, a blush casting her face in a pink glow.

"Given his age, I rather imagine Lord Cougham will look to take a wife during the Season," Elizabeth said, attempting to lighten the suddenly uncomfortable atmosphere. "Will you as well, Lord Hartwell?"

Richard exchanged quick glances with George. "Once I'm better established here in town, I think I shall endeavor to consider eligible young ladies," he hedged. He thought better of asking who those young ladies might be, fearing Lady Vivian might volunteer herself. He couldn't decide if she was angling for the position or if she was behaving as she was to ensure she wouldn't be considered.

"Then we must be sure you're invited to all the entertainments," Christina said with some excitement. "Mother?"

Elizabeth dimpled. "I will see to it, of course," she assured those at the table, at the same moment she waved for the footmen to see to the next course. "Once my mother knows, though, all of the *ton* will know," she added, referring to Adeline Carlington, Marchioness of Morganfield.

"Am I to understand your father is the Marquess of Morganfield?" Richard asked, remembering some of what his host had told him before inviting him to dinner.

"He is," Elizabeth replied. "My brother is Christopher, Earl of Haddon. He's finally taken a wife, so you needn't be concerned with having to compete with *him* for a lady's attention."

"Not that there were many of those," Vivian said under her breath.

"Vivian," Christina hissed, shocked by her friend's words. "It's true that Uncle Christopher wasn't behaving as himself these past few years, but he's back to the way he was, and it's all because of Lady Juliet. I mean, Lady Haddon," she quickly amended.

"And a bump on his head," Vivian said, her eyes rounding at seeing the dinner set before them. "Three hours ago, I could have eaten all of this, I was so hungry."

Christina's eyes rounded, but she wasn't about to ask what had happened three hours ago. "Will David come home for the start of the Season?" she asked, her query directed to her father.

"He will not," George replied. "Your brother is determined to finish his studies before he heads for the Continent. I told him he should do his Grand Tour whilst he was young enough to enjoy it. He's especially looking forward to a tour of the Kingdom of the Two Sicilies."

Christina sighed. "He'll get to meet all of grandmother's family long before I ever do." When she noted Viscount Hartwell's expression of curiosity, she added, "The Marchioness of Morganfield is from Italy. My grandfather met and married her when he was on his Grand Tour."

"So romantic," Vivian said dramatically, a hand going to her heart before she giggled.

"Was it, Mother?" Adeline asked, managing to keep from laughing at Vivian's antics. "Romantic?"

Elizabeth regarded her youngest daughter with a wistful expression. "According to your grandmother, your grandfather fell in love with her when he was standing near one of the fountains. She splashed water on him because she thought he looked entirely too serious."

Christina struggled to withhold a giggle. "That's not what *he* said." Noting how Viscount Hartwell was staring at her, she quickly sobered. "Although he did mention the fountain."

"I understand Italy has become the favorite place for newlyweds to go on their wedding trips," Richard said, his attention turning back to George.

"Apparently so. One of our fellow viscounts—Torrington's heir—just returned with his bride. He was very impressed by all the art and the fine weather. He was smart to go during the winter months. It's much cooler in Rome and on Sicily."

Richard seemed to consider his comment for a time. "I suppose my plan to wed at the end of the Season may not be a wise one if I'm to take a bride to Rome shortly thereafter."

"You can always wait and take your trip after the Little

Season," Elizabeth suggested. "I hear travel can be rather trying on newlyweds."

"I would insist on taking my wedding trip immediately after the vows," Vivian announced. "No matter the heat in Italy or Greece."

"Greece?" Christina repeated, stunned to hear her friend's comment.

"I expect we shall visit both countries, since I will insist on it," Vivian said with glee.

Given she was sitting next to her best friend, Christina couldn't manage to direct a glower at Vivian and not be noticed by the dinner guest who sat across from them. She did notice him blinking as his head jerked back slightly. He was obviously as shocked by Vivian's boast as she was, which had her deciding a giggle was necessary.

Christina giggled. "Oh, Viv. You're such a tease. Poor Lord Hartwell will believe everything you said if you're not careful," she claimed, waving a hand as if she was swatting a fly.

When Vivian was about to offer a rebuttal, Christina kicked the side of her leg while maintaining a grin. She was relieved to see her mother had already ordered the next course be served. Leaning forward, she said in a quiet voice, "Lady Vivian is merely nervous at having met a new acquaintance."

Richard's eyes darted to Vivian before he allowed a nod. "As am I."

"Oh, you needn't be, my lord," Christina assured him. "We don't bite."

"At least, she doesn't," Vivian put in, her lashes fluttering.

Adeline, quiet up until this point, inhaled sharply and held her napkin to her mouth in an attempt to suppress the rest of what was about to come out.

George was quick to take over the conversation. "I think you'll find Tuesday's session of Parliament rather sedate. Our speaker is well aware there is an important ball to attend and will see to it we are dismissed in time for us to return to our homes to change clothes."

"I was surprised to have received an invitation to Lord Weatherstone's ball," Richard remarked. "I suppose I have you to thank for that?"

George nodded to the other end of the table. "Actually, my lovely wife saw to it," he replied.

Richard turned his gaze on the viscountess. "Much obliged, my lady," he said with a nod.

"You're welcome, Lord Hartwell. Of course, you'll be expected to dance with my daughters," Elizabeth teased.

"I shall be honored to do so," Richard said. He noted Vivian's sudden look of hurt and said, "Along with Lady Vivian." He blinked at seeing how her face lit up.

"You're very kind, sir," Vivian offered, the second hint of humility she had shown that evening.

Richard leaned sideways as a footmen delivered the main course, and conversation returned to matters of Parliament and events of the Season.

When the ladies retired to the parlor so he and George could enjoy their port and engage in more serious discussion, Richard felt profound relief.

CHAPTER 8

EXCUSED FOR NOT-SO-VERY PROPER BEHAVIOR

A half hour later

"She's not usually like this," George murmured as a footman set glasses of port before the two viscounts.

"Pardon?"

"Lady Vivian," George murmured. "She has always been the most prim and proper young lady in all of London. Tonight it was as if... as if she was a different person."

Richard sipped the port and made a sound of appreciation before he said, "She struck me as rather... *bold*. Not at all what I would expect of a properly raised young lady." He paused a moment before he added, "I find Miss Christina a breath of fresh air, though."

"Oh?" George responded. He crossed his arms on the edge of the table and leaned forward. "She's not had many suitors."

"I find that a surprise," Richard replied. "She has had her come-out?"

George nodded. "Oh, yes. She makes friends easily, boys as well as girls, so I think the young men haven't seen her as a potential wife is all. I'm not concerned. I expect I'll be paying her dowry by the end of this Season."

Richard furrowed a brow. "I was serious when I mentioned *my* intention to wed by the end of the Season," he murmured. Although he didn't mention Christina specifically, his meaning was clear.

"You are in an unfortunate position," George commented. "I take it there are no young ladies in Lincolnshire who have turned your head?"

Richard said, "None I would consider appropriate to the station of viscountess. Perhaps... perhaps I am too demanding."

Furrowing his brow, George said, "You can be as demanding as you need to be. Best you be happy with your wife, though. You'll be less likely to seek a mistress."

Richard winced. "I have discovered since arriving here in the capital that employing a mistress is a common practice among the *ton*."

"For some," George agreed. "Not for all. It can be expensive and costly, though."

A quizzical expression crossing his face, Richard said, "Is that not the same?"

George shook his head. "Hardly. You will pay good coin, and you will likely lose the love of a good wife should you decide to have both."

"Spoken as if you learned the lesson first-hand," Richard remarked.

George once again shook his head. "I let my mistress go before I married. At her insistence," he replied. "I know of too many others who did not and have since paid for it by being cuckolded by their wives."

The warning seemed to have the younger viscount reconsidering his options. "I take your meaning," Richard replied, his gaze suggesting he was studying something in his mind's eye.

"Do you have someone in mind to be your viscountess?" George asked carefully. "There's no shame in marrying a woman from your district," he added.

Richard regarded the older man for a moment before he said, "Although there might have been one ten years ago, there is no one now."

George winced at hearing the comment. Any young lady that Hartwell might have considered ten years ago would have no doubt married another before her twenty-eighth birthday. That seemed to mark the official year of spinsterhood for those who lived in the country.

"Before I begin the search for a viscountess, I do have matters to complete regarding my late father," Richard said.

"Matters of estate?"

"Indeed. By chance, are you familiar with a solicitor named Andrew Barton?"

Guffawing, George said, "I am. The offices of my wife's charities are next door to his in Oxford Street."

Richard looked relieved at hearing this bit of news. "I have completed everything necessary up in Lincolnshire, but my solicitor there mentioned my father had a separate solicitor here in town. Someone to oversee his business whilst he was here for the Season, I suppose."

"Not so unusual," George said. "I have one in Sussex as well as in London." He paused and then added, "If you're not comfortable with continuing his employment, you should know that Mr. Barton has a son who is also a solicitor. Andrew is getting on in years. He's still sharp, but it's probably time he take his retirement and leave the office to his son."

"Good to know," Richard replied. "I sent word yesterday that I would be paying a call and was surprised when a note arrived early this morning confirming the appointment."

George nodded. "As I said, he is still sharp." When he noted the younger viscount's look of concern, he asked, "Did you find him otherwise?"

"Oh, I've not yet had the pleasure. I am merely bothered by something he wrote. Besides the usual papers that require my signature, apparently my father left a box that needs to be delivered to someone here in the capital. I have to wonder why Mr. Barton hasn't already arranged its delivery."

Shrugging, George considered possibilities. "Perhaps it's

personal. Or... more likely, he wished for you to meet the recipient?" he guessed.

Richard nodded. "Perhaps. I suppose the mystery will be solved on the morrow. My appointment with him is in the late morning."

"Have you a town coach?"

"I do," Richard hedged. "My father's, although there was a note mentioning it was in need of repair. A wheel, I think. It's being seen to and due back from Tilbury's any day now.

"And a staff of servants?"

"They were a nice surprise. Turns out I have a groom who is also the driver, a housekeeper, and a couple of maids. Then there is a cook and a butler who is also a valet."

"Ah, the best kind," George said. "He'll keep you apprised of the London gossip as well as keep your house in good stead." He eyed his empty glass and said, "The ladies will be wondering if we have fallen asleep in our port."

His eyes rounding, Richard asked, "Are we to see them again?"

Nodding, George explained, "It is customary to join them in the parlor. They're probably still enjoying a cup of tea or two."

"And you say this is... customary?" Richard asked.

George stared at Richard a moment, reminded the younger viscount hadn't been raised in a home with a mother. With a viscountess. Perhaps the late viscount didn't entertain often. "It is. But not required should you prefer to take your leave," George offered.

"I would not," Richard replied.

"Then let us head back up to the parlor," George said as he pushed back his carver.

Richard joined him as they made their way to the stairs and then into the parlor. They bowed as the three ladies stood and curtsied.

"Well, it's about time," Vivian murmured, loud enough to be heard by both men.

"Apologies, my lady," Richard said. "I was not familiar with the practice of returning to the parlor after dinner."

Vivian's chin went up a notch. "I suppose it's not done in Lincolnshire?"

"Vivian," Christina scolded in a whisper.

"It might have been had there been a lady or two present," Richard said, secretly glad when he overheard Christina's quiet rebuke.

If her father gave him permission, he would be paying a call on the young lady.

CHAPTER 9
CATCHING UP AT THE CLUB

*M*eanwhile, at White's, St. James Street, Mayfair

Sebastian stepped down from his father's town coach and regarded the exterior of White's with a wary eye. Despite having been gone from England for four years, he found the venerable men's club looked exactly the same as it had when he had last seen it.

Apparently not everything had changed during his absence.

His father and mother certainly had, their aging features reminding him of their mortality—and his own. Given his five-and-thirty years, he needed to find a young lady to marry and to start his nursery.

Considering the circumstances, he rather wished he could work on the latter first. He hadn't been in the company of a woman—in *that* way—for two years.

"Cougham?"

The familiar voice of Sir Randolph Roderick brought Sebastian out of his reverie. He stared at his friend from an earlier life for a moment before he blurted, "You have gray hair!"

Randolph laughed out loud, drawing the attention of several young men who were about to enter White's. "Only at my temples, and it's well earned, I assure you," the knight and oldest son of Randall Roderick, Marquess of Reading, replied with a grin. "Between children and horses, there is never a dull moment." He angled his head to one side. "Have you brought back a future countess from Italy with you?" he added as he turned toward White's.

Sebastian fell in step with the gentleman who was only a few years older than him—and a few inches shorter. "I have not, but then I wasn't looking for a wife," he replied.

Horses and the desire for speed had made them fast friends at university. Randolph's first marriage at the age of twenty and the birth of his son only a year later tempered his desire to engage in acts of derring-do, especially given his wife had died in the childbed.

His position with the Foreign Office may have had something to do with his more mature behavior as well.

Half-expecting Randolph to return to his more reckless behavior, Sebastian was disappointed when Randolph married a widowed viscountess and added two more babes to his nursery in just four years. "I suppose you have a full house these days?" he added.

Randolph climbed the few steps up to the black door of the club, nodding to the footman who held it open for them. "There are six of us now," he said proudly. "Xenobia has made a wonderful mother, and she would probably give me more, but..."

Sebastian made a sound of disgust as he allowed a footman to see to his greatcoat. "Locked you out of the mistress suite, has she?" he teased.

Furrowing a brow, Randolph said, "Hardly. We happily share a bed, in fact. But I dare not risk her death with the birth of another," he explained.

It was Sebastian's turn to furrow a brow. "How...?"

Randolph rolled his eyes. "I would have thought *you* of all men would be familiar with French letters," he said as he led them through the first room. Gentlemen of various ages were standing or seated in groups, engaged in quiet conversations while they drank from crystal cups. Two were smoking cheroots, and the scent of tobacco permeated the room. Only a few stopped to acknowledge their arrival.

"I know *of* them, of course," Sebastian said, nodding to those who called out his name. "Never thought of using them to prevent a child."

"They work as well for that as they do to help prevent nasty diseases," Randolph said. He entered the next room and headed directly to the betting book. "You're no doubt here to collect on the wagers you placed before you took off on your extended leave."

Sebastian's eyes widened. "I've won a bet?" he asked in surprise.

Randolph gave him a quelling glance. "Five, in fact. Nothing like refilling the coffers after a long trip," he said as he pointed to the tally sheet.

His eyes rounding, Sebastian stared at the amount above Randolph's fingertip. "I cannot even remember what I was betting on," he whispered.

"Bachelors who married sooner than they claimed they would, the age at which Lady Angelica would marry, the number of legitimate sons my father would sire before his twentieth wedding anniversary—which was two, by the way—and the age at which Alexander Tennison would lose his virginity."

"He's lost it?" Sebastian asked in surprise.

Randolph waggled his brows. "He's marrying Margaret Ewen. An *older* woman," he whispered with a grin.

Sebastian's look of confusion was almost comical. "I've no idea who that is," he murmured.

"She's the gemologist at Ewen and Ewen Jewelers in Ludgate Hill."

Sebastian merely shrugged. "Can't say I've spent much time shopping in Ludgate Hill of late," he admitted.

Once again, Randolph laughed. "You will if you intend to take a wife anytime soon. And you'll continue to do so if you want to ensure your wife doesn't make you a cuckold."

"I resent that remark," Sebastian said, as he moved to

collect his winnings. "I'll have you know I was quite accomplished when it came to pleasing a woman in bed."

"Was?" Randolph repeated, an eyebrow arching.

Sebastian glanced around before he leaned toward his friend and said, "I've been living the life of a monk for the past two years—"

"Two *years?*" Randolph blurted.

"Two years, two months, three weeks and a day, but who's counting?" Sebastian whispered hoarsely.

"You, apparently," Randolph countered. "What the hell happened?" He watched as Sebastian surreptitiously pocketed his winnings before moving to the next room.

"I was living with monks... while I was convalescing."

The humor left Randolph's face in an instant. "Monks? But... why?"

Sebastian allowed a sigh, but he refrained from answering when a footman appeared to take their drink order. "An ale for me," he said, which had both the footman and Randolph staring at him. "You do serve ale, do you not?" Sebastian asked, sounding impatient.

The footman nodded. "Yes, sir."

"Brandy for me," Randolph said, his look of worry increasing as he stared at the viscount. When the footman took his leave of the room, he leaned toward Sebastian and said, "You're not the same man who left London four years ago, are you?"

Sebastian gave a one-shouldered shrug. "I am not the reckless, hell-bent-for-leather boy I once was, it's true," he admitted. "But I'm still *me*."

"What happened?"

The footman reappeared with their drinks, and Sebastian took a long draught from his mug while Randolph barely sipped his brandy.

"I've an appreciation for living a long life given I nearly died whilst skiing," Sebastian said quietly. He moved to take a seat in a wingback chair near the fireplace.

"Skiing?" Randolph repeated. He took the adjacent chair.

"In the Alps. It's exhilarating. A very fast means to get down a snow-covered mountain," Sebastian explained

"I know *what* it is," Randolph said. "Why were *you* doing it?"

"For sport. For the thrill," Sebastian replied. He took a long sip from his cup. "Certainly not to crash into a tree and end up with broken bones."

Randolph winced. "Someone was with you then? To get help?"

Sebastian shook his head. "I was alone. I had been with someone, but he had already headed down the mountain. I was to follow, but once you're moving, there's no easy way to to stop."

"Then, who—?"

Rolling his eyes, Sebastian said, "I was rescued by two large dogs. Alpenmastiffs. Owned by the—"

"St. Bernard monks," Randolph finished for him. "I've heard about them." He eyes rounded. "You convalesced in their monastery?"

Sebastian nodded. "I did. And I can assure you, there is nothing so humbling as having to put your life into someone else's care for over a year."

Randolph nodded his understanding. "And the rest of the time? You mentioned it had been over two years since—"

"By the time I recovered, it was winter and there was no way off the mountain. Truth be told... I liked it there. Not at first, of course. Mostly because I was in so much pain. Except when I was drunk on their ale. They make an excellent ale." He indicated his almost empty cup. "Not like this piss water."

"What changed?"

Sebastian inhaled softly. "I found I liked the quiet. There wasn't a need to prove myself. I didn't have to compete with anyone. I just had to... *be*."

Randolph furrowed a dark brow. "Was it a religious experience for you?"

The viscount seemed to think on the query for a time

before he said, "Not particularly. Spiritual, perhaps. Not at all like a Sunday at St. George's."

Nodding, Randolph took a sip of his brandy before he asked, "So, why did you return to England?"

Grunting, Sebastian said, "Duty. Responsibility. I am an only heir. My father is getting on in years. I've never learned anything I'll need to know about the Weatherstone earldom, and I thought it was past time I start."

"You know I'm about to faint at hearing you say all this," Randolph replied, his words not sounding at all like a jest.

"What? Did you place a wager on when I would come to my senses?"

About to respond, Randolph closed his mouth and dipped his head. "I didn't. But I do believe others have."

Allowing a guffaw, Sebastian drained the rest of his ale. "Well, the first duty I must see to is taking a wife."

Having just taken a sip of his brandy, Randolph nearly choked on the fortified wine. "Attend your father's ball on Tuesday night, and you can have your pick of pretty young ladies," he said when he'd finally recovered from his fit of coughing.

"I don't want a pretty young lady," Sebastian replied.

Randolph was glad he hadn't attempted to drink any more of his brandy. "Wot?"

"I want a prim and proper young lady. Preferably one who is... a bit older. Not straight out of the schoolroom," he explained. He had the perfect woman in mind, but he knew time had changed them both. That and what he'd almost done to her the last night he was in London. The night before he had left for Italy. "The one I warned everyone not to go near, way back when I was still in my twenties," he murmured.

"Good God, you really have changed," Randolph remarked in surprise. "You'll have to settle for someone who's almost a spinster. Someone who has already reached their majority and may not need to wed," he warned. "May not *want* to wed. Which means..." He stopped speaking and grimaced.

"Which means *what*, exactly?"

"You'll have to convince her you're worth it," Randolph said, his voice tinged with doom.

Sebastian boggled. "I *am* worth it," he countered. "Besides, I'm the sole heir to an earldom. That has to be worth *something*."

Randolph shook his head and displayed an expression of sadness. "You're going to find things are a bit different than when you were last in London," he said in a quiet voice. "There are rich tradesmen and merchants who can offer a young lady a higher standard of living. A happier living."

"How?"

"They don't have to deal with the petty jealousies of their peers," Randolph replied. "The endless gossip. The infighting. The backstabbing."

"Oh, my God. Just what have the women of the *ton* been doing whilst I was on the Continent?" Sebastian asked in alarm.

Randolph shrugged. "Nothing they weren't already doing when you were last here," he replied.

Suddenly doubting his prospects for a quick marriage, Sebastian sighed and shook hands with his friend. "You've been a fount of information and a killjoy, too."

"Glad I could help," Randolph deadpanned.

Sebastian took his leave of White's in a much more sober mood than when he had arrived. At least he had a full purse from his winnings.

Apparently he would need it in his pursuit of the perfect wife.

Or at least his idea of a perfect wife.

CHAPTER 10

SCOLDING A FRIEND

*M*eanwhile, in the Bostwick town coach

"Whatever has gotten into you on this night?"

Vivian had barely settled into the squabs of the Bostwick town coach when Christina put voice to the scolding query. "I don't know what you mean," Vivian replied, wrapping her shawl about her shoulders more tightly.

Scoffing, Christina rolled her eyes. "Your behavior was appalling. You'll have no chance of making a match with Lord Hartwell—"

"I don't want one."

"—or anyone else, for that matter," Christina continued before she jerked as if she'd been slapped across the face. "Whatever do you mean, you don't want one?"

A heavy sigh escaped Vivian, one that sounded as if tears might be imminent. "Oh, Tina. For once I behaved boldly, and I liked it. If Lord Hartwell did not, then I shan't expect him to pay a call on me."

"If you're not careful, *no one* will pay a call on you," Christina countered. "If there had been a gossip among those present at dinner this evening, you might have discovered how easy it is to become *persona non grata* in this town."

"I wasn't *that* bad," Vivian replied. She leaned forward.

"Was I?" she added, sounding entirely too enthusiastic in the darkened coach. "I had such a good time. I felt free and unfettered. I didn't care what anyone thought. I said *exactly* what I was thinking."

Christina didn't respond right away, so shocked was she by Vivian's claim. Despite having discussed it before dinner, Christina didn't think Vivian would actually change her behavior as much as she had in the presence of the new viscount.

She only hoped he would not hold his poor opinion of Vivian against her, since Christina had decided she rather liked the gentleman. Although she had pretended to be listening to her friend whilst they were in the parlor after dinner, she had overheard Lord Hartwell's comment about Vivian being fast.

Should he share that opinion with other lords, Vivian's chances of making a good match would be forfeit. No self-respecting aristocrat wanted a wife who was seen as a consummate flirt. Or who behaved badly.

Well, there might be one, but could Lord Cougham really be considered a self-respecting aristocrat?

Upon overhearing Lord Hartwell's assessment of Vivian, Christina nearly gasped in horror. She had been forced to swallow her reaction, though, and pretend all was well as they continued drinking their tea. She was relieved when the viscount made his excuses and announced that he needed to take his leave. Apparently, he still had business in Westminster before he could officially take his seat as Viscount Hartwell on Tuesday for the first session of Parliament.

The look on her father's face suggested George Bennett-Jones was disappointed, as if he had realized they might never again have the new viscount's company.

Would Vivian's behavior cause Lord Hartwell to avoid further socializing with her father? If so, Christina couldn't help the sick feeling that had her stomach roiling.

Or it could have just been due to the amount of tea she

had drunk after dinner, hoping it had been laced with something alcoholic to help tone down Vivian's brashness.

No such luck.

"Your boldness might have ended a friendship, which I believe my father welcomed. Which *I* welcomed," Christina said in a quiet voice.

Vivian stiffened before she settled back in the squabs, attempting to hide a sniffle with her hanky. "I apologize, Tina. I did not consider that others might suffer for my behavior. No one else should."

Christina sighed. "Apology accepted." After a moment, she added, "Perhaps you'll have an opportunity to explain your behavior to Lord Hartwell."

"But why?"

"So that he won't be left with a permanently poor opinion of you," Christina replied. "Don't you see? I am one-and-twenty. You are—"

"Old," Vivian interrupted, making the word sound as if it were two or three syllables. "Another year or two, and I'll be a spinster. Boo-hoo."

"Viv!"

"I don't care, Tina. I am tired of being perfect. Of doing every little thing I'm supposed to and not having it count for anything. I have wasted four... nay *seven* years for *what*?"

"For the opportunity to marry well," Christina murmured, now wishing she hadn't pressed her friend. She was practically making her argument for her.

"You don't think that opportunity is long gone? I'm too damned *tall*, Tina," Vivian hissed. "No one wants me to be his wife, or he would have courted me when I was twenty and before I grew another two inches."

Christina winced at hearing the curse. Winced again at hearing the vehemence in Vivian's voice. "That's not true," she whispered. "It's not."

"Name one man in London who wants to court me," Vivian countered.

Remembering Vivian's earlier comment about Sebastian

Peele, Viscount Cougham, Christina leaned forward and said, "Bash."

Vivian gasped, apparently not expecting *him* to be mentioned. "Name another."

Christina sighed. "I won't because there isn't another man for you, Viv. You won't give another man a chance."

"That's not true," Vivian claimed.

"Isn't it?"

About to argue, Vivian clamped her mouth shut for a moment. "The Weatherstone ball is Tuesday night. I will be on my very best behavior for that night only. If I don't receive a proposal by midnight, I'm going to behave as I want, Miss Pipkins be damned."

Christina gasped at hearing the curse. "Midnight?" she repeated. "Can't you see fit to making it more like... Friday at midnight? Give a young man the opportunity to court you for a few days after the ball? Marry you on your birthday?"

Vivian scoffed. "The young men have had *seven* years to court me. But if you insist, I'll behave until Friday."

"I insist."

Vivian gave a start. "Friday is my birthday," she said in awe.

Christina furrowed a brow. "Isn't that why you chose it as your deadline? Because you will have reached your majority and can claim your inheritance?"

"I'll be five-and-twenty," Vivian agreed, acting as if she hadn't heard the rest of what Christina had spoken.

As the coach came to a halt, Christina gasped. "Oh, that was quick," she said, always surprised by how fast a carriage ride was when there was someone with whom to converse.

She only wished this night's conversation had been a more pleasant one.

"Promise you won't depart for the Kingdom of the Two Sicilies. At least... not without me," Christina said, trying to make her voice sound light.

"If I don't see you before, I'll see you Tuesday night,"

Vivian said before she stepped down from the coach, the driver holding out his hand for her.

"But you will. You're coming to Lady Morganfield's garden party on Saturday, are you not?"

Vivian scoffed. "Yes, I'll be there," she said with an exaggerated sigh. "Then I'll see you Tuesday at the Weatherstone's ball. But don't expect me to be wearing white."

"Why ever not?"

Vivian gave her a quelling glance from where she stood in the street. "I warned the modiste if she made something white, I would tell everyone she's a terrible seamstress."

"Vivian!"

"I didn't really, but it sounded so good thinking it out loud," Vivian teased. "Good night."

"Good night," Christina replied as the driver escorted Vivian to the front door of Roth House.

Worried about what her friend might be plotting next, Christina settled back into the squabs and tried to think of something more pleasant.

Someone more pleasant.

She grinned all way home as thoughts of the dashing Lord Hartwell flitted across her mind's eye.

CHAPTER 11

PILLOW TALK ABOUT A
DAUGHTER AND A
VISCOUNT

ater that night in the master suite, Bostwick House
"This is my favorite time of the day," George
whispered, his slurred delivery suggesting he would
be sound asleep in only moments. That night's round of lovemaking had been slow and satisfying and then quick and
quiet. He had almost fallen asleep atop Elizabeth when her
response had his eyes rounding.

"He's too old for her, George," Elizabeth murmured.

"Who? What... what are you talking about?" he asked as
he rolled off of her. Landing on his back, he took a deep
breath and pulled her closer.

"Hartwell."

George blinked, his mind finally understanding where
hers was. How could she think of their dinner guest at a time
like this? But George had learned very early in their marriage
that Elizabeth Carlington Bennett-Jones was capable of
accomplishing much in a single day. Apparently lovemaking
wouldn't be the last of her endeavors on this one.

"You think Hartwell is too old for Lady Vivian?" he asked,
realizing she meant their daughter but deciding he would
tease her. The thought that she might have spent any of their
intimate time together thinking of the other viscount had

him feeling a bit jealous. He was a good looking man who didn't appear as old as the record in *Debrett's* claimed he was.

"For Christina Charlotte, of course," Elizabeth whispered, not displaying one iota of annoyance at hearing his query. "I think it was quite evident that he's smitten with her."

George sighed. "He's five-and-thirty," he murmured, remembering the date of his birth as being sometime in 1804.

"Exactly," Elizabeth replied, apparently glad to hear his response.

"She's one-and-twenty."

When Elizabeth didn't say anything, George turned his head to find her brows furrowed. "Surely this must sound familiar to you?"

Her look of confusion had him displaying a smirk. "If you'll recall, there's quite a difference in age between *us*."

She scoffed. "It's not the same at all," she argued.

Not ready for a lesson in logic—sleep was threatening to take him from the here and now—George bussed her on the cheek and said, "Let's wait until breakfast to discuss this further. I should like to hear our daughter's opinion before I decide anything."

"You're already asleep, aren't you?" she whispered.

"Not quite," he replied. "Tell me, my love. Is their age difference your only objection to Hartwell?"

Elizabeth moved her head to the small of his shoulder and wrapped an arm across his chest. "I haven't yet decided."

George chuckled. "Then think on it, and we shall discuss it over breakfast." He closed his eyes as he moved a hand to rest atop the one she had placed on his chest. "I love you."

For the longest time, her breathing stayed even as she lay tucked against his side, so George decided it was safe to go to sleep. He was nearly in slumber when her whisper had him stirring.

"I'm not sure I *like* him."

Jerking, George blinked several times. "Why ever not?" Having experienced many a night in long discussions like this one, George had learned to respond as best he could or risk censure in the morning.

He didn't like being censured in the mornings.

His second favorite time of the day was when they woke and she was practically atop him, ready to ride St. George.

He liked playing St. George.

Hell, he'd play the dragon if it meant another opportunity to make love to his wife.

"He seems... *lost*. As if he doesn't really know anything about being in polite company. Being in Society."

The comment wasn't at all what he expected, but he found he couldn't disagree with her. He'd had the same impression upon meeting the viscount. "That's because he is lost, my love," George whispered. "As one who was once in his position, I remember that time well."

Elizabeth lifted her head from his shoulder. "What do you mean?"

"I remember the day my uncle died as if it were yesterday. That feeling of loss? Confusion? I had no idea what I was supposed to do. Where I was supposed to go," he murmured. "If it had't been for..." He clamped his mouth shut, about to mention Josephine, his one and only mistress. The woman he had been with for many years before he had inherited the Bostwick earldom from the rich uncle who took after King Midas in how he managed his money.

"Mrs. Theisen," Elizabeth whispered. "You can say her name. I don't mind," she added as she tightened her hold on him. "I think my father still seeks her counsel when he doesn't know which way to vote in Parliament."

"Josephine," George said aloud, referring to Josephine Theisen. At the behest of his uncle, he had hired her as his mistress and stayed with her for years before Joseph Bennett-Jones' death.

With George's inheritance of the Bostwick properties and the viscountcy title, Josephine had announced that it was time George seek a wife. From her years of providing Elizabeth's father, the Marquess of Morganfield, with political insights and recommendations, Josephine encouraged George to consider the marquess' daughter to be his wife.

"I don't believe Hartwell has a mistress or anyone he can go to for counsel," George said, thinking that he had valued Josephine for those qualities. "What's worse is, everyone in London has mistaken him for Sir Randolph, and I'm beginning to think..." His voice trailed off again as his body stiffened.

"What? What is it?" Elizabeth asked, once again lifting her head from his shoulder.

"What if... what if Hartwell isn't what he seems?"

She blinked as she regarded her husband, his gaze on his mind's eye. "You think him an imposter?" she asked in alarm.

"No. Not exactly," George murmured. "At least, if he is, he's an innocent imposter."

"Innocent? Whatever are you saying?"

George pulled her head back down to his shoulder. "What if... what if he's really one of Sir Randolph's many illegitimate brothers?" he asked in wonder. "Placed into the arms of a bereft father whose wife and heir had perished in the childbed?"

Elizabeth gasped and then sat up, taking most of the bed linens with her. "George!" she scolded, even as she was left thinking his supposition a possibility.

"His wife did die in the childbed," George said by way of bolstering his argument. The death date of Hartwell's mother matched his birth date.

"I suppose he is of an age to *be* one of the illegitimate brothers," Elizabeth whispered. "Reading had so many of them."

"Four, but Hartwell is not as old as Sir Randolph, so he's probably not his identical twin," George reasoned, now wide awake.

"Isn't Sir Randolph the oldest?" Elizabeth asked.

George nodded. "I don't know the names of all of the rest of them, but I rather imagine they all have names that start with an 'R.' That seems to be the way with Reading's offspring," he explained.

"Richard," she whispered as she inhaled.

"Rachel, Robert, Raymond, Reginald," George said, reciting some of the names he knew were children of Randall Roderick, Marquess of Reading.

"Hartwell could be the son of a marquess," Elizabeth breathed, her eyes rounding in delight.

"He could be," George agreed, rather liking how her opinion of Richard Hartwell seemed to change considerably.

For the better.

"Which means our daughter would not only be a viscountess, but a wife to the son of a marquess," he reasoned.

"Oh, George," Elizabeth breathed. "How appropriate for her." That her oldest daughter would end up married to an aristocrat was expected. The other connections would have to remain secret, though.

"We cannot tell a soul," he warned, realizing anything she might say in a Mayfair parlor could be both a boon and a detriment to the newly-minted viscount.

"My lips are sealed," she agreed. She settled back onto his body and took a deep breath. "I do so love being married to you," she whispered. "And I think I shall be a willing prisoner of your dragon in the morning," she murmured.

Grinning in the dark, George decided their conversation had been well worth having to give up a few minutes of sleep. He managed to buss his wife on the cheek before closing his eyes.

Sleep did not come easily, though.

CHAPTER 12

MIDNIGHT IN THE STUDY

*M*eanwhile, *at Weatherstone Manor in Park Lane* William, Earl of Weatherstone, made his way down the marble steps and to his study, a glass of brandy dangling from one hand and a silver-topped cane in the other. He nearly dropped the glass upon discovering someone was in his study.

"Apologies, Father. I didn't mean to frighten you," Sebastian said as he looked up from a letter he had been reading.

"I thought you were at White's," William said as he moved to his chair behind the desk. His son was ensconced on one of the leather sofas positioned near the fireplace, a silver salver of correspondence sitting to one side and the read missives accumulating in a pile on the other.

"I was. I stayed for an hour."

"An hour?" his father repeated in disbelief.

"Yes. I had a drink with Sir Randolph, collected some winnings from bets I made four years ago, and took my leave," he said.

"Anything... wrong?" his father asked as he leaned back in his leather-upholstered chair.

Sebastian furrowed a brow. "Not that I'm aware of," he answered carefully.

"You've been gone from British shores for four years. I

would have expected you to have moved into White's for the night and most of tomorrow morning," William said. "Placed a dozen bets, played a few hands of whist or hazard, accepted a challenge to drive a coach-and-four along the Serpentine or some such—"

"I've changed, Father," Sebastian interrupted. "None of those activities appeals to me any longer."

William slumped against the back of his chair, his brandy forgotten. "You were telling the truth earlier this afternoon?" he whispered.

Suspecting a trap, Sebastian merely nodded. "I've much to see to since my return, not the least of which is responding to all this correspondence. Were you aware Haddon got married?" he asked as he held up an engraved invitation.

"Of course. Your mother and I attended the wedding."

"To Juliet Comber?" Sebastian said in disbelief. "He's old enough to be her father."

"And she's old enough to have learned how to wrap him around her little pinky, or so that's what your mother claims. Bumped his head, you see, and now he's all right in the head again. He behaved like an arse before that."

Sebastian furrowed a brow, never having known Haddon to behave badly. "Is Lady Morganfield happy she has a new daughter?" he asked, referring to Haddon's mother.

"Treats her like royalty. Why, you never saw a happier mother-in-law in all your life."

Sebastian guffawed. "And what's this about Hexham? He married Ann Wellingham?"

"Indeed. They returned from their wedding trip only a few days ago. He's accepted a writ of acceleration and will be taking his father's place in Parliament this year," William explained. "Before you ask, yes, Gabe Wellingham has married a potter from the museum."

"You still love to gossip," Sebastian accused.

"I *live* for it," his father acknowledged.

"Which is why you're immortal," his son teased.

"You wish," William countered, a grin brightening his weathered face.

"Well, I suppose you know who will be announcing their betrothals at your ball, too?"

"Oh, yes. And some marriages as well. These civil services make it more difficult to know what's going on, though, since the banns aren't always read," Weatherstone complained.

"Such a pity," Sebastian deadpanned. "I suppose you're making arrangements for those recent marriages to be announced by the butler? During the ball?"

William's eyes widened. "What a capital idea," he replied happily.

"I was joking."

"Well, I'm not. It's an excellent idea, son."

Sebastian rolled his eyes. "How many are you expecting will be announced?" He'd been away for four years, and although gossip did make it's way across the Channel, it hadn't made it to the monastery.

William furrowed a bushy white brow. "Well, let's see. Thomas Grandby has taken Lady Victoria—Somerset's youngest—to wife."

Sebastian blinked. "Tom Grandby got married?" he asked in disbelief.

For the first time that evening, William laughed. "To a duke's daughter, no less. He bought Fairmont Park for her and will allow her to continue her work with horses." He paused and then said, "Graham Wellingham is finally getting married to Hannah Simpson. That's a union that took entirely too long to happen."

Blinking, Sebastian gave his head a shake. "I thought she was married to a baron."

"She was. He died, so she's a widow, which had Graham returning from Boston. He'd been in America running the import business there ever since she wed the first time," his father explained.

"Good for him. Of course, now he probably has to take over his father's business here."

"Wellingham Imports, yes," William agreed. "Lots of money there. Old and new," he added.

"Who else?"

William blinked, as if he didn't understand the query.

"Married?"

"Oh, her brother, Henry is marrying a portrait painter of some renown."

"Anyone else?"

William nodded. "Alexander Tennison is marrying a jeweler's daughter. Margaret Ewen of Ewen and Ewen in Ludgate Hill."

"Randolph mentioned that. Is Alexander even old enough to wed?" Sebastian queried. "I ask only because I managed to win a bet that had to do with him."

His father gave him a quelling glance. "Smart man, if you ask me. He's too damned handsome to be allowed out after dark." He paused a moment, as if deep in thought. "I don't think I've missed anyone."

His son shook his head. "What of Lady Vivian? Who has captured her hand?"

William furrowed a brow before a grin turned up the corners of his mouth. "You will, no doubt."

Sebastian gave a start. "Me?" he repeated.

"Yes, you. She's an earl's daughter. Perfectly suited to be a countess. And the only woman in London you won't have to bend over double to kiss on the lips," he teased.

"Father," Sebastian scolded. He was quiet a moment. "Are you quite sure she's not spoken for?"

"Very sure." William took a sip of his brandy, a wan smile appearing before he added. "You saw to it she wouldn't have any suitors and now you'd be wise to court her before she decides to take her inheritance and use it to travel to the Continent. She's of an age to do so."

Sebastian dropped the letter he'd been holding. "She wouldn't," he breathed.

The earl arched his bushy brows. "Agnes claims she despises her companion. That she'll do almost anything to be rid of her," he said on a sigh. "Poor thing is so tall, most men in London only think to proposition her rather than propose to her."

A growl erupted from Sebastian's throat. An expression of anger replaced that of befuddlement. "Lady Vivian is far too proper to be propositioned," he argued.

His father merely shrugged. "My thoughts exactly," he replied before he drained his brandy. "Well, I'm off to bed. I trust you will be soon, too?" he half-questioned.

Sebastian's attention wasn't on his father, though, as he began to read the next missive from the pile on the salver. In fact, he didn't even notice as the earl made his way out of the study and up the marble stairs, a satisfied grin lighting his face.

CHAPTER 13

A VISCOUNT MEETS HIS SOLICITOR

The following morning, Friday, March 29, 1839
His thoughts on his dinner with the Bennett-Joneses the night before, Richard Hartwell watched from the window of a hansom cab as it made its way east in Oxford Street.

Although his butler had offered to arrange for the chariot to take him, Richard declined, claiming his appointments would have the driver waiting a long time. Better he was in the stables behind the Hartwell townhouse seeing to his late father's horses. He was sure the mare would be foaling within the week.

Richard noticed the shingle for *Lady E's Finding Work for the Wounded* before that of the solicitor's appeared just beyond. A few men in clothing befitting laborers entered and departed Lady Bostwick's charity while he watched, one limping and another with an arm in a sling. He winced at thinking he might have been one of the wounded had he fought on behalf of Greece in their war for independence, or in one of the other skirmishes that seemed to keep the world at war.

His father had forbidden him from going to Greece. As an heir—the only heir—to the Hartwell viscountcy, it would have been irresponsible for him to participate.

When the hansom cab halted in front of the next office, Richard stepped down and paid the driver.

"Would you like me to wait, sir?"

Richard shook his head. "I expect I'll be here too long, but I thank you for the offer." He turned around and regarded the neatly painted gold and black lettering on the glass in the door.

The name, *Andrew S. Barton, Esq.*, had recently been amended to add *and Son* beneath it. He entered, introducing himself to a young man who turned out to be the son.

"Andrew Barton, Junior, my lord," the young man said as he stood and offered his hand. Richard shook it. "My father is ill today, but he has apprised me of what needs to be done."

Richard glanced over the items on the desk. When he noted there was no box, he said, "I understand there is an item I am to deliver to someone?"

Barton waved Richard to a chair in front of another desk and joined him on the other side. "Yes, sir." Andrew opened a drawer and pulled out a folio along with a small box. He offered the box to Richard, who took it and regarded it with a furrowed brow. From its size, he was fairly sure it held a ring.

"May I open it?"

Andrew shrugged. "The instructions for its delivery are in here," he said as he pulled a sheaf of papers from the folio. He handed a handwritten note to Richard, who immediately recognized his father's penmanship.

He held the parchment to the desk's candle lamp and began to read.

Dear Richard,

I have proposed marriage to her every year for the past ten years, but she turns me down every time. Despite her rejections, I still love her and wish for her to have this. See to its delivery, and I shall be forever grateful.

Please do not fault her for what she once did for her living. She is a brilliant woman, and should you become acquainted, you will find she is worth knowing. Be careful with your words, son. Had I gotten my way, she might have been your stepmother.

Your father, Hartwell

Beneath the script was written *V. Higgins, The Queen of Hearts, Stafford Street, Mayfair*.

The sound of a clearing throat had Richard lifting his head from the curious note. "Is there a problem, my lord?" Andrew asked, a paper held in one hand as if he'd been waiting for some time for Richard to return his attention to him.

"Who is this *V. Higgins?*" Richard asked as he indicated the name at the bottom of the missive.

The solicitor brightened. "Ah. She's the Queen of Hearts, sir. She's the proprietress of The Queen of Hearts. The men's club in Mayfair."

Richard glanced again at his father's note before he took the lid off the small box. He gave a start at seeing a rather large ruby set in gold. The solitaire was surrounded by a circle of small diamonds mounted on a gold ring. "Good God," he whispered in awe.

A brief thought of a stack of letters in his desk back at Hartwell House had him realizing his father *had* been carrying on with a woman in London. He couldn't think about the letters right now, though. There was business to see to. Papers to sign. An estate to clear up.

*D*eciding his client wasn't expecting an answer to his statement, Andrew continued to hold out the paper. "This has to do with the unentailed properties belonging to your father. They pass to your possession, of course, whilst all the entailed properties remain with the viscountcy."

"Unentailed properties?" Richard questioned. "But... there are none," he said as he finally took the paper in hand.

Andrew cleared his throat. "The townhouse was purchased ten years ago, sir. Fully staffed and furnished."

"From whom?"

The solicitor leaned over to study something on another paper before he looked up. "Seems your father let it from the Earl of Torrington for several years before buying it," he explained as he held out another paper. "And then there is the property in Kent."

"Kent?"

"A hunting lodge, sir."

"But... my father didn't hunt," Richard argued.

"No, but he gambled on occasion. He won it whilst playing whist."

Richard was about to say his father didn't gamble, but thought better of it.

The solicitor would probably inform him that his father owned a gaming hell.

He studied the deed to the hunting lodge. "Who lost it?"

The solicitor took back the paper and scanned the bottom. He pointed to the signature. "Randall, Marquess of Reading."

Scoffing, Richard gave his head a shake. "I was sure my father didn't gamble."

"Given your father's paramour, it's unlikely he could avoid it."

Richard blinked and then remembered the mention of The Queen of Hearts. A men's club.

"*She* owns the gaming hell," Andrew said as he leaned over the desk and pointed to the name at the bottom of his father's handwritten note.

Scoffing—his father had never once mentioned he was involved with a woman when he was in town for Parliament—Richard arched a brow. "Was *she* included in any sort of settlement?" he asked, knowing her name didn't appear in the will that had been read back in Horncastle. The solicitor there had simply said that Richard owned everything his father had in his possession at the time of his death. With no other heirs or close relatives, the settlement was rather straightforward.

"Unnecessary, sir. Mrs. Higgins is probably worth more than most of the aristocrats and tradesmen in London, so any bequests she receives are simply given to the charities of her choice."

Blinking at hearing this particular information, Richard dared a glance at the ring. Surely she wouldn't give away a ruby ring. The jewel had to be worth a fortune.

"Then I hope she has someone to inherit *her* estate," Richard murmured, not expecting an answer. If Mrs. Higgins had turned down his father's offer of marriage every year for ten years, then perhaps his father had been a fortune seeker.

Except that there had been that mention in the note that he loved her.

Andrew Barton stared at him with the oddest expression on his face before he said, "Her two children will inherit everything, of course, sir."

Rather surprised the gaming hell owner would even have any children, Richard arched a brow. "Lucky bastards," he murmured.

No response came from the solicitor, but the young man regarded him a long moment before giving his head a shake. "We're nearly done, sir," he finally said as he passed several more sheets of parchment across the desk. He explained the purpose of each one as he did so and indicated where Richard needed to sign.

Richard wrote out his name on the papers where he was told to do so, his mind in a whirl.

When they were finished, some of the papers from the stack were shoved into the folio and given to Richard while the rest were collected into another folio. "I'll keep these copies safe, sir. I would recommend you do the same with yours if you would, sir," Andrew said. "And should you require our services, we'll be happy to represent you."

"Thank you," Richard murmured. "And the invoice for your services today?"

"Already paid, sir. Your father saw to it when he arranged all this."

Richard gave a start. "When? You said that as if… as if he knew he was going to die," he accused.

The solicitor inhaled softly and nodded. "Everyone dies, sir."

As if in a daze, Richard took his leave of the solicitor's office, the folio tucked into one arm and the ring box in his greatcoat pocket. He was barely aware he had hailed a hackney until it pulled up to the curb in front of him.

He didn't pay attention as it took him back to the townhouse.

His townhouse.

Now that the sun was peeking out from behind the clouds that had spit rain all morning, he regarded the domicile in a whole new light. He owned the building and all the furnishings within. The mews in the back included the horses and chariot contained therein. The staff was his to command.

His mind turned to other matters, such as the entailed properties of the viscountcy. The other unentailed property he owned outright. A hunting lodge in Kent, the solicitor had said.

The ruby and diamond ring box tucked into his pocket.

For the first time in his life, Richard Hartwell felt wealthy. And very alone.

CHAPTER 14
ROOTED REBELLION GROWS

*M**eanwhile, at Roth House, Park Lane, Mayfair*
Vivian stared at the sampler she held in one hand, frustrated by the number of mistakes she hadn't bothered to fix. A skein of embroidery thread lay in her lap, and another was suffering the attentions of her mother's cat, Felix. Once he grew bored hooking the threads with his claws, it would be worthless.

"That's the third one this week you've allowed him to ruin," Miss Pipkins said from where she was seated, knitting needles rhythmically clacking.

Stiffening, Vivian fought the urge to agree and instead said, "And I'm quite sure it won't be the last."

The knitting needles dropped to Miss Pipkins' lap. "What did you say?"

Vivian looked up from the sampler and said, "I'm quite sure it won't be the last." She returned her gaze to the linen fabric, rather pleased she hadn't simply agreed with the companion. The poor weather—it had been drizzling all morning—and gray skies only added to her blue mood.

"I heard what you said," Miss Pipkins remarked.

Mentally girding her loins—Vivian imagined pulling the fabric of her skirts through her legs and tying them up around her hips—she sighed loudly and said, "Then it was unnecessary for you to ask what I said, wasn't it?"

Miss Pipkins' mouth dropped open. "Young lady, you will apologize this instant!"

Her eyes narrowing and then darting to the swords above the fireplace mantel, Vivian remembered her bold behavior the night before and said, "I will not, Miss Pipkins, for there is nothing to apologize for. You, on the other hand, will desist from remarking on the cat's doings given it is neither my cat nor a creature over which anyone has any control. Do I make myself clear, Miss Pipkins?"

The companion's eyes widened in disbelief. "Wh... what?"

"What, indeed? In fact, what *am* I doing here? Certainly nothing of value to anyone." Vivian stood up, tossed the sampler to the settee, and shook out her skirts, pretending they had been tied up around her hips. "I'm off."

Miss Pipkins' eyes rounded. "To where?"

Vivian shrugged. "I think I shall pay a call on a gentleman, and your presence is not welcome nor required."

With that, she took her leave of the parlor, well aware Felix watched her with as much interest—and was that respect?—as Miss Pipkins did with horror.

*O*nce she reached her bedchamber, her breaths coming in short pants from the quick climb up the stairs, Vivian placed a hand on her chest. She could hardly believe what she had said to Miss Pipkins. She could hardly believe how satisfying it had been to see the older woman's reaction. Why, her eyeballs had nearly popped out of her head, they were so round and bulging.

Vivian grimaced at the image her mind's eye had conjured and hurried to her wardrobe. Flinging the doors open, she paused a moment as her gaze darted over the selection of gowns. When she spotted the purple satin ballgown, she pulled it from its peg and shook the skirts as she held it in front of her body.

Although it was terribly out of fashion—it had been her mother's—it had made a perfect costume to wear when she had joined her finishing school classmates in putting on a play.

Vivian quickly stripped off her day gown and pulled the purple satin over her head, wincing when one of the fasteners caught in her bun and pulled a few strands out of place. "Damnation," she whispered as she regarded her reflection in the dressing table mirror.

Stepping back, she turned her head and gave it a shake. Another strand broke loose from its pin. Using a thumb and forefinger, she pulled a matching strand from the other side of the bun, rather liking the messy look of the bun. She continued to loosen strands here and there until the tight bun had doubled in size and one particularly long lock hung over one shoulder.

Vivian pinched her cheeks. Before she could determine if any color appeared, she began a search for her potted lip color. Although she wasn't supposed to own any cosmetics, she had surreptitiously acquired a few pots over the years, including a mouche she now applied high on one cheek and kohl that she used to darken her lashes.

Blinking a few times, she regarded her reflection. She practiced grinning, arching a dark eyebrow as she planted a fist onto one hip. Liking how that particular move had her bust pushed forward and the tops of her breasts on display, Vivian practiced several other expressions, frowning before attempting a 'come-hither' look.

She might have laughed at her antics, but she found she rather liked what she saw in the mirror. The image was still her, but it was a version that looked happier. More daring.

Seductive.

Her eyes widened when she discovered that particular pose, and she wondered if Lord Cougham would find it so.

The thought of Sebastian had the oddest sensation passing through her body. Excitement combined with a hint of pleasure. One of her hands rested on her belly, and she glanced down in wonderment.

How could the mere thought of Bash have her insides feeling as if a flock of flutterbies were tumbling about?

The very thought of the word 'tumbling' brought about an entirely different image, and she gasped as her insides blessed her with an entirely new sensation.

Her abdomen seemed to contract in a manner most unexpected. Not at all like it did when she was experiencing her monthly courses, but rather in a way that had her wishing she could experience it over and over.

Try as she might, she couldn't recreate the pleasurable sensation. Sighing in frustration, she moved to the wardrobe and pulled out her hooded mantle.

If she was going to be successful with what she was planning to do, she knew she couldn't be seen wearing a gown twenty years out of date and a messy bun and a mouche on her cheek.

Once the mantle's hood covered her head, she took her leave of her bedchamber, helped herself to an umbrella in the vestibule, and rushed out of Roth House. Although she could have requested a carriage be brought 'round—the light drizzle had just then stopped falling—she opted instead to walk the short distance to Weatherstone Manor.

CHAPTER 15

A VISCOUNT MEETS A MATRON

An hour later in Westminster

Having left the parcels he had collected from the solicitor at his townhouse, Richard learned the next meal at Hartwell House wouldn't be served until seven o'clock that evening.

"Pardon, my lord. Had the cook known you would be returning, she could have prepared a—"

"It's all right," Richard interrupted as he held up a hand. "I've yet to apprise the household of my schedule. I'll do so once I've discovered what it will be."

His stomach growled in protest when he recalled the sumptuous meal Lady Bostwick had arranged the night before.

Feeling ever so peckish—the more he thought of his father and what the man had been doing the past ten years whilst he was in London, the more irate he felt—Richard knew he needed sustenance. He thought of the The Three Bells as he hailed a hansom cab. He looked forward to another meal there, even if someone might think he was Sir Randolph.

Once he was settled in the squabs, his thoughts went to the night before. Did Viscountess Bostwick always serve multi-course dinners? He had the distinct impression she had seen to an extra special menu for the prior night's affair, and yet the mannerisms of the others at the table suggested they were enjoying a dinner similar to any other night.

Was she one of the matrons he had been warned about whilst he was still in Lincolnshire? A meddling mother whose daughter was in need of a husband? Her manner certainly hadn't seemed calculated. She hadn't espoused Miss Bennett-Jones' favorable attributes, nor those of the younger sister.

But then, she hadn't needed to.

He had found Christina Bennett-Jones a perfect young lady. Pleasant to look upon and a pleasure to engage in conversation. She'd obviously enjoyed an education beyond that of most her age.

Not at all like her friend, Lady Vivian.

He shuddered at the thought of the tall young woman, so brash and bold with her opinions. How could she expect to land a husband?

Perhaps she didn't wish to.

Perhaps she was deliberately acting poorly as a means of ensuring she wouldn't end up married. It wasn't unheard of. One of the women in his parish in Horncastle aspired to spinsterhood, claiming she looked forward to freedoms her married counterparts could not enjoy.

He remembered how his face and neck had heated at the thought of what she meant until she clarified her comment with a remark about being able to spend her own funds as she saw fit and travel when she was of a mind to do so. Nothing was said about taking a lover or sharing a man's bed.

He hoped Miss Bennett-Jones wasn't of a similar mind. He had spent his last waking moments the night before thinking of her. Remembering her auburn hair and happy manner. Her aquamarine eyes and teasing grin. Her bow lips and how they formed an 'o' when Lady Vivian made some callous remark.

He thought of how those lips might feel when pressed against his own. How much he might enjoy such a kiss. What he might do to ensure she enjoyed it, too.

His body had responded to those thoughts, his cock hard-ening so it tented his bed linens. For the first time in a long time, he had taken his member in hand and brought himself to a quick and exquisite ecstasy.

He had been as shocked by its intensity as he was by the pleasure he had experienced, the name 'Tina' repeated over and over as his release took hold. When his breathing had returned to normal, he almost felt shame at what he had done. At who he had imagined beneath him on the bed.

The hansom cab came to a stuttering halt near a corner, and Richard was jerked from his momentary reverie. Glancing down his front, he cursed at seeing how his cock was pressing against his pantaloons. Then he remembered he wore a long topcoat. Although the pleated skirt of it flared at the bottom, it was more than long enough to cover his crotch when he stood, and he secretly thanked his tailor in Horn-castle for having made it to the current fashion.

He paid the driver and donned his top hat. About to head up the street, he couldn't when he nearly collided with a woman.

"Pardon me," he said as he took a step back and gave a slight bow.

The woman who stood before him was staring at him, her large blue eyes widening in wonder. "Richard?" she asked in a hoarse whisper. "Richard!"

Richard blinked. He had expected her to call him 'Sir Randolph.' That she knew his given name had his brows furrowing. She wasn't the least bit familiar to him, but the oddest sensation passed through his body as she regarded him, obviously awestruck. "Yes," he finally admitted, the comment coming out as almost a question.

"Richard! Oh, my," she breathed. Her gaze went from the top of his head to the tip of his boots and back up again. "I always hoped I might finally meet you. I had nearly given up hope of ever *finding* you."

Richard glanced about, wanting to be sure they weren't blocking traffic on the pavement before he returned his attention to the matron. "Forgive me, my lady, but you have me at a disadvantage."

It was her turn to blink. "Oh, of course I do." She reached out and placed a hand on his arm as she turned to face the same direction as him. "May I walk with you? What is your destination?"

Richard's eyes rounded at feeling her arm atop his. Were most women in London so bold? "The Three Bells, my lady," he replied hesitantly. "For a luncheon." For a moment, he thought she might be a thief—a pickpocket who was using this opportunity to relieve him of his purse.

His coins were safely stowed in said purse, and it was stuffed into his waistcoat pocket—an inside pocket. For her to get to it meant she would have to lift the skirt of his topcoat, reach up past his waist, slide her hand between the waistcoat and his shirt, and pull the purse up and out of the interior pocket, all without being noticed.

A highly unlikely maneuver, unless she had a double-jointed elbow and very long fingers.

Well, she had long fingers, five of which were resting on his forearm. As for her elbow, it looked perfectly normal. Her eyes, however, had rounded upon hearing his destination and a huge smile appeared to display perfect teeth. "A very good choice, sir."

For a moment, he experienced the oddest sensation.

Familiarity.

And yet he was sure he had never seen the woman before.

The words the waiter had said in The Three Bells the day before came back in a flash. The words identifying the owners of the public house. "Are you... Mrs. Merriweather?" he asked with a good deal of suspicion.

The smile widened, and all at once, Richard recognized features he possessed. The same eyes. The same shaped lips. The same hair color.

"Oh, now, you really must afford me a few minutes of your time. Please, allow me to treat you to a luncheon," she insisted.

"I can hardly allow you to buy me a meal," he replied.

"You can, actually, seeing as how my husband owns this public house. I would introduce you to him this very moment, but he is meeting with one of his vendors. The butcher, I think."

Richard opened the establishment's door and inhaled deeply at the scents of grilling meat and a number of spices he could not identify. His stomach once again growled, reminding him he hadn't eaten breakfast that morning.

"Our chef is making his favorite today," she said as she caught the attention of a waiter and then pointed to a table in the back corner.

The young man acknowledged her with a firm nod as she led Richard to the table. The waiter arrived shortly after they did, a menu board stuffed under one arm. The fact that his white linen apron was still white made it apparent they had come in before the usual luncheon crowd. He asked what he could bring them.

"Tea for me," Mrs. Merriweather said. "And some shortbread."

"An ale for me," Richard said as a menu board was pressed into his hand. "And whatever the chef's favorite is."

"Good choice," Mrs. Merriweather said. "I would join you in eating, but..." She allowed a titter. "I was the very first to eat luncheon today, so I'm not yet hungry. I'm always the one who must test our cook's concoctions, you see."

"Then you must live somewhere nearby?" Richard guessed.

She nodded as she lifted a finger and pointed to the ceiling. "Upstairs. We have three floors of rooms and an office. I finished yesterday's accounting and was off to see to another establishment's books when I ran into you." Her eyes widened. "Oh, and Mother is going to be..." She paused at seeing Richard's upraised hand and straightened in her chair.

"My lady, forgive me, but I really must make it clear that we are not... we *cannot* be related to one another," he said, deciding he best sound apologetic. The poor woman seemed so sure of herself.

Her face fell as a brow furrowed. She inhaled, and her back straightened even as she leaned forward.

For a moment, Richard had the impression she was girding her loins, and he attempted to prepare himself for a verbal assault. Once she began to speak, he was glad he had.

"My name is Rachel Roderick Merriweather," she stated. "I am the only illegitimate daughter of Randall, Marquess of Reading. My twin brother Richard and I were born to his first mistress. Upon our birth, Richard was taken by our father and given to another aristocrat to be raised as his heir. I was left in my mother's care, but Lord Reading saw to all my expenses until I agreed to marry Mark Merriweather, second son of the Earl of Middleton."

Richard leaned back in his chair, stunned by her recitation. "And... you think *I* am your twin brother?"

"I am quite sure of it. If you could meet my other brothers—there are *eight* of them—you would understand why it is you *must* be a Roderick."

Deciding two could play at the game she had begun, Richard inhaled slowly. Clearing his throat, he said, "I am Richard Hartwell, son and the sole heir of Abraham Hartwell, Viscount Hartwell. I was born in Horncastle, Lincolnshire on the thirtieth of—"

"May, eighteen-oh-four," Rachel finished.

Richard gave a start. "How do you—?"

"I am your twin sister. Don't you see?" She stopped speaking as the waiter set a cup of tea on a saucer before her along with a plate of shortbread. Two lumps of sugar were perched on the saucer's edge.

Another waiter stepped forward and placed a plate of sliced beef and boiled potatoes covered in a savory gravy in front of Richard. Still another followed with a wooden board bearing a steaming loaf of brown bread and a bell of butter.

The three waiters gave slight bows before they hurried

off, unaware of Richard's wide-eyed stare following them. "This is a veritable feast," he murmured in awe.

"It's supposed to be," Rachel replied. "Enough to last you until dinner at eight." She reached over and sliced the bread, placing a few pieces on his plate and pushing the butter in his direction.

Richard nodded his thanks and then furrowed his brows at seeing the flat, white biscuit on the plate set before her. "What is that?"

"Shortbread," she replied with a grin. "The day cook is from Scotland. We're the only public house in all of London to offer it. Would you like a taste? It makes the most delightful accompaniment to tea."

Richard shook his head. "Thank you, but no," he murmured, staring at the odd looking biscuit as if it might bite him. "I think I have enough food here to last me well past eight o'clock."

He watched as she added the two lumps of sugar to her tea and then gently stirred it with the silver spoon that had been resting on her saucer. Her fingers reminded him of Christina's, and he struggled to clear his mind of the viscount's daughter lest his manhood react as it had earlier in the hansom cab.

"I understand if you don't believe me," Rachel said after she took a sip of her tea. "I understand the repercussions. I do—"

"Repercussions?" Richard repeated, after he'd taken a bite of the beef. He had to resist the urge to moan at how good it tasted. Even the parson's wife back in Horncastle didn't make a gravy as good as what was on his plate.

"You were no doubt raised as the only son of Viscount Hartwell—"

"I *was* the only son of Abraham Hartwell."

"And now some woman comes along and claims to be your twin sister, which means you were not the natural son of Viscount Hart—"

"But I was. My mother died giving birth to—"

"To a son who then died," she interrupted. "Our father gave you up so that the Hartwell viscountcy could survive. I'm sure of it."

Richard took a moment to swallow several bites of his beef before he shook his head. "Did your father tell you all of this?" he asked, annoyed by her words but rather taken with how sure she was of her information. Someone had an active imagination, and now he was wondering if it was her or her father.

Rachel inhaled softly before her shoulders slumped. "He did not," she finally admitted. At Richard's sound of disgust, she added, "I have sorted most of it myself."

"Indeed? But... how? Why?" Richard asked before taking a bite of the bread. The warmth and yeasty flavor had him almost sighing with pleasure, and he hadn't even added any of the soft butter. Food in London was obviously far better than what he'd been served in Lincolnshire.

"You were the only entry in *Debrett's* with the same birthdate as me," Rachel claimed.

Richard blinked. "You read all of *Debrett's* searching for my birthdate?"

"*My* birthdate," she countered. "And yes. It took me several days when I should have been seeing to my accounting tasks."

Rather impressed by her fortitude, Richard asked, "May I ask what the other business is for which you do the books?"

Rachel broke off a piece of the shortbread and held it up. "Our mother's business."

He furrowed a brow, struggling to remember if she had mentioned a name. "Your mother has a business?"

"She does. She is the Queen of Hearts," Rachel said proudly.

Richard blinked but didn't say anything at first. He'd seen those words in print. Heard them in the solicitor's office. He might have sorted more just then, but Mrs. Merriweather was obviously expecting a response. "A matchmaker, from the sounds of it?" he guessed.

Rachel scoffed. "You have not heard of The Queen of Hearts?" she asked in disbelief. "The gaming establishment? How long have you been in town?"

Clearing his throat, Richard said, "I have been in London three days."

Sighing, Rachel said, "It's a gaming hell in Stafford Street. Across from The Jack of Spades. Along the same stretch of St. James Street where all the gentlemen's clubs are located."

His brows furrowing, Richard's mouth dropped open, and not only because she had used the word "hell" in her response. "Your mother owns a gaming establishment?"

The ring in his greatcoat pocket was to be delivered to someone at The Queen of Hearts. A woman of some means. A woman who was wealthier than most aristocrats, Barton had said.

"*Our* mother does, yes," Rachel replied. "And it's a very *lucrative* business. I should know. I keep the books."

Richard shook his head and turned his attention back to his meal. He didn't want to consider what she was claiming. It was bad enough his father had dealings with the woman in question.

Enough dealings that Abraham Hartwell had wanted to make her his wife.

A strange sound erupted from Richard's throat as he considered the repercussions. Surely Mrs. Merriweather was merely confused. His father and her mother had engaged in some sort of *affaire* that had addlepated his father enough to have the man proposing marriage.

Every year for ten years.

He did the arithmetic in his head. He would have been almost five-and-twenty when the two had begun seeing one another. He almost asked the woman who sat across from him if she was aware of the liaison and then thought better of it.

The suggestion might only make her more determined he believe her fantastical story.

"I shall pay for your tea and your shortbread, my lady," he

said. "As well as my wonderful luncheon. I shall even make this a regular place in which to enjoy a meal whilst Parliament is in session," he added. "And as much as I like you—and I do like you—I cannot be your twin brother. I am *not* your twin brother."

He finished his meal and regarded her with a worried look, for she seemed to be on the verge of tears. "Thank you for sharing my luncheon, given I am a complete stranger to you. Good day, my lady."

Richard stood up and tossed a five pound note on the table before giving a short bow. He took his leave of The Three Bells well aware that Rachel Merriweather watched his departure until he disappeared from view.

CHAPTER 16

A CHANCE MEETING IN THE PARK

*M**eanwhile, in Hyde Park*

"I thought we might see more people out today," Christina said as she and her lady's maid walked on one of the crushed granite paths near the Serpentine. The early afternoon was fine despite the earlier morning drizzle. The gray overcast had parted to reveal an early spring sun and wispy white clouds made so by the wind that had accompanied the morning storm.

"Perhaps they are all preparing for tonight's entertainments," Perkins suggested. Although she was Christina's age, her time as a kitchen maid had aged her so she appeared far older.

"Perhaps," Christina responded, her gaze sweeping the shoreline to see that most of the boats were moored. "If there were any scheduled," she murmured with a sigh. Next week, London would be brimming with entertainments, the most anticipated being that of Lord Weatherstone's annual ball on Tuesday night.

In the meantime, these few days were the calm before the storm. A time to mentally prepare for the nightly entertainments and the daily calls. A time to simply walk and enjoy the early spring days in the park.

If only she didn't have the oddest sense she was being watched.

Christina dared a glance behind them as they made their way, surprised to discover they weren't being followed. As she turned her head to concentrate on the path in front of them, she didn't see anyone watching them, but she couldn't shake the feeling someone was spying on them.

A few children darted about, their nurses lounging on blankets spread out on the green lawn. When she sighed and directed her attention to a nearby hedgerow, she nearly stumbled.

A gentlemen was seated on one end of a park bench, his gaze directed to the ground in front of him. His expression suggested sorrow, his slumped shoulders accentuating his general poor mood.

Christina was about to redirect her attention to the path before them, but realized she recognized the man. She paused and made her way to the park bench.

"Lord Hartwell?" she asked in a quiet voice. He seemed lost in thought, and she dared not startle him.

Richard lifted his head and stared at Christina, blinking several times before he quickly rose from the bench. He tipped his hat. "Miss Bennett-Jones," he said in surprise, his expression immediately changing to one of delight.

"I do hope I did not disturb you?" she asked, dipping a curtsy as the viscount reached for her hand.

"Not at all. Actually, your presence is quite welcome right now." He lowered his lips to her gloved hand and then held on to it far longer than was usual. "Would you care to join me?" He waved to the bench with his other hand.

Christina gently pulled her hand from his. "I can for a time, I suppose." She turned and gave a wave in Perkin's direction. The lady's maid's eyes widened a fraction, but she quickly recovered and slowly ambled toward another bench farther along the hedgerow. "You looked as if you were quite lost in thought," Christina said as she watched him use a handkerchief to dust off the bench. "Why, thank you," she added, rather touched by the courtesy.

"You're most welcome." Richard waited until she was seated before he settled back onto the bench. "I *was* lost in thought, I suppose. I've experienced a most unexpected incident, and I'm not quite sure..." His voice trailed off as he turned to regard her.

"Whatever has happened?" Christina asked in alarm, now well aware the viscount had been on the verge of tears.

He dipped his head and said, "It's possible... nay, probable, that the life I have led has been one of deceit. Of a fraud not of my doing."

Christina inhaled softly before her brows furrowed. "Does this have anything to do with your uncanny resemblance to Sir Randolph?"

Richard gasped and stared at her. "You think so, too?"

She angled her head to one side and finally nodded. "He is older than you, but otherwise you two could be twins," she said with a wan grin. She sobered, though, when she noted his reaction. "Trust me when I tell you that I meant no offense by the comparison. Sir Randolph is an upstanding gentleman. Rather handsome and well regarded by those who own horses. His wife is a baron's widow."

"Oh, I am well aware of his attributes," Richard replied. "Having spent nearly an hour in his sister's company earlier today."

Christina considered the comment before her eyes widened. "Oh, you must have met Mrs. Merriweather," she said happily. "She is well regarded, too. An accountant of some skill, I understand."

"Indeed," he agreed. "And she is convinced I am her twin brother." This last was said as if he might have initially thought such a situation impossible but was now reconsidering.

Christina stared at him. "Twin?"

He nodded. "She looked at me as if she knew me. Knew who I was. Called me 'Richard' and gripped my wrist and stared at me with the happiest of expressions," he explained as he shook his head.

"She is the daughter of the Marquess of Reading," Christina said, hoping she didn't sound inane saying it. "If you were her twin, then you would have to be one of his sons."

"And I cannot be," he whispered quickly. "Don't you see? I am the sole heir to the Hartwell viscountcy. How could I be... how could I be the bastard son of Reading *and* the legitimate son of Abraham Hartwell?"

Christina winced at hearing the bitter words. At hearing the anger behind them. "It is rather unbelievable," she agreed.

"Exactly," he said.

"But... is it possible?"

His immediate reaction suggested it was impossible, but his gaze returned to the ground in front of him. "It would explain a few things I've always wondered about," he murmured.

"Such as?" she prompted gently.

Straightening on the bench, Richard seemed to consider his answer before he said, "I look nothing like my father. Nothing like any of the prior viscounts going back to the first in sixteen-fifty-six. All their portraits hang in a gallery at Hartwell House in Lincolnshire."

Christina considered his comment a moment before she asked, "Do you resemble your mother? Or any of her siblings?" The memory of his mother's family came to her in a flash, but she thought it best not to mention the Earl of Greenley. "Your cousins?"

He shook his head. "I never knew her. She died when I was born." Pausing, he rolled his eyes, as if he had just then sorted how it was possible he could be someone else's son. "Her portrait hangs in my father's... in *my* study," he corrected. "I... I look nothing like her."

"Family resemblance isn't always evident. My brothers and I look nothing alike."

He gave her a grin and said, "For which you are undoubtedly glad."

"I am," she agreed with a giggle.

"While you and your sister are obviously sisters," he countered.

She sobered and said, "I suppose without any siblings, it makes the comparing harder to do."

"It's always just been my father and me," he acknowledged.

"And now it's just you," Christina said as she placed a hand on his arm. They sat in silence for a time before she inhaled softly. "Would it really be so bad if you were Lord Reading's son? As well as Lord Hartwell's?"

He inhaled and regarded her with an expression of uncertainty. "I am the sole heir to the Hartwell viscountcy. If word should spread that I am—"

"It will not," Christina said, her hand gripping his arm. "Mrs. Merriweather is not a gossip. Nor am I," she added. "If it's true... if you are Reading's son, well, you might have lost a mother you never knew and the father who raised you, but..." Her eyes widened. "But you will have gained a father, and lots of half-brothers, two sisters... and a stepmother you would find quite interesting given her knowledge of horses," she gushed.

"You say that as if you wish it to be true," he accused, his brows furrowed.

Christina found she didn't have an immediate response. "Oh, it matters not to *me*, but as I asked before, would it really be so bad? To have a *secret family*?"

A mix of emotions played out on the viscount's face before he suddenly stood, scoffing. "Indeed it *would*, my lady," he replied, anger tingeing his words. "Secret family," he repeated in a harsh whisper. Louder, he said, "I trust you will keep this fantasy to yourself?"

"I won't say a word," she whispered.

"I must go. Good day." He tipped his hat and, without a backward glance, he hurried off toward Park Lane, his boot heels crunching the crushed granite.

Her shoulders slumping, Christina leaned against the back of the park bench and immediately regretted her query.

Why, oh why had she thought it necessary to reinforce what Mrs. Merriweather had probably already said to the viscount? Surely Rachel Roderick Merriweather knew she had a twin brother somewhere in the world. Otherwise, why would she have brought up the topic with Lord Hartwell?

Wishful thinking?

A desire to know the identity of her long lost twin brother?

Christina sighed and looked up to discover her lady's maid standing in front of her.

"The viscount didn't seem very happy when he took his leave," Perkins remarked, her gaze turning to follow the retreating back of the aristocrat.

"He had his reasons," Christina murmured, tears brightening the corners of her eyes. She had only hoped to assuage his concerns, not put his parentage and inheritance into question. Now he was probably angry with her. Any hope she might have had of forging a relationship with Lord Hartwell...

Christina blinked as she straightened.

Whatever was she thinking? Lord Hartwell was far older than she was. By at least ten years. Mayhap fifteen.

So why was she experiencing such a sense of loss at his sudden departure? A sense of sorrow at realizing she had angered him?

"I thought he was sweet on you," Perkins said absently, her gaze still directed to the east.

Inhaling softly at hearing the lady's maid's remark, Christina turned to direct her attention on the departing back of the viscount.

He cut a fine form in his black cape coat, his black Hessians hugging calves that she knew weren't enhanced with stuffing. The shape of his muscles had been apparent beneath the pantaloons he had worn to dinner the night before, no doubt built up from his work with horses.

The thought of the four-legged beasts had her hoping he

might find solace with one. He could do with a ride to help clear his head.

At the moment, she could do with a ride.

"Perkins, we're going riding," she announced as she stood from the bench.

"Riding?"

"Indeed. I wish to better my skills on a horse."

Her brows rising in surprise, Perkins allowed a shrug and said, "Well, then, I suppose we need to find some horses, my lady."

Christina gave her lady's maid a quelling glance before setting off, her pace quick as they made their way to Park Lane.

Viscount Hartwell might well be concerned that his life as a viscount could be near an end, but she knew better. She intended that he know it, too.

CHAPTER 17

A SEDUCTRESS ON
THE HUNT

eanwhile, in Park Lane

Vivian reached up to push the hood away from her face in an attempt to learn exactly where she was in Park Lane. She had thought the walk to Weatherstone Manor from Roth House would take but five minutes. Instead, she was sure she had been walking for an hour.

Had she passed the house that hosted nearly every aristocrat for the first ball of the Season?

Apparently not, for she discovered she was standing directly in front of the manor house.

Allowing a huff, she marched up to the front door. Ignoring the brass lion's head knocker, she pounded a gloved fist on the carved wooden door and stepped back. When it didn't open after five heartbeats—she had discovered they were an excellent way in which to gauge the passage of time —she stepped up and used the knocker. Before she could even pound it a second time, the knocker was pulled from her grip when the door opened from within.

The ancient butler, who would normally maintain a stoic expression befitting his station, actually recoiled before he managed to recover. "Yes, my lady?"

Vivian was rather glad the hood cast her face in shadow, for she was dumbstruck.

What was she supposed to do now?

Bash.

She was there to seduce Bash—even though her slippered feet ached from her walk and the mouche she had applied had migrated from the top of her cheek to somewhere near her chin.

"Is Lord Cougham in residence?" she asked.

The butler had the audacity to peek out the front door and look left and right before he gave her a second assessing glance. "He is not. Might you have a... a calling card?" he asked, lowering his voice to a near whisper.

"Why are you whispering?"

Straightening as much as his hunchback would allow, the servant said, "Aren't you a bit... early?"

Vivian blinked. "For what?" Realizing the butler didn't recognize her, she pushed the hood from her head with a huff. "It's me, Gilbert."

His eyes rounding, the butler doubled over in a deep bow. "Forgive me, my lady. I did not recognize you."

"You're forgiven," Vivian replied, her brows furrowing as she continued to wonder what he meant by his response. "Will he be long, do you suppose? I was hoping I might..." She clamped her mouth shut, realizing she really shouldn't be telling the butler what she intended to do once she had Sebastian in her sights.

Just the thought of pushing him down onto a Grecian sofa and straddling him had those strange flutterbies fluttering about her insides, sending all sorts of other strange sensations shooting through her midsection.

As excited as she was, she might have simply employed her wiles on the servant, but given his stooped stature, she was sure Gilbert would break.

"You were thinking you might... *what*, my lady?"

At the realization of what she was thinking—of what she was imagining—Vivian let out a strangled cry. Seduction wasn't something she could manage. Especially now that she knew her mouche had become detached from her chin and was now resting atop the first fastening of her mantle.

She plucked the black velvet circle from its new home using her thumb and forefinger. "I was thinking I need to find a different way to attach this to my cheek," she mused.

"Ah. Lady Weatherstone buys hers with a resin-based mastic applied to the back," Gilbert said, sounding ever so proud of his mistress.

Vivian furrowed a brow before she realized what expression it might convey. The last thing she wanted to do was seduce the butler. "And if I don't have a resin-based mastic on the back of mine?" she asked, rather intrigued the butler would know anything about mouches.

The butler shrugged. "Lick it and stick it on, my lady," he replied.

Not about to admit that was exactly what she had done to begin with, Vivian placed the black velvet dot on the end of her tongue and then pushed it onto her cheek. "I don't suppose Lord Cougham is available now?" she asked.

Shaking his head, the butler said, "He is not, my lady. Would you like to leave a calling card?"

Not having brought any cards with her—she hadn't considered this a social call—Vivian sighed. "I do not." After a pause, she turned to take her leave. Gilbert was quick to open the door for her, and when he offered to let the viscount know she had paid a call, Vivian shook her head. "Oh, please do not."

The butler furrowed his pair of bushy gray brows and said, "Very well, my lady."

He lingered at the front door as Vivian took her leave of Weatherstone Manor.

Neither he nor Vivian were aware they were being watched as Lady Vivian made her way down the front walk and then back to Roth House.

CHAPTER 18

A DEJECTED DAUGHTER
TELLS ALL

eanwhile, at Bostwick House

From inside his study, George Bennett-Jones knew when his daughter had returned from her walk in the park. There was the usual commotion in the vestibule as redingotes were shed and gloves were removed. The muted voices weren't expected, though, and the fact that her lady's maid went upstairs with the garments and Christina practically ran into the library had him on alert.

Curious, George stood from the leather-clad sofa and dropped the book he'd been reading. From the study's threshold, he could make out the faint sounds of keening.

He winced.

Although it didn't happen often, he knew when his wife was crying. She made that same high-pitched sound in between her struggles to breathe.

Pulling his handkerchief from his pocket, he marched into the library and stopped short. Christina wasn't visible from where he stood, but he heard her sob and made his way between a row of bookshelves. He found her clear at the back of the wood-paneled room, leaning against the end of a bookshelf. One hand covered her mouth in an attempt to stifle the sounds of her crying while the other was wrapped around her middle as if she had to use it to hold herself up.

"Who is it that I must impale with my foil?" he asked as he pressed the handkerchief against her cheek.

Her eyes widened at realizing she wasn't alone. She gingerly took the linen as her sobs became more violent. A moment later, and both her arms were around her middle as she stepped into his hold.

"I shouldn't have said... have said... any.... anything," she stammered, gasping for air.

"To whom were you speaking?" He pulled away, grimacing when he could feel the sobs wracking her body.

"Lord... Lord Hart... Hartwell," she managed to get out before the next round of keening started.

"When... when were you speaking with Lord Hartwell?" he asked in surprise. The viscount was the very last person he would have expected her to mention as a reason for her to cry.

"In the... the... park." She panted a couple of breaths. "It was just by... by chance that we found each other. He was... vexed because everyone calls him... 'Sir Randolph'," she explained in between sobs.

Wincing, George allowed a long sigh. "He bears an uncanny resemblance to the man, it's true," he murmured.

Christina sniffled. "Mrs. Merriweather saw him at The Three Bells and claimed he's her brother. Told him who their real father was, which meant Lord Reading had to have arranged for him to become the Hartwell heir."

George gave a start, blinking in shock. "Oh, damnation," he muttered. A memory of his conversation with Elizabeth the night before came flooding back. "Are you speaking of Reading's daughter, Rachel?"

She nodded as she blew her nose. "I think he was cordial with her, but by the time I spoke with him in the park, he'd had time to think, and..." Her words were once again interrupted by a sob.

"Whatever did he say to make you *cry?*" George asked, now befuddled.

The keening started again, and Christina hiccuped several

times before she said, "I was only … try… trying to help. Would it really be so bad if he was Reading's son? Rachel's twin?" she whispered. "Hartwell doesn't have any family any longer. I told him he could be the son of a… a… marquess and would have brothers. Lots of them. And a stepmother and two sisters—"

"And he did not take it well," George finished for her.

She shook her head and new tears welled up once again.

"Oh, daughter. I suppose the fact that you're crying like this means you thought him an agreeable sort after last night?"

She nodded. "I thought he liked me, too. He seemed so very happy to find me in the park."

George once again pulled her into an embrace. "Did you run, or did he?"

Christina jerked in his hold. "He did. He was angry and hurt that I would say such things. I was only trying to help."

"Where was he going when he took his leave of you?"

Hiccuping again, Christina at first shrugged, but then said, "I think to his townhouse." She sniffled. "Mayhap Lord Reading's townhouse," she murmured, thinking he might wish to confront the marquess. "Is it so very hard to believe he could be Reading's son?"

George cleared his throat. "Not for me or for your mother," he replied dryly. When Christina's wet eyes widened, he added, "And after hearing me put voice to my suspicions last night, she had to agree it's a possibility. But know this," he said in a voice filled with warning. "There are people in this world who are entirely unrelated who still look like someone else. It's very possible it's just a… a coincidence that he happens to look like Sir Randolph."

Nodding her understanding, Christina dried her tears on the handkerchief. "I should apologize to him."

"Oh, no," her father replied, his head shaking from side to side. "He made you cry. He's the one who should apologize."

Christina's eyes once again rounded. "Are you going to threaten him with a sword?"

George cleared his throat. "I was thinking I might try a tongue lashing before I challenge him to a duel."

The keening almost started again, but Christina swallowed and straightened. "*I* was thinking this might be the year I accept a marriage proposal," she whispered. "Now... now I suppose I'll have to wait another Season."

Allowing a huff, George said, "If he hasn't come calling with his tail betwixt his legs by this time tomorrow, then I shall seek him out."

Christina nodded her understanding. "Don't be too hard on him, Father," she whispered. "It cannot be easy to be new in town *and* learn he might not be who he has been raised to believe he is."

George bussed her on the forehead and took a steadying breath. "He would have been a very lucky man to have you as his wife," he stated.

The two made their way out of the library at the same moment Elizabeth was making her way down the stairs. "Why you won't believe who I've just seen riding horses into the park from the upstairs window," she said before she noted Christina's reddened eyes. She exchanged glances with her husband before she added, "Oh, dear."

"Oh, dear, indeed," George whispered.

"I was thinking I might like to go for a ride," Christina said between soft sobs.

George exchanged a quick glance with his wife. "On horseback?" he asked in alarm.

Christina winced. "It seemed like a good idea at the time," she murmured.

"Blackie will know you're upset the moment you mount him," her mother warned. "Whereas the phaeton is being pulled around to the front of the house as we speak."

"Are you going for a ride with father?"

George cleared his throat. "I think perhaps you two could do with a ride," he suggested. "I can follow on horseback." He leaned over and kissed Elizabeth on the cheek. "Don't wait for me. I've got some correspondence to see to first. I'll catch up."

With that, he headed toward the back of the house while Elizabeth regarded her daughter. "You heard your father," she said. "There will be no changing clothes, but do fetch your redingote and a hat."

"Yes, Mother," Christina replied as she hurried up the stairs. She had no idea what her parents had in mind, but she thought it best she learn it first hand.

CHAPTER 19

A BUTLER IS GRILLED FOR
WHAT HE KNOWS

*M*eanwhile, at Weatherstone Manor

"Was that Lady Vivian who paid a call a few minutes ago?" Sebastian asked as he allowed Gilbert to take his great coat. Having watched a young lady take her leave of Weatherstone Manor only a few moments ago, a hood covering most of her head, he wasn't entirely certain.

"I'm quite sure I don't know who you mean, sir," the butler replied, his attention on the wool garment and the short top hat Sebastian had tossed onto a nearby chair.

"Oh, come now. She's only the tallest woman in all of London," Sebastian countered, a teasing grin appearing to youthen his appearance.

Gilbert finally acquiesced. "It was she, my lord, but you didn't learn that from me."

Sebastian blinked. Why ever would Lady Vivian ask a butler to keep her visitation a secret? "Did she come for tea with my mother?"

The butler shook his head. "Lady Weatherstone is paying calls this afternoon. I believe she's at Carlington House, helping Lady Morganfield plot the particulars for her garden party tomorrow."

Sebastian straightened to his full height, knowing the

butler couldn't begin to unfold himself in order to look up that high. "Did Lady Vivian ask for my father?"

"No, sir."

A slow grin spreading over his face, Sebastian felt a glimmer of excitement at thinking Vivian Wentworth might pay a call on him at his place of residence. "She was looking for me, then," he reasoned. "And she didn't even have a lady's maid or her companion with her."

A rather bold move on the young lady's part. Perhaps the companion had come up lame and been left on the side of the road, or Lady Vivian had walked too fast. Given her long legs, it was possible she would leave a lady's maid in the dust.

When the butler didn't confirm nor deny his comment, Sebastian planted his fists on his hips, knowing the move would cause his chest to puff out and his biceps to bulge in a manner befitting a bare-knuckle boxer. "Lady Vivian would never do such a thing," he murmured, loud enough for Gilbert to hear. "Why, if anyone spotted her, her reputation as Miss Prim and Proper would suffer."

Gilbert's hands clasped behind his back, but he glanced left and right before he finally allowed a long sigh. "It was she, sir. She asked for you. Seemed quite determined to speak with you until she discovered her mouche was behaving badly."

Sebastian blinked again. "Mouche?" he repeated, his brows furrowing. "Lady Vivian was wearing a beauty spot?"

The butler's eyes darted sideways. "Only when she departed."

The brows rose in response, and Sebastian's face took on an expression of confusion. "Where was it before that?"

Gilbert allowed a shrug. "She had managed to capture it with a thumb and forefinger, although I cannot say exactly where she put it after that. I told her she should lick it and stick it."

Not for the first time since his return to London, Sebastian felt as if he was in a different world. One that was upside down and inside out. "Lick it and stick it... where, exactly?"

His eyes widening, Gilbert said, "Well, on her face, of course, sir. I'm quite sure it started somewhere high on her cheek before it took on the migratory path of birds."

"Birds?" Sebastian asked, realizing too late he really shouldn't have responded.

"They fly south in the winter, sir."

"It's spring, Gilbert," Sebastian countered.

"Ah, then their migratory pattern in the autumn, sir," the butler quickly amended.

"So... low on her cheek?" Sebastian guessed.

Gilbert sighed. "Her chin, sir. It was not a pretty sight."

Wincing, Sebastian tried to sort why Lady Vivian would think she needed to wear a beauty spot in the first place. She had never displayed any scars from smallpox or sores from syphilis. She didn't need cosmetics. She was gorgeous without them. Tall and lithesome and the only woman on the planet who might cause him to forget his two years at the monastery. Forget his promise that he would never again behave as the scoundrel he had been prior to his departure from London.

Just the thought of Lady Vivian had his nether region responding in a most unmonkish manner.

"Sir, I'm to tell you the countess wishes a word with you before dinner this evening," Gilbert said, interrupting his reverie.

His nether region reacted in a most monk-like manner, which had him feeling profound relief. "Where might I find *her*?" he asked.

"Her private salon, sir."

Sebastian nodded and hurried through the grand hall and up the stairs, images of Lady Vivian wearing a mouche on the top of her cheek threatening his sanity.

CHAPTER 20

PLOTTING WHAT TO DO NEXT

A bit earlier, in Hyde Park

As Richard walked with purpose toward his townhouse in Park Lane, a myriad of emotions played out over his face. Had anyone paid him any mind, they might have thought him angry and then sad, frustrated and then determined, sorrowful and then despondent. He felt all that and more as he made his way, his stomping steps softening to a more reasonable walk and finally slowing to a leisurely stroll.

Why hurry when he had no real destination in mind? He would no doubt end up at home—his very own townhouse—but what would he find there that would provide him any solace?

Nay, the solace he sought would have to come from somewhere else. Something else.

Someone else.

He cursed when he considered how he had left Christina Bennett-Jones' company. How he had responded to her gentle queries. She hadn't meant to anger him—only to make him see that his situation need not be as bad as he was imagining.

A loss of identity was certainly cause for concern. He had always been Richard Hartwell, heir to the Hartwell viscountcy. He had always been his father's only son. His father had always treated him as if he was his progeny. Always been fair with him. Never raised a hand to discipline him, although there hadn't been a need to do so.

Richard had been a good son, eager to please and determined not to embarrass the only aristocrat within thirty miles of Horncastle. He never set foot in a brothel, nor had he ever employed a mistress. Even at school, he avoided fraternizing with boys who were prone to finding trouble—or causing it.

From the time he was breeched, he'd been encouraged not to call attention to himself. To remember he had been born into a life of privilege that most did not share. To remember that to be a viscount—to own land that helped sustain others—meant he had a responsibility to them and to king and country.

He also had to find a wife and sire an heir, whether or not he was really Abraham Hartwell's son. As far as everyone in Parliament knew, he was the new viscount. He needed to behave as such.

Could his title even be taken away if the truth was revealed? For he was coming to realize he probably wasn't the son of Abraham. There were a growing number of reasons for him to be the son of Randall Roderick, Marquess of Reading.

An image of Christina Bennett-Jones flitted across his mind's eye. She had tried so hard to console him. So hard to show him the positive side of his probable parentage.

Rachel Merriweather hadn't tried to convince him, apparently deciding he needed to work it out for himself. She had probably had to do the same for herself at some point in her past.

Had she known from a young age that she was illegitimate? Had she known Reading when she was a child?

There was only one man in London who could give him the answers he needed.

He could make an appointment—he really should send word ahead—but Richard feared any advance notice might have that man replying with an excuse to avoid such a meeting.

Reaching Park Avenue, Richard waved when he spotted a

hansom cab. The equipage pulled to the curb, and the driver asked, "Where to, guv'nor?"

"Might you know the location of Lord Reading's residence?"

A thoughtful expression crossed the older man's face. "Reading House, you mean?" he asked. He lifted a gloved hand and pointed in the direction of the nearest street that intersected with Park Lane. "Why, it's just a few streets up Curzon, sir."

"Take me there, won't you?" Richard tossed a coin and the driver caught it.

"Right away, guv'nor."

Richard stepped into the cab and settled into the black leather squabs. If the Marquess of Reading's townhouse really was only a few streets to the east, Richard realized he didn't have long to rehearse what he planned to say.

Instead of thinking of how he might change his mind and tell the driver to go to The Queen of Hearts—Mrs. Merriweather had mentioned she had an office there—he concentrated on what he would say to the man who might be his real father. What questions he might ask to learn the truth of the matter.

Given the short trip—Reading House was indeed close to Park Lane—Richard found he had very little time to think. No time at all to come up with suitable questions. No time to consider the consequences of what he was about to do.

And not a moment to feel regret.

CHAPTER 21

A REUNION GOES AWRY

*M*eanwhile, at Roth House

Her feet aching and her mouche once again taking its leave of her cheek, Vivian plodded up the walk to Roth House.

Not a single person had given her a second look when she passed other pedestrians. As if it were perfectly acceptable for a woman her age to be walking in Park Lane without a lady's maid or a companion. As if everyone thought she was a spinster or a widow or a... a courtesan given her errant mouche, out for an afternoon walk.

So despondent was she, the feather on her hat drooping with her mood, she didn't hear the carriage that stopped on the street behind her.

"Lady Vivian?"

The male voice had her pausing in mid-step. She turned around to discover a yellow-wheeled high-perch phaeton had parked directly in front of Roth House. A Cleveland Bay stood in front of it, and atop it sat Sebastian Peele, Viscount Cougham.

"Bash?" she said, the word barely audible.

The viscount descended from the phaeton's bench, his height allowing him to easily negotiate the single step of the sporting vehicle. "Vi of My Eye," he said as he approached. He reached for her hand and bowed over it.

"Lord Cougham," she acknowledged, shocked at hearing one of his many forms of address for her. She managed to dip a curtsy at the last minute. "Good afternoon."

"Afternoon," he replied as he stepped back and let go of her hand. "I am sorry I was not home when you paid a call a while ago," he said.

Vivian shook her head. "Oh, I did no such thing," she replied. "I've just been out to take some air."

Sebastian opened his other gloved hand. In the middle of the kid leather palm was a black velvet circle. "I think this might be yours?"

Vivian blew out a breath that sent the curls at the top edge of her coiffure flying up. "If I said I'd never seen it before, would you believe me?"

His brows furrowed and he shook his head. "No."

She inhaled deeply. "Gilbert promised he wouldn't say anything," she complained.

"It's not his fault, my lady. I beat it out of him. Trust me when I tell you, it was painful for him to relay what had happened."

"No doubt," Vivian replied as she rolled her eyes. She took the mouche from his outstretched hand and examined it as she held it between her thumb and forefinger. "This is far larger than any beauty spot I possess," she claimed, her eyes widening as she turned her attention back to Sebastian. She found him attempting to stifle a grin. She scoffed. "Bash!"

"I could not help it. Mother has dozens of those damned things. I merely borrowed one of them." He quickly sobered at seeing her expression of hurt. "Are you well?"

She shrugged. "I suppose. And you?"

"Alive," he replied with a curt nod.

Her brows furrowing at the curious response, Vivian asked, "Was there a chance you would not be?"

It was his turn to shrug. "Given my past acts of derring

do, and quests for speed, and desire for danger, it's rather remarkable I am," he said with some awe.

"And all this time, you could have been a model of perfect behavior, like me," she retorted. "Forced to spend your days with a sourpuss for a companion with nothing to do but ruin perfectly innocent skeins of embroidery thread and look down your nose at men several inches shorter than you."

Sebastian gave a start at hearing her uncharacteristic response. "You needn't make it sound so awful," he murmured. "Besides, I already do that thing with looking down my nose at shorter men. Hard not to given I'm so tall." He moved a step closer when his words didn't seem to have the effect he was hoping for. "What's wrong?"

"I promised Miss Christina Bennett-Jones that I would behave myself until Friday."

His gaze darted sideways a moment before he said, "You make that sound as if it will be difficult."

"It will be. In fact, I've already broken my promise, seeing as how I went to your house to pay a call on you without the benefit of a companion."

"The sourpuss?"

"Yes. Miss Pipkins."

"She's still your companion?" he asked in disbelief.

"She is."

"You... you could have fired her," he suggested.

"How? I wasn't the one who hired her."

He shrugged. "You could have married someone."

She angled her head and gave him a quelling glance. "That would have required that someone court me and propose to me."

Sebastian was careful to keep a passive expression on his face despite having learned what he came for. "You could have found *her* a husband," he suggested, a grin appearing before he could hide it behind a hand.

"A capital idea. Why don't you propose to her?"

Dipping his head, Sebastian said, "I apologize. I merely wished to renew our acquaintance. Not make you upset."

Her lower lip extended in a pout, Vivian regarded him a moment before she said, "Apology accepted."

"Now, what's this about you having to behave until Friday?"

She rolled her eyes. "I'm tired of being prim and proper," she whispered.

"But... you're so good at it," he replied. "If you weren't prim and proper, what would you be?" This last was asked in a voice that suggested he was panicking.

"Engaging in acts of derring do? Seeking a means to go faster? Desiring danger?" she responded, remembering his words of a few moments ago.

"It's not worth it, Vivian," he replied, giving his head a shake.

Vivian lifted her chin a bit. "Says the man who seems to enjoy that lifestyle very much."

"I'm not like that any longer, Viv."

She gave him another quelling glance and was about to argue when the front door opened behind her. She visibly stiffened, as if she knew what was to come.

"My lady, it's not seemly for you to be conversing without a chaperone," Miss Pipkins stated in her harshest voice.

Well aware Vivian was about to say something entirely unladylike—her eyes were ablaze and her expression had turned rather stern—Sebastian hurried up to the companion and dipped a low bow. "Miss Pipkins, so good to see you again," he said in a silky voice as he reached for her hand.

The startled companion boggled in response as she watched him kiss the back of her knuckles. "Lord Cougham?" she replied in a breathy voice.

"Guilty as charged. Lady Vivian was being so kind as to remind me of the upcoming entertainments. I've only just returned to town, you see, and I knew she could fill me in on where I need to be. I trust we'll see you at the...?" He turned to Vivian. "What's the next social engagement?"

"Lady Morganfield's annual garden party," Vivian replied,

taking great delight in seeing his momentary wince. "One o'clock tomorrow."

Sebastian turned back around, forcing a pleasant expression. "At the garden party," he said.

"Tomorrow, yes," Miss Pipkins nodded, nearly salivating at the attentions the viscount was showering on her.

"Very good, then. I shall see you there." He turned around and bowed to Vivian. "My lady," he said before he lifted her hand to his lips. "I look forward to seeing you tomorrow. Wearing a mouche, perhaps?" he whispered, his eyes settling on her cheek.

Vivian might have slapped him across the face except he moved too quickly. He was up and on his sporty phaeton before she could lift her arm.

About to stomp a foot, Vivian decided it hurt too much already and simply made her way into the house.

Friday could not come quick enough.

CHAPTER 22

A MAN MEETS HIS FATHER

eading House, Curzon Street, Mayfair
Richard stepped down from the hansom cab and gave the white stucco townhouse an assessing glance. Neat flower boxes, painted a dark blue to match the shutters, hung beneath the lower rows of windows. A riot of colors was depicted in their floral display. The front door, painted the same dark blue, sported a brass lion's head knocker.

"Should I wait for you, sir?" the cab driver asked from his perch. The single horse let out a whinny, obviously impatient at having to stand still for more than a moment.

Richard quickly examined the horse. He thought the Cleveland Bay especially well formed and wished he'd had a carrot or an apple to give the beast. He turned his attention to the black-clad driver and said, "That won't be necessary, but I do appreciate the offer."

As Richard approached the Reading House door, he almost hoped the marquess wouldn't be in residence. In that case, Richard would simply walk home—his townhouse wasn't far at all.

Before he could change his mind, though, the blue door opened to reveal a portly butler whose thinning hair was nearly white.

"Good afternoon, Sir... sir," the butler said as he bowed his head.

"Afternoon. Might Lord Reading be in residence?" Having noted the butler's initial intention to call him Sir Randolph, he handed the servant his calling card.

The butler, Giles, gave the card a cursory glance and waved him in. "He's not in the house at the moment, my lord, but he is on the grounds. Do you wish to wait in the front salon? Or I can take you to him," he offered.

Richard furrowed a brow. When did a butler ever take a visitor to his master without first clearing it with him? "He is... nearby?"

Nodding, the butler said, "He's in the stables, my lord. He and his marchioness will eventually depart on horseback for the park."

"Eventually?" Richard repeated.

"They spend a good deal of time *reviewing* their horses, sir. Even seeing to some of the tasks a groom really should be doing." He added this last with a sniff, as if he found the practice appalling.

"Ah," Richard replied, glad to know another lord shared his appreciation for good horseflesh. "To the stables, then," he said.

"Very good, sir."

The butler turned and led Richard through a great hall tastefully decorated with caryatids bearing marble busts. A round rosewood table, whose middle displayed a bouquet of flowers that might have come from the window boxes out front, stood in the middle of the hall. Beyond it was a carpeted marble staircase.

Given his own townhouse's front hall appearance was nearly identical, Richard wondered if his father and Lord Reading had used the same decorators.

Before Richard could direct his gaze up past the landing, they were beyond the stairs and walking through a wide gallery featuring large portraits. He did a double-take upon seeing one that looked entirely too familiar.

He stutter-stepped and then halted, staring at a man who could have been him. Given the height of the painting and the manner in which it was hung, it was like looking in a mirror. Richard frowned at seeing the garb the subject wore, though, for it was obviously from a time over a hundred years ago. Two-hundred years, even.

"If I may say so, you bear a remarkable resemblance to the second marquess, sir," Giles said. The servant had backtracked to stand next to Richard as he gazed at the painting.

"I do," Richard replied in a quiet voice. For a moment, he thought to turn on his heel and take his leave. Curiosity had him staying, though. He would never know the truth unless he confronted Lord Reading.

When the butler realized the visitor had had his fill of the painting, he resumed the trek to the back door. As they passed open doors along the corridor, Richard swiveled his head to take in the decor beyond their thresholds.

The brief glances had him realizing the marquess was wealthy and his marchioness had good taste. Nothing was overdone. Furnishings were appropriate to their rooms. Walls were sheathed in silk or paneled in wood. Floors were tiled in marble or covered with Turkish carpets. Gas lights hung from the ceilings in the form of crystal chandeliers and decorative globes.

Richard considered the townhouse he now called home. Other than the front hall, he doubted his father had ever had the benefit of a woman's help in decorating the house. A brief thought of what Christina Bennett-Jones might choose to redecorate the townhouse had him wishing he hadn't been so dismissive with her.

She had only been trying to help, he realized. Trying to make him see that he was still *him*, even if he might not be the real son of Abraham Hartwell.

He owed her an apology.

Before he could consider when and where he might find her to extend such a courtesy, the butler exited the house and followed a paved path to a large stables that ran the length of the back of the townhouse's property. The odors of fresh hay and manure assaulted his nostrils, reminding him of the Hartwell stables in Horncastle.

The oddest sensation passed through him just then. A familiar sensation. The sensation of being home.

"She'll drop hers before the month is over," a feminine voice said from somewhere to his right.

"Nonsense. She's probably just carrying twins," a deep voice replied.

Richard stared at the couple who were doting on a very pregnant mare that was tied to a pole in the back garden. The woman was brushing the Thoroughbred while the man was examining its teeth.

The butler cleared his throat, which had Lord Reading turning to regard first his servant and then Richard with a look of surprise.

"Lord Hartwell," he called out happily. "Come join us."

Stepping back, the butler returned to the house while Richard hurried over to the marquess. He quickly removed his glove and held out his right hand, and Reading shook it.

"I hope I haven't come at a bad time, sir," Richard said as he bowed.

"Randolph! I didn't realize..." The older woman's words trailed off as she regarded him a moment, the brush she held in her right hand resting on the mare's withers. "Oh, I apologize, sir. I've mistaken you for someone else."

"It's quite all right, my lady. You are not the first on this day to refer to me by your... your stepson's name," Richard replied, hoping he had the relationship sorted and that she was, indeed, the Marchioness of Reading. He had never in his life imagined he would find a woman of her station brushing a horse.

Constance Fitzwilliam Roderick handed the brush to a groom and stepped forward to join her husband in greeting Richard.

"Lady Reading, may I present Richard Hartwell, Viscount Hartwell?" Randall said. "He's new to Parliament this Season, and he is... well, truth be told, he is my third son. Rachel's twin, in fact."

Both Constance and Richard turned to stare at Randall, looks of shock apparent in their widened eyes.

"Sir?"

"Randall?"

Randall grimaced. "That is why you have come, is it not?" he asked as he regarded Richard. "Because you have come to realize the truth? Surely not because... because someone told you?" he added carefully.

Richard felt as if a rock had dropped into his stomach at the same time he felt relief at not having to be the first one to broach the subject. "Your reaction is unexpected, as are your words." He glanced over at Lady Reading, fearing she would be staring at him in a less than cordial manner. Her face displayed a look of awe, though, her head angled as she gazed rather lovingly at her husband. "It is good of you to... to admit such a truth, sir," Richard said. "If it is the truth?"

Randall allowed a one-shouldered shrug. "It is."

"Now I find I am left in a quandary not of my making."

"Of course, you do." Randall replied, a worried expression replacing that of the happiness he had displayed only a moment ago. "You are owed an explanation, and I shall provide one. The question now is how and where that explanation will occur. Are you up for a ride in the park?"

Richard glanced down at his suit of clothes. Although he wasn't wearing attire specifically suited to riding—he wore a long top coat and leathern breeches tucked into Hessians—it would do in a pinch. "I am, sir." His gaze went to a black horse in a stall at the far end of the stables. "Do you have another mount in need of exercise?"

Constance tittered. "We have a number of horses who would like nothing more than that," she replied. "I see you have your sights on Midnight. He's spirited, a bit ornery at times, but you'll do fine on him. I understand you have an impressive stable in Lincolnshire."

Richard's eyes widened. "I do, my lady," he replied, realizing she knew of the Hartwell stables from the horse racing circuit.

"You can call me Connie," she countered, one of her gloved hands coming to rest on his arm. "As one of my husband's sons, you are family, and I will always treat you as such. That means you are not exempt from scolding should you do something stupid, however," she warned with a quirk. She turned and motioned for a groom to join them.

A guffaw escaped his lips before Richard could bring it under control. "I understand, my lady... Connie," he corrected, deciding he rather liked the marchioness. How Lord Reading had managed to find a woman who would not only tolerate his many bastard sons—Rachel had said there were four—and treat them like family had him believing she was not born and bred among the usual London aristocracy.

When Constance indicated Midnight, the groom nodded and hurried off to saddle the stallion.

"I *am* sorry for your loss, Richard," Randall said in reference to Abraham Hartwell. "He was a good man. A better viscount. If you've learned half of what he knew about managing lands and tenants, you'll make a fine aristocrat."

Richard sighed. "I hope I have learned all of it, sir."

Randall gave him a curt nod before he moved to a stall and hooked his gloved hand into the reins of a white Thoroughbred. "Abraham was all about duty. All about seeing to the welfare of his people. I appreciated that about him," he said, as he pulled the Thoroughbred to stand next to the pregnant mare. The two horses seemed to acknowledge one another. "He's the sire to the twin colts she carries," he added. "Speed, agility, endurance... we'll have not one, but two entries in the major races in a few years," he boasted.

"You're forgetting about Aries," Constance said with a roll of her eyes. "He's a Thoroughbred in our Reading stables," she added, directing her comment to Richard. "We used to keep all of our racers there, but..." She shook her head. "I like to have the racers close when they are young, so I can help oversee their development. Two of our two-year-olds are up in Fairmont Park, just north of London. Lady Victoria... I mean, Lady *Grandby*... sees to their training. She has a track on her property."

"Both Constance and Victoria are very hands-on horse-women," Randall said with an arched brow. "I learned that about Constance the first year of our marriage."

Remembering the story George had told him about the marchioness borrowing his stallion, Richard couldn't help but grin. These two were not at all what he expected in highborn aristocrats. Not at all what he expected if he truly was Randall Roderick's son. "They'll have to compete against two of mine," he warned. "Both the sires and the dams have been winners."

Randall guffawed, and Richard was struck by how at ease he felt in the older man's presence.

"Steeple chases? Or the Derby?" Randall countered.

"Distance has always been the strength of the Hartwell stables, my lord."

Constance winced and leaned in to whisper, "He *loves* being called 'father' by his progeny."

Richard's eyes widened. From her words, it was apparent she already knew about him. He would have expected the wife of a former rake to give him the cut direct.

Apparently, the surprise showed on his face, for she added, "Randall told me all about his four illegitimate sons before we married," she explained. "Although he did leave out the particulars about *you*, I am just beginning to understand why."

Richard furrowed a brow. "You are not *angered* by my presence?"

Constance shook her head. "I am relieved, in fact. I admit I have been most vexed at not having made your acquaintance before now. I feared you two were estranged. Now that I understand the truth of the situation, I am even more impressed that you would see fit to make *our* acquaintance," she explained. "You have every right to be angry with Reading, especially if today is your first day at learning the truth of the matter."

Richard considered her words. "I admit that I was angry with... with the *world* earlier today," he murmured, now doubly worried at how he had left things with Miss Bennett-Jones. "I might still be," he added, keeping his voice low lest the marquess overhear his claim. Randall was seeing to leading another mount from the stables.

"Well, we'll know the particulars shortly. Randall does not mince words, nor does he want there to be any misunderstandings."

The groom appeared with Midnight in tow, the stallion appearing rather docile while sporting a black leather saddle on his back. "He's going to buck a bit, isn't he?" Richard asked rhetorically.

"Mount him quickly, and show him who is boss, my lord," the groom countered. "He's happy for the opportunity to get out." He leaned in closer. "That mare?" he whispered, indicating the one who carried twins. "She was his the year before last, so he's none too happy a different sire had her this past year." He arched a brow to emphasize his point. "Jealous one, he is."

Richard indicated he understood and then asked, "Which one was he a stud for this year?"

The groom shook his head, and Richard rolled his eyes. "Out to pasture already?"

"Her ladyship has plans for him, and has told him as much, but he still has his nose out of joint."

Richard couldn't help but laugh. "You didn't have a two-year-old he could have mounted?" he chided.

The groom shook his head. "They're all at the stables in Reading," he said. "So it was fortuitous when one of the lords brought his mare to be bred. Midnight took to her immediately, and she'll have his colt in a few months."

"Sounds as if that mare needs to pay a call on your stables," Richard hinted.

The groom's eyes widened. "Why, I think you might be right, sir."

Constance overheard some of what the two men were discussing, a smirk appearing when the groom returned to the stables.

"It seems you've proven yourself to him rather quickly," she said. "Would you like a cup of tea before we ride?" she asked, ever the consummate hostess.

Richard considered accepting the offer, but the horses were growing impatient. "Perhaps after we ride?" he countered.

"Very well."

Richard watched as Reading helped his marchioness onto her horse—she didn't bother with a mounting block but allowed her husband to simply lift her onto her bay—before he quickly mounted Midnight. As he expected, the stallion protested. Once it was apparent he would be allowed the rein in a few minutes, the horse settled down.

When Reading was on his mount, the three headed off down the alley towards the park.

CHAPTER 23

MEETING WITH A CONCERNED MOTHER

Meanwhile, back at Weatherstone Manor

"You wished to see me?" Sebastian said as he poked his head around the open door of his mother's private salon.

"Bash," Agnes said with a broad grin. "Why, I didn't expect to see you until dinner."

"Gilbert seemed to think otherwise," Sebastian countered, reeling a moment from having heard her use Vivian's nickname for him. Well, his close friends had called him Bash as well, but mostly because of his reputation.

"He's a good butler, darling. One you'll want to keep on should he outlive your father," she chided.

"Of course, Mother," Sebastian replied. "Besides, doesn't he just come with the house?"

"Well, there is that," she agreed. After a moment of displaying a teasing grin, she sobered. "Are you going for a ride in Rotten Row?" she asked, admiring his hunter green topcoat and riding breeches.

Sebastian glanced down at his riding habit. "What gave it away?"

Agnes tittered. "You'll want to see your tailor about some adjustments," she remarked. "You've lost some weight."

Pausing a moment, she seemed reluctant to say what was next on her mind.

"What is it, Mother?"

"Adeline is hosting a garden party at Carlington House on the morrow," she said, referring to the Marchioness of Morganfield. "When she learned you had returned, she insisted you attend and apologizes profusely for not having sent an invitation. You will attend, won't you?"

Sebastian's initial reaction was much like it would have been years ago—annoyance. The older matrons all seemed to think it was a young aristocrat's obligation to attend Society events so there might be an even number of males and females. He had found most of the fêtes tedious, mostly because they didn't involve anything fast or dangerous.

Having been forewarned about the event only the hour before, and knowing Lady Vivian would be in attendance, he experienced an epiphany.

His father had said something the night before. Something about a warning.

Sebastian inhaled. Years ago, he had made it known to every bachelor he knew at White's that Lady Vivian wasn't to be courted by anyone. That she was off-limits to all but him. His edict had obviously worked since Vivian was still unwed and apparently didn't have any suitors.

She certainly wasn't fast or dangerous, but he had put the need for excitement behind him. Miss Prim and Proper would make a perfect wife, and the garden party a fitting event to make his intentions known to the *ton*. "I'll be happy to attend the garden party," he said with a grin. "One o'clock, isn't it?"

His mother looked as if she might faint. "One o' clock," she agreed in wonder.

"So... one-fifteen?" he replied, remembering the need to be fashionably late.

"Perfect," she murmured, her eyes rounding in shock.

"You needn't look so stricken, Mother," he scolded.

"Oh, but I must," she argued. "Where might I send a

generous donation to the St. Bernard monks who saw to your care whilst you were recovering?"

Sebastian furrowed one brow. "I'm not sure if they're able to receive regular posts," he replied, "given where they're located in the Alps."

Agnes Peele shook her head. "Pity. I've a mind to leave them my entire dowry," she said with a sigh. She continued to regard him with a wistful look.

"What is it?" he asked, uncomfortable with how she gazed at him.

"Do you suppose there's any chance you might marry before you inherit? I know this sounds terribly selfish of me, but I would like to meet a grandchild or two before I die."

"Mother," Sebastian sighed. "I'm quite sure you'll meet more than one or two," he said gently.

Once again, the countess' eyes rounded. "Have you taken a wife since we last spoke?"

Sebastian guffawed. "Not as yet, but..."

"You have someone in mind?"

He nodded. "I do," he admitted, afraid her reaction might be too enthusiastic. "If I hadn't left for Europe when I did, I might already be married to her." He inhaled softly, deciding it was safe to finally tell her just why he had left so suddenly all those years ago.

"Oh. What a pity."

Clearing his throat, Sebastian sighed and said, "If I had stayed, I would have ruined her, Mother. Ruined her *thoroughly*. There would have been a scandal. It's why I had to leave. I wasn't... I wasn't ready for the parson's mousetrap."

Instead of the look of shock he expected to see, Agnes Peele beamed in delight. "Oh! Well, that's exactly what your father did with me," she happily claimed as she clapped her hands together. "He was such a scoundrel, your father."

"He was?" Sebastian's eyes rounded as much as his mother's had a moment ago.

"Oh, goodness, yes. But I had set my cap on him from the moment I first saw him. Vowed I would do *whatever* it took to land him as my husband." She waggled her eyebrows to emphasize her point.

"You did?" Sebastian tried to imagine his mother seducing his father and had to give his head a shake. The image of the two of them together—in that way—wasn't one he could abide.

Then he remembered the portraits of them that hung in the gallery on the ground floor. Portraits that had been done when they were both much younger. Handsome and beautiful, his parents were the perfect aristocratic couple—his father the son of an earl and his mother the daughter of a marquess. It was easy to imagine the two of them *in that way* when they were newly married.

"Indeed. In fact, I do believe you were already on your way when we wed," his mother went on, ignoring his look of shock. "Once we were betrothed, we had sexual relations wherever we could find a place. Mother's salon, the library in this house, Father's study, the parlor—"

"Mother."

"—Oh, the guest bedchambers, of course. And the gardens. We cannot forget the gardens. The hedgerows weren't as tall back then, but—"

"Mother."

"I usually wore an especially large shawl so we'd have something to put down on the ground, and—"

"Mother."

"Then your father would always be sure to bring something to cover his backside. You know, for privacy—"

"Mother!" Sebastian shouted as he came to his feet, his hands going to the sides of his head so he could cover his ears.

Agnes grinned as she glanced up at him, obviously enjoying herself. "I might have been Miss Prim and Proper at one point in *my* young life, but your father made sure I understood when I didn't have to be," she said, loud enough for her words to be heard despite his attempt at drowning them out.

"Are you saying you did all that *before* you were wed?" he asked in alarm.

Her eyes darting to the side, Agnes nodded. "And after. Still do, actually. There's an especially comfortable sofa in the library—"

"La la la la la la la," Sebastian recited as he squeezed his eyes shut. Despite his attempt at not imagining what she was describing, he couldn't help himself.

His parents having sexual intercourse on the leather-clad sofa in the library.

The very same sofa that was apparently used by every randy couple that had attended the Weatherstone ball over the years. The one that would no doubt be occupied during the ball they were hosting Tuesday night!

"Why, I certainly wouldn't expect *you* to be any different given your reckless behavior," Agnes accused gently. "You do have a reputation, young man."

"Mother!" he scolded again. His experiences with sexual intercourse had never required secret meeting places or especially large shawls. Widows weren't like that. They preferred encounters in their bedchambers. When he was considerably younger, there had been the serving wench at The Crown and Anchor, and she didn't care if anyone watched whilst she was being tupped.

When he finally took a wife and made love to her, it would be in his or her bedchamber.

"Oh, don't be mothering me," she replied. "But do tell me who it is you're on the cusp of ruining." She held up a gnarled finger. "And it had better be Lady Vivian."

Sebastian gave a start. "Why is that?" he asked, his mouth dropping open.

She gave him a quelling glance. "You're too tall for anyone else. And besides..." She allowed a shrug. "She's been waiting for you for a very long time."

Sebastian stared at his mother for a while before he finally nodded. "Has she been courted by anyone?"

Agnes shook her head. "Of course not. You saw to that

with your *edict* a long time ago," she accused, one of her gray brows arching as if in a scold. "She's been propositioned many a time, though."

"What?" he asked in alarm, both at her accusation and the mention of Vivian being propositioned.

"Her height, darling. Men find it especially intriguing. Why, you can just see how they're trying to imagine what tupping her would be like with those long legs wrapped around their backsides and her bosom in their—"

"You've made your point, Mother," Sebastian stated. "I'll put an end to it soon. I promise."

Agnes clasped her hands together on her lap. "Oh, good. Now, the front salon is usually available should you ever need it for a liaison."

Rolling his eyes, Sebastian couldn't help how his face reddened. "Mother... I'm going riding." When he noted her look of mischief, he added, "In the park, Mother."

Managing one of her naughty grins, Agnes watched as Sebastian bowed and took his leave of the salon.

Once the door was shut, Sebastian rested his head against it a moment as he considered what had just happened. He had actually admitted in a rather round about way that he wished to take Lady Vivian to wife.

Apparently, his mother wanted her for a daughter, for he had seen the gleam in her eyes when he had assured her he would see to it.

He loved making his mother happy. Making Lady Morganfield happy by attending her annual garden party would only be icing on the cake.

And an opportunity to spend time with Lady Vivian.

An opportunity to make his intentions known.

He wondered at the whereabouts of Lady Roth and took his leave of Weatherstone Manor.

CHAPTER 24

AN EXPLANATION AND REGRETS

A half hour later in Hyde Park

Although Richard had expected the ride in Hyde Park would involve no more than a quick trot for the horses, he was pleasantly surprised when the marquess said, "Once we hit the turf, we'll let them run for a while."

Midnight apparently knew the routine, for as soon as his hooves were on the lawn, Richard felt the beast's wish to surge ahead. He gave the horse the rein and reveled in the excitement of the run.

Or rather the race.

For Midnight was flanked by his stablemates, and they were just as anxious to run as he was.

Knowing he couldn't be heard over the thundering sound of the horses, Richard simply enjoyed the ride. When they neared the Serpentine, he noted how the marchioness aimed her horse to the south, and he followed suit. His gaze darted to the area where he had parted company with Christina Bennett-Jones earlier that afternoon, almost wishing she were still there so that he might show her who he was with and make his apologies.

Even if he wasn't quite sure what to believe, he wanted her to know that he had made the effort to learn the truth.

The park bench was empty, though.

When they passed through a row of tall trees, Richard was forced to pull back on the reins. The Readings did as well, given the number of carriages and riders they came upon parading down a dirt track.

"This is the King's Private Road. Better known as Rotten Row," Constance explained as they merged into the traffic of riders on horseback. "Every day at five o'clock during the Season, aristocrats form a parade of sorts and ride around."

"Not so private any longer," Richard remarked after he turned and looked back, stunned at the number of barouches, phaetons, and coaches that traveled on the road that lay directly to the left of the path that they followed. Beyond the carriages was a walking path, where dozens of ladies walked arm-in-arm and couples pushed perambulators or strolled next to each other, the lady's arm on her husband's.

An image of him walking with Christina Bennett-Jones flitted past his mind's eye, and he gave a start.

"Do you see someone you know?" Constance asked, her gaze on those who strolled on the crushed granite path to the south.

"Not from this vantage," Richard replied. The walking path was a distance from where they rode. "You?"

Constance grinned. "The Norwicks, of course. Daniel is my cousin. He and Clarinda prefer to walk over riding," she replied, referring to the Earl and Countess of Norwick. "While their twin daughters tend to ride with whomever has shown them any attention during the last entertainment." She glanced around as if in search of the girls who were still unclaimed in the Marriage Mart.

Richard struggled to remember who they might be, his recent perusal of *Debrett's* having left him confused.

How was he supposed to remember all the names?

"Diana and ... Dahlia?" he guessed.

Constance regarded him with delight. "Dahlia prefers to go by Davida in honor of her late father, and I should have known you would have paid particular attention to those who are not betrothed," she teased.

Hoping the rim of his top hat hid his reddening face, Richard thought to counter her claim, but her words were true. He had spent a good deal of time since his thirtieth birthday considering the eligible young ladies of the *ton*.

There were few in his part of Lincolnshire who could be called suitable. Some girls were barely out of the schoolroom and were the daughters of tradesmen. Another was nearly as old as him, a widow who now owned her own estate home in the country. She preferred her widowhood and the money she had inherited upon her husband's death, claiming no amount of attention from a member of the opposite sex could entice her from a life of independence.

Richard found he couldn't blame her. Besides, she couldn't ride a horse and didn't wish to learn.

"I know I must wed soon and start a nursery," he said in response to Constance's ribbing.

"If you're Rachel's twin, as I believe you are, then you are the same age Randall was when he decided to take me to wife," she replied.

Richard stared at her a moment, one brow furrowing. "You say that as if you didn't have a say in the matter."

Constance giggled, which had the marquess turning to regard her with a huge grin and Richard wondering if he had said something wrong.

"I almost didn't," she replied. "I fainted when he told me how many sons he had fathered."

"I caught her before she could hit the ground," Randall said proudly. "Not far from here, in fact."

The marchioness rolled her eyes but displayed a prim grin. "Randall was very persistent. Didn't even tell me he was a marquess at first. Wanted to discover if I might be convinced without the promise of a title and a coronet."

"She would have married me if I'd been a pauper," Randall claimed, his voice loud over the sound of the horses.

"Oh, I don't know about *that*," Constance countered, her teasing grin brightening her face. Her blush was apparent despite the fashionable hat she wore.

Randall turned his attention to Richard. "From the moment I saw her, I knew she was the one for me."

Richard regarded his possible father for a moment before he said, "You believe in love at first sight, sir?"

Nodding, Randall turned his attention back on the road in front of them. "I suppose I do. I experienced it more often than most men," he added with a quirked lip. "Connie knows this, so you needn't be too shocked on her behalf, but I loved every one of the women who are mothers to my sons and my daughter," he claimed. "Your mother," he added quickly, ignoring Richard's wince. "When I hit my mid-thirties, though, I knew I had to mend my rakish ways. Take a wife. Settle down. Adopt monogamy, which I gladly did once I finally convinced Connie to be my wife."

"He had to, for I would have refused him otherwise," the marchioness claimed.

Sure his face was bright red at hearing the marquess' admission, Richard gave his head a shake. "I am nothing like you, sir," he murmured, managing to keep his disgust from sounding in his words.

"Thank the gods," Randall replied. "I knew Hartwell would raise you right. Instill you with good values and respect for others. I made him promise me he would."

Richard nearly pulled back on the reins, shocked at hearing the manner in which the marquess referred to his real father.

The man who had raised him.

His facial expression must have given him away, for the marquess sighed and then gave his head a shake. "I don't blame you for not believing me," Randall said as he pulled on the reins to slow his mount. Once his horse was behind those of his marchioness and Richard, he hurried his mount forward until he was riding to the left of Richard. "But know this. Your father was an honorable man, but once his wife and heir died in the childbed, he was desperate."

"You think he was honorable?" Richard countered, anger tingeing his voice.

"To his viscountcy, yes," Randall answered. "He's not the first, and he won't be the last to do what he had to do in order to ensure a line of succession. Desperate men do desperate things, Hartwell."

Richard grimaced at hearing his new honorific said as part of such a serious remark. He took a steadying breath, glad his horse didn't seem to notice his discomfort. "What if I don't believe you?" he asked, his words barely audible.

On the other side of the marquess, Constance's expression betrayed her thoughts on the subject, which had Richard frowning. Surely *she* could not be happy learning he was one of Reading's bastards, and yet she seemed bereaved at hearing his words of doubt.

"It's your right not to," Randall replied. "I know it's a lot to take in—"

"What of your other bastard sons?" Richard interrupted. "Do *they* accept you as their father?"

"My oldest, Sir Randolph, does. He was born to a viscount's daughter shortly before she met the man she would marry. A baron from Northumberland who has since died," he explained. "Randolph always knew, I think, especially when his mother insisted he attend Oxford," Randall explained. "Her husband was a Cambridge man," he added with a quirked brow. "By then, Randolph knew he wasn't eligible to inherit the barony, and he returned to London once he completed university."

"Did he seek you out?" Richard asked.

"A bit of both. His mother had sent me a letter apprising me of his plans, so I knew to look for him. He's a horseman, of course, and runs the Reading stables that are located to the west of Richmond."

Richard nodded his understanding. "What of the others?"

Taking a deep breath, Randall said, "Reid's mother also married a baron, and they live in the country. I've not seen him since she took possession of him, but she writes on occasion with word of his accomplishments. He supposedly knows nothing of me, but I cannot help but hope we might one day meet," he said, his words barely heard above the sound of the horses. "Now Reginald, on the other hand, is an entirely different matter. A man who enjoys digging in the dirt. Apparently he was a mudlark back in his early years. Once he finished university—"

"Oxford?" Richard guessed.

Randall grinned. "Indeed. Once he finished university, Reginald headed up to northern England to excavate some ancient Roman artifacts near Hadrian's Wall. He would have probably preferred to continue as an archaeologist—he was apprenticed to the Duke of Westhaven's brother for a time— but decided to return to London when Darius Stewart moved to Sicily," Randall explained. "Reggy oversees my other London stables whilst he researches antiquities for the British Museum."

When Randall didn't continue his recitation, Constance cleared her throat. Loudly.

"Oh, and my marchioness has gifted me with two legitimate sons. You'll meet them when you come for dinner."

Richard listened intently, realizing the marquess was talking about men who could be his brothers.

Half brothers.

Five of them!

He'd never had siblings. His father had never remarried, although Richard was now sure he had the company of the woman mentioned in the note—for at least the last decade. He had always suspected there was a widow in London, and his suspicions had been confirmed when he discovered a packet of letters in his father's desk drawer. From the few lines he had read in the most recent letter, he realized his father had loved the woman. As to her identity, he'd had no idea at the time. There was never a return address, and the signature was always a simple v-shaped flourish.

Now that he'd spoken with the solicitor, now that he'd been given a note and a box to pass on to the woman—a box containing a rather expensive ruby ring—he realized she had to be the one.

Mrs. V. Higgins.

As far as he knew, the woman had never been to Horncastle. Never been a guest at Hartwell House.

But his father had obviously loved her. Proposed to her ten times, if the note the solicitor had given him could be believed.

Why had his father kept his *affaire* with her from him, though? Was he embarrassed? Or did he fear his dalliance in London would make for tawdry gossip in Lincolnshire?

There were no secrets in Horncastle.

Which had Richard wondering if others in Horncastle questioned his parenthood. Did anyone else in Horncastle know what his father had apparently done on behalf of the Hartwell viscountcy? Did anyone else know Richard wasn't truly the son of Abraham Hartwell?

Richard furrowed his brows when he remembered that no strangers had paid a call after his father's death. No females had been at the funeral, either, but then most women didn't usually attend such affairs.

Did his lover in London even know Abraham Hartwell had died?

The thought had Richard rethinking everything that had happened in the past year. Everything he had thought was true and real in his life.

"How many people knew?" Richard asked, his attention turning to the marquess who rode alongside him.

Randall furrowed a bushy brow. "Your father, of course. The nursemaid I hired for you. The midwife, who died only a few years later." He paused before giving his head a shake. "No one else that I know of."

Scoffing, Richard shook his head. "The woman who supposedly gave birth to me?" he countered, annoyance evident in his voice.

"Your real mother knew I was making arrangements on

your behalf. She couldn't see to two babes, so I left Rachel in her care whilst I delivered you to Hartwell," Randall explained. "Your mother wants to meet you, by the way. She's never really forgiven me for having taken you away."

Richard continued to frown. At no point during his conversation with Rachel Merriweather had she mentioned her mother's name. "Who is she?"

"Violet Higgins," Randall replied as his face brightened.

Once again remembering the note, Richard gave a start. *V. Higgins* had been the name of the woman to whom he was to deliver the ring. "The Queen of Hearts?" he murmured in disbelief.

"Oh, Violet Higgins *is* the Queen of Hearts," Randall affirmed. "She certainly broke mine," he added, an apologetic glance aimed in his marchioness' direction. "Depending on the day, she either hates me or adores me, but we both agree we've done right by your twin, Rachel, and on occasion, she admits we did right by you."

Richard considered his time with Rachel Merriweather. Remembered how sure she was that he was her twin brother. Remembered the look of adoration when she had stared at him and said his name in wonder.

Richard.

Who wouldn't want a sister who held him in such high regard? Despite not knowing a whit about him?

"A matchmaker?" Richard asked, feigning no knowledge of Violet Higgin's gaming establishment. He had said the same thing to Rachel, and he was curious as to how the marquess would describe her avocation.

"An astute businesswoman," Constance countered. "She runs one of the most lucrative gaming hells in all of Mayfair."

Richard stared at the woman who could be his stepmother. This time he didn't wince at hearing the curse word said in association with a business. "You say that as if... as if you *admire* her," he replied, rather stunned by her comment.

Constance arched both of her eyebrows. "That's because I do," she claimed. "She has parlayed a life of pleasing men into a popular business concern, and now she's... she's *rich*. And yet, because of the costumes and wigs she wears, no one knows her true identity when she's outside of her club. I cannot tell you how thrilled I was to finally meet her in person."

Richard stared at the marchioness. "Perhaps I shall pay a call at her establishment this evening," he said.

Randall's eyes widened. "Mayhap you would allow me to introduce you?"

Richard allowed a long sigh. To believe everything the marquess and his marchioness had said meant he had to let go of his beliefs of how he had been born of a viscount and a woman who had died in the childbed.

Or maybe he didn't.

What would be the harm in accepting the Marquess of Reading's truth of the matter but holding onto the memories of his life as Abraham Hartwell's son? Holding onto the image of his supposed mother, gowned in red satin and wearing a white wig, that had been captured so beautifully in the portrait that graced the hall in Hartwell House in Horncastle. In the miniature he had tucked into his traveling trunk prior to leaving Lincolnshire.

"I have much to think about," Richard said to no one in particular.

"And plenty of time in which to do it," Constance said, an understanding smile brightening her face. "You're always welcome at Reading House and at Reading Manor and in any of the Reading stables," she added. "Should you wish to bring one of your own mounts to London, you're welcome to stable him with ours."

"But know this," Randall interjected. "Our horses will beat yours in every horse race."

"Randall!" Constance scolded.

The two men grinned as they directed their horses to complete the circuit of the King's Private Road.

. . .

*I*t was while they were headed back east when Richard noted a high-perch phaeton on the adjacent path. A phaeton driven by a woman familiar to him, her passenger even more familiar. He was about to call out, but realized his attempt would be drowned out by the sounds of spinning wheels and horses' hooves.

And by the hooves of a horse upon which was mounted a young gentleman. He appeared to be having a conversation with the young woman who rode with her mother, his general good cheer and attentions those of a possible suitor.

An unfamiliar sensation—jealousy—rose up so suddenly, Richard nearly pulled back on the reins. Miss Bennett-Jones seemed to be enjoying the young man's words, her face lit up in delight.

"Would you like an introduction?" Constance asked, noting his attention on the Bostwick phaeton.

Richard shook his head. "Not necessary," he replied. "I was a guest for dinner at Bostwick House last night. I find I need to make my apologies to the young lady, though," he said, relieved when the young buck's mount sped on ahead of the phaeton.

Constance furrowed a brow, but then her face brightened. "There is nothing keeping you from doing so right now," she replied.

Blinking, Richard dared another glance towards the phaeton. "But... her mother is with her."

"Exactly," Constance responded, one eyebrow arching.

Richard blinked again and realized there was a price for behaving like a prize idiot. A price it seemed he was willing to pay.

He aimed Midnight in the direction of the phaeton and felt excitement when the horse closed the distance to the equipage.

CHAPTER 25

AN APOLOGY MADE MOST DIFFICULT

A moment later

Richard discovered Midnight made for a perfect cohort in crime as he aimed the horse in the direction of the Bostwick phaeton. Trouble was, the mare pulling said phaeton seemed determined to set a speed record on the King's Private Road. Almost as if she knew she was being chased.

By the time Richard was able to pull up next to the speeding equipage, it had begun to slow for the turn to either head to the southeast corner entrance or loop around once again to head west.

Richard thanked the gods the horse headed north to stay on the King's Private Road, and he was able to pull up alongside the phaeton. "Good afternoon, Lady Bostwick," he called out.

Elizabeth slowed the gray mare that pulled the phaeton as she turned her attention on him. "Why, Lord Hartwell. What a surprise. And what a beautiful mount you have there," she remarked.

"He is borrowed, my lady," he replied, attempting to look around Elizabeth in an effort to catch the eye of Christina. "Might I have your permission to speak with your daughter?"

Elizabeth lifted her chin as she slowed the horse another

notch. "That all depends, Lord Hartwell. What are your intentions toward my daughter?"

Richard cleared his throat. "To bestow an apology, my lady."

At how her head swiveled on her neck, Richard knew he had surprised the viscountess. For only a fraction of a second, he had caught sight of Christina. Caught sight of her look of awe and her reddened eyes beneath the brim of her hat.

Did she suffer from some sort of malady due to the early spring weather? Or had she been crying on his account? Crying because of what he had said to her?

His insides in a turmoil, Richard waited with baited breath for the viscountess' reply.

"You're allowed, my lord."

Rather than attempt to speak across the front of her lady-ship, Richard slowed his mount and then aimed Midnight to come up along the right side. When he was abreast of the phaeton, he made sure Midnight's pace matched that of the gray mare.

"Good afternoon, my lady," he shouted.

Christina afforded him a nod. "Good afternoon, my lord."

"Miss Bennett-Jones. I wish to apologize for my conduct earlier this afternoon," he said with as much contrition as he could manage. "I was wrong. I was..." He paused and waited for her to turn her head completely in his direction. "I was a fool," he murmured.

Even if she couldn't hear his last words, she apparently could read his lips, for her red-rimmed eyes rounded. "Did you learn the truth of the matter?" she asked in awe.

He furrowed a brow and finally nodded. "A possible truth," he acknowledged. "A probable truth," he quickly amended.

"You are not angry?"

He shook his head. "*Disappointed* is more the thing," he admitted. "I feel as if I've been hoodwinked."

She nodded and seemed to contemplate her response

before she said, "I accept your apology, my lord. And I look forward to seeing you at the entertainments this Season."

Richard felt a stab of disappointment at hearing her curt response, although he wasn't sure what he expected.

For her to rise up and launch herself from the equipage and into his arms? Mayhap beg her mother to bring the phaeton to a halt so they could speak face to face? So they could kiss one another? Make it apparent she would marry him if he proposed marriage?

The last thought had him blinking.

He'd only just met the young woman the night before! "You will afford me two dances at all the balls, I hope?" he said, hoping he didn't sound as desperate as he felt.

A thought of what Reading had said about desperate men doing desperate things came to mind.

Christina seemed to regard him with uncertainty before she allowed a nod. "Of course, my lord."

"Richard," he said then. "Please, call me Richard. I don't wish there to be any formality betwixt us."

A flash of something seemed to light her eyes for a moment, but then it was gone as quickly as it appeared. "That's very kind of you, sir. I look forward to dancing with you at Lord Weatherstone's ball."

He nodded. "As do I with you. Twice if you will allow it. Perhaps I might be allowed to pay a call on you—"

"Good day, Lord Hartwell," Elizabeth called out before she gave the gray mare the reins. Released from its easy trot, the horse broke into a run, leaving Richard Hartwell and his mount far behind.

Although Midnight wanted to run with the yoked mare, Richard deliberately held him back, murmuring words of encouragement as he allowed his gaze to sweep the track to his left. When he finally spotted the Marquess and Marchioness of Reading, he gave the Thoroughbred the rein to run as fast as he could to catch up to his stablemates.

For the rest of the ride in Hyde Park, Richard worried. He had erred terribly with Christina Bennett-Jones—and apparently with her mother, as well. Now he wondered how he could ever make it right with her.

"Mother!" Christina scolded when the phaeton pulled well ahead of the viscount. "What are you doing? He apologized!"

Elizabeth lifted her chin and allowed a prim grin. "Determining just how determined Lord Hartwell might be when it comes to courting you, darling," she responded.

"He is sorry for what he said to me," Christina argued. "He showed suitable contrition, I thought."

"Oh he did," Elizabeth agreed, her grin widening into a brilliant smile. "He did."

Scoffing, Christina turned to stare at her mother. "Then why—?"

"Let's discover exactly how *interested* he is in you," her mother said. "Should he truly wish to court you, he will make his intentions known to your father on the morrow."

Christina regarded her mother with widened eyes. "Do you think he will?"

Elizabeth aimed a quelling glance in her daughter's direction. "He's heels over head in love with you," she said. "He would be a fool not to speak with your father."

Gratified at hearing her mother's comment, Christina straightened on the bench and enjoyed the breakneck speed at which they traveled. For a moment, she understood why Sebastian Peele had engaged in driving fast horses. The experience was positively exhilarating.

Until they took the turn at the end.

"Mother!" she shouted as she was sure the phaeton angled onto two wheels and threatened to topple over.

"Hang on, darling!" Elizabeth shouted happily. "I've always wanted to do this!"

As if in slow motion, Christina watched as the horizon seemed to tilt at a most unusual angle. Meanwhile, she was forced to angle her body in the opposite direction, and she was sure she shouted something before her mother let out a most unladylike curse and the ground appeared to rise up to her right.

Sensing the need to jump, she did so, tucking her bent arms tight against her body as the horse whinnied and the phaeton hit the dirt. She rolled several times, aware when her hat came free of its pins. Other than the sickening sense of rolling over and over, she felt no pain as she came to a halt on her side near the edge of the turf.

She knew almost immediately her mother wasn't so lucky, for she saw from the corner of her eye as the viscountess tumbled from the phaeton, skirts and petticoats flying.

"Mother!" she shouted as she struggled to right her skirts and get to her feet. She ran to kneel next to her mother's prone body, well aware there were a number of horses nearly upon them.

The phaeton dragged another twenty feet before the hobbled gray came to a halt and attempted to rear up in her yoke, whinnying loudly.

All at once, shouts sounded from behind and to the side of the road. Christina was deaf to it all. "Mother," she whispered as she turned the woman onto her back.

Seeing her mother's chest rise and fall despite the redingote she wore, Christina gave a shout of relief.

Elizabeth opened first one eye and then the other before a grin appeared and she turned her attention to the horse. "Promise you won't tell your father," she said as she turned back to Christina, giving her a wink.

Her eyes wide with worry, Christina shook her head. "I will do no such thing, Mother," she replied before strong arms lifted her from the dirt and wrapped around her shoulders at the very same time someone else saw to lifting her mother from the road. A few carriages came to a stuttering halt to the right and left of them, horses complaining with loud neighs and their drivers shouting in alarm.

"Oh, good God, are you all right?"

Christina leaned back to regard her rescuer. "I am," she

replied, relieved to see it was Lord Hartwell who held her. "But Mother..." She turned to see Lord Reading holding her mother. "I think she might be hurt."

"Reading's got her," Richard said as he lifted Christina into his arms and hurried to the side of the road. Still on horseback, Constance had gathered up the reins of their mounts and was leading the two horses to safety.

Wrapping her arms around his neck, Christina regarded Richard with wide eyes. "I can walk," she claimed, her attention going to two grooms who were already seeing to the phaeton. With the help of two more men, the equipage was set upright while another groom was seeing to holding the horse and checking the rigging.

"Are you sure?" he asked, as if he found her words a disappointment.

"I'm leaving dirt all over you," she whispered, noting how her redingote and skirts had collected a combination of soil and mud from her tumble from the phaeton. "I'm ruining your top coat," she added in dismay.

"It's fine, really," he assured her as he set her on her feet and straightened, although he didn't give up his hold on her. "Your hair is so long."

Christina's eyes widened when she realized that with her hat having been torn from her head in the fall, most of the pins holding her hair up had come out. Waves of dark mahogany hair spilled over her shoulders and down her back. "My hat," she whispered.

Richard finally tore his gaze from her and gave a start. "Oh," he said in alarm before he rushed out onto the turf in front of an oncoming curricle. He snagged the hat and quickly moved out of the path of the vehicle, though its driver had already slowed in deference to the number of people who had stopped to help with the downed phaeton.

He hurried back, examining the hat before holding it out to her. "It doesn't seem to have suffered too badly," he murmured. "Are you sure nothing's broken?"

Touched by his concern, Christina regarded him a

moment before she gave her head a shake. "I am fine, truly, but Mother... I think she might have hit her head."

Richard glanced over to where Lord Reading was helping the viscountess gain her feet. "She did seem rather amused by the ordeal," he commented. "Probably suffering from shock."

"And she was terribly excited. Almost as if she wanted it to happen." Christina blinked, realizing her mother might have caused the accident deliberately. Might have done it to discover how Lord Hartwell would respond.

Her worry turning to dismay, Christina rolled her eyes and allowed a huff.

"What is it?" Richard asked, offering his arm as they made their way to the viscountess and marquess. Having tied up the horses to a nearby post, Lady Reading had joined them and was fussing over Elizabeth, asking the same sorts of questions Richard had been asking of Christina.

"I may have a more managing mother than I thought," Christina replied quietly.

Richard darted a glance in her direction before he nodded to Viscountess Bostwick.

"I am fine, truly, although I probably won't be once my lady's maid sees what's happened to my gown," Elizabeth Bennett-Jones said as she waved a gloved hand down the front of her body. "Oh, dear. When George learns of this, he'll never let me drive again."

The Readings gave each other a quick glance. "Well, *I* would never tell, but unfortunately a number of others have seen what's happened," Constance warned as she looked around. "If anyone should make a comment of it over tea, we shall have to remind them that the horse was spooked." She glanced over at the gray mare, who was obviously enjoying the attentions—and an apple—provided by a groom. "Besides, it's spring. She could be... she could be in heat. She could have attracted the unwanted attention of a nearby stallion."

Richard dipped his head and dared a glance in Christina's direction. Heartened she still had her arm on his, he leaned over and whispered. "You're sure you're not hurt? Now that the excitement has worn off... an injury may have made itself apparent," he suggested.

Christina inhaled softly and shook her head. "Did you ever roll down a grassy hill as a child?" she asked, a wan grin accompanying her query.

Richard furrowed a brow. "I recall doing it, but I didn't fall hard to the ground prior to doing the rolling, and I certainly didn't do it on bare ground," he countered.

"Well, it was much like that," Christina said with a sigh. "Do you suppose the phaeton is drivable?" she asked as her attention returned to the equipage. "And is the horse all right?" A groom was leading the horse toward them, the mare pulling the phaeton behind as if nothing had happened. Except for the swath of mud and layer of dirt on one side, there was no evidence of the accident.

Glancing toward the opposite end of the road, Christina looked in vain for her father. He had said he would be joining them on horseback. That he would catch up to them.

"She looks rather proud of herself," Richard remarked, noting how the mare was high-stepping as the groom pulled her along.

"She was probably in cahoots with Mother," Christina whispered.

Richard's head jerked in her direction before a look of amusement crossed his face. He placed a hand over the one on his arm. "If you're agreeable, and I'd understand if you were not, I'd like to pay a call on the morrow," he said in quiet voice. "Ask your father for permission to take you for a ride in the park? A proper ride?"

Christina's eyes rounded. "On horseback?" she asked, an expression of excitement appearing.

"Possibly. Seems I know a stables where I can find a mount whenever I want to go riding," he said as he indicated the Readings.

"I would like that very much," Christina replied. Then she remembered the garden party. "It would have to be later in the day, though. My grandmother—Lady Morganfield—is hosting a garden party at Carlington House at one o'clock."

"I know. I have an invitation," he replied, a brow furrowing when he remembered it was Lady Bostwick who had given it to him. "So... after that?" he prompted.

"Perhaps... perhaps you'll share with me what's changed?"

Richard nodded, his contrition apparent. "I've learned much on this day," he admitted. "And I fear there is more I must face."

"At least you won't have to do it alone."

He allowed a wan grin. He seemed about to lean down to kiss her when the sound of a clearing throat caught their attention.

"It seems we can resume our ride, darling," Elizabeth said from where she sat on the phaeton, holding the reins. She had the equipage pulled up to to where they stood. "Everything appears to be in working order."

Christina blinked. She gave Richard a quick glance before he helped her onto the phaeton bench. "Good day, Lord Hartwell."

He lifted his top hat from his head and bowed. "To you as well, Miss Bennet-Jones."

Watching him until the phaeton was well past where Richard and the Readings stood, Christina finally turned her attention to her mother. She had a thought to scold her—and the mare—but her mother's earlier look of self-satisfaction had been replaced by one of worry.

"What is it, Mother?"

Elizabeth sighed loudly. "I really don't wish to lose my driving privileges."

Christina regarded her mother for a long moment before she said, "Mayhap Lord Hartwell will put in a good word for you when he pays a call on Father tomorrow."

Her lips forming an 'o,' Elizabeth was about to turn and hug her daughter, but Christina used a gloved hand to push her cheek forward.

"Eyes on the road, Mother," she scolded. "Father is riding in our direction at this very moment."

Elizabeth immediately straightened on the bench and then waved enthusiastically.

George rode up and turned his horse to head in the same direction as they were going. "From your flushed faces, it appears you've had a good time this afternoon."

Christina exchanged a quick glance with her mother. "Oh, yes. It was quite exhilarating, Father. And Lord Hartwell found me and... he apologized," she said, well aware she sounded as if she was babbling. As long as her father stayed on the other side of the phaeton, he wouldn't notice the mud caked on her side of the equipage.

George scoffed. "Sounds as if I'll be denied the opportunity to challenge him," he teased. His gaze swept the phaeton before his brows furrowed. "You've been racing again, haven't you?"

Elizabeth inhaled sharply. "Mayhap," she replied. "What gave it away?"

"The layer of dust you seem to have acquired since you left the house," he replied.

"She beat Lord Hartwell, although she had a head start," Christina offered, ignoring her mother's grunt of protest.

Furrowing his brows, George's suspicion was apparent, but he said nothing in response.

They made it back to Bostwick House without further incident, and with a surreptitious bribe from the lady of the house, a groom saw to cleaning the equipage.

CHAPTER 26

A NEAR-DEATH EXPERIENCE
CHANGES A MAN

An hour later, at Weatherstone Manor

"Why, I thought you went riding in the park this afternoon," Agnes Peele said when she discovered her son reading in the library.

Sebastian pulled his chronometer from his waistcoat pocket. "I did," he said, wincing when he saw that it was well past six o'clock. "Did you go?"

She nodded as she pushed a book into an opening in one of the bookshelves. "I did, and it was quite exciting. Elizabeth lost control of the horse that was pulling her husband's phaeton—"

"Oh, dear God. How did I miss that?"

"—and of course it overturned. Her poor daughter was with her. Why—"

"Charlotte Christina?" Sebastian asked in alarm, halfway out of his chair. "Is she all right?" He set aside the book he'd been reading and stood.

Agnes regarded him with an arched brow. "*Christina* is, yes. Lord Hartwell—have you met him yet? He is such a quick thinker. He had her up and off the turf in the blink of an eye, whilst Lord Reading saw to carrying Elizabeth out of danger. They're both right as rain."

Sebastian relaxed some. "And the horse?"

"She's fine. The phaeton is a bit muddy on one side, though."

Sebastian displayed a look of relief, while he briefly pondered the identity of Christina's rescuer. Although he hadn't yet met Lord Hartwell, he was fairly sure he knew what he looked like.

Given what he had witnessed in Hyde Park earlier that day, he had been left with the impression that there would be no more interaction between Miss Christina Bennett-Jones and the new viscount. After what appeared to be a rather long and clandestine meeting on a park bench, he had watched as the dark-haired man had stomped off, as if giving Christina the cut direct.

Before that, he was sure the two were engaging in a secret meeting. Their heads had been bent together, their words kept quiet as they conversed. Obviously the young lady had said something not to the viscount's liking for him to leave so suddenly, though.

So angrily.

That Hartwell would then risk bodily harm to rescue Christina from the King's Private Road had him wondering if the two had reconciled. Wondering if the two had come to some sort of understanding.

Wondering if they were betrothed.

If only he would be given such a chance with Lady Vivian. Should she end up tossed from a phaeton and lay prone in the dirt, he knew exactly how he would respond. Why, he would scoop her up and carry her to the nearest secluded spot and kiss her senseless.

Well, he would see to it she wasn't injured first and *then* kiss her senseless. Mayhap help her straighten her skirts and kiss her even more senseless.

Which would have him entirely senseless.

He liked the idea of being senseless with Lady Vivian.

Sebastian was about to go on imagining other things he might do with Lady Vivian once his senses were back when he realized his mother was watching him with baited breath.

She was expecting a response to whatever it was she had said.

What had they been talking about?

Overturned phaetons. Damsels in the dirt.

"Bostwick won't scold Lady Bostwick too badly, will he?" he asked, thinking any other man would. A high perch phaeton was usually a gentleman's prized possession. To have it overturn on a ride during the parade in Rotten Row seemed rather unusual.

Rather unlikely.

Whatever would spook a horse in Rotten Row?

Agnes gave him a prim grin. "Well, if he did, he would soon be taking it back and apologizing profusely."

"What do you mean?"

She tittered again. "Darling, they're much like your father and me. Their differences aren't solved over the dinner table."

Sebastian blinked. "Oh," he replied. His eyes rounded as his face reddened. "Oh!" he said louder when he sorted what she meant.

Agnes watched him settle back into the chair as she took the one next to it. "By the way, you needn't refer to Christina by both of her given names any longer, darling."

His gaze darted to the book he held. "Oh? Did she decide she didn't like to be called Charlotte Christina?"

Shrugging, Agnes crossed her arms and said, "I think it was more that there are so many Charlottes her age," she replied with a sigh. "Besides, Christina suits her." She paused and seemed to consider what she was about to ask before she finally said, "From your earlier reaction, am I to suspect you have feelings for her?" Her expression suggested dismay.

Sebastian shook his head. "Not like that, Mother. It's just... she's a good friend of Lady Vivian's, and for a moment, I feared Viv might have been with her on that phaeton."

"Oh, I see," Agnes replied, her face lighting up in a combination of relief and delight. "Well, I've spent some time discussing your accommodations with Mrs. Landau, the housekeeper. I was thinking it might be time for you to move into the other apartment upstairs. The one at the other end of the corridor from ours."

Confused by the change of subject, Sebastian stared at his mother a moment. "All right," he replied slowly. "Any particular reason?"

She lifted a shoulder. "It's past time you have your own suite of rooms and a... mistress suite for your future countess," she replied. "You *are* going to marry this year, are you not? Given our discussion earlier, why I thought a proposal was about to happen."

He nodded. "I am going to marry, yes," he admitted. Although the words might have frightened him in the past, he felt relief in putting voice to them now.

"Well, are you prepared to propose?"

Sebastian blinked. "What?"

Agnes rolled her eyes. "Have you a ring?" she asked in dismay. Holding out her left hand, she said, "I would give you this one, but I'm still using it," she added, referring to the ruby and diamond ring his father had bestowed on her when they had finally married.

"Uh, no," he replied, his brows furrowing. "What's the current fashion for such things these days?"

Angling her head to one side, Agnes allowed a prim grin. "I hear rubies are quite expensive these days, so... rubies."

Sebastian chuckled. "Father obviously had good taste."

"He still does," she said as she held out her other arm to show off a ruby bracelet. "He gave this to me for our most recent wedding anniversary."

"Do I need to get her one of those, too?" Sebastian asked, his expression showing worry.

Agnes tittered. "You could for a wedding present," she suggested.

Sebastian continued to display his concern. "I'll have to check with Father to be sure my allowance will cover it," he murmured.

Her silver brows furrowing, Agnes said, "You needn't worry about the cost, darling. Even if it was a hundred pounds, your father will be so thrilled to learn you're finally getting married, he won't bat an eye."

Sebastian's gaze darted to the side. "But I do worry. It would be... it would be irresponsible to spend more than I'm allowed," he argued.

Agnes blinked. A strange expression crossed her face. "You really *have* changed, haven't you?" she murmured. "Bash, I must admit, I hardly recognize you. It's as if you're a completely different person in the guise of my son."

Sebastian sensed a trap. "But... I've changed in a *good* way, right?"

She was about to answer and then straightened in her chair. "Are you still my son at heart?"

Inhaling softly, Sebastian found he was at a loss for words. "I'm still *me*," he finally said. "Regrettably, at times."

"What's that supposed to mean?" The countess shifted forward so she sat on the very front edge of her chair.

He gave a shrug. "I did something. Before I left on my Grand Tour." He rolled his eyes. "I apologized. And I know what I have to do to make it right, and I want to. Make it right," he stammered.

Realization dawned on his mother. "Oh. You're referring to ruining a young lady," she said. "What we were discussing earlier?"

"I didn't *ruin* her," he argued. "At least, not... completely," he hedged.

She scoffed. "Well, you best get to it. You're not getting any younger, and neither is she." Displaying a satisfied expression, Agnes was about to rise from her chair when she suddenly sobered. "We *are* talking about Lady Vivian, are we not?"

His brows furrowed with suspicion. Had she thought there was another? "And if we weren't?"

Agnes' eyes rounded. "There's *another* you've ruined?" she asked in alarm.

He shook his head, relieved she didn't think there was. "*Nearly* ruined. And no. Not that I'm aware of," he replied carefully. He gave his head another shake. "No."

"You're sure?"

"I'm sure."

"Well, then, it's well past time you see to ruining Lady Vivian," she said happily. "Well, after you propose marriage, of course."

"Of course, Mother." He stood when she did and watched her nearly dance her way out of the library. When he sat back down, he nearly fell into the chair as he considered the odd conversation.

At least he had made his mother happy, even if he had never actually mentioned Vivian's name. Which had him wondering why she had decided Vivian was to be her future daughter-in-law.

What did she know?

What had she said earlier? About an *edict*?

Had his father told her about the announcement he had made a few days after Lady Vivian's come-out? That no one was to court Lady Vivian or risk his wrath and a duel?

He winced at the thought that someone might have challenged him. That he might have died by a bullet discharged during a duel.

Did Vivian even know of his devotion to her? Know that he had secretly held a candle for her from the first moment he had spied her from across the Weatherstone Manor ballroom, her gorgeous oval face the only one appearing above the heads of every other member of the aristocracy in attendance that night? Know that she had haunted his dreams with her beguiling eyes and teasing grin? Her luscious dark hair and creamy white skin? That she gave him someone to imagine when he was engaged with women for whom he had no feelings?

He might have felt bad for those women, except the randy duke's daughter admitted she only wanted him for a tumble, and the rich widow didn't wish to attend a ball without an escort.

Sebastian winced at remembering those encounters.

How different life would have been if he *had* ruined Vivian that night before he left for the Kingdom of the Two Sicilies.

For if he had, he never would have left for the Continent.

He never would have engaged in the meaningless encounters with the duke's randy daughter or the rich widow who insisted on a tall man to accompany her to a count's ball in Rome.

He wouldn't have agreed to go skiing with the randy daughter's husband in the Alps. A woman who was, unbeknownst to him, married.

He wouldn't have suffered the accident that resulted in his two years at the St. Bernard monastery.

Sebastian inhaled softly.

Perhaps it hadn't been so much an accident as payback. He was sure the encounter with the woman was clandestine —that no one else knew of their secret meeting in a secluded bedchamber in a wing opposite from where the duke's family resided.

Perhaps she had been followed.

Perhaps he had been followed.

He thought of how he would feel if he learned his Vivian had sneaked off in the middle of the night and lain with a guest of his father's. He would be livid. Hurt, too, but angry enough to wish the man dead. Jealous enough to challenge the man to a duel.

Sebastian rolled his eyes and settled back in the chair with a groan. If that had been the husband's intent—to see to it Sebastian died—then he had nearly succeeded. Sebastian had suffered for the indiscretion. Despite not having feelings for the young woman, he had enjoyed the spirited tumble if only because he had spent the entire time imagining her to be Vivian. They looked enough alike that it was easy to believe.

He had probably even called her 'Vivian' whilst in the throes of passion.

At the moment, he couldn't even remember her name. Only that she had been the one to initiate the *affaire*. The one who had flirted and flitted about as if she was still an unmarried woman. He hadn't even known she was married until the husband introduced himself and mentioned the opportunity to ski.

After crashing into a tree, Sebastian had nearly died that day on the mountain. Once the dogs had found him, they dragged him to the safety of a structure built into the mountain, some of it carved out of the stone. He didn't remember learning he was in a monastery until he had been there for several weeks, most of that time spent on death's door. Day after day of pain had followed.

But he hadn't died.

Thoughts of Vivian had kept him alive. Thoughts of Vivian had kept him warm during the bitter winter months. Thoughts of Vivian had kept him sane. Given him something to look forward to. Something to hold onto as he reconsidered how he had been living his life.

She had been his salvation. She would be his salvation for the rest of his life, once they were husband and wife.

The possibility of her ending up with another man hadn't come to mind back then. In fact, he hadn't considered she might marry someone else until he was lying on a cot in a small room made of stone walls. A fear that his edict hadn't been honored kept him alive. Kept him breathing through the pain.

That it had been honored now had him feeling at peace with the world.

He would finish what he had started with Vivian that fateful night. He would propose marriage. Make her his viscountess and eventually his countess. Make love to her morning, noon and night.

Well, maybe just once a day. He was older now.

But first, he had to court her.

And check on the status of the ring he was having made by a jeweler in Ludgate Hill. He might have pretended ignorance with his mother, but he was well aware of how important a ring was when it came to a betrothal.

As for a wedding present, it seemed a bracelet was necessary. He left the library in search of his father.

CHAPTER 27

MEETING A FAMILY FOR THE
VERY FIRST TIME

ater that night, Reading House, Curzon Street, Mayfair
Having accepted the invitation to dine at Reading House in Curzon Street following his ride with the Marquess and Marchioness of Reading, Richard Hartwell wondered if he had made an error in judgement.

Constance Roderick had been so insistent with her invitation, and remembering he hadn't left instructions at the townhouse for his dinner that evening, Richard acquiesced with the proviso that he be allowed to change into suitable clothes.

From the look on her face now, he had the impression she thought he would never appear. But appear he did, dressed in his finest dinner clothes and shoes appropriate for a *ton* ball. Expecting to have to wait some time in a parlor somewhere, Richard was surprised when Constance appeared directly after the butler saw to his greatcoat and top hat.

She was dressed in a coral gown topped with gold sarcenet and trimmed in gold lace. If he hadn't already known who she was, he would have guessed she was the Queen of England.

"Thank you so much for coming tonight," she gushed as she placed a hand on his arm and allowed him to lead her upstairs to the main parlor. "The boys are so excited to meet you."

"They know?" he asked in alarm.

"Only that we're having a dinner guest," she said quickly. "They're home because Sunday is Easter, and I insisted they be here in London for it."

"Ah," he replied as they climbed the stairs.

"I've invited two other couples," she said carefully.

"A dinner party it is, then?" he replied, a grin lifting the corners of his lips. "I appreciate the opportunity to meet new people before Parliament begins on Tuesday."

"Then you'll no doubt attend Lord Weatherstone's ball that night?" she said, making it more of a statement than a question.

Richard regarded her a moment as they took the turn at the top of the stairs and headed toward the parlor. "You recommend I do? An invitation was delivered yesterday." For some reason, he trusted that the marchioness had his best interests at heart.

"I do. It's the first ball of the Season and a perfect enter-tainment at which to dance with your future wife," she replied, her eyes twinkling in delight. She sobered and added, "But I'm told Lady Vivian—she's an earl's daughter—is not included amongst your choices."

Richard stiffened. Did everyone think the two of them would suit? "I met her only last night. I cannot say she would be my first choice, but pray tell, has she received an offer since then?" If so, he couldn't imagine who might have proposed to the bold, brash young lady.

"Not that I'm aware, but I understand one is forthcom-ing. I only know this because my jeweler is making the betrothal ring for Lord Cougham," she explained. "As for the rest—"

"You're not going to pester me with a parade of eligible young ladies, are you?" he countered, unfamiliar with the name she mentioned.

"I am not," she assured him. "Their mothers will, howev-er," she added as they stepped into the parlor.

Six sets of eyes turned to meet his, and he gave a start.

So did those who were in possession of those eyes.

"By the gods, I'm seeing double," Mark Merriweather said as he stood and regarded first Richard and then Sir Randolph, his mouth open in shock.

"Mark," Rachel scolded before she hurried over to greet Richard. "It's so good to see you again, Lord Hartwell." Instead of simply extending her hand so that he might bring it to his lips, she lifted herself onto tiptoes and kissed him on the cheek. "Thank you for coming this evening."

Behind her, Mark stepped forward, his right hand held out. "May I present my husband?" Rachel went on. "Mark Merriweather, proprietor of The Three Bells."

"Sir," Richard said as he gave the man a half bow. "Excellent public house. The luncheon was very good. Middleton's son, are you not?"

Mark nodded. "I am. He's getting along in years, so my older brother, Viscount Wessex, has accepted a writ of acceleration. He'll be joining you in the House of Lords on Tuesday."

"Good to know," Richard said, immediately feeling a sense of relief. "I feared being the only new lord in the House."

"And this is Lady Xenobia Roderick and my older brother, Sir Randolph," Rachel said as she hooked an arm into the man's elbow and pulled him forward along with his wife.

Richard stared at Randolph much the way Randolph stared at him. "My God," Richard murmured with a grin.

"My *reflection* is more like it," Randolph replied as his wife stepped forward and dipped a curtsy. "I thought Rachel was exaggerating when she told me about you."

"Me, as well," Richard replied, suddenly nervous. If everyone in the room believed he was another illegitimate son of Reading, it would be impossible to keep the secret. Given what he'd heard about gossip in London, he feared how he would be received by the other lords in Parliament.

He bent over Xenobia's hand and brushed his lips over the back of it. "It's very good to meet you, my lady."

"Oh, this is delightful," she replied, her smile infectious.

"Why, I've a mind to show up at the Weatherstone's with you on my arm just to see if anyone notices you're not my Randolph."

"He's a bit taller than me," Richard whispered in warning.

Randolph turned to Rachel. "Are you quite sure I'm not *his* twin?" he teased gently.

A brilliant smile appeared to brighten Rachel's face even more than it already was. "He's not, you brigand. He's mine. All mine," she said as she stared at Richard.

"Lord Hartwell, would you allow me to introduce my sons?" Constance asked, her gaze sweeping those who crowded around Richard.

"Of course, my lady," Richard said as he nodded and took a step back.

Two young men, both of whom appeared old enough to be in university, regarded him in wonder. The youngest bore a remarkable resemblance to Richard while the older looked like a younger version of his father.

"Raymond and Robert, this is Richard, Viscount Hartwell," Constance said proudly. "He's new to the capital."

"It's very good to meet you, my lord," the young men said in unison.

"You as well. But..." He turned his attention to Raymond. "Aren't you... the Earl of Farring...?" He winced, thinking the oldest son of a marquess would have an honorary title, but he couldn't remember it from his recent reading of *Debrett's*.

Raymond shrugged. "Farringdon, but I'll answer to my given name."

When all the eyes in the room focused their attention on something behind him, Richard turned around to discover Randall, Marquess of Reading, standing on the parlor's threshold.

"Hartwell. So good of you to join us," Randall said as he moved to take Richard's hand.

"I appreciate the invitation, sir," Richard said as he shook hands with the marquess, well aware the others in the room moved to reclaim their seats.

"I take it you have met everyone?"

"I have, sir."

"If my marchioness hasn't already told you, please know that you are welcome here any time, Hartwell," Randall said as he accepted a drink from a footman and took another, handing it to Richard. "As are your horses."

"That's very kind of you, sir."

Randall gave him a quelling glance. "Call me Reading, please." He glanced around before he lowered his voice and said, "I have warned your sister she isn't to say anything about you outside of this house. The others simply believe we are distantly related, and that's what everyone else in London will learn. Common ancestor."

Richard's eyes widened. "I appreciate that, sir... Reading."

Randall inhaled softly. "If it's not too late after dinner tonight, might I suggest you pay a call at The Queen of Hearts? Violet will want to meet you, and..." He paused and allowed a long sigh. "If she learns that I know you are in town and haven't made arrangements for the two of you to meet, she will have my bullocks on a plate, no doubt prepared by her French chef in a wine sauce."

Richard winced. "Understood." He hadn't considered going to the gaming hell that night, but he supposed he may as well meet the woman who Randall claimed was his mother. He had a delivery for her.

"Do you play billiards?" Randall asked.

His eyes widening, Richard nodded. "I do, although I haven't since Father..." He stopped speaking and cleared his throat.

"We'll play later," Randall stated.

The butler appeared on the threshold and announced dinner.

The marquess gave Richard a nod as Constance stepped up and placed an arm on her husband's arm. "Apologies for the uneven numbers this evening," she whispered. "But I wasn't sure if you had met any young ladies yet." Her arched brow suggested she thought he might be sweet on someone.

She had paid witness to his behavior toward Christina when the Bostwick phaeton had overturned that afternoon.

"No apology is necessary, my lady," he replied, reminded that he still wished to converse with Christina. With all the hub-bub, he'd been unable to have a private conversation with her after moving her to the lawn next to the turf.

Given how late the hour would be after dinner and a game of billiards, he knew it would be unwise to pay a call at Bostwick House later that night.

Deciding his call would have to wait until another time, Richard joined the others as they made their way to the dining room.

Three hours later
Despite attempting to kiss the back of Rachel's hand before his departure from Reading House, Richard found it was easier to simply allow his supposed sister to have her way. She once again kissed him on the cheek.

"Would you like me to come with you?" she asked as the butler helped him with his greatcoat. "To meet mother?"

"This time of the night?" he asked in alarm.

"I am the daughter of a gaming hell owner," Rachel countered with a shrug. "The wife of a man who owns a public house. For me, this is not so late," she said with a shrug, her hand waving to a clock mounted on a caryatid in the Great Hall.

Although it wasn't yet midnight, it would be by the time Richard's coachman would deliver him to The Queen of Hearts. "Please don't think ill of me, but I shall decline your offer."

She sighed, but her eyes widened. "When you ask for her, do tell the young lady who is hostess this evening to mention that I sent you."

Richard furrowed a brow. "Not Reading?"

A glimmer of something that might have been mischief danced in her eyes when Rachel grinned. "If you mention him, she will claim Mother isn't on the premises," she claimed.

He considered her comment and wondered if the two were estranged. "Understood," Richard replied. He gave her a bow and took his top hat from the butler before he made his way out of Reading House and towards his waiting town coach.

"Where to, sir?" the driver asked as he held the door for his master.

"The Queen of Hearts."

"Very good, sir."

His stomach full and his mind in a whirl, Richard settled into the squabs and wondered at the sudden loneliness he felt. Having spent the evening in the company of such a close —and boisterous—family, he had felt as if he was among old friends. No one stared at him as if he was some long lost prodigal son. Randolph hadn't stared at him—overmuch— although Richard had caught his wife, Xenobia, casting curious glances between Randolph and him. Conversation had come easily. The marchioness had never once put on airs and neither had Xenobia.

He'd even been allowed to win a game of billiards, but having watched Randolph beat the marquess—the lord hadn't been allowed a single opportunity to sink a billiard ball— Richard knew not to challenge the knight to a future game.

He wondered what kind of luck he would have at The Queen of Hearts.

CHAPTER 28

MEETING THE QUEEN

A *half hour later, The Queen of Hearts, Stafford Street, Mayfair*

Richard regarded the front doors of The Queen of Hearts with trepidation. From the window of his town coach, he had watched a number of noisy young men enter the establishment followed by several older gentlemen, all dressed as if they had just come from dinner.

Well, at least he wasn't underdressed.

A footman opened one of the doors for him, and he was suddenly surrounded by rich reds and gold gilt. He blinked several times as his gaze swept the large room before him. Several felt-covered tables were occupied by quartets of card players while a few female faro dealers ruled over their tables.

"Good evening, sir," a petite blonde called out from where she stood next to a gilt-clad podium. She was dressed in a red satin gown that was entirely too tight in the bodice. There were obviously panniers on her hips, for the gown looked as if it might have been worn by a randy grandmother in the last century. "Sir Randolph?" she added, before she gave her head a quick shake. "Apologies," she added. "You look so much like him—"

"I do," he acknowledged, for once not annoyed by the comparison. Having spent the evening in the man's company, he had decided any comparison could only reflect well on him. "I wondered where I might find…" He paused to pull the handwritten note he had acquired from the solicitor from his waistcoat pocket. "V. Higgins?" Reading had referred to her as 'Violet.' He remembered Rachel's instructions. "Mrs. Merriweather suggested I meet her."

The young woman's eyes widened. "Her Highness is…" She glanced around the gaming room. "Not in this salon," she murmured as a blonde brow furrowed.

"I'm happy to make an appointment," Richard offered.

"Oh, I shouldn't think that would be necessary." The woman waved to a similarly garbed brunette, who hurried over and bent her head as the hostess spoke in low tones.

"Good evening, sir. My name is Annette, and I should be happy to take you to the queen. Might I learn the reason for your call?"

Richard was sure his face was as red as the woman's gown as he considered how to respond. "A private matter. I've a delivery for her from my late father," he added as he patted his midsection.

"Very good, sir. Follow me," she said as she headed toward the back of the huge salon.

Richard's attention darted left and right as Annette led him through a set of double-doors and into a dining room. Despite the late hour—it was half-past eleven o'clock—the scents of grilling meat and something savory assaulted his nostrils. If he hadn't just consumed a seven course meal at Lord Reading's house, he would have been tempted to take a seat at one of the small tables placed against the walls. In the middle, tables for four, six, and eight, dressed with white linens, crystal, and silverware, were crowded with gentlemen of all ages. A few glanced in his direction, some with curiosity, while others displayed boredom.

He nearly collided with Annette when she stopped in front of a burly man in the back corner.

"This gentleman wishes a word with the queen," she said as she indicated Richard. "Rachel sent him."

"Richard Hartwell," he offered, "Viscount Hartwell. It's a private matter."

Despite the bald man's lack of eyebrows, Richard knew he had lifted one as he regarded him. "One moment."

The man disappeared through a panel—a jib door—and Richard blinked. He was sure there hadn't been a door there.

Annette turned to him, her red lips affording him a prim grin. "Are you new to London, sir?"

Surprised at her attempt at conversation, Richard nodded. "I am. Here for the Season," he replied.

Her smile widened. "Should you ever require companionship, we offer a number of ladies of various ages and... *experience*, with whom you might wish to spend an evening."

Richard regarded her for a moment. If he hadn't met Christina Bennett-Jones and seen her gorgeous mahogany hair freed from its pins, he might have been tempted by the woman's words.

For some reason, all he could think about was how Christina would look like beneath him on a bed with her hair splayed out on a pillow, her arms wrapped around him as he made slow, quiet love to her. "Thank you for the information," he replied, tempted to ask if there might be a way for him to watch someone engaged in sexual intercourse with one of the young women in the brothel. Although he had read a number of books on the subject, his lack of actual experience would no doubt become apparent on his wedding night.

No matter who he took to wife.

The burly guard reappeared but held the jib door open for him. "The queen will see you in her parlor. Down the hall and to the left," he said in a low voice.

From the expression on Annette's face, Richard knew he had gained a rare audience with the queen.

He passed through the panel door and paused to allow his eyes to adjust to the darker corridor in which he found himself. At the end, a chandelier lit what appeared to be a vestibule. When he turned to the left, he inhaled sharply.

"Lord Hartwell?"

The words were said by a matron who could have been thirty or sixty. Although he expected her to be garbed much like Annette and the hostess, she was dressed in a modest blue day gown and wore her brown locks in a simple bun.

"My lady," he replied as he bowed.

She stared at him as she approached, her breath obviously held until she was close enough to touch his arm. "You look exactly like your father did when I first met him," she murmured in awe. "Oh, Richard, it's so good to finally see you again."

Richard stared at her a moment, touched by how she regarded him with a combination of awe and relief, her eyes bright with tears. "I suppose you're referring to Lord Reading and not to Abraham Hartwell?" he half-asked.

She furrowed a dark brow. "You've spoken with Reading?"

He nodded. "I had dinner with him and his family this evening."

A hand went to her breast as she sighed with relief. "I am Violet Higgins, and I am your mother," she said as the tears collected in the corners of her eyes. "You've obviously met Rachel—"

"She was the first to inform me," he replied, a pained expression crossing his face. "Although there was a hint of the situation contained in this note," he added as he once again pulled the note from his waistcoat pocket. "My father wanted you to have this," he said as he took the small box from his top coat and handed it to her.

Although she gingerly took the velvet covered box from him, she didn't immediately open it, apparently well aware what was contained within. Tears streamed down her face then, and Richard struggled to pull a handkerchief from a pocket. "Please, don't cry."

He had already made one woman cry on this day, and he didn't want another one turning into a watering pot.

"Did he know you were my mother?" Richard asked, suddenly wondering if his father's attentions toward her were because of him or because he was truly besotted with the gaming hell owner.

Violet opened the hinged box. "Oh!" she replied as she regarded the ring. She looked up, her furrowed brows aging her several years. "He must have," she breathed as she accepted the handkerchief and shook her head. "But he never told me about *you*," she complained. She dabbed at the tears and cleared her throat. "I would have accepted his offer of marriage if he had, if only to be your stepmother," she said as new tears fell. "Can you imagine? Me? Your real mother as well as your stepmother?" she asked rhetorically, managing a watery grin.

"You must have made him very happy," Richard replied. "He always looked forward to returning to London for Parliament, but he never told me why." For some reason he couldn't quite place, he felt the need to pull her into his arms. Hold her a moment until her tears subsided.

When he did so, Violet practically fell against him. "Oh, you even smell like him," she whispered.

"I haven't yet paid a call at Floris," he murmured. "I understand I should acquire a scent of my own."

Violet shook her head. "You needn't. It suits you," she said as she rested her head against his shoulder. "Abraham hated Parliament, you must know. Despised the incessant arguments and illogical behavior so many of the lords displayed. Not your real father, of course, though. Reading and Abraham got along quite well. Reading has always been one of the better lords," she quickly added, finally pulling her head away to regard him with wet eyes.

"Good to know," Richard said, his gaze taking in their surroundings. Not at all garish as was the gaming hell, Violet's parlor was a model of restraint and elegant decor. Green and peach, and furniture in light colored woods were perfectly arranged around a fireplace mantel made of marble.

"Will you keep the ring?" Richard asked. "The solicitor suggested you donated bequests to your favorites charities."

Violet arched an elegant brow as she lifted the ring box

and regarded the jewel within. She pulled it out and slid it onto the fourth finger on her otherwise bare left hand. She splayed her fingers and sighed in awe. "I will keep this. And I'll wear it every day," she promised in a whisper.

"So, you miss him?" Richard asked, prepared to discover she was merely a harlot his father had hired to warm his bed on cold nights.

"Very much," she replied as tears once again threatened. "I know you must think I entertain all manner of men in my position, but your father was my only this past nine... ten years," she said as she regarded him with tear-filled eyes. "He was always so proper. Never once treated me like anything other than a lady," she claimed. "Took me for rides in the park, ices at Gunters, and dinners at Rules Restaurant," she went on. "And every year, on the anniversary of our first outing, he would ask for my hand in marriage and present this ring," she whispered. She sighed audibly. "I was a such fool not to accept."

"Rachel would claim you were only acting as a good businesswoman would," Richard replied. "Protecting your hard-won assets."

Violet regarded him with sad eyes for a moment before she said, "That was true the first few times he asked," she acknowledged. "But after that..." She allowed the sentence to trail off as she stepped back. "It was just more comfortable to keep things the way they were, I suppose."

"Mayhap for the both of you," Richard murmured, thinking of how another marriage would have upended Abraham Hartwell's neat and tidy life in Horncastle. Especially if word got out about Violet Higgin's identity as The Queen of Hearts. He could just imagine how the women in the village would react. How many would faint or claim to have the vapors in his presence. How many would no longer support his father's attempts to make life in Horncastle better for those who worked for him. For everyone.

"Come. Have a seat and join me for a drink?" Violet half-asked. "I think champagne is called for on this night."

Richard gave a start. "You have champagne?"

She gave him a quelling glance. "There are some in London who think I bathe in it," she replied with a teasing grin. "I do not," she quickly added.

"Good to know." He was about to sit down in the chair she indicated, one that was near the fireplace, but he remained standing when she moved on to a sideboard situated on the opposite wall. Soft flames danced about in the fireplace, adding a golden glow to the already well-lit parlor.

"Now that you know the truth of the situation, I cannot help but think you must despise me," she said as she pulled a bottle from a bucket.

The sound of shifting ice startled Richard. "Here. Let me get that for you," he offered as he moved to take the champagne from her.

"You've opened champagne before?" she asked in surprise.

He twisted the cork and jerked at the violent reaction of the bottle. Although foam threatened to escape, he quickly moved the bottle so its top was over a glass. "Actually, this is my first time," he admitted as he chuckled.

"Well, you're better at it than the butler," she said with a grin. She indicated the two glasses he should fill, and he did so, aware he needed to do so slowly.

"Is it always this foamy?"

"It would not be champagne if it was not," she replied, studying his features.

Richard noticed her gaze and rolled his eyes. "Yes, I look like Sir Randolph."

"And one of your younger brothers," she murmured.

"You've met them?" he asked in surprise, wincing when he realized how he must sound.

She nodded. "Reading brought them for dinner one night. His marchioness was spending the night in a barn waiting for her favorite mare to foal."

Richard furrowed a brow. "You're not joking," he said with some consternation.

Violet shook her head. "I am not. Reading found the

perfect wife in her," she said as she took one of the glasses he offered. She touched the rim to the one he still held. "To life in London," she said.

"To you," Richard countered before he took a sip of the champagne and seemed to contemplate whether or not he should swallow.

"It's delightful if you don't drink it all at once," she said, moving to take a seat in a floral upholstered chair next to the fire.

"It's... quite unexpected," Richard replied, taking the chair she had originally offered.

"You've never drunk champagne before?"

He shook his head. "Brandy, scotch..." he allowed a grimace, "...a variety of ales, and some tasteless concoction made in Russia," he went on before taking another sip of the champagne.

She grinned. "Vodka," she murmured. "We serve it in the gaming rooms," she added with a grin. After she took another sip, she said, "Champagne will be served at nearly every ball you attend this Season, along with lobster cakes and midnight dinners that may or may not leave you with a sour stomach."

Richard grinned. "Are you warning me about some of the London cooks?" he asked in shock. "Because the dinner at Reading's house was magnificent," he said.

Violet grinned. "That's because he has an excellent cook. Now, have you been invited to Lord Weatherstone's annual ball?"

He nodded. "I have. I've already promised dances to two young ladies."

Violet gave a start. "How long have you been in London?"

Dipping his head, Richard said, "I had dinner at Bostwick House last night."

Her eyes rounding in delight, Violet said, "And?"

Richard sobered and suddenly appeared uncomfortable. "I find I'm rather attracted to Miss Christina Bennett-Jones," he admitted.

Violet angled her head to one side as her face took on a

grin of delight. "Oh, Richard. She would be perfect for you," she murmured. "She's the daughter of a viscount, grand-daughter of a marquess, and the perfect age to marry," she gushed.

Richard's eyes rounded. "I expected you would put voice to an argument."

"What sort of argument?"

"That I should pursue a duke's daughter," he replied with a shrug. "Or accept nothing less than a marquess' daughter."

Violet tittered, the giggle sounding quite at odds with her age. "I do not believe that a man should attempt a higher standing in Society by way of an advantageous marriage," she countered. "You would just be miserable as would be your wife."

Richard furrowed a brow. "You say that as if you have paid witness to such unions?"

She nodded. "I have. I have lived in London my entire life," she explained. "My mother, may she rest in peace, was a very good teacher. A good judge of character."

"A courtesan?" Richard guessed.

Violet nodded. "She was born in the palace. Her father was a royal duke. Her mother his favorite."

Blinking at hearing her claim, Richard settled back in his chair. "And you?"

Inhaling softly, Violet finally said, "Similar, although I had more options than she did."

"Options?"

She rolled her eyes before she waved at the ceiling. "My father made sure to settle a dowry on me. A settlement I was able to parlay into this establishment."

Richard's eyes rounded as he considered her words. "I think Reading believes one of your—"

"He believes what I *allow* him to believe," she interrupted. "Only you know the truth, as anyone else involved in the settlement is long since dead." When she noted how he stared at her, she added, "It's all right if men believe I earned this place while on my back, or acquired it by way of a bequest made by a man who had lost his mind. But the truth of the matter is, I've only ever shared a bed with men I loved. Or thought I did."

Richard stared into his half-empty champagne glass. "You loved Reading?"

A brilliant smile lit her face. "He was my first. I loved him truly. Madly. But I quickly learned to hate him after I gave birth to you."

Wincing, Richard, placed the glass on the side table next to his chair. "He claims you could not have taken care of two babes."

"And he was correct," she acknowledged. "He did right by all of us. Your father, me, you. But I still hated him for taking you from me. I was your mother, after all."

Richard nodded his understanding. "Do you still hate him?"

She allowed a prim grin. "Not a bit. He knew what was best. For all of us." After a pause, she added, "Including Hartwell, apparently." Her eyes rounded. "If only I had known. Things could have been so different."

Richard frowned. "So you would have married my father if you had known about me?"

Violet sighed softly. "Probably," she whispered.

Finishing his champagne, Richard regarded the empty glass a moment before he asked, "What will you do now?"

She allowed a shrug. "Continue as I have. As I did whilst your father was in Lincolnshire," she replied.

"There is not another man who has captured your heart?"

She shook her head. "Although I am not dressed for it, I am still in mourning. It hasn't even been three weeks since his death," she argued.

Richard dipped his head. "Apologies. I did not—"

"It's all right," she interrupted. "Besides, if you'll allow it, I should like it very much if we can spend time together. Perhaps you'll take me to Gunter's or for a ride in the park?"

"I could do that," he replied, hesitance evident in his voice.

"No one knows who I am when I'm not garbed as The Queen of Hearts, so you shouldn't be concerned for propriety's sake."

"Oh, it's not that," he assured her. "I was thinking of Miss Bennett-Jones. I'm sure she would be amenable to joining us, but would *you* be all right if the three of us took the air together?"

Tears brightened Violet's eyes. "Oh, Richard. Of course. I would enjoy it immensely," she gushed. The tears streamed down her cheeks.

Richard reached for his handkerchief, glad he had remembered to ask his valet for a clean one after having used his other to wipe off the bench in Hyde Park. He offered it to her as he said, "There's no need to cry, Mother. In fact, I'm beginning to wonder if making women cry is to be my lot in life here in London."

When Violet's head jerked up and she stared at him in surprise, he recoiled slightly. "What is it?" he asked in a whisper.

"Nothing," Violet replied as new tears threatened. "Nothing at all. Everything is fine. Everything is wonderful."

Realizing at that moment what he had said to have her reacting so—he had called her 'Mother'—Richard sat back and allowed a long sigh.

"So... you would approve of me courting Miss Bennett-Jones?"

Violet nodded, dabbing at the corners of her eyes. "Oh, yes. Very much. In fact, you must bring her here for dinner. Tomorrow night, if you can. I'll have my chef make us his very best meal."

"Promise me you have not bedded her father."

"Richard!" she scolded before she rolled her eyes. "I have not, nor would Bostwick seek out anyone to be his mistress," she claimed.

"You seem awfully sure."

"That's because I am. Everyone knows Lord Bostwick is hopelessly devoted to his viscountess."

Remembering how the two behaved with one another the night before, Richard realized her words were true. Now that memory seemed as if it had occurred a fortnight ago, and weariness settled over him as he considered everything that had happened the night before. Everything that had happened on this day.

He didn't even notice when Violet took his empty glass from him, spread a quilt over his body, and kissed his forehead as he slept.

CHAPTER 29

ATTENDING A GARDEN
PARTY

*The following day, Lady Morganfield's annual garden
party, Carlington House, Park Lane, Mayfair*

"I think every matron in Mayfair must be in attendance,"
Christina whispered to Vivian as they drank lemonade and
watched a myriad of couples promenade along the length of
her grandmother's gardens. Adeline Carlington, Marchioness
of Morganfield, was holding court at a nearby table,
surrounded by countesses and viscountesses, including her
daughter—Christina's mother, Elizabeth, Viscountess
Bostwick.

"As well as the most handsome gentlemen," Vivian whispered, her gaze following a young man whose arms were held
out for not one, but two young ladies whom he led past a row
of boxwoods fronted with red tulips. "How is it I don't know
them?" she asked in dismay.

Christina allowed a smirk. "You will after the first ball of
the Season," she replied. "After they've all filled your dance
cards and stepped on your very best slippers a time or two."

Vivian shuddered. "Oh. I forgot about that," she replied
with a huff. "An unfortunate consequence of being taller than
they are."

Her head angling to one side, Christina asked, "I take it
Lord Cougham never stepped on you?"

Vivian's eyes widened. "Never," she replied. She nearly added what he *had* done to her, but clamped her lips shut as she remembered the night before he had left for the Continent.

What if he *had* finished what he had started? What if he hadn't come to his senses and realized what he was doing?

How different would their lives be now!

Would he have gone to Italy?

Vivian's brows furrowed in wonder. "He knew if he stepped on my feet, I would have stepped on his," she said with a grin. Their behavior with one another had always been tit for tat. Which had probably been why their last night together had been so... complicated. Why their brief reunion had been so stilted.

"Vivian," Christina scolded in a quiet voice. "You wouldn't."

"I would stomp on his feet, and I..." Vivian paused, her look of delight changing to one of consternation. She had overheard her name mentioned at the next table over, and she furrowed a brow at the words that were being said about her.

Unkind words. Words which implied something for which she wasn't guilty. Couldn't be guilty.

She lifted her gaze to regard the speaker, feeling a good deal of satisfaction when the old biddy noticed and quickly ended her comments with, "At least, that's what I've heard on the matter."

"What is it?" Christina asked in a whisper, well aware Vivian's attention was no longer on their conversation.

Vivian continued to stare at Viscountess Pettigrew, a woman whose aged face, overly large ears, and beady eyes had paid witness to over seventy-five years worth of London gossip. Her pinched mouth had then repeated every last tidbit, usually enhancing the *on-dit* to make it that much more enticing for whoever would listen to her.

"Lady Pettigrew," Vivian said with gritted teeth, her eyes still on the viscountess, "is under the impression I am guilty of having done something with a certain viscount with whom I have in fact done *nothing*." Her words grew louder as she said them, so loud, in fact, that several of the older matrons turned their attention to her with expressions of alarm.

"Were you saying something, Lady Vivian?"

The syrupy voice of Lady Pettigrew had Vivian stiffening in her chair, which had Christina's eyes rounding with worry. At any moment, she was sure Vivian was going to say—or do —something that would be the exact opposite of prim and proper. "Viv! It's not yet Friday," Christina whispered.

Vivian settled in her chair slightly before she said, "Why, Viscount Cougham and I did indeed renew our acquaintance only yesterday. Why, right out in front of Roth House," she said, directing her words to the others around the same table. "Such an ordeal he had to endure in the Alps. Poor man. I wanted desperately to kiss him, if only as a mother would."

Several sets of rounded eyes stared at her before blinking almost in unison. "Ordeal?" Lady Roderick repeated.

Lady Comber asked, "Whatever happened?" before Lady Chamberlain could.

Aware she had the attentions of everyone seated around Lady Pettigrew's table, Vivian angled her head and gave it a shake. "A skiing accident. He very nearly died."

A chorus of gasps and shocked expressions greeted her claim, and Vivian calmly turned around and faced those at her table. "Now, what were we discussing?"

Christina might have given her a quelling glance, but she was attempting to hide her humor behind a quickly unfurled fan. "Vivian," she whispered.

"It's true. He was rescued by the dogs of the St. Bernard monks and spent two years recovering in their monastery."

Blinking several times, Christina shook her head. "Did you just make that up?" she asked in a whisper.

It was Vivian's turn to blink. "I did not. He suffered broken bones. Nearly froze to death. Lord Weatherstone told me all about it when I arrived today. I was trying to avoid Miss Pipkins and he took pity on me."

"Lord Cougham. In a monastery? For two years?" Christina countered in disbelief. An image of Sebastian Peele teaching the monks how to play cards flitted through her mind.

Vivian nodded and lowered her lips so they were near Christina's ear. "He's changed, Tina. He's not at all how we remember him."

Scoffing, Christina turned her head so she could whisper into Vivian's. "Father says he collected winnings from five wagers when he was at White's the other night." A dark brow arched, as if that alone negated what Vivian was claiming.

"Wagers I'm quite sure he won after his departure from the capital four years ago," Vivian argued, her hoarse whisper nearly audible to those around them.

"Perhaps," Christina acknowledged as she realized it was unlikely he could win a wager the same night it had been made. "Did he say anything about Tuesday night?"

Vivian's good cheer seemed to dissipate. "Should he have?"

Christina blinked. "Well, did he ask you for a dance?"

Sighing, Vivian squared her shoulders and straightened in her chair. "I'll be dancing *twice* with Cougham," she announced, her voice loud enough to be heard by everyone at the table and mayhap a few at the next table over. "Whether he asks me or not."

"Vivian!" Christina hissed. Her eyes quickly lifted and then lowered, her brows furrowing at the same time. When it happened again, Vivian leaned toward her friend, about to ask if she had something in her eye.

Then, from behind her, a deep voice filled with humor said, "Now it sounds as if I really must attend the Weatherstone ball."

Vivian stiffened at hearing Sebastian's teasing voice. She slowly turned around, looked up, and gave him a prim grin. "You're incorrigible, my lord," she accused, batting her lashes.

A round of titters sounded from the adjacent tables as Sebastian gave an exaggerated bow. "Ladies," he said as he straightened. "I do hope you're all well on this fine afternoon."

Affirmative murmurs sounded in reply as Sebastian placed a hand on the back of the empty chair next Vivian. "May I?" he asked.

Vivian, her cheeks bright pink, said, "Please do."

Once he was seated, he helped himself to her hand and lifted it to his lips. "Do you have plans for a good Easter?" he asked.

Sure she was being watched by everyone at every table around them, Vivian merely angled her head and nodded. "Of course, my lord. And you?"

"I'll be attending the service at St. George's. I'm sure it will be quite enthralling," he replied. "Given my time with the monks, I now have an appreciation for what our Lord had to endure to atone for my sins."

Vivian blinked, well aware of the stunned silence that greeted the viscount's claim. Most probably thought Sebastian Peele would oversleep and miss the church service. "Have you written to them to let them know you have arrived safely back on British shores?" Vivian asked, well aware she needed to keep up her end of the conversation.

"My post left on the *Fairweather* this morning," he replied. "It set sail before dawn."

"You were there?" Vivian asked in surprise, thinking he had probably ended a night of card playing and drinking by going to Wapping.

Sebastian's eyes darted sideways before he leaned closer and said, "A footman saw to it. I was... still asleep."

A shiver shot down Vivian's spine when she realized he still held onto her gloved hand. "Did you send your regards to the dogs as well?"

He nodded. "There is a crate of biscuits for them on the same ship. Biscuits our cook assures me will be well received by the Alpenmastiffs, based on how my mother's precious dogs appreciate them."

Another round of sighs erupted from the matrons who sat

at the nearby tables, and Vivian dared a quick glance around to discover everyone seemed intent on hearing Lord Cougham's words. "How kind of you," she murmured. "Will you pay a call on them when you're next in the Alps?"

He cleared his throat. "I will indeed."

Vivian's eyes rounded. "You're going back?"

He gave a one-shouldered shrug. "Not to ski, but I expect I will go there as part of my honeymoon," he replied.

A rock seemed to drop into Vivian's stomach, rendering her unable to speak.

Noticing her sudden discomfort, Christina quickly picked up the conversation. "Then you must have found the Kingdom of the Two Sicilies diverting?"

"Very," Sebastian replied. "The Greeks have left their very best mark on the island of Sicily. The art in Rome is... amazing. The cathedrals are testaments to what mere mortal humans can accomplish when inspired. The wine is most appealing and the food... well, I am considering hiring an Italian chef."

Christina gave him a brilliant smile. "Mother will never give hers up, so don't even try to hire Antonio away from Bostwick House," she said. "Or you shall risk her wrath."

Sebastian arched a brow. "I know better than to risk the wrath of anyone of the fairer sex," he replied, his response directed to Vivian. "But I do appreciate the warning," he added, turning his attention back to Christina. He glanced around. "I suppose I should make the rounds," he murmured as he tipped his top hat. "There never seems to be enough of my sex at these parties."

He stood up from the table, gave a slight bow, and went off to another table surrounded by older matrons.

"When has he ever risked the wrath of you?" Christina asked in a whisper.

Vivian gave a start. "He... he hasn't," she stammered, looking as if she was on the verge of tears.

"What's wrong, Viv?"

Blinking several times, Vivian said, "I think I must have

something in my eye. Would you pardon me?" She stood up and made her way to the house.

Not about to allow her friend to escape, Christina went after her. She caught up with her in the portrait gallery, beneath a portrait of the Marquess and Marchioness of Morganfield that had been painted upon their return from their honeymoon. On any other occasion, Christina wouldn't have given the painting a second glance—she'd seen it hundreds of times during her youth when the Bennett-Joneses had dinner with her grandparents. Now she paused and regarded the image of Adeline Carlington as if seeing it for the first time.

Tall, brunette, and bearing cheekbones that made her appear as if she were carved from marble, the marchioness looked every bit the aristocrat she was. Her deep scarlet gown, a late Georgian era confection, featured panniers on the smaller side and a stomacher that enhanced her rising moons. A parure of red jewels decorated her neck, ears, fingers, and upswept hair.

As the oldest daughter of an Italian count, she had been born to her position.

She also appeared no older than Christina.

"What is it?" Vivian asked, a hanky held to the side of one eye as she sniffled.

"Look how tall *she* was," Christina whispered in awe. "Taller than you."

Vivian's gaze turned onto the painting, and she stepped back. "Lady Morganfield is still rather tall," she murmured as she admired the couple depicted when they were much younger. "She looked like a queen even back then."

"He looks rather regal, too," Christina murmured, her gaze going to her grandfather. "Where do you suppose this was painted?" She had never before noticed the background, but it appeared as if it were somewhere in Rome.

"In the parlor, actually," a baritone voice said from somewhere to their right. "The artist exercised a good deal of license when it came to the background, but then, he was Italian."

Vivian and Christina gasped and whirled around to discover David Carlington, Marquess of Morganfield, leaning against the wall with his arms crossed over his chest. "Your grandmother insisted on it."

Christina grinned. "Grandfather. How do?"

"I am well, and in answer to your question, I *felt* rather regal whilst it was being painted," he added with a grin as he pushed away from the wall and bowed.

"Good afternoon, my lord," Vivian said.

The two young ladies dipped curtsies and blushed at having been overheard.

"It's a beautiful painting," Vivian said as the marquess took her hand.

"It looks as if was painted by a Master," Christina chimed in.

Morganfield regarded Vivian a moment longer than he did Christina. "You aren't quite as tall as Adeline, but almost," he said with a wink.

"Pardon, sir, but did you mind that your marchioness was so tall?" Vivian asked, ignoring the jab to her ribs that came by way of Christina's elbow.

Pulling his chin into his neck, the marquess gave a look of disbelief. "Hardly." His brows furrowed. "Have you been led to believe *your* lack of an offer of marriage is because you're *tall?*"

Vivian inhaled in preparation to answer, but Morganfield added, "Because your height has nothing to do with it, my lady."

Blinking, Vivian nearly cried out when Christina's hand crushed hers in its hold. "Oh?" she managed, the single syllable barely audible.

The marquess seemed to realize something and then shook his head. "Oh, forgive me. It's been so long since Roth's passing that I forget you don't have a father to apprise you of such particulars."

"Particulars?"

He ran a hand across his forehead. "The man who intends to ask for your hand made it clear to the rest of the eligible bachelors that they're not to give you a second look," he explained. "Of course, I'm not sure if those outside of London were given the same edict, but I suppose they come to learn it should they give you more than a passing glance."

"Wot?" Christina asked, her mouth left open with the exclamation.

Vivian looked as if she might swoon, but she suddenly straightened to her full height. "Oh, really?" she replied, her voice filled with indignation. "How long ago was this?"

Carlington seemed to consider his answer a moment too long before he said, "Five... six years, mayhap?"

It was Christina's turn to look as if she might swoon. "Was there no expiry date for his... warning?" she asked, earning her an appreciative nod from Vivian.

Allowing a shrug, her grandfather said, "Why would there be? The last I heard, he still intends to take you to wife." His attention going to someone who had just entered the corridor, the marquess' face split into a brilliant grin. "Ah, I must take my leave of you two," he said as he bowed, his gaze on the woman behind them never leaving her.

Christina turned around to watch him take her grandmother's hands—both of them—to his lips before he kissed her quite thoroughly on the mouth. Due to the marchioness' height, he barely had to bend down to kiss her.

A thought of what it would be like if Lord Hartwell did such a thing to her every time she entered their house had Christina's insides doing funny little flips that left her blushing profusely.

She could only imagine what the marchioness must be experiencing.

"Oh," Vivian sighed softly. "He must *love* her," she whispered.

"Oh, he does," Christina replied as she watched the older couple go out to the gardens. Although she knew David

Carlington despised garden parties, he would always make an appearance to please his wife. Of course, he expected a reward of a carnal nature later, but Christina quickly put that thought from her mind when she noticed Vivian's expression.

"Mother says you shouldn't frown like that," she warned. "Your face might freeze in place."

Vivian gave her a quelling glance. "Someone's face will be looking far worse when I discover just who told all the men in London they couldn't court me," she said in a huff.

"Vivian. You said you would behave. At least until Friday," Christina countered.

Her friend let out a sound of frustration, which reminded Christina of how she had felt the day before in the park. That moment when she realized she might have feelings for Richard Hartwell. How she had felt later that afternoon, after he had rescued her from the King's Private Road and apologized.

She hadn't seen him since, and she wondered if he had learned anything about his true parentage. Even thoughts of him now had her body responding in a myriad of confusing sensations, including lust.

Her gaze went to the open door through which her grandparents had just exited. "Grandfather lusts for my grandmother, and she him, which is probably why he doesn't have a mistress."

Vivian's eyes rounded. "How do you know such a thing?"

Wincing, Christina said, "Mother has mentioned it on occasion. I expect they will continue their naughty ways Tuesday night during Lord Weatherstone's ball."

Curious, Vivian leaned down. "Pray tell, doing what?"

Christina gave her a quelling glance. "Enjoying one another's company in the library, of course," she replied. "Tupping, whilst other couples wait in line outside the door. Why, Mother claims they nearly missed her wedding because they... lost track of time."

Vivian blinked. A thought of Sebastian Peele tupping her on the leather sofa in Lord Weatherstone's library came to mind, and the most delightful sensations shot through her midsection. She inhaled softly, her eyes nearly closing from the pleasure she envisioned experiencing.

"You're imagining him making love to you, aren't you?" Christina whispered.

"What? Who?" Vivian blinked several times, as if she still had something in her eye.

Christina rolled her own. "He wants to, you must know."

Vivian stilled. "How do you know that? Did he... did he say something?"

Staring at her friend, Christina sobered. "He didn't have to," she replied softly. "I saw the way he looks at you. As if he regrets something and knows he must make it right."

Her attention going back to the painting, Vivian took a deep breath and sighed. "He *did* do something, although..."

Christina gasped. "Did he ruin you?" she asked in alarm.

Vivian shook her head. "I rather wish he had, but no. He... he stopped before he could take my virtue. And then he left for the Continent the very next day."

She pretended nonchalance, but Christina could tell her friend felt hurt by the memory. "He could be the one, Viv. The one my grandfather mentioned."

Vivian frowned again. "Then he had better be prepared for what I'm about to do to him," she vowed.

Blinking several times, Christina realized Vivian would not be keeping her promise to behave until Friday. The young woman was already headed toward the front door.

Instead of following her, Christina went out the back door. In search of Lord Cougham—hoping to warn him that Vivian would be paying a call—Christina allowed a long sigh of frustration when she learned from her mother that the viscount had already taken his leave.

"As will I in a moment. There are several of us here that have been invited to afternoon tea at Lady Weatherstone's," Elizabeth said in delight. "Her son was escorting her home only a moment ago. She's promised to show us the progress her footmen have made in transforming her ballroom for Tuesday night's ball."

Relieved Vivian couldn't do anything unseemly in the presence of the others in attendance at the garden party, Christina was about to take her leave when she realized she had no escort. No chaperone.

She turned around, about to ask her mother what she should do. She couldn't, though, given the man who stood before her.

Lord Hartwell.

CHAPTER 30

AN ATTEMPT AT SEDUCTION
GOES AWRY

A half-hour later, near Weatherstone Manor, Park Lane, Mayfair

Vivian had thought the walk down Park Lane would do her some good. Clear her head. Help her forget what she had overheard at the garden party. Instead, it merely had her feeling frustration. Anger.

Did a lifetime of behaving as Miss Prim and Proper account for nothing?

Well, apparently not. The old biddies all seemed to know something she didn't. Seemed to think she'd done something not so prim and proper even though she had behaved her entire life.

Well, except for Thursday night, when she'd been a guest at Bostwick House.

She inhaled deeply and finally took in her surroundings. Directly to her left was Weatherstone Manor.

This couldn't be a coincidence. It was a sign. A sign she needed to read.

Well, there wasn't an actual sign to read, but she had to believe that there was a reason she had ended up in this particular spot at this particular moment in her reverie.

Bash.

She was determined to discover if he was the one who had

warned all her possible suitors to stay away from her. It was time she learned for certain what his plans for his future—and hers—entailed.

She marched up to the pair of front doors, wishing her gloves didn't muffle the sound of her hard knock. She shook out her hand, annoyed that she had probably bruised her knuckles.

The door opened, as did the eyes of the butler who beheld her. Apparently he remembered all too well the incident with the mouche and was relieved to see there wasn't one on her face today.

"Is Lord Cougham in?"

If it was possible, the butler's eyes widened even more as he waved her into the vestibule. "I will see if he is, my lady. Whom shall I say is calling?"

Vivian was tempted to say "his future wife," but thought better of it. She was already upset with the viscount, and the fact that the butler behaved as if she hadn't just been there the day before had her even more miffed.

She would be positively peeved if Bash was the one who had warned off all her potential suitors.

To think, her height had nothing to do with why she'd been shunned all these years.

Besides, did she really believe all that had supposedly happened to Sebastian Peele whilst he was on the Continent? Was it really why he behaved so strangely now? His tale of living with monks seemed so outlandish, she was sure he had made it up.

"Miss Vivian Wentworth," she replied, forgoing her title. She certainly wasn't behaving as a lady should by calling on a gentleman in the middle of the day. Two times in two days. Miss Pipkins would pop a blood vessel and suffer a coronary if she learned what Vivian was doing.

Gilbert nodded and disappeared from view as Vivian stood in the middle of the entry. As she removed her redingote, she glanced around, remembering how she had passed through this small chamber a half-dozen times over the years, always to attend the Weatherstone ball.

Never had she stopped to admire the wall coverings—moire silk in a soft mauve—or the white painted woodwork and plasterwork that graced the corners and the ceiling. Above the bin for umbrellas was a small painting of a folly, and above the long shelf that held a few top hats was a landscape painting of rolling hills and stone fences with sheep scattered about.

Rarely did she look to see if she could decipher an artist's signature, but after the time she had spent with Christina in the portrait gallery in Carlington House, she leaned closer to stare at it.

S Fitzsimmons.

"Lady Plymouth painted it during her first year as a marchioness," a voice said from her left.

Vivian gave a start and turned to see the reason for her visit staring at her. "She was quite an accomplished painter," Vivian said when she found her voice.

Sebastian gave a bow as Vivian dipped a belated curtsy. When he reached for her hand, she allowed him to grip it, but she quickly moved to stand in front of him so their bodies were nearly touching. As a result, he was prevented from kissing her knuckles.

"We need to talk," she whispered, her head tilted back for one of the few men in London who was taller than she.

Appearing nervous, Sebastian glanced around the vestibule. "Where's Miss Pipkins? Or... or your lady's maid?"

"I don't know. I don't care," she replied, sounding breathless.

Sebastian furrowed his brows before he pulled her into the adjacent room, a large salon decorated entirely in creams and golds. From the white silk-covered furnishings and low table in front of the settee, he decided it was the downstairs parlor his mother had mentioned.

He quickly shut the door and leaned against it, rather

startled when he could see his reflection in the polished marble floor.

Vivian thought of girding her loins, but she wasn't there to fight him.

The very last thing she wished to do with Sebastian Peele was fight. Not given how her body responded to the man who stood before her, looking not at all like the rogue he had been prior to his trip to the Continent. Instead, he appeared clean-shaven and groomed, his hair combed perfectly into place. His top coat was even buttoned.

She reached up and speared two fingers into the front of his hair, dislodging a forelock so that it sprang out from whatever held it into an unnatural position. It settled onto his forehead.

"That's better," she whispered as she grinned. "Now you look more like the man I remember."

But Sebastian wasn't amused. "Do you know how long it took my valet to tame that?" he asked rhetorically.

"Perhaps it shouldn't be tamed," Vivian replied, an eyebrow arching. She leaned in closer and sniffed. "You smell different," she added in awe. "I like it."

*S*ebastian made a sound in the back of his throat that might have been frustration. "It's an Italian cologne I found in Naples. I used up what I took with me, and.... well, I haven't had a chance to pay a call at Floris," he replied, now wishing he had purchased more of the Italian cologne. An entire crate of it. "What's this about, my lady?" he asked in a quiet voice.

Vivian pointed to the nearest piece of furniture—a chaise lounge—and said, "May we sit, please?"

Sebastian didn't respond, but he did wave to the chaise. He waited for her to take a seat, and she did so right in the middle, which forced him to sit entirely too close to her.

Vivian angled her body in his direction and inhaled softly.

"I like that scent very much. Perhaps one of the perfumers at Floris can recreate it for you," she whispered.

Sebastian cleared his throat. "I... I'll see what I can do."

"It's rather good of you to consider my thoughts on the matter," she replied. She reached up and cupped a hand along his cheek and then smoothed a finger down along his jawline. "And I must say, I prefer you without the whiskers."

"It was past time I stopped allowing them to be seen in public," he murmured, his gaze following the fingertip. A fleeting thought of how his whiskers might have scraped her thighs when he made love to her had him blinking quickly. He then imagined the fingertip drawing down his growing manhood, and he struggled to breathe.

"I expected you would be all bronzed from your time on the Continent, and yet..." Her gaze followed the contours of his face, down his cravat-wrapped neck, along his impossibly broad shoulders and down to where his bare hand was pressed into the cushion of the chaise. "You look as if you never left England."

"I... I spent my last two years indoors," he stammered.

"The heat was that bad?" she asked, her voice still a whisper. She reached out and undid the two buttons of his top coat.

"No... I was... I was in the mountains," he replied, watching her long fingers as they spread open his top coat. "The Alps, in fact."

"Take this off," she ordered.

"Why?"

Vivian scoffed, her eyes rolling as she straightened. "Because... because I told you to." She winced, obviously aware she sounded entirely too much like Miss Pipkins. The thought of Miss Pipkins ordering a man to remove his top coat was so outlandish, she had to stifle the urge to grin.

Sebastian shed the top coat, but carefully folded it before he draped it over the edge of the chaise.

Vivian's eyes rounded and then narrowed. The Sebastian

she knew would have tossed the coat to the floor and then moved to do the same with his waistcoat.

Only her pleas and whimpers of fright had stopped him from doing so the last time they had been this close.

She reached out and undid his waistcoat buttons, noting how they weren't straining against their holes as they had done so in the past. "You've lost weight," she murmured.

"Some," he agreed. When she had finished undoing the buttons, he removed the waistcoat and slowly set it aside. "It was necessary and only fair to the others."

"Others?"

He nodded. "Those I shared quarters with for the past two years. They barely had enough to eat but were still willing to share."

Vivian stared at him a moment, confused by his words. "Are you all right?" she asked, displaying her sudden concern as she undid the knot of his cravat. She had never undone a cravat before, and she marveled at the intricate way in which the ends had been tied.

He cleared his throat again. "I won't be when my valet sees what you've done. What you're doing."

Vivian unwrapped one of the ends of the cravat from around his neck, which forced her to lean against him. The oddest sound erupted from his throat as one of her breasts pressed against his arm.

The warmth of him seeped through the thin fabric of her gown, and Vivian inhaled softly. "You feel as if you might have a fever," she murmured. She moved a hand to his forehead, her fingers tangling with his forelock as she pressed her palm against him. "Ooh," she whispered before moving the same hand behind his head so she could pull it down. She pressed her lips against his forehead before saying. "You are feverish."

"I can't imagine why," he said, obviously struggling with his breathing.

"Perhaps you should lie back," she suggested, giving his chest a slight push with the palm of her hand.

Sebastian settled against the small back of the chaise and

gripped the carved wood edges as Vivian readjusted her position on the chaise.

"Now, that's better," she said, continuing to press her hand against his chest.

"I'm not sure how," he grunted.

Vivian leaned over him, her lips hovering mere inches from his. "I thought you'd wish to continue what you started before you left for your Grand Tour," she murmured, as one hand spread open his shirt to reveal the top of his chest. Two fingers barely touched the dark hair that was revealed with her moves.

"You want me to?" he asked in surprise. Memories of their last night together flitted before his mind's eye. Memories of how he had seduced her. Almost taken her virtue. Memories of her wide eyes and frightened expression reminded him of why he had stopped when he had. Why he had finally simply kissed her thoroughly and then promised to write whilst on his trip.

Up until that moment, Sebastian had been thinking of cancelling his belated Grand Tour. He had been thinking he would simply ruin her and then promise her she would one day be his wife.

But the thought of marriage, of settling down and becoming the responsible heir he would eventually have to become, had him fleeing London the following morning. He had never before come so close to ruining a young woman, and he certainly didn't want Vivian to suffer for his indiscretions.

"Of course I *want* you to," Vivian said in a hoarse whisper. Her brows furrowed. "I thought you would be more... participatory," she accused. She pulled her hand from his chest, the move betraying her sudden suspicion.

Sebastian took advantage and captured the hand in his, kissing her knuckles one after the other. "I thought so, too," he murmured, struggling to maintain the self-discipline he had worked so hard to learn during his time with the monks. "But I'm not like that any longer."

Vivian blinked. "What?"

He groaned. "I'm trying very hard to be good here," he said. "I have been good for over two years."

Scoffing, Vivian pulled her hand from his grasp and then used both hands to spread open his shirt. She had to stifle a gasp at seeing his bare chest and the cloud of crisp curls that covered most of it. "You can't have been all that good, or you would have written to me."

His eyes widening in alarm, Sebastian gave his head a small shake. "Didn't you receive my letters?" he asked. He swallowed, his gaze darting down to her parted lips and then below to discover he could see down the front of her gown. See the space between her breasts—what little there was. He groaned. He wanted nothing more than to cup those breasts in his large hands. To strip her of the gown that barely covered her charms and then cover them with his mouth. To use his considerable experience to prove to her that he was the only man in all of London who could pleasure her until her toes curled. To prove to her he had acquired his experience for one purpose—so that she might cry out *his* name at the height of her ecstasy.

Selfish on his part, yes, but he was determined she be his and only his.

Vivian pulled back a bit. "Three letters, as I recall," she replied, her voice no longer a whisper. "Two were rather wicked, and the third..." She straightened. "Well, the third was quite unbelievable. Rather apologetic. Not like you at all."

"I've changed," Sebastian said, hoping no one would walk in on them. In their current positions on the chaise and given his state of dishabille, he was sure he would be accused of the same sorts of antics of which he'd been guilty prior to his stay with the St. Bernard monks. "I'm not the man you remember, my lady."

Of all the times in his life to decide he was no longer going to be a rogue—now he almost regretted his decision to live the life of an honorable man.

Vivian furrowed her brows. "'My lady'?" she repeated in disbelief. "And yet you allowed me to undress you—"

"Yes, yes, I did," he agreed. "I am a man, Viv. I cannot change that," he added on a sigh. If her hand moved one inch to the left of where it rested on his thigh, she would discover just how much of a manhood he possessed. He'd been aroused from the moment she had him on the chaise. He was hardening more now that she was poised over most of his body, like a tigress about to pounce. At any moment, he was sure she would, and he would be powerless to stop her.

He didn't want to stop her.

*V*ivian crossed her arms and gave him a quelling glance. Then her gaze darted down to the bulge behind his pantaloons. Her hand had been not an inch away from the evidence of his arousal!

Shock had Vivian backing away, scooting down the chaise to the end.

What had she been thinking to come here?

Seduction.

She had thought to scold him if he was indeed responsible for her lack of suitors. Then, out of spite, seduce the heir to the Weatherstone earldom. Perhaps be caught in the act in an effort to secure an offer of marriage.

A memory of her conversation with Lord Hartwell came to mind. Friday she would be of an age when she could declare her independence. She could request her dowry. Let a small townhouse and live the quiet life of a spinster. Or she could travel. She could take her own tour of Italy and Greece. Invite Christina along to be her companion. Meet interesting people. See amazing sites. Be squired about by counts and marquis, dukes and princes—at least those who weren't intimidated by her unusual height.

"I must go," she said as she leaned forward to stand.

"What?" Sebastian straightened on the lounge, his feet moving to the floor so that he was sitting so close, his thighs nearly touched hers once again. He hooked her arm so she couldn't escape the chaise. "Please, don't go," he said, breathless. "I cannot live without you," he said in a harsh whisper. "Every woman I have been with since I left England, I imagined she was you," he claimed.

Vivian's mouth dropped open at the same time her brows shot up in surprise. "Bash!" she said in protest. "That's... that's *disgusting*."

"I thought you'd be honored to know that," he argued. "I thought of no one but you, Viv. I thought of how when I returned to England, I would bestow you with the largest sapphire ring I could find and make you my wife," he claimed.

Despite his hold on her, Vivian stood up and then turned to stare down at him. "And yet, you've been home for... for almost a week," she countered. She held out a bare hand and wiggled her fingers. "No ring. No proposal." She held out the other and did the same, giving him a quelling glance.

"It's under construction," he replied, straightening on the lounge. "I have the very best jeweler in all of London working on it."

Vivian rolled her eyes. "Next, you'll be telling me that you're going to take me to the Kingdom of the Two Sicilies for our honeymoon," she argued.

"Agrigento on Sicily, actually, but we can go to Rome, too," he said. "After a tour of Palermo and Naples, of course."

Her brows furrowing, Vivian almost believed him. The idea of independence had her reconsidering, though, and she shook out her skirts. "Oh, Bash," she whispered in frustration as she pulled on her gloves.

Vivian turned and made her way to the door, stomping as much as her slippers would allow. She opened it to discover Elizabeth Bennett-Jones, Lady Bostwick, standing on the other side.

CHAPTER 31

A RESEMBLANCE IS
REMARKED UPON

A half-hour before, at Lady Morganfield's garden party

"Lord Hartwell!" Christina said in surprise. Her thoughts of the viscount seemed to have conjured him into existence. She dipped a curtsy. "How do?"

He bowed and took her hand in his. "Miss Bennett-Jones. I am much better now that I have found you," he replied before his lips brushed over the back of her gloved hand.

Christina furrowed a brow. "Has something happened?"

He regarded her with a look of bemusement before he said, "Many things have happened. Might I be allowed to escort you on a walk in the park?" he asked. "I know we spoke of a ride, but... I find I am without two horses at the moment."

A shiver of excitement coursed through Christina before she remembered permission would be required. She angled her head to the side, bending slightly to discover her mother's gaze on them. "Mother?" she asked, realizing Elizabeth Bennett-Jones had overheard the viscount's query.

"Oh, course you can, my dear. Do be home in time for dinner," Viscountess Bostwick replied, beaming in delight.

Christina blinked. Dinner wouldn't be served for at least five hours!

The viscount cleared his throat. "My lady, if I might have a moment of your time?"

Elizabeth paused as she moved to rise from her chair. "Yes?"

"I already spoke with Lord Bostwick on the matter. Miss Bennett-Jones and I have been invited to dinner," he said. "If you've no objections, I should like to extend the invitation to her and come for her at six o'clock this evening."

Her eyes widening in wonder, Elizabeth gave Christina a brief glance. "I've none," she replied. "But you'll have her home no later than eleven o'clock. We have church in the morning."

"Of course, my lady. I shall have her home before ten o'clock."

Elizabeth's eyes widened in appreciation. "Well, do enjoy the evening," she replied, allowing the viscount to kiss the back of her gloved hand.

Christina watched as her mother stood and passed them on her way to the back door of Carlington House. Several other matrons were saying their farewells to Lady Morganfield as they, too, took their leave of the garden party. Most were on their way to Weatherstone Manor for tea and a look at the ballroom.

Christina turned her attention on the viscount. "Apparently, you are once again in my mother's good graces," she said with a brilliant smile.

Richard no sooner offered his arm and Christina had placed hers on it before Lady Pettigrew's voice sounded over all the others at her table. "Why, I was sure that was Sir Randolph."

Christina felt Richard stiffen beneath her arm.

"He merely bears a *slight* resemblance to the knight," another at her table remarked. "I should know, since I am *married* to Sir Randolph," Lady Xenobia Roderick countered with a happy grin.

Richard turned and gave a deep bow. "Ladies."

A collective gasp sounded from the others at the table as

they regarded him. He gave a one-shouldered shrug. "We share a common ancestor," he said with a lopsided grin.

"You look so much like him," Lady Chamberlain remarked.

"You two could be twins," Lady Comber chimed in, quickly adding, "except you're so much *younger* than Sir Randolph," when she noted Christina's glower.

"Given the knight is so well regarded for his handsomeness, I shall take your comments as compliments, my ladies," Richard said with another bow. He turned to Christina, a fleeting expression of panic appearing before he said, "Shall we?"

She nodded quickly. When they were through the long corridor of the house and out the front door, Christina dared a glance in his direction. "From what Lady Roderick said, I take it she knows?"

He nodded. "She does, as do my two youngest brothers, my sister, Rachel, Sir Randolph, Mr. Merriweather, Lady Reading, and probably all the staff at Reading House. Oh, and my mother." He gave a sidelong glance in Christina's direction before they crossed Park Lane.

"Your mother?" Christina repeated once they had made it to the other side. "You found your mother?"

Richard allowed a chuckle. "She was never lost," he countered. "She is also who will be hosting us for dinner this evening."

"Oh," Christina replied. When she noted his expression of worry, she asked, "Why is it you don't seem happy about it?"

Chuckling, Richard considered how to respond. "Her identity has been a source of... consternation for me," he admitted.

"How so?"

"She owns a gaming hell... hall... den," he quickly amended. "Pardon the curse."

"Oh, I understand," Christina replied. "One of the better ones, or—?"

"The Queen of Hearts." He watched her closely, as if he expected her to react with derision.

Christina just stared back at him. "I've never been in it, but it looks well kept from the street," she remarked.

"There is more red and fake gold behind those doors than you shall find in any other building in all of England," he replied with a smirk.

"You did not like it?"

"Oh, it was fine," Richard replied. "*She* was fine. Not at all what I expected and yet..." He sighed.

"Familiar?" Christina guessed.

"Yes," he whispered softly. "I made her cry."

Christina stopped walking, which forced him to pause. "Right away, or—?"

"She was ever so glad to finally meet me," he said with a shrug. "It's been five-and thirty years. I think she had given up believing we would ever be in the same room together."

"She must have been so happy," Christina murmured.

"If my father had been successful with one of his ten marriage proposals to her, I might have met her far sooner."

"Marriage proposals?" Christina repeated. Her face betrayed her confusion. "Lord Reading *proposed* to her?" she asked.

"My father...Lord *Hartwell*... proposed to her. He even had a ring made, which I gave to her last night. I think that might have made her cry even more than my being there."

"Oh, Richard," Christina breathed, not even aware she had used his given name. "Now *I* might cry."

"Well, you needn't to on my account," he replied as they resumed their walk. "Miss Bennett-Jones, I know I overreacted yesterday afternoon—"

"You didn't," she interrupted. "News such as this had to be a shock. I cannot even imagine how I might have behaved if I had learned I had been living a lie not of my making."

Her thoughts briefly went to Vivian. To the words her grandfather had said when they were in the portrait gallery.

Someone had warned all of Vivian's potential suitors to stay away from her.

Poor Vivian!

Or not, if she was doing what Christina was afraid she was doing.

Confronting Lord Cougham.

Because even if he wasn't the man who had warned off possible suitors, then he would surely be bearing the brunt of Vivian's displeasure.

Or perhaps he would be declaring his love for her. Why else would he have warned off all possible suitors if not to have Vivian all to himself?

"You would have handled it with far more grace than I," Richard said, a brow furrowing when he noticed her sudden discomfort. "What is it?"

Christina allowed a wan grin. "Lady Vivian learned only a half-hour ago why it is that she has not had any suitors since her come-out." When Richard didn't say anything, she added, "She always thought it was because she is so tall."

He failed at suppressing a chuckle. "And the truth of the matter?" he prompted.

"Someone warned off all her suitors five or six years ago. Told them she was his, and they were to stay away," Christina explained.

"Ah, that would have been Lord Cougham," Richard said with a nod.

Christina gasped. "How do you know that?"

Remembering Lady Reading's comment about Lady Vivian, a ring, and Lord Cougham, Richard dipped his head. "Lady Reading mentioned it before dinner. Said I wasn't to consider Lady Vivian for courting. Apparently Lord Cougham hasn't yet proposed to the lady because the ring isn't ready."

The way Christina's mouth opened and formed an 'o' had him wishing they were somewhere more private. Somewhere he could kiss her. Somewhere he could do far more.

His comment was obviously welcome news for her.

"So it *was* Lord Cougham who warned everyone away

from Viv," she breathed. "Oh, I do hope she's not blistering his ears this very moment," she added.

"Should we be in fear for Lord Cougham?" Richard asked, a brow furrowing in confusion.

Christina couldn't decide whether to laugh or cry at hearing the query. "He'll be fine," she finally replied. "He's tall. He's large. He can take care of himself," she went on, her head bobbing to reinforce her words.

Or to convince herself they were true.

Richard chuckled. "I met Lord Cougham in the gardens today," he said.

"You did?"

He nodded. "He was... *watching* your table from behind a hedgerow."

"You mean spying on us?" she countered, her eyes round.

He chuckled. "I am amused now, but at the time, I was not. I didn't know *who* he was watching so intently."

Christina eyed him with suspicion. "Oh, now you really must explain yourself."

His gaze darted around the area where they were walking, and he winced when he noted that the park bench where he had left her during their last encounter in the park was up ahead. "I was jealous," he admitted.

"Of Lord Cougham?"

Richard inhaled and said. "I was convinced he was watching *you*," he went on.

It was Christina's turn to chuckle. "Oh, he would have been watching Vivian," she assured him. "Those two are... well, they are perfect for one another, but I was never sure if they knew it." A frisson skittered through her body when she comprehended his comment then.

He had been jealous.

She paused, and he once again moved to stand in front of her. "Why would *you* be jealous?" she asked.

Dipping his head so the rim of his hat touched hers, Richard closed his eyes a moment. "I have been thinking of you. Ever since we met," he whispered. "I even mentioned you to Mrs. Higgins. To the woman who is supposedly my mother," he clarified before he straightened.

Christina held her breath. "I don't think I've met her."

Richard shook his head. "I would hope not, except I find myself in a bit of a quandary."

"What sort of quandary?"

He inhaled to answer and then seemed to reconsider what he was about to say.

"Tell me," she urged, giving him a nudge.

Amused she would shove him, Richard pushed her back. "Well, it seems she would welcome an invitation to ride in the park. Or to go to a place called Gunter's, I think she said?"

"Gunter's Tea Shoppe. It's in Berkley Square," Christina replied, a look of delight accompanying her words. "They serve ices and sugary confections."

Richard's face lit up with understanding. "Ah. Well, that explains it. She was hoping I might take you both there. At the same time."

A smile brightened Christina's face even more. "I should like that very much," she replied.

"Even if she is.... a gambling den owner?" He asked the question in a lowered voice, as if he were saying a curse.

Continuing to grin, Christina said, "A successful business owner, don't you mean?" she countered.

He opened his mouth as if he was about to respond and then closed it. "Yes. You have the right of it," he finally agreed, remembering what Lady Reading had said.

The two continued their walk near the Serpentine. Despite the ease of their conversation so far, Christina knew Richard was nervous about something.

She was fairly sure she knew it had to do with his new family, but she thought to let him be the one to bring it up.

Meanwhile, she enjoyed their outing and imagined what it would be like to do this with him every day.

CHAPTER 32

A SEDUCTRESS IS NEARLY CAUGHT IN THE ACT

eanwhile, at Weatherstone Manor, ground floor parlor

Years of training had Vivian dropping into a deep curtsy and a proper greeting for Elizabeth Bennett-Jones, Viscountess Bostwick. Mere minutes of improper behavior, and she was about to be ruined.

Thoroughly ruined.

She could only hope Sebastian Peele was seeing to closing his shirt and pulling on his waistcoat. If not, she would be hopelessly ruined.

"Lady Vivian," Elizabeth said, as a smile replaced her initial reaction of surprise. "I'm so glad I am not the first of Lady Weatherstone's callers on this beautiful afternoon. I wasn't aware you'd be interested in seeing the ballroom whilst it was still empty."

"Oh, of course I am. I might one day host such an *affaire*," she claimed, now thinking she wouldn't be allowed such an honor. When word got out that she had removed most of Lord Cougham's clothing, she would be forced to move to a small cottage on a cliffside, overlooking the Channel as she lived the quiet, desperate life of a ruined woman. Or she would be on her trip to the Kingdom of the Two Sicilies, carrying on with a count who had lost his fortune and needed hers to shore up his lust for living, leaving her to rusticate in one of his rundown estates on one of the seven hills of Rome.

At least there would be wine. No doubt from the count's private vineyards.

Vivian blinked away the odd thoughts and gave the viscountess a brilliant smile. She could only imagine what might be happening behind her. Either Sebastian was hurriedly redressing, or he was determined she be caught in a trap of her own making and was lounging contentedly in the Greek chaise.

A quick glance behind her had Vivian realizing neither one of her suppositions was correct.

Sebastian was no where in sight.

"You are not the first to arrive on this beautiful afternoon, of course," Vivian replied, opening the door wider. "I thought to let some air in. I hadn't even realized the door was closed."

Elizabeth gave her a dubious glance and made her way into the parlor. "I hope you haven't been waiting long," she said as she took a seat in one of the white upholstered chairs. "The trip from the gardens at Carlington House was very quick. Even quicker for you, it would seem."

"Oh, I only just arrived a few minutes ago myself. I haven't paid a call on Lady Weatherstone in an age, and thought to join you all in admiring her arrangements for the ball." She paused and glanced towards the door. "Didn't Christina come with you?"

"Oh, no. She's off for a walk," Elizabeth replied. She watched as Vivian took a seat on the Greek chaise lounge.

"Oh? By herself?" She nearly winced, realizing she had left her friend in the portrait gallery.

"Lord Hartwell invited her to go for a walk in the park. He seems... interested," Elizabeth hedged.

"Oh, he would be *perfect* for her," Vivian said. "Other than she would have to move to Lincolnshire," she added as her brows furrowed.

"My thoughts exactly," Elizabeth agreed. "Although... I do think she'd be more amenable to the idea if she knew her best friend was suitably settled here in London." She paused, gauging Vivian's reaction. "As opposed to traveling to Rome all alone. Ripe for the plucking by some destitute count in need of a dowry."

Vivian's eyes widened before tears brightened their corners. "Oh, that's so kind of her," she murmured. "However, I *am* thinking of taking a trip before I consider any offers of marriage. But I rather doubt I shall consider an offer from a destitute count."

"Oh? Do you have a particular destination in mind?" Elizabeth asked, at the same moment a maid appeared with a tea tray. She was followed by Lady Weatherstone and Lady Roth, who displayed a look of surprise at seeing her daughter.

"Why, the Kingdom of the Two Sicilies, of course. Mayhap Greece," Vivian replied as she stood and then curtsied to the new arrivals.

"Why, Vivian, it's so good of you to come," Agnes Peele said as she returned the curtsy and made her way to a chair next to where the tea tray had been set.

"Hello, Mother," Vivian added as she directed her gaze to Grace Wentworth.

"Vivian. I'm... I'm surprised to see you here," her mother replied. She glanced around. "Where is Miss Pipkins?"

Vivian shook her head. "At Roth House, I should think. I merely wished to see the ballroom before it is filled with guests," she gushed, as she turned her gaze onto the elderly matriarch. A thought that Lady Weatherstone could one day be her mother-in-law had her briefly wishing it could be so. Agnes Peele had always been one of her champions, scolding those who made disparaging comments about her height and reminding everyone she was the epitome of prim and proper.

Vivian wondered what Lady Weatherstone would think if she had known what she had been doing with Sebastian—doing *to* Sebastian—only a few moments ago.

Attempting seduction and failing miserably.

"I'm so glad you think so, especially since you're going to

have to host these balls at some point in the future," Agnes replied happily.

These balls?

As in *the Weatherstone balls?*

Vivian stared at Lady Weatherstone for several seconds before a gray curtain surrounded her vision. Before she could put voice to a response, everything went black.

CHAPTER 33

A PROPOSAL IN THE PARK

Meanwhile, in Hyde Park

After Christina had taken a moment to remove a stone from her slipper, she threaded her arm around Richard's and allowed him to lead her along the crushed granite path near the Serpentine. Although she had been left with the impression they would be allowed this walk without requiring a chaperone, she couldn't help but imagine someone was watching them.

Should Richard do so much as attempt a peck on her temple, she feared someone—probably her father—would spring from the nearby trees and behead him with a sword.

"I wanted you to know that I am truly sorry for how I left you when we were last here," Richard murmured as they passed the park bench on which they had been sitting.

"As am I—for having supposed you would welcome my thoughts on the matter." When a sad expression settled on his face, Christina added, "We'd only just met. It was not my place to say such things."

He furrowed his brows, making him appear far older than his years. "I was angry," he admitted, "but not at you," he added, a gloved hand settling over hers on his arm.

Touched by his gesture, Christina inhaled softly. She was about to ask where his anger had been directed when he said,

"I was hurt at the time. My sister..." He rolled his eyes. "I felt as if I'd been ambushed, and yet in her defense, she had no time to plot what happened yesterday." When he noted Christina's quirked lip, he said, "Wot?"

"She's had her entire life to plot what she might say when she finally met you," she teased gently. "For you to appear before her—unexpectedly—set her off on one of probably ten different scenarios she had imagined for the occasion." She winced. "You had every right to feel ambushed."

"You're not speaking very kindly of one of your sex," he accused lightly.

She gave him a sideways glance. "That's because I am the granddaughter of one of the doyens of the *ton* who live for gossip. I have a sister. I have many friends who, as nice as they can be, sometimes choose to say things that are not always kind."

Richard made a sound deep in his throat. "I cannot imagine you would say anything unkind to anyone."

Scoffing, Christina said, "That's because you were not in Carlington House when I was scolding Lady Vivian earlier this afternoon," she replied. She gave her head a shake. "I fear her recent rebelliousness will result in her ruin."

Richard angled his head. "Or a betrothal," he murmured, a grin youthening his face by at least a decade.

Christina's eyes rounded. "You say that as if—"

"Lord Cougham has warned off every possible suitor because he intends to take her to wife. Soon, I think."

"He warned *you* off, too?" Christina asked in surprise. The viscount hadn't yet been in London for an entire week. How did he know of Sebastian Peele's edict?

"He didn't need to, but I was informed I should steer clear. By then, it wasn't an issue for me, since I already knew I was not interested in courting *her*," he explained.

"Because of what happened over dinner?"

He nodded. "Well, that, and a much better opportunity had already presented itself," he hedged.

"A much better opportunity?"

Now that they were well beyond the end of the Serpentine, Richard led them to a secluded park bench. "A much better option, yes," he said once he had cleaned off the bench with a handkerchief. The two sat and Christina waited for him to explain his comment.

"I spoke with your father earlier today. Before the garden party. That's how I learned you were at Carlington House," he said. "He gave me his permission to court you as well as to ask you to dinner."

"You wish to court *me*?" Christina replied, her voice barely above a whisper.

"Actually, I was thinking to simply propose to you. Especially after I saw that young man speak with you yesterday. Before the accident with the phaeton."

Christina eyes rounded. "Oh, you mean Gabriel Wellingham? He works at the British Museum cataloging Greek antiquities."

"Was he looking to catalog you?"

Laughing, Christina said, "He is married, Richard. He was merely telling my mother and me of a new exhibit that's being unveiled at the museum this week. He knows I happen to appreciate Greek antiquities."

Feeling ever the fool—he seemed to be doing that too much of late—Richard dipped his head. Then he remembered how the main hall of his house was decorated and he felt a surge of pride. "I'd hate to discover that some young buck had met you at the ball tomorrow night, and swept you off your feet, and left me—"

"Richard," she whispered.

"Oh, I do so like the way you say my name."

"Oh!" she said as her eyes rounded. "I should probably call you by your title," she whispered.

"But you will continue to call me Richard when we're alone?"

She nodded. "If you'd like."

"I must warn you. I've very little experience spending

time around women," he said. "Not having had a mother or sisters—"

"I understand."

"No nieces or aunts."

"Of course."

"No grandmothers to set me straight when I've done something unpardonable."

"Are you asking me to set you straight should you do something unpardonable?" she asked with a grin.

"If you could be kind when you do so," he replied with a wince.

Christina gave him a brilliant smile. "I shall." When he didn't say anything else but merely stared at her, she added, "Would you like to kiss me?" She quickly squelched the thought that she sounded rather bold just then.

He nodded. "I don't suppose *you* have any experience with the matter?"

She shook her head. "Other than seeing my parents do it every day of my entire life, I should hope not. Although, I have tried practicing on the base of my thumb," she offered, raising a hand to her lips to show him what she meant. "But I'm sure it's not the same."

"I find myself quite jealous of the base of your thumb," he murmured.

When he didn't make a move to lean toward her, Christina did so toward him, her lips barely touching his until he had an arm around her waist and had bent his head slightly. The closer proximity meant she could relax in his hold as his lips finally captured hers.

Awkward at first and all too brief, their initial kiss was barely finished before Richard seemed to understand what to do.

All at once, Christina found her lips open to his, felt the tip of his tongue against her teeth and the front of his body against hers. Had it been freezing cold in the park, she would not have noticed. Her entire body was warm, her insides molten. Desire overwhelmed her. Her breasts seemed to swell, their nipples tightening into buds behind her corset. The space at the top of her thighs began to throb, and she felt liquid heat form there.

A small moan of appreciation sounded from her throat as his hand moved up the side of her torso and his thumb pressed against the side of her breast. When it lifted higher, so it was wrapped around her shoulder, she mewled her disappointment.

When Richard finally ended the kiss, he left his lips hovering over hers. "I cannot help but think I should apologize," he whispered.

"But, why?" she countered, her voice sounding ever so breathless.

"I've taken liberties I'm not yet allowed."

Christina gave him a pretend pout. "My mother says when I am betrothed, I'm to allow my future husband to ruin me, so I hardly think bestowing a kiss is taking liberties."

Richard's eyes widened. "I rather doubt your father would agree."

She grinned then. "And yet he probably ruined her before they were wed," she argued as she straightened on the bench. A quick look around showed they were still alone, the only witnesses to their kiss a few birds in the branches above them.

Richard considered her comment. The idea of spending time with her for the purpose of ruining her didn't sit right with his principles, but he had to admit to curiosity.

Thoughts of taking Christina to his townhouse—he wanted to give her a tour—had him imagining what else he might do with her. To her.

There was much he needed to learn, though. Probably much she needed to learn.

"Are you thinking you might wish to make love to me before the wedding?" Christina asked, her voice kept to a whisper.

"I want to make love to you, of course," Richard admitted, rather shocked they were discussing it. "But I think it's best we keep our activities to kissing. At least for a few days," he added.

"Of course," Christina replied, looking ever so relieved.

"Did you like it? The kiss, I mean?" Richard asked in a quiet voice.

She nodded. "Oh, very much. And you?"

He nodded, sounding breathless when he said, "It was rather intimate," he admitted. "Even after we're wed, do you suppose we might do it often?"

Christine gave him a brilliant smile. "I should hope we do it every day. Every night," she replied.

"So, you will marry me?"

She angled her head to one side and reached up to kiss him on the corner of his mouth. "Yes. Yes, I will marry you. Hopefully before you meet all those beautiful young women who are about to have their come-outs," she replied. "They might have you changing your mind about wishing to wed me."

He let out a breath he'd apparently been holding a long time, which had Christina giggling and him chuckling. "Thank you. And I won't be paying any of them any mind," he claimed. "I want *you*." He glanced around and frowned. "This is not exactly how I imagined I would be doing this," he admitted.

"What did you imagine?"

Richard dipped his head. "The parlor at Bostwick House? With a proper ring." He paused a moment. "As a different person. The person I was."

Christina stared at him. Apparently he had decided to ask for her hand before he learned anything about his true parentage. "You still *are* Richard Hartwell," Christina countered. "That hasn't changed even if other truths have."

He straightened on the bench as his attention went to something in his mind's eye. "There is something to be said for the truth," he murmured. "As much as I didn't want to learn it, I am relieved to know it now." He paused to consider his next words. "Relieved and, well, *worried*. For no one can know, Christina. I don't want my father's memory to suffer for something he had to do for the sake of the viscountcy."

Christina nodded her understanding. "I will keep the secret because I must," she said. "For the sake of our children and for the viscountcy."

His brows furrowed. "And how will we explain my resemblance to Sir Randolph? To my younger brothers?"

An impish grin appeared. "The same as you did today at the garden party," she replied. "You have common ancestors, of course," she reminded him. When she saw his hesitancy, she asked, "What is it?"

"How did *you* sort it?"

She inhaled softly. "I know I wasn't supposed to know, but I just *knew*," she murmured. "And it makes no difference." Beneath the arm that still rested on his, she could feel him stiffen. "It will make no difference to anyone."

"It does to me," he replied on a sigh. "I almost feel as if I've been made a fool—"

"You have not."

"Or poorly used."

Christina grimaced. "You're allowed that, I suppose," she murmured. "Now that you *have* met some of your real family, does it help to know that you have a sister who loves you? A father who is still alive? And all those brothers and another sister who might not yet know the truth, but are still your immediate relations? A stepmother who would never deny you anything, including her love? Surely that makes it more bearable."

Richard inhaled and let the breath out slowly. "Other than it's been so much to take in, I suppose you're right." He turned to regard her again, his expression one of dismay. "I would understand if you change your mind about marrying me, once you've had more time to think on it."

Christina stared at him in shock. "Richard," she scolded softly. "Even if you weren't the son of a marquess, I would still find you a perfect match for me," she replied with a quirked lip.

He scoffed. "Even if our children can never know the truth of the matter?"

Christina inhaled softly, a smile slowly lightening her face. "Mayhap we could tell them on our deathbeds?" she suggested. "What an interesting tidbit of information to impart with our dying breaths," she added. "*You are the grandchildren of the Marquess of Reading,*" she said in a hoarse whisper.

"The *late* Marquess of Reading," he corrected her. "Given his age, I rather doubt Reading will still be alive when *we're* on our deathbeds," he added.

"*You are the grandchildren of the late Marquess of Reading,*" Christina announced with a grin, her voice once again taking on the serious manner of an actress on the stage.

"That's more like it," Richard agreed, a brilliant smile appearing for the first time that day. "I suppose you are right. I have been looking at this all wrong."

"You have every right to be angry with your father," Christina said quietly.

"But I'm not," he replied on a sigh. At seeing her look of disbelief, he added, "He did what he had to. For the viscountcy. I understand that now."

"If he hadn't... would there still have been a Hartwell viscountcy?" she asked. "Without you?"

He shook his head. "I am it until I sire an heir," he replied. "There are no cousins. No distant relatives who could inherit."

"Which means the Hartwell viscountcy would have gone back to the Crown."

Richard shuddered. "Father did right by his responsibility, it's true."

Christina turned her head toward him and allowed a grin. Reaching up, she kissed him on the cheek. "And so shall you."

"Said as if you look forward to being a mother," he teased.

"Oh, I do, Richard. I almost wish I could have twins, just so I can hold babies all day long."

Richard dipped his head and then leaned over to kiss her

on the temple. "I can imagine you doing so," he said as his grin widened. "Does that mean you wish to marry soon? Or should we... wait?"

Christina dimpled as she considered his query. "Although I am old enough to marry without my parents' permission, and if I wasn't the oldest daughter of Elizabeth Carlington Bennett-Jones, I would suggest you whisk me off to Gretna Green on the morrow," she began.

"Not today?" he countered playfully.

She rolled her eyes and grinned. "But..." Her eyes suddenly widened. "Her wedding was quick," she said then. "Quite quick. Why, if I merely reminded her of that fact, she wouldn't object to ours being soon. That is, if *you* wish to marry soon."

Richard leaned over and kissed her on her forehead. "It matters not *when* so much as that it simply happens. Preferably before Parliament retires for the summer. Then I can take you to Lincolnshire. Take you on a wedding trip."

"To the Continent?" she asked in awe.

He sobered a moment. "We could. I've never been. I suppose you'd like to go to Italy?"

"I would, of course, but didn't you go there as part of your Grand Tour?" she asked in surprise.

He shook his head. "I did not. I... I was not allowed given what was happening in Greece. And the Revolution of 1820 had just occurred in the Kingdom of the Two Sicilies. Father worried I might be injured or die, so he forbid me from going." When he turned to face her, he found Christina regarding him with bemusement. "What is it?"

"You've only just proposed, and we've already decided where we're going on our wedding trip."

"And it sounds as if we're going to have twins," he said with a chuckle.

"Where will the four of us live?"

"Ah," he said as he held up a finger. "I happen to own a townhouse. In Park Lane."

"You do?" she asked in surprise. "I thought you said you were letting one?"

"I thought I was," he replied. "Turns out my father purchased it some years ago. I also own a hunting lodge in Kent—"

"You like to hunt?"

"I do not, but seeing as how my father won it from Lord Reading in a card game, I think I shall keep it."

Christina giggled. "It sounds as if your late father left a few surprises for you."

Richard nodded. "He did indeed, not the least of which was his *affaire* with Mrs. Higgins." He sobered as he considered the woman who he now knew was his real mother.

"I'm glad you've met her," Christina murmured. "I look forward to making her acquaintance, as well."

His eyes widened when he once again remembered the invitation to dinner his mother had put forth. "I'm to bring you to her house for dinner this evening. She said she will have her chef make us his very best meal."

Christina grinned. "I'm sure it will be fine. What time will you come for me?"

"Six o'clock? I'll send word to let her know we're coming."

"The ride to her house will give us more time for conversation."

Richard sighed. "If you insist," he said, somewhat dramatically.

Christina giggled. She inhaled softly and then noted the afternoon sun. "Oh, dear. If I'm to dress for dinner with your mother, then I do believe we need to be getting back."

"You're right," he said as he pulled out his pocket watch. "I surely don't want the Hartwell viscountcy ended because your father decides to off me with a fencing foil," he teased.

They resumed their walk, taking a different path back toward Park Lane and walking quickly as they did so.

There was news to share.

CHAPTER 34

A PENDING MARRIAGE IS MADE PUBLIC

eanwhile, back in the front salon at Weatherstone Manor

"There now, no sudden moves, my sweeting."

The voice came to Vivian as if it was from far away. As if the source of it was in another room. She would have opened her eyes, but then she was sure her pleasant dream of being held by a warm, solid body who smelled like Sebastian would dissipate.

At the moment, she wanted to imagine that he was holding her. Murmuring sweet nothings in her ear as hushed comments of concern buzzed at the edge of her consciousness. Wanted to imagine that this is what it would be like to be held by him in the middle of the night, after he'd made mad, passionate love to her in a hotel room overlooking a palazzo in Italy.

Or in their shared bed.

The location didn't matter as long as she woke up in his arms.

"Vivian?"

Well, that was definitely *his* voice, sounding all concerned and worried. Vivian slowly opened her eyes, rather happy to discover him staring down at her. "There's my girl," he whispered. "You gave us quite a fright," he added.

Vivian's gaze darted sideways to discover a number of matriarchs of the *ton* staring down at her. "Oh!" she said as she struggled to rise.

"Careful, my sweet," Sebastian said as he helped her to a sitting position on the edge of the Greek chaise.

Vivian buried her face in her hands. "Oh, dear," she murmured. She felt his lips press against her temple, and she knew a blush colored her neck and face.

"I didn't mean to embarrass you, my dear," Agnes said as she held out a cup of tea. "But I suppose the prospect of marrying my son is rather overwhelming. Hopefully not too frightening," she added, aiming an arched brow in his direction.

"Mother," Sebastian gently teased. "Lady Vivian is well aware that I am not the same man I was four years ago," he claimed. "She is, in fact, looking forward to becoming my wife."

Vivian was about to counter his words, but he was regarding her with such an interesting expression. One filled with concern. One filled with longing.

One filled with love.

"Your wife?" she whispered as she accepted the tea.

He lowered his lips to her ear. "Please, I beg you, don't deny it," he whispered. "Or I shall have a good deal of explaining to do." Such as why he'd been able to appear as if out of nowhere when his mother had let out a cry of, "Help!" when Vivian had fainted dead away on the chaise lounge.

Ever since Lady Bostwick had arrived, he had been hiding behind the thick drapes at the end of the room, carefully buttoning up his waistcoat and top coat. Rearranging his cravat had been far more difficult, sure he hadn't been able to properly pleat it before wrapping it around his neck as surreptitiously as he hoped. Since no one directed their attentions to his end of the parlor, he was fairly sure his presence had gone unnoticed by his mother's guests.

If it had become necessary, he could have sneaked out through the French doors and into one of his father's many gardens, made his way around to the back of the house, and then into the house by way of the kitchen door.

Vivian's eyes scanned the collection of older matrons who sat around the parlor—there were now six of them—all delicately sipping tea and daring occasional glances in her direction as they spoke of the Season's gossip and entertainments.

It wasn't until she took a sip of her tea that she realized Sebastian was sitting impossibly close. So close, his thighs were pressed against hers. One of his arms was even wrapped around her waist, as if he was holding her upright.

Perhaps he was.

"Do you really wish to marry me?" she asked in a whisper.

His lips once again kissed her temple. "After what you nearly did to me? I should think that would be evident," he murmured.

"What *I* did to *you*?" she countered, as if she had forgotten her attempt at seduction only the half-hour before.

"Made me fall in love with you?" he said, his voice not quite as quiet as it should have been given the current company in the parlor.

A series of contented sighs sounded in response to his words, and he gave a winning smile to those who surrounded him. "I have always loved Lady Vivian," he announced proudly. "It's true. I teased her mercilessly when she was younger, but only because she had me so vexed I could not think straight. Other than I knew I would one day make her my wife."

Vivian inhaled softly as she stared at him. "You bounder," she whispered.

He directed his grin to her and then kissed her forehead to a responding chorus of nervous titters.

"Now, Sebastian, that's quite enough," his mother scolded. "You'll have your future wife displaying a blush until well past your wedding day if you're not careful," she added in warning.

"I want all of London to know," he replied defensively.

"Well, given those in attendance today, I should think

everyone in England *will* know by tomorrow afternoon," she responded happily.

All those in the parlor giggled as hands were raised to cover their lips and teacups jiggled on their saucers.

Deciding a solo trip to Italy wasn't in her immediate future, Vivian sighed and sipped her tea.

CHAPTER 35

A WEDDING IS DISCUSSED

*M*eanwhile, in the study at Bostwick House George Bennett-Jones regarded his fellow viscount and future son-in-law with a grin. "So... dinner with your mother?" he asked. "Tonight?"

"Indeed. Mrs. Higgins wishes to meet my future wife, and Christina is amenable to the idea," Richard explained.

"Fine with me. What's your other request?"

"A quick wedding," Richard stated, sounding a bit more forceful than he intended.

"How quick?" George asked, suspicious.

The younger viscount inhaled slowly and said, "Besides my age—I'm not getting any younger—the sooner I can secure the future of the viscountcy, the better." He paused and added. "And I fear if I do not announce my intention to marry your daughter on the morrow, some young buck is going to ruin her so he can have her. Probably during Tuesday night's ball, given all I've heard about what happens in the gardens behind Weatherstone Manor."

"Not that Christina would do such a thing, but I see your point," George countered.

Richard dipped his head. "I suppose her mother will want to arrange a wedding of some note."

"No doubt," George agreed. "Although..." He paused as he

seemed to reconsider. "There is always Adeline, if she cannot do it for Christina."

Richard's eyes widened. "What are you suggesting?"

George pulled his Breguet from his pocket and raised a brow. "If you go now, you can make it to Doctors' Common in time to secure a special license. I can take you on my phaeton. It's already hitched up for the parade in Rotten Row."

"Not too damaged from the accident, I hope?" Richard asked.

George rolled his eyes. "Nothing a good washing couldn't cure," he replied before a look of suspicion crossed his face. "It would serve her right," he murmured, realizing why it was the phaeton overturned.

"Pardon?"

Giving his head a shake, George said, "You two can marry Tuesday—"

"But, we have Parliament."

"Before the ball. Here in Bostwick House. It will give Elizabeth something to do all day besides worry about which gown she should wear. Weatherstone will be thrilled to have the marriage announced as part of the festivities."

"But what about your viscountess? I shouldn't wish to start out on her bad side," he argued.

"Leave her to me," George argued with a sly grin. "She's about to learn a lesson about repercussions."

Richard was about to put voice to another protest, but George was already up and out of his office, heading for the front door. When Richard followed him, he paused and turned around to discover Christina standing next to the study's door, a grin lighting her face. "You heard?" he asked.

She nodded. "I did."

He hurried to pull her into his arms. "A wedding on Tuesday?"

She nodded. "I know exactly which gown I'll wear," she whispered.

He kissed her, intending for it to be quick—George was

already out the front door—but his lips lingered on hers when she opened her mouth to him. When he finally pulled away, he left his forehead pressed against hers. "I shall never grow tired of doing that," he whispered.

"Neither shall I. Now, you must go. You haven't much time," she said as she pointed to the hall clock. "I will still see you at six?"

"You shall." He bowed and hurried off through the front door.

Christina watched him go as she leaned a shoulder against the wall and grinned in delight. A moment later, the butler opened the front door again and Elizabeth entered.

"Where is your father off to?" her mother asked as she pointed toward the street. "I was sure I arrived in time to change for our ride in Rotten Row."

Stiffening, Christina straightened and considered how to respond. "He won't be long," she said. "He and Lord Hartwell just have to pay a call in Doctors' Commons."

"Oh," Elizabeth replied with a wave. She was halfway up the stairs before she paused. Holding onto the rail, she turned and said, "A special license?" she guessed, her face lighting up in delight.

Christina's expression matched hers. "Indeed, Mother. I'm getting married on Tuesday. Before the ball."

Her smile faltering slightly, Elizabeth inhaled sharply and seemed about to put voice to a protest when Christina said, "You can arrange a large wedding for Adeline, Mother."

Elizabeth seemed to think on the comment a moment before she nodded. "True," she replied. "But if you think for one moment you will get the short shrift for yours, think again, young lady. Yours will not be the first quick wedding I've arranged in my time."

Her eyes widening, Christina watched as her mother continued her ascent.

For a few seconds, Christina wondered if she should be worried.

CHAPTER 36

A PROPOSITION IN THE GARDENS

*M*eanwhile, *in the Weatherstone gardens*

"I was thinking of taking you to Sicily for our wedding trip," Sebastian said quietly. He and Vivian were walking amongst his father's most recent blooms in the bulb garden.

"Sicily?" she repeated in surprise.

"Agrigento to start—to see the Greek ruins—and then Palermo. Cross the channel and make our way to Naples and then to Rome," he continued. "We can spend as long as you'd like before we sail to Greece."

"Greece?"

"Maybe take a ferry to a couple of the largest islands?" he suggested. "Crete? By then, I should hope I would have gotten a child on you," he said as his brows waggled. "And if not by then, definitely there."

"Bash!" she scolded, her smile resplendent in the late afternoon sunshine.

"Father claims I can make love to you whenever I want, now that I have secured your promise of marriage," he said in a quiet voice. "As much as I wish to do so, I think I should—"

"Do so tonight," Vivian interrupted.

Sebastian stopped in his tracks and turned to stare at her.

"Tonight?" he repeated in surprise. "I am willing to wait," he added.

She shrugged. "Mother warned me. Said that now that I had agreed to marry you, I should expect that you would wish to take my virtue."

Sebastian frowned. "It's not that I wish to take your virtue," he argued. "I want to, of course, but only to ensure that no one else will lay claim to you."

Vivian rolled her eyes. "No one else will lay claim to me," she countered. "I'm entirely too tall."

He leaned down so that his forehead touched hers. "You have no idea just how enticing your height is to randy men," he replied.

"Are you a randy man?" she asked, not quite sure what the word implied.

"Indeed," he replied. "But only for you these days," he quickly added. "Now, we must decide where it is I'm to make love to you."

"Somewhere private," she said, as she turned to move along on the path.

Bash quickly joined her, offering his arm. "Of course."

"Somewhere where no one will hear us," she added.

"That might be a problem," he murmured.

"What?"

He gave her a quelling glance. "I intend to have you begging for me quite loudly," he said. "Good thing my parents are nearly deaf."

"Bash!" she scolded.

"But first, you're going to tell me what's gotten into you."

Vivian swallowed. "Into me?"

Sebastian sighed. "When I left London, you were known by everyone as Miss Prim and Proper," he claimed.

"I was not," she countered with a huff. At seeing his quelling glance, she sighed. "Oh, I suppose it's true. And I was, until..." She paused, thinking of how angry she had been with Miss Pipkins this past week. How rebellious she had felt of late.

Furrowing a brow, Sebastian prompted, "Until?"

"Until I learned *you* had returned."

Sebastian scoffed. "Whatever do you mean?"

It was her turn to give him a quelling glance. "You were known for your rakish behavior, Bash. Driving coach-and-fours at breakneck speeds at four o'clock in the morning—"

"It was never past two," he argued.

"Bedding widows—"

"I was always thinking of you."

Vivian inhaled and stared at him. "That's disgusting."

"Perhaps, but it made it more... *tolerable* for me."

She was about to argue the tolerable part, but thought better of it. Perhaps he really didn't enjoy bedding widows. "And gambling until dawn... I hated you," she whispered.

"I know," he said on a sigh. "But I also knew you would one day have to forgive me."

She scoffed. "Oh, did you now?"

He nodded. "We've always known we were going to end up together. Married. Parents to a brood of misbehaving children."

Vivian gasped. "*We* have not always known that. At least, no one informed me. And what's this about misbehaving children?"

Grinning, Sebastian brought her hand to his lips and kissed her palm. "I thought you would sort it from my teasing you all those years."

"You did tease me. Terribly," she agreed.

"As an only child, I speak from experience when I say we should have more than one."

"Wait. All that teasing meant you *liked* me?" she asked, ignoring the comment about having more than one child.

She hadn't even married him yet.

"Uh-huh," he said with a grin. He kissed her forehead when she displayed a look of confusion.

"It certainly wasn't obvious," she whispered.

He arched a brow. "We men are terribly obtuse," he agreed. "And speaking of indecipherable behavior—"

"Were we?"

"What accounts for *your* sudden change in behavior?" he asked after a pause. "And don't say it's because I've returned."

Vivian gazed at him a moment, a slight grin appearing when she noted how the errant forelock she had pulled from his perfectly combed hair now rested on his forehead, all thick and curly. She reached up and used two fingers to pull it straight and then let it go. The curl bounced back, finally settling into place on his forehead, and she giggled. "I wanted to be more like you," she replied. "So you might notice me."

"I *had* already noticed you," he argued. "The very first day I met you. Hard not to given how tall you were even when you were younger," he claimed. "Right there in my line of sight," he said as he held the flat of a hand to his forehead and pretended to look out toward the horizon. "Besides, I thought you knew that when you were twelve."

She rolled her eyes. "I meant... notice me in a *different* way. In a way that might suggest I could join you for a midnight ride in Richmond, and that you might even allow *me* to drive—"

"Not at midnight," he said in alarm. "*I* won't even do that any longer."

Vivian's eyes rounded. "Why ever not?"

"Because it's irresponsible," he answered without pausing. "I could be in a terrible accident and die. You'd be rid of me then, and the Weatherstone earldom would... well, it would go to my oldest cousin, I suppose," he admitted.

"Well, that never seemed to bother you before."

Sebastian paused in front of a stone bench near the statue of Cupid. He had watched many a young couple experience their first kiss on the bench. Many a young woman stare at the statue whilst saying prayers for a future marriage. Many a young man curse the chubby-cheeked marble for having shot an arrow in their direction, but not at their true love.

He indicated she should sit. "Have you ever talked to him?" he asked as he settled next to her and pointed toward the statue. He wrapped an arm around her shoulders and pulled her close.

Vivian rested her head on his shoulder. "Twice," she admitted.

Sebastian frowned. "To curse him or—"

"Cursed him. Both times," she admitted.

"Over me?" Sebastian asked with a combination of humor and dread.

"As a matter of fact, yes. He shot me, but he didn't shoot you," she complained. "At least, not in the right place or at the right time."

"Oh, he shot me. Got me good," Sebastian claimed as he pounded his chest with a fist.

"You're teasing again."

"Am not," he replied. "I'm in love with you, Vivian Wentworth, and I shall take you to wife and prove it to you."

She grimaced. "I thought you were going to prove it to me first."

"First and last and every day in between," he replied. "Maybe mornings and nights. We'll see if I still have the stamina to make love twice in one day, since I'm so old and it's been so long."

"What, a fortnight?" she teased.

Sebastian inhaled and let the breath out slowly. "More like two years," he whispered. Before Vivian could display her disbelief, he added, "I lived with monks, Viv. I learned to be pious and quiet and to appreciate the life I had here in England. I realized I missed you, and you are the only reason I left the monks to come home." This time, her look of disbelief appeared, so he had to add, "You and the earldom, I suppose. I will eventually have that responsibility."

Vivian winced. "So while I was aspiring to be bold and audacious, you were... you were already Mr. Prim and Proper?"

His eyes darted sideways. "Something like that," he admitted. He hugged her closer so her head fell into the small of his shoulder. "Mayhap we could meet in the middle?" he suggested. "That is, if you're not inclined to continue being too bold with others?"

"What's the middle for you?" she asked, suspicious.

He sighed. "An occasional night at the club. Say... twice a week and home by one?"

"No more Four-in-Hand Club?"

"No," he replied. "I'm not a member any longer."

"No more bedding widows?"

He shuddered in disgust. "Please, spare me," he begged.

Her brows arched. "Agreed. What about gambling? I wouldn't mind unless you lost our... our house or our first-born son."

"Only small wagers," he agreed. "And only on the nights I'm at the club." He paused before asking, "What's the middle for you?"

Vivian straightened on the stone bench. She hadn't had a chance to be truly bold, at least not in her actions. "I suppose the widowers shall have to do without me," she murmured.

"They had better," he agreed. "Or there will be pistols at dawn." At seeing her widened eyes, he added, "I've never shot a pistol, so—"

"I'll become one of those randy widows you so abhor."

"Swords. Swords at dawn," he said quickly. "I'm very good at impaling my victims."

Vivian squirmed on the bench. "I can only imagine."

"Oh, please do. You'll enjoy it immensely, but only with me."

Smirking, Vivian considered what she might do that would be bolder than anything she had ever done but not so bold as to make her the bane of Society. "I shall only partici-pate in card parties with other matrons once... maybe twice a week."

Sebastian nodded several times. "I'll be sure you have adequate pin money for those occasions."

Her eyes rounded. "Does that mean there's wagering?"

He chuckled. "Your mother hasn't told you about those card parties, has she?"

"Oh, I am so going to beat her at cards," Vivian vowed.

"What else?" he pressed.

She sobered. "I don't wish to ever have to see or hear Miss Pipkins again. *Ever*," she replied.

"Agreed."

"Then my answer is yes. I'll marry you."

Sebastian rolled his eyes. "I suppose we could have started with Miss Pipkins and been done a half-hour ago?" he queried.

Vivian nodded. "True, but it's good to have the other particulars sorted."

Sebastian leaned over and kissed her on the lips. When he pulled away, he said, "Indeed."

"So when do we do whatever is necessary to start your nursery?" she asked.

Sebastian was up and off the bench in a heartbeat, pulling her up with him. "I thought you'd never ask," he teased as he led her toward the house.

CHAPTER 37

A WHIRLWIND WEDDING IN
THE WORKS

eanwhile, back at Bostwick House
When George Bennett-Jones returned from Doctors' Commons by himself, Christina was waiting. "What have you done with Richard?" she asked.

George quirked a lip. "Richard?" he repeated in a teasing voice.

"He gave me permission to use his given name," Christina countered. "Now, what have you done with him?" she asked again, worry sounding in her voice.

"I haven't stabbed him with a fencing foil, if that's what you're concerned about," he teased, chuckling at her expense. "I'm to give you his regards and to tell you that he will see you here at six o'clock."

"He got the license?"

George nodded. "He did. In the knick of time. The bishop's office was about to close when we arrived, but it seems Hartwell wasn't the only one after a license this late in the day," he explained. "Seems Weatherstone's ball has provided an incentive to others like Hartwell. I dropped him at Hartwell House, by the way. Which it turns out he owns."

"He told me," Christina said, her relief apparent as she moved to give him a hug. "As well as a hunting lodge in Kent and the main house in Horncastle."

"Ah, he didn't mention the hunting lodge," George murmured.

"His father won it from Lord Reading in a card game."

Her father's face screwed up in a look of suspicion. "Or Reading lost it deliberately," he said quietly.

"I thought the same," Christina replied. After a pause, she said, "Mother saw you leave. I told her about the wedding."

George stiffened. "And?"

Christina inhaled to answer and then gave a shrug. "I think she took it as a challenge." She watched as her father's eyes darted to one side. "What is it?"

"She arranged a quick wedding for one of her best friends. Hannah—"

"The Countess of Gisborn," Christina finished for him. Her eyes widened as if she understood what was about to happen. "She really needn't go to all that trouble," she whispered.

"Do you want Lady Vivian to stand with you?"

Christina nodded. "Of course."

"Then you best send her a note. Something tells me she might be getting married any day now as well."

"How do you know that? Was Cougham at the archbishop's office, too?"

"He was at the jewelers' yesterday when I went to pick up your mother's gift for Tuesday night. I must admit, I hardly recognized him. He looked like a right proper gentleman," he murmured. "He was ordering a ruby ring."

Christina heaved a sigh of relief before her eyes rounded. "What if they're marrying Tuesday as well?"

George chuckled. "Well, there is this viscountess I know who can see to arranging a quick wedding." He glanced up to see that the woman in question was hurrying down the stairs. "Are you ready for our ride?" he asked, directing his query to Elizabeth.

"Oh, don't you play coy with me, you scoundrel," Elizabeth scolded gently. She gave Christina a wink before she placed her hand on his arm and practically led him to the front door. "Why, it will probably already be dark by the time we get there."

George glanced back at his daughter and winked before he escorted his wife to his phaeton.

Not sure which parent she should pity at the moment, Christina hurried up to her bedchamber and settled herself at a small escritoire. Pulling a sheet of parchment from the drawer, she considered what to write to Vivian. If she hurried, she could have a footman deliver it and receive a response back before Richard came for her at six.

She dipped a pen into the ink pot and wrote,

Dear Vivian,

After your Lord Cougham took you from my presence this afternoon, Lord Hartwell gained Mother's permission to walk me to the park. It seems he had also gained Father's permission to court me, after he confessed his affection for me. This courtship is to be a brief one, since he has already proposed marriage and secured a special license!

We are to be wed Tuesday before Lord Weatherstone's ball.

Will you stand with me?

Is there a chance you are to wed your beloved Bash soon? I ask only because Mother, who has experience with overseeing quick weddings, implied a double wedding could be arranged. I'm quite sure Lady Weatherstone would be thrilled to have her son wed before the ball, and by now, you two have sorted your differences and probably enjoyed a chaste kiss in the Weatherstone gardens.

Do respond as quickly as you're able. I look forward to learning what you have been doing on this most wonderful of spring days.

Your friend always,

CC

Christina reread her script, wincing when she realized she had made no mention of Lady Roth. Vivian's mother would no doubt wish to be involved in any wedding arrangements—Vivian was her only daughter. And what of Miss Pipkins?

Grimacing, Christina decided against mentioning the paid companion in her postscript.

P.S. Lady Roth and my mother might wish to speak on the matter.

Showering the sheet with sand, Christina curled the paper and watched as the sand flowed back into the bowl. She carefully folded the corners in, dripped wax onto the middle, and pressed her seal into the puddle. On the other side, she wrote "Lady Vivian" and hurried off to find a footman.

CHAPTER 38

AN ATTEMPT TO FINISH
WHAT WAS STARTED

Meanwhile, at Weatherstone Manor

Sebastian led Vivian into Weatherstone Manor by way of the kitchen door, gratified to see the cook and scullery maid had their backs to them as they made their way past the opening and then up the servants' stairs.

Although he tried hard to keep his footfalls quiet on the wooden stairs, Sebastian found it nearly impossible. Vivian's slippered feet barely made a sound, though, so when he emerged onto the second floor, breathless, Sebastian took a quick look in both directions. Upon seeing a chamber maid depart his parents' apartments, he ducked back into the stair-well and waited until the corridor was clear.

Vivian could barely contain her humor, although nervousness was quickly replacing it as she considered what they were about to do.

Finish what he had started all those years ago.

The mere thought had her insides tumbling about in anticipation. The apex of her thighs seemed to throb in a manner most unfamiliar. Her corset, already too tight given how Bales, her lady's maid, had tied it that morning, seemed to constrict even more. At the same time, her breasts seemed to have swelled, their nipples obviously remembering what had been done to them that fateful night before Sebastian had left for the Continent.

Sebastian tugged on her hand, a sign the corridor was clear. She followed him to a door at the opposite end, and the two slipped into an apartment before he closed and locked the door.

"If you're amenable, these rooms will be ours after we marry," Sebastian said as his wave indicated the sitting room before them and the bedchambers to the left and right. There were two facing settees and floral upholstered chairs in the middle of the room along with a small table for two and a fireplace. "We can have our breakfast here if we wish."

"The bedchambers aren't connected?" Vivian asked, her disappointment evident.

Sebastian allowed a devilish grin. "They are, in fact, by way of the dressing room and a bathing chamber. They're directly behind this sitting room," he explained as he pointed to the opposite wall. "Which bedchamber would you like to look at first?"

The oddest of sensations deep in her belly had Vivian momentarily breathless. "Whichever one you're going to make love to me in, of course," she replied.

Blinking, Sebastian glanced first left and then right before leading her into the bedchamber to the left. "I haven't been in either of these rooms in an age," he said, waiting until she was well into the room before he closed and locked the bedchamber door. He turned to find her staring in awe. He followed her gaze to the four poster bed and then to the other furnishings, relieved to find they weren't garish or pink.

"I adore this color of green," Vivian murmured. "It looks like the emeralds in my favorite necklace."

Sebastian winced, wondering if it was too late to have her betrothal ring's rubies swapped out for emeralds. Before he could respond, he watched as she made her way around the bed and through the room's other door.

He quickly followed her, as if he feared she might be

trying to escape. She had already made it through the empty dressing room, though, and into the other bedchamber.

"Oh, but I do love scarlet even more," she breathed as she spun around the master suite. "I don't suppose you would let me have this bedchamber as the mistress suite?"

Relieved he didn't have to pay another call on the jeweler—what other stone but a ruby would be close to scarlet in color?—Sebastian said, "As long as you let me in, you can have whichever bedchamber you want," he replied. "Take both if you'd like."

He glanced at the bed, hoping it was long enough for them. He imagined their feet hanging over the end, their toes tangling after an especially spirited round of lovemaking.

Vivian tittered and moved toward him, her fingers spearing his hair as she pressed her body against the front of his and kissed him on the lips. "I'm ready," she breathed, when she finally let go of him.

Sebastian blinked, and then his eyes darkened. "Are you?" he whispered.

Excitement skittered up Vivian's spine. "I suppose you're going to want me naked?"

A growl erupted from Sebastian's throat. He couldn't recall ever having bedded a completely naked woman before. Apparently his cock understood her query for it was hardening enough to tent his pantaloons. "Is that an option?" he asked, his voice an octave higher than usual.

"Will *you* be?"

His eyes darting to the side, Sebastian considered the query. "I suppose I will be if you remove all my clothes."

The look of delight that appeared on Vivian's face had him letting out a guffaw. "So much for Miss Prim and Proper," he accused in mock dismay.

Her fingers were already undoing his topcoat buttons. "We're meeting in the middle, remember?" she whispered.

"And staying there for the rest of our lives," he replied as he helped to remove the outer garment.

Vivian paused while unbuttoning his waistcoat. "What if...?" Her eyes stayed fixed on his middle a moment.

"What if what?" he asked, using his forefinger to lift her chin until he could see her eyes.

"What if we don't suit?"

Sebastian glanced toward the bed. "But... we already know we do," he replied. "Haven't we both known we were destined to be together? I remember the moment I spied you at your first ball, glancing around as if you were looking for someone. Your face appeared above the sea of heads when I did the same," he teased. "I knew you were the one for me."

"As I recall, you made a rather rude gesture," she countered, her face coloring into a bright pink. "Had Miss Pipkins paid witness, she would have blistered your ears with a rebuke and ushered me right out of your parents' ball."

Quickly sobering, Sebastian grunted. "I was rather immature," he admitted, remembering very well how he had teased her by using his fingers to pantomime sexual intercourse.

"You were eight-and-twenty," she argued.

"As I said, I was immature." He gave his very best look of contrition. "And it wasn't as if anyone else saw me. We were well above the fray."

"Still, I was so embarrassed," she said, "I had no desire to meet you."

"It's a good thing I saw to that," he whispered. "Do you remember the moment we first met? I knew then, Vivian. I knew you would one day be my countess."

Vivian gave a start at hearing his query. She had certainly hoped they might one day wed, but she hadn't known he felt the same. "What if we don't suit?" she asked again. "I mean, in *that* way," she added, her head nodding in the direction of the bed. "Intimately."

Scoffing, Sebastian kissed her on the forehead and pulled her into an embrace. "Are you worried that I have imagined bedding you so many times that I'll be disappointed now that I'm finally able to do it for real?"

She glanced up and nodded, a blush coloring her face at

hearing his claim. "Something like that," she whispered. "I've never done this before." She resumed her work on his waistcoat.

"Actually, you have," he replied. "As I recall, you had me half undressed in my mother's front salon." He grinned when he remembered his mother mentioning he could use the room if he required a place for an illicit meeting. He was fairly sure she didn't mean for him to use it moments before a bevy of aristocratic matrons descended on it for tea and a tour of her ballroom, though.

"You thought it funny?"

He shook his head. "I thought you rather daring. Fast. You took me completely by surprise."

"So... you hated it."

"Oh, I assure you, I did not. My only concern was that we would be discovered. That you would be forced to marry me," he said in a low voice. "Rather than *wanting* to marry me," he quickly amended, realizing how she might interpret his comment.

From the look of hurt on her face, he realized he had been too late with his last words. "I love you, Vivian."

"You do?" Her eyes widened in wonder.

He nodded. "I shouldn't have run away to Italy. I should have stayed. I should have ruined you thoroughly when I last had the chance."

"Bash!" she scolded.

"We'd have been married for four years by now. We could have had five children."

Vivian's eyes widened. "I would have had to have a couple of sets of twins," she argued, well aware he was walking her backwards toward the bed.

"Three then?"

She tittered as she unwrapped his cravat from around his neck. "Two with one on the way," she countered as she pulled the length of silk away and let go. It fluttered to the carpeted floor as she spread open his shirt.

"We have some making up to do," he said between labored breaths.

She glanced down at his pantaloons and the boots below. "I haven't done this part before," she said, her voice sounding breathless.

"I should hope not," he countered, his eyes wide.

"But you have."

"True, but it's been a long time." He almost mentioned just how long but thought better of it. She would know he had bedded someone on the Continent.

"How long?"

He sighed. "Two years, two months, three weeks, and five days." He shed the waistcoat.

"You've kept track?" she asked in disbelief.

"Well, I was thinking of *you* the entire time, and it left quite an impression," he replied, taking her shoulders with both hands to turn her so he could undo her buttons.

"Will you teach me what to do?" Her head turned so her chin rested on her shoulder.

Sebastian nodded. "Something tells me you'll just know what to do," he murmured.

"Oh? And why... why is that?" she asked, as he turned her back around and pulled the sleeves from her arms and pushed the gown down.

"Because you've no doubt sneaked into the library and found all the books with the color plates. The ones from France," he accused. Then he inhaled softly as his gaze traveled down the front of her body. "By the gods, you are gorgeous," he murmured, as he traced a fingertip along the top edge of her corset.

Vivian shivered at his touch, her slight inhalation of breath barely audible. "Promise me you won't be disappointed," she whispered.

"By what?"

Her confidence faltering, Vivian wrapped her arms in front of her breasts. "Me," she answered in a huff.

"I promise, I will not be disappointed."

"Bounder," she accused.

His forehead pressed against hers. "There's only one way to find out," he whispered, an eyebrow arching suggestively.

A frisson shot through her middle, and Vivian inhaled at the same moment his lips took hers. She was forced to uncross her arms as he pulled her body against his, but then her hands were where they needed to be to pull the hem of his shirt from his pantaloons. Even as he plundered her mouth, she was practically tearing the linen from his body and then undoing the fastenings of his pantaloons.

Sebastian pushed her gown down as far as it would go, frustrated by the layer of petticoats that impeded his progress. He managed to undo the ties that held them up and around her waist.

He broke the kiss a moment to murmur, "Hold on," and then lifted her into his arms. Yards of fabric cascaded to the floor.

"Well, that was efficient," she said in a startled whisper.

Sebastian wasn't about to mention he'd had practice with that particular maneuver, especially when he noted she wasn't wearing any drawers. "Did your drawers already come off with the petticoats?" He glanced down, as if he was surveying the collection of muslin and crepe de Naples fabric that had pooled at their feet.

Vivian's eyes widened. "I'll have you know I don't wear drawers," she said in a huff.

Blinking, Sebastian felt his manhood harden even more. "Never?"

"Of course not," she replied. "I think they're scandalous. Don't you?"

Sebastian blinked again. Every woman he had ever bedded had worn drawers. "Do you realize how hard it's going to be for me knowing you're not wearing drawers? I'll *be* hard. All the time."

"What do you mean?" Her eyes widened in fright.

"I'll be walking around with a stuffed pego. All the time."

It was Vivian's turn to blink. "What's a pego?"

Sebastian took one of her hands and placed it against the hard ridge outlined in the front of his pantaloons.

"Oh!" she breathed in shock. "Bash." Her eyes widened more as her hand gripped the ridge through the fabric. She ignored the groan that erupted from deep in his throat. "However are you supposed to get *that* into me?"

He was about to say, "Practice," but thought better of it. "I'll make you ready, I promise," he whispered as he started to push his pantaloons down. Then he remembered he still wore his boots and swore softly.

"What is it?" Vivian asked in a whisper. Despite wearing only a chemise, corset, and stockings, she had given up trying to hide from him.

He fell onto the edge of the bed and bent a leg so he could pull off the boot. "You have me so discombobulated, I'd forgotten what order clothes need to come off," he replied. He bent his other leg over the opposite knee and pulled off the second boot.

Vivian couldn't help the bubble of laughter that erupted from her lips just then. "Should I send for your valet?" she teased.

"Oh, I'll not give him the benefit of even the slightest peek of you undressed," he replied, tossing his boots far away from the bed. His gaze remained on her corseted torso, her stockings and the ribbons that held them up, the only other clothing left on her body.

Her arms moved to cross over her body again, but she caught the expression on his face and glanced down. "What is it? What's wrong with me?"

Sebastian shook his head. "Nothing. Viv, you're perfect," he said as he pushed the pantaloons down, leaving his smalls still in place. Even if he had wanted them to come off with the pantaloons, they wouldn't have been able to given how they were perched on his erect member.

He reached out and drew the back of a fingertip down the side of her thigh, which left her shivering. "You've the most beautiful limbs," he murmured. "I thought I had imagined exactly what they would look like, but I was wrong."

Vivian bent over and glanced down again. "I've never liked my knees," she murmured, as she bent one and turned it to the side. She pointed the foot beneath it so her toes were buried in the Aubusson carpeting.

She was doing her best not to stare at the obvious ridge that had now taken on a more dimensional shape behind the thin fabric of his smalls. Nearly gasping when she was sure it moved of its own volition, Vivian quickly averted her gaze.

"Oh, but why not?" he asked in disbelief, referring to her knees. "They have such a remarkable angle to them, and the limb below is so long." He grunted again, imagining what her legs would feel like wrapped around his back. With calves as long as hers, she would be able to lock her ankles together as he made love to her.

The thought had him groaning again.

"You don't think the space between them is too large?" she asked, placing her legs back together so her knees were side by side.

Sebastian nearly fell to the floor in his attempt to kneel before her. He reached out and pulled the ribbons at the top of her stocking. "You're not bow-legged if that's what you're worried about," he said as he rolled her stockings down her calves. "My, this is quite a pretty pattern," he added as he used his fingers to fold over the top hem of one lavender stocking. He used two fingers and his thumbs to roll the hem down her thigh and over her knee. "Harlequin, is it not?" His voice sounded a half-octave higher than usual, and he struggled to clear his throat.

Vivian inhaled softly at the feel of his hands against her bare skin. At the sensation of the stocking slowly rolling down her leg. "I think of them as diamonds," she whispered. "Like the ones on the playing cards." Her gaze settled on his bare back. She held her breath when she noticed how his muscles bunched around his shoulder blades, the pair moving in harmony on either side of a spine whose bones weren't apparent. Then she noticed how the muscles at the tops of his shoulders moved like liquid beneath his pale skin.

A shiver of excitement traveled down her spine and right to her core, turning her insides molten and her legs into jelly.

"I hadn't thought of them that way, but you're right," he murmured, referring to the diamonds woven into her knit stockings. "Hang onto me," he said as he placed his palm behind one foot and gently lifted it.

Vivian was forced to place her hands on his shoulders lest she fall onto him as he popped the stocking off her foot. Meanwhile, the top of his head pressed firmly against her belly as his lips connected with an upper thigh.

"I've been wanting to kiss you there all day," he whispered. He turned his head slightly and kissed the other thigh.

"What?" she managed to squeak. Any thoughts of playing cards had long since left her head and were now replaced with images of what his back muscles would be doing when he was atop her. How they might bunch and bulge as he moved. She was sure no other man in Park Lane could claim such a physique.

Her attention darted to his arms as he went to work on the second stocking, and she inhaled sharply. There were even more muscles evident in his upper arms. All round and curvy. Shifting up and down as his hands performed their magic on the insides of her thighs and on her knees and calves.

When he gripped her foot to lift it, she offered no resistance. The knit stocking sprang from her toes and rolled away.

"Are you intending to leave me branded by your fingernails?" he asked as he settled his head on the back of his neck to look up at her.

Dropping her head to regard him with a furrowed brow, Vivian had no idea what he meant until she noticed how she was gripping his bare shoulders with her fingers. She let go, revealing a series of half-moon impressions in his skin. "I'm so sorry," she said, moving her hands to either side of his head.

"Minx," he accused with a grin.

She continued to frown. "Are you saying that in a good way, or... or are you scolding me?"

"Which would you prefer?" he asked, his eyes darkening with desire.

Vivian inhaled sharply at the same moment one of his fingers delved into the space at the top of her thighs, the tip tracing the folds that hid her sex. "Do I have to choose?" she managed to get out as the fingertip separated her folds and teased whatever it was that had been throbbing since he had undressed her.

Without thinking, she shifted one of her feet farther from the other, giving his finger more room to wiggle. She knew what would soon happen. She remembered well the sharp sensations of pleasure that resulted from what his finger was doing. From what his thumb was about to do. The anticipation would kill her if he didn't press just a bit harder and move his finger a wee bit faster.

"Bash," she hissed. "Please don't make me wait..." She gasped and held her breath at the same moment Sebastian's gaze lifted.

He watched with satisfaction as her head fell back and her body quaked with the waves of pleasure his simple movements had set off. She mewled and moaned, struggled to breathe, and then seemed to lose her ability to stand of her own volition.

"Never, my sweet," he whispered as he quickly rose to his feet and moved to stand behind her.

Vivian's head ended up on his shoulder as he undid the ties of her corset and pushed it from her body. The chemise came off after the corset, the tie at the top of it long since undone. The translucent silk billowed to the floor as Sebastian lifted her into his arms and then placed her on the bed.

He knew she was ready for him. Lust had him wanting nothing more than to impale her. Claim her. Make her his. But Sebastian thought it best he provide her more pleasure before he saw to his own. Before he saw to his duty to create the next generation of Peeles.

"Where are you going?" she whispered as he covered her body but then moved down the front of it, his lips teasing her breasts and belly.

"Not far, darling," he whispered from somewhere south of her left hip.

Vivian squeaked when his hands slid beneath the globes of her bottom and lifted. Her knees, already feeling disconnected from the rest of her body, fell apart in a manner most improper.

A manner that reminded her of what he had almost done to her that night before he left for his Grand Tour, when one of his fingers had entered her most private place, sending delicious sensations cascading through her core. He had added a second finger to the first, which had her mewling first in invitation and then in panic. For something had happened or been said that brought her back from the brink. Something that had incited reason. Brought her back to the prim and proper miss she was supposed to be.

Perhaps Sebastian sensed it before she could put voice to a protest, for he had ceased his movements and slowly pulled his fingers from her. Drenched with her ambrosia, they rested on her mound a moment as Sebastian seemed to struggle to catch his breath—and his sanity. Another moment later, and her skirts were down, and he was sitting on the bed next to her.

There had been a knock at the door back then. A knock and a woman's voice calling out.

Just as there was at this very moment.

CHAPTER 39

LIKE-MINDED MOTHERS

Meanwhile, at Roth House

"This was just delivered for Lady Vivian," Thompkins, the Roth House butler, said as he held out a silver salver for the Countess of Roth. Christina's letter was in the middle of the tray.

Having just returned from paying witness to Sebastian Peele proposing to her daughter in Lady Weatherstone's salon, Grace regarded the folded parchment a moment before she set it down. "Word certainly spreads quickly in this town. It's no doubt a congratulatory note regarding Vivian's betrothal," she said with some delight.

"The footman who delivered it is awaiting a response, my lady," Thompkins said as he nodded in the direction of a liveried young man whom he had seated in one of the front hall's chairs.

"Response?" she repeated. She removed her gloves and popped the wax from the parchment. Unfolding the letter, she quickly read the missive and the postscript, an elegant brow arching as she considered the news.

Miss Pipkins appeared in the hall from the salon, her face pinching upon seeing the footman. "How did you find Lady Weatherstone's arrangements for her ball?" she asked. Although she had been in attendance at the garden party, she hadn't been included in the contingent of matrons that had been invited to tea at Weatherstone Manor.

"Quite satisfactory, of course. Lady Weatherstone could hold a ball in her sleep, she's done it so many times," Grace replied.

Miss Pipkins glanced into the vestibule. "Where is Vivian?"

Grace grinned in delight. "No doubt enjoying a chaste kiss in the gardens with Lord Cougham," she replied, using the words Christina had written in her letter.

"*What?*" The companion's violent response and wide eyes were almost frightful.

"My daughter's welfare shall no longer be any of your concern, Miss Pipkins. She is to be wed to Lord Cougham. On Monday or Tuesday, if his lordship saw to a special license, as it seems Lord Hartwell has done for his marriage to Miss Bennett-Jones."

Miss Pipkins' eyes rounded even more. "But... she wasn't even being courted by anyone," she argued. "How could you just let her agree to wed... *Cougham*, did you say? Why, he's a... a rake... a gambler... a—"

"Perfectly acceptable heir to an earldom," Grace interrupted, her eyebrow once again arching. "A reformed one, at that."

"Rakes aren't capable of reform," Miss Pipkins argued.

"Who has been in love with my daughter since her come-out," Grace went on, ignoring the companion.

"You're just going to... to *give* her to him?"

Grace lifted her chin and looked down her nose at Miss Pipkins. "Along with her *dowry*, if you must know. Now, I'll need to write a character for you followed by letters to Lady Bostwick and Lady Weatherstone. I've a double wedding to help arrange," she said with some delight.

Looking as if she was about to cry, Miss Pipkins said, "You seem happy about this."

Lady Roth gave her a brilliant smile. "Oh, I am, for if Vivian didn't gain an offer by this Friday, she was going to use her dowry and travel to the Continent," she explained. Her eyes suddenly widened. "She might still, but as Viscountess Cougham."

"I could have gone with her. As her traveling companion," Miss Pipkins whispered.

"Oh, I don't believe that would have been an option," Grace replied with a shake of her head. "Now, you'll want to see to packing your bags this evening. You can spend the night here, but of course I'll see to it you're situated in a suitable boarding house until you can arrange another position."

Miss Pipkins blinked. "Of course. Thank you, my lady." She dipped a curtsy and watched as Lady Roth moved to stand before the footman.

Upon her approach, he quickly stood. "Tell Lady Bostwick I shall meet with her Monday morning regarding the arrangements."

The footman furrowed a brow. "I was to take an answer back to Miss Bennett-Jones," he replied, confusion apparent on his face.

"Oh! Yes, well, you can tell her we're working on it."

His eyes darting to one side, the footman bowed and said, "Yes, my lady."

He took his leave of Roth House as the countess hurried up the stairs, shouting instructions to the butler and the housekeeper as she went.

CHAPTER 40

CAUGHT IN THE ACT

*I*n the apartment of the future Earl and Countess of *Weatherstone*

"Damnation!" Vivian cursed aloud, which had Sebastian's head popping up and his brows furrowing. She listened intently, expecting the woman's voice to sound out again.

"Deja vu, is more like it," he growled. He didn't move to get off the bed, but listened intently. "What did she say?"

"Didn't you lock the door?" Vivian asked in a hoarse whisper.

"That's not what she said."

Despite the seriousness of the situation, Vivian tittered at hearing his response. She couldn't help it. Given how her pulse pounded in her ears, she was surprised she could hear anything at all.

Meanwhile, there was pulsing of a different kind at the top of her thighs, one that she was sure was about to be rewarded with attentions of a more carnal nature. The sudden loss of fingers and a thumb left her feeling bereft. Unfulfilled. She was sure Sebastian was about to do something very improper with his tongue.

Blinking to clear his glazed eyes, and apparently his addled brain along with them, Sebastian nodded. "I locked the door to the suite and the door to the other bedchamber," he replied, his brows both furrowed in concentration.

"But not this one?" she asked, sounding as if she was on the verge of laughing out loud at his expense.

Not finding humor in the situation, Sebastian said, "I didn't get that far, remember? Besides, you were closer." Then he lowered his head between her thighs and flicked the tip of his tongue over her womanhood.

Vivian inhaled sharply as her chest rose from the bed. "Oh!" she let out, making no attempt to keep her voice down.

"On top of that, how did whoever she is get *into* the suite?" Sebastian asked as his head popped up from between her thighs.

Her brain now addled from what he had just done to her, Vivian had no answer for his query, but she did give him a brilliant smile. "Will you do that to me *after* we're married?"

Sebastian grinned. "Do you want me to?"

"Oh, yes," she whispered before she sighed, her arms stretched out on either side of her.

Torn between staying on the bed and seeing to whoever was at the door, Sebastian allowed his gaze to linger a moment. "You look like an angel. And not a very prim and proper angel," he murmured, his lips lowering to her belly once more.

She giggled. "I don't feel the least bit angelic," she said, covering her bare breasts with one arm.

About to say something about her devilish behavior, Sebastian couldn't when the knocking resumed from the other side of the door. The two turned to stare at it. "Who is it?" he called out, making sure to sound annoyed.

An indignant gasp could be heard through the door. "Is that you, Alonyius? Mrs. Landau will blister your ears if she learns you're tupping the kitchen maid again."

Vivian giggled. "Alonyius?" she whispered.

Sebastian rolled his eyes. "Footman. Rather tall and apparently still popular with the maids," he whispered back.

"Oooh," Vivian replied happily.

"You are *not* a maid," he said, seriousness returning to his voice. "I'd better never catch you and him in the same bed together."

Sobering, Vivian shook her head. "I would never," she assured him.

Rising from the bed, Sebastian moved to the door. About to open it, he heard Vivian's gasp and turned around. "What?"

"You're *naked*," she reminded him, her gaze taking in his entire body for the first time since he had undressed her. At least his manhood wasn't as prominent as it had been when he was still wearing his smalls.

"Oh." He reached down and grabbed his shirt from the floor, wrapping it around his midsection before he moved to open the door.

"Wait!" Vivian commanded.

When Sebastian turned his head to ask why, he found her scrambling to get beneath the counterpane and bed linens, her body bent over the edge of the bed so her bare bottom was aimed in his direction. He struggled to keep from growling and to keep his cock from reacting more than it already was.

"What is it?" Vivian asked when she had the covers pulled up to her neck.

"Will you do that for me after we're married?" he asked.

Her brows furrowed in confusion. "Do what?"

"Never mind." He opened the door with more force than he intended. "What?" he said in his most lordly voice.

The chambermaid who stood on the other side let out a squeak and backed up three full steps as her hands went to her chest. "Lord Cougham." She dipped a curtsy.

"Alonyius isn't here," he said as he leaned a forearm against the door jamb while holding his shirt with the other.

Her face red with embarrassment—the maid didn't seem to know where to look given the expanse of bare chest directly in front of her—she let out a groan. "Pardon, my lord, but Mrs. Landau said that Lady Weatherstone had asked that these rooms be serviced, seein' as how you're to occupy them," she explained. "I'm so sorry. I didn't know you had already moved in."

Sebastian allowed a shrug. "Apology accepted, miss. You can come back tomorrow after... noon?" he offered. Then he glanced down to see that she held a key in one hand. "I'll take that," he said as he plucked the key from her grasp. "I would have hated for you to have walked in on me, especially if you were expecting Alonyius."

Her eyes widened, but before she could put voice to a complaint, Sebastian said, "When the outer door is unlocked, it means we have left the apartment, and you can service the rooms."

"Yes, my lord." She blinked. "*We*, sir?"

"I will inform my wife of the arrangements."

Her eyes rounding even more, the maid said, "Apologies, sir. I didn't know there was a *Lady* Cougham. Mrs. Landau didn't say anything about it."

"The public announcement hasn't yet been made," Sebastian said, realizing word would spread through the staff at that evening's dinner if he didn't put a stop to it. "Civil service," he said in a lowered voice, remembering such marriages were now allowed. "Let's give her ladyship a few days to settle into the apartment before anything is said below stairs, shall we?"

The maid nodded. "Of course, sir. I shan't say a word." She curtsied again and hurried off, closing the apartment door behind her.

Sebastian followed, driving home the bolt to lock the door. When he returned to the bedchamber, he shut the door, locked it, and tossed the key atop a bureau. "Apologies for the interruption," he said. "Now, where were we?" he asked as he dropped his shirt to the floor.

His words faded away when he discovered the bed was empty.

CHAPTER 41

PUTTING THE HORSE BEFORE
THE CART

*M*eanwhile, *at Bostwick House*
Having changed into her best dinner gown for that night's engagement with Lord Hartwell and his mother, Christina returned to the front hall in anticipation of the footman's arrival. When he appeared in the vestibule only a moment later, she regarded him a moment before she asked, "What did she say?"

Breathless, the Bostwick House footman inhaled to respond before he said, "Lady Vivian wasn't in residence."

Her attention turning to the hall clock—it was nearly six —Christina's eyes widened. "But you have news?"

Knowing he had important information, the footman straightened to his full six-foot height and said, "Well, I'm to tell Lady Bostwick that Lady Roth will meet with her Monday morning regarding the arrangements, and I'm to tell *you* that... that they're working on it."

Christina blinked. "*They're* working on it?" she repeated.

Had her mother already met with Lady Roth?

"The 'it' being the wedding?" she asked in confusion.

"Yes, miss. Which had one of the servants most upset. She was arguing with the countess about the character of Lord Cougham, and now she's being sacked," he said with some excitement. "But with a character."

"Sacked?" Christina repeated. "As in, *fired* from her position?"

He nodded.

"Which servant?"

The footman seemed to think on it a moment. "Well, she wasn't wearing livery, so I expect she is a governess or a companion of some sort?" he guessed.

"Miss Pipkins?"

"Aye. I think that was her name," he affirmed.

Well, Vivian would certainly be glad to learn the former governess would no longer be around to criticize her every action. "She's worked in that household for years," Christina murmured.

He nodded. "Her ladyship is going to write a character for her, though, and see to a place for her to live after she moves out of Roth House. I thought that rather generous."

Christina inhaled softly. "I'm sure she'll land a new position then," she said before she dipped her head. "Was there anything else?"

The footman seemed to hesitate before he said, "Am I to understand best wishes are in order, miss?"

Blushing, Christina nodded. "Lord Hartwell has proposed marriage, and I have accepted. We're looking forward to a wedding next week."

"The gentleman that was here for dinner this Thursday past?"

"The very same," she replied.

"Well, then, best wishes, Miss Charlotte Christina."

"Thank you," she said, just as her parents came through the front door continuing whatever conversation they had been engaged in during their ride in the park.

The footman bowed and hurried off to his station while Christina moved to intercept her parents.

"Lady Roth will meet with you Monday morning regarding the arrangements," she blurted.

Elizabeth exchanged a quick glance with George, and the two chuckled. "That's a relief," her father said.

"We will be in good company," her mother added, "for we came upon the Weatherstones in the park a while ago. Agnes is over the moon happy about Cougham finally marrying. Apparently he secured a marriage license before today's garden party and told her he intended to wed before next Friday," she explained.

Christina's eyes widened. "Friday?" She knew the significance of that particular day. "Vivian's twenty-fifth birthday," she added. "If she didn't have an offer by then, she was going to leave on a trip to the Continent."

"With Miss Pipkins?" Elizabeth asked in surprise.

"Oh, no. Never," Christina replied as she shook her head. "To get *away* from Miss Pipkins. But now that Vivian is to marry Bash, Miss Pipkins has been sacked."

Elizabeth murmured, "I'm sure I'll learn more about *that* from Grace. She never felt like she could get rid of the woman whilst Vivian remained unmarried."

"So... did you see Vivian and Lord Cougham whilst on your drive?" Christina asked, thinking the two would be sharing their good news while on the drive in Rotten Row.

Her parents shared sideways glances. "We did not," Elizabeth replied.

"Oh," Christina murmured, disappointed. "Might I be allowed to pay a call on Roth House when I return from dinner later this evening?" she asked. "I know it will be late, but—"

"Of course, darling," her mother replied. "Speaking of which, you look especially lovely for your dinner this evening."

Christina glanced down at her teal silk dinner gown, the simple ruffle at the hem and tiny ruffle around the neckline the only decoration. "I worried it might be too plain," she said.

"It makes you look like a viscountess," her father remarked. "I half-expected you would already be gone."

As if on cue, the butler opened the front door. Christina watched as the silhouette of Richard appeared, backed by the oranges and reds leftover from that evening's sunset.

"I need to change for dinner," Elizabeth said to her husband. She gave his attire an assessing glance. "You, on the other hand, could show up in your banyan and still appear appropriately dressed."

George chuckled. "After the last of the children have been married off, I might consider doing just that," he said with a grin. "See you later this evening," he added before bussing Christina on the cheek.

Christina watched her parents as they headed up the stairs. Sighing as she imagined doing much the same with Richard Hartwell, she decided she could start right then.

From where he stood just beyond the vestibule, Richard seemed to be thinking the same thing.

"Good evening, Richard," she said as she dipped a curtsy.

Richard bowed before his gaze darted up the stairs, as if he feared one of her parents might see him as Christina stood on tiptoes and kissed him on the cheek. He returned the greeting by kissing her on the forehead. "You look especially lovely," he murmured.

She dimpled. "I think taking the air at the garden party helped," she replied.

He sobered. "Not the marriage proposal?"

Giving him a brilliant smile, Christina kissed him on the corner of his mouth. "That made all the difference."

"So you haven't changed your mind?"

"Of course not."

"I've been told that's a common characteristic among those of your sex," he murmured. "Changing your mind, I mean."

Christina shook her head. "Does the fact that I usually don't mean that I am stubborn?"

He frowned. "I think it means that you will not leave me guessing."

"Which you'll appreciate," she countered as she dimpled.

His grin widened. "Indeed." He glanced around the hall. "Are you ready to leave?"

"I am."

He offered his arm and then helped with her mantle before leading her out to the Hartwell coach.

"Is it true you've already secured a marriage license for us?" she asked, once they were settled in the squabs. Although she had hoped they would sit next to one another, he had taken the seat across from her, his back to the direction of travel.

From the faint odor of leather, she wondered if the town coach was new. It was certainly clean, and the large wheel she could see as she boarded seemed as if it had received a fresh coat of paint.

"Of a sort," he replied. "We have some freedoms regarding when we marry, but we may be limited to *where* that can happen."

"I understand," Christina replied. "We should be sure to invite your mother," she added, her mind awhirl with thoughts of who might wish to pay witness to their nuptials.

"I think she would like that very much," he replied. "It's very kind of you to think of it."

Nervous, Christina inhaled softly. "Should I know anything about her before we arrive?"

Richard suddenly seemed at a loss for words. "Truth be told, I hardly know her. She likes champagne, but she does not bathe in it."

Christina tittered. "I should hope not."

"She and my father—Hartwell—they were... *together* for an entire decade. I know he loved her because..." He paused and dipped his head. "I found their letters in his desk. Back at Hartwell House."

"Love letters?" Christina guessed with some excitement.

He nodded. "And yesterday, when I met with the solicitor, he gave me a small box to deliver to her at my father's request."

Christina inhaled softly. "A ring?" she guessed.

"Indeed. It seems he proposed marriage to my real mother every year for the past ten years," he explained.

Gasping, Christina blinked. "Your adoptive father wanted to marry your real mother?" she asked in disbelief. "So, that means he knew her identity?"

Richard sighed. "I have to believe that he did. It's too much of a coincidence otherwise."

"But Mrs. Higgins didn't know he was your adoptive father?"

He shook his head. "She did not." At Christina's quiet cry, he added, "Had she known, she said she would have married him."

"Oh, how sad for him," Christina murmured. "If only he had told her what he knew, they might have enjoyed ten years of marriage."

Richard leaned forward. "Which is one of the reasons why I proposed so quickly," he said. "I'm quite sure there are others who wish to court you—like that man who was speaking with you yesterday in the park—and I feared if I waited, you would be saying your vows with someone else." He dipped his head. "I do not wish to experience my father's fate. To love another but not *be* with them."

Christina stared at him in the dim light from the carriage lamp, wondering at his last words. He spoke of love, but how could he possibly know that he loved her? They had only known one another for two days!

She reached out a hand and gripped one of his, pulling on it as she slid to one side of the seat. "Come. Sit next to me," she encouraged. "It will make kissing you so much easier," she added when she sensed his hesitancy.

If he had been hesitating, her words certainly removed his doubt, for he quickly changed seats, settling next to her so their thighs barely touched. Reminded of how her parents sat together in their town coach, she angled her body much like her mother would and used a gloved hand to cup his jaw.

Christina half-expected she would have to be the one to touch her lips to his, so she was pleasantly surprised when he accepted the invitation and kissed her lips. He barely opened his mouth, so she merely followed his lead, hoping she was doing it right. He had pulled away slightly and then begun another, longer kiss, his lips opening wider in invitation, when the town coach slowed and finally halted.

Although Christina would have welcomed another, shorter kiss—a peck—Richard straightened and took a breath. "We're already here."

The coach door opened, and he stepped down, turning to help her. Christina glanced around in an attempt to gain her bearings.

Before them was a rather tall house, well lit from within and without—there were two gas lamps on either side of the short walk to the front door—with a number of buildings across the street. "Are we in Picadilly?"

"We are," he affirmed.

Before they reached the door, it opened to reveal a liveried footman. Beyond him stood a matron of indeterminate age dressed in an exquisite dinner gown of blue silk with a silver sarcenet overskirt. Her brown hair, shot with streaks of chestnut and golden gray, was swept up in a smooth chignon held in place with a diamond-encrusted comb. Diamonds hung from her earlobes, and several decorated one of her fingers. The only piece of jewelry that seemed out of place was a ruby ring.

Christina was struck by two thoughts at once.

This was the Queen of Hearts. The owner of The Queen of Hearts. She looked like a queen, her bearing suggesting she had just risen from her throne.

She was also Richard's mother, and from the expression on her face, she knew the woman was as nervous as she was. Nervous and excited.

"I'm so very glad you've come," Violet said as she stepped forward. The footman saw to their wraps and then disappeared.

"Good evening, Mrs. Higgins," Richard said.

Dipping a curtsy at the same time Richard bowed,

Christina sensed a calm settle over him. When he straightened, he not only kissed Violet's hand but followed it with a kiss to her cheek, which had the matron beaming in delight. "Mrs. Higgins, may I have the honor of presenting my betrothed, Miss Christina Bennett-Jones?"

"Oh, of course," Violet gushed as she opened her arms and pulled Christina into an embrace she wasn't expecting. "I cannot tell you how happy I was to learn Hartwell had not only met you, but wished to take you to wife," Violet murmured. She stepped back and regarded Christina with a watery grin.

"It's very good to meet you, ma'am...," Christina stammered. "You have a very lovely home."

"Oh, there will none of that," Violet replied with a chuckle as she turned to lead them further into the house. "Call me Mother, if you'd like. Or Violet."

Christina exchanged a quick glance with Richard, whose expression of bemusement put her at ease.

Even before they were seated in the peach and green parlor, Christina caught the faint whiff of grilled meat and some sauce she couldn't place. She was about to say something about it, but Richard beat her to it.

"Whatever your cook is making smells even more delicious than what's served at The Three Bells," he remarked.

Violet tittered as a footman served them champagne and placed plates of nuts next to where they were seated. "That's because Mr. Merriweather..." she turned to Christina, "He's my daughter's husband..." She once again faced Richard to add, "He hired Mrs. Baker, who used to be the cook here. I had to let her go when I acquired my French chef—Jean-Claude, you see—so I was relieved when she landed a position at such a fine establishment." She turned back to Christina. "I don't just say that because it's owned by Rachel's husband. The Three Bells really is an excellent public house."

"I look forward to eating there," Christina said. "And to meeting your daughter. Perhaps you and she and Mr. Merriweather can attend our wedding?"

Violet's eyes widened. Her gaze darted to Richard before her mouth dropped open. "That's very kind of you," she murmured.

Richard was quick to say, "I was able to acquire a special license. Miss Bennett-Jones and—"

"You can call me Christina, darling," Christina said as she dimpled.

Blinking, Richard seemed at a loss for words for a moment before he continued. "Christina and I hope to wed this week."

"So soon?" Violet replied in surprise. "You're just like your sister," she added with a brilliant smile. "Once Rachel made up her mind to accept Mark's offer—which took a good deal of convincing on his part, by the way—those two were insepar-able. That he's an earl's son had absolutely no bearing on it."

Richard inhaled softly. "So he's truly an earl's son?" he asked. He hadn't been sure what to believe when Mrs. Merri-weather was telling him about her situation.

"He's Middleton's second son," Violet explained. "Wessex —he's the heir—already has his heirs, so Mark knew he wouldn't be needed to carry on the title."

"So he went into business," Christina said with awe. "That seems so unusual, but I suppose it's no different from the business associated with having an earldom."

"What do you mean?" Richard asked.

"Well, an earldom cannot survive without funds," she replied. "I suppose most of the money comes from its land. From farming or... or from mining. But those are businesses of a sort, wouldn't you say?"

Richard and Violet both gave her looks of appreciation. "I hadn't thought of it like that, but you are right. The Hartwell viscountcy relies on the funds from farming. From sheep and horses. We have an interest in the canal, of course—"

"The canal?" Violet asked, her attention briefly flitting to a servant who was motioning to her.

"The Horncastle Canal," he clarified. "Connected our

little market town to the Wash and made it possible to transport goods in and out," he explained.

"Well, it seems dinner is served," Violet said as she moved to stand.

Richard was actually the first on his feet, offering a hand to their hostess.

Violet gave him an appreciative glance. "Your father certainly saw to it you were raised as a gentleman," she murmured, as she watched him do the same for Christina.

He offered his arms to them both, much as he had done for Vivian and Christina the night he had dined at Bostwick House. "I'm relieved to learn I'm doing this right," he replied. "For there is much he didn't see to teaching me."

Although Christina's expression suggested she didn't understand his meaning, Violet's expression indicated she knew exactly what he meant. "There are some things that are better learned without instruction," she said as they approached a small dining room. "Some things that are better learned by doing," she added with an arched brow.

All at once, Christina understood her meaning.

CHAPTER 42

AN IMPROPER PROPOSAL

Meanwhile, in the Cougham apartment in Weatherstone Manor

"Vivian?" Sebastian called out, hurrying through the dressing room to the other suite.

Still naked and holding her gown and underthings over one arm, Vivian stood at the end of the bed looking as if she might faint. "I have to go," she said.

"No. No you don't," he said as he moved to pull her into his arms. "What's wrong?"

Vivian didn't fight his hold, but rather seemed to melt into it. "*Lady Cougham?*" she whispered.

Sebastian grinned. "I rather love the sound of it, don't you?"

"You told her we were *married*," she accused.

"And we will be. I've already paid a call on an archbishop and a registrar of some sort," he stammered. "As soon as a certain jeweler finishes his part of it, we shall wed."

Vivian's eyes rounded. "A certain jeweler?" she repeated.

"Well, yes. The betrothal ring," he replied. "You have to have a suitable ring."

Her mouth dropped open in wonder, and Sebastian took the opportunity to kiss her. When he finally came up for air, he placed his forehead against hers. "I wanted the ring to make a proper proposal," he whispered. "Which is why... which is why I haven't exactly asked for your hand. I do have your mother's permission, though."

"My mother?"

He nodded. "Seeing as how your father probably wouldn't answer from the grave, I thought it best to ask her," he explained.

"When did you do that?"

"Today. At the garden party."

Vivian inhaled softly. "And if you had the ring?"

Sebastian stepped back and took hold of the yards of fabric that separated them. He tossed it all onto the end of the bed, leaving her once again naked. Then he lowered himself on one knee and angled his head back. Before he said anything, he leaned forward and kissed her belly and then took both her hands in his. When he heard her slight inhalation of breath, he grinned. "Lady Vivian Wentworth, would you do me the honor of becoming my wife? My viscountess and eventually my countess? I promise I shall always be faithful and a good father to our children."

Swallowing, Vivian stared down at him, her gaze going beyond his face to see that his manhood was clearly as anxious for her response as Sebastian was. "I will," she replied with a nod. She allowed a brilliant smile. "I will. Now will you make love to me?"

Grunting with the effort as he came to his feet, Sebastian embraced her before he thoroughly kissed her. "I thought I had been doing so, but yes," he whispered. He lifted her into his arms and took her back to the other bedchamber. Before she was even settled on the bed, he was over the top of her, murmuring incomprehensible words and kissing her face and neck and shoulders.

When she spread her legs in invitation, he entered her. His movements were slow while he worried one of her nipples with his lips. His manhood stretched her barrier until it finally gave way. He paused when he felt more than heard her hiss. Felt her chest rise and her breath hold.

"Why did you stop?" she whispered.

"I don't want to hurt you," he replied.

She moved her hands down the sides of his torso and to his hard bottom, cupping it and pulling until his manhood was nearly all the way into her.

He groaned. "You are an angel," Sebastian murmured as he pulled out a few inches and then pushed into her as far as he could go. "Oh, my stars," he whispered, glancing back to see that her legs were wrapped around his back. "Oh, my love," he whispered, dropping his head to her shoulder.

"What do I do?"

"I won't last long enough for you to *do* anything."

"Bash," she whispered in complaint.

"When I push into you, you push up," he said between labored breaths. He growled when she managed a counter thrust to his.

"Like that?"

"Exactly like that." He inhaled sharply when she did it again.

"It's not as hard as I thought."

He paused and stared down at her. "I assure you, it's harder than it's ever been in my entire life."

Vivian's eyes widened. "I didn't mean *that*," she replied. "I was referring to *this*." She lifted her hips again.

"You minx," he groaned. Another thrust met his, and his body stiffened as his orgasm gripped him. At the last moment, he moved a hand between their bodies, his thumb rubbing over her sex until he felt the ripples of her orgasm pulling him into her.

She inhaled as if to scream, her eyes widening at the same moment his movements ceased. She watched as he seemed to hold his body suspended over hers. His head lifted with his ecstasy, the cords of his neck showing in relief. Then, all at once, he collapsed atop her, his head ending up on the pillow next to hers while his chest pressed onto her torso.

At some point, Vivian remembered to breathe. Her arms wrapped around his back as she slowly lowered her feet to the bed. "Are you... are you dead?" she asked in a whisper that sounded calmer than she felt.

Vivian felt his chuckle rumble in his chest before he lifted his face from the pillow. "Not yet, but when I do die, that's how I wish to go," he said as a grin split his face. At seeing her look of alarm, he said, "When I'm eighty or ninety years of age."

She gave him a quelling glance. "I rather doubt I'll live that long, which means you'll be doing this with someone else," she accused.

He couldn't help but chuckle again. "You are the only one I will be doing this with for the rest of my life," he said on a sigh.

"It's quite... exhilarating," Vivian whispered.

He stared down at her and then kissed her nose. "So... do you suppose we can do it often?"

She seemed to think on it a moment before she nodded in the pillow. "First thing in the morning? Last thing at night?"

He blinked. "I...I was thinking once a day, but I'll see what I can manage."

"I thought you'd want to do it several times a day. I can certainly understand why."

He blinked again. "I'm five-and-thirty," he countered. "I'm not I'm capable of such frequent couplings."

Vivian sighed dramatically. "There's always Alonyius, I suppose," she teased.

She squealed in delight when his mouth covered one of her breasts, and she felt him harden inside her. Her eyes widened as his darkened, and she lifted her legs to wrap them around his back. "Do your worst, you devil," she whispered.

"I intend to do my *best*, my lady," he replied as he thrust into her and reveled in the pleasure.

Perhaps he wasn't as reformed as he had imagined.

CHAPTER 43
DINNER WITH THE QUEEN

*M*eanwhile, back at the private residence of Violet *Higgins, Piccadilly Street, Mayfair*

Christina knew the moment Richard realized his mother was a wealthy woman. She knew it because she felt his arm stiffen beneath her hold. Knew because she was seeing the same elegant dining room as he was.

The walls were upholstered in a deep gold silk, and a crystal chandelier hung above a Chippendale dining table with four matching chairs. A marquetry console flanked one wall—it appeared to be Italian, its top adorned with Wedgwood pottery and a collection of crystal glasses and a decanter. On the back wall stood an enormous carved buffet, the perfect furniture from which to serve a breakfast. Beneath it all was a dark, thick Aubusson carpet.

Dressed in a linen tablecloth shot with metallic threads, the table displayed place settings of china, crystal goblets, silver, and tiny fruits made of marzipan on silver salvers. The gaslight from the chandelier cast the room in a golden glow.

"What a beautiful room," Christina breathed.

"A more recent addition to the residence," Violet commented as Richard finally stepped over the threshold. He took Violet to one end of the table and Christina to the middle, holding their chairs before he took the carver opposite his mother. The placement of the chairs meant that none of them had their backs to the door. "Hartwell insisted, really, since he preferred we take our dinners in private." She pointed to the west wall. "Before I met your father, I simply ate with the employees in the The Queen of Hearts dining room," she explained.

"What was this room before?" Christina asked as footmen entered carrying carafes of wine and bowls of soup.

"My office. It's the closest room to the business, so it made sense to have it in here. I've since taken over a bedchamber on the first floor to use as my office. I really do prefer it since it has windows, and Rachel seems to like it. She spends a couple of hours every afternoon in there seeing to the books for the business."

The footmen finished pouring the wine and took their leave.

"Did you take in the Season's entertainments with him while Lord Hartwell was in town?" Christina asked.

Violet took an experimental sip of her wine. "Not often. Given the time of day I had to be on the gaming hall floor, it was rare that we were able to attend the theatre or a *musicale*," she explained. "I do enjoy a bit of anonymity when I am not dressed as The Queen, though, so I didn't have to be concerned with being recognized whilst we were out together. I certainly didn't want people thinking Hartwell was consorting with a courtesan. Most just thought I was a widow."

"Whatever do you mean?" Richard asked in surprise.

Violet grinned. "When I am The Queen, I wear a good deal of cosmetics, a huge white wig, and a red satin gown from the last century," she explained. "It's only a costume. The hostesses and faro dealers in the club wear the same sort of gown, although I don't insist they wear the white wigs."

Christina grinned at the description. "Have you ever been in The Queen of Hearts?" she asked Richard.

He nodded. "Just last night, but only to pay a call here. I had the sense I was only seeing a very small portion of the club and the dining room when I was brought here," he explained. "Something tells me I should come just for the dinners, though," he added.

"You probably found the decor rather gaudy. Red carpet, red papered walls, and lots of faux gilt," Violet claimed with a grin. "It's truly not to my taste, but it suits perfectly for such an establishment as that."

Between sips of his soup, Richard suddenly furrowed a brow and asked, "When Hartwell met you, were you in your costume?"

"I was," Violet replied. "As I recall, he would arrive at the club for games of hazard with some other gentlemen, but after they finished playing, he always found an excuse to come speak with me," she said in a wistful voice. "It was quite some time before he worked up the courage and asked me to attend a *musicale* with him."

"How romantic," Christina said on a sigh. "You did go with him?" she added.

Grinning, Violet said, "I think it was his third invitation that I finally accepted. We attended the theatre. Some naval reenactment. After that, we continued to see one another whilst he was in London for Parliament."

"And when he wasn't? Here in London?" Christina asked, her brows furrowed.

Violet seemed hesitant to reply, but said, "We exchanged correspondence, but if you're asking if he ever invited me to Horncastle, then no. Nor did I ever take a trip there of my own volition. I haven't been outside of London in an age," she added.

For a moment she seemed ready to resume eating, but then said, "I remember the second year Hartwell paid calls on me, he insisted I have my portrait done while I wore my costume. Said he wanted something for one of his walls back in Horncastle." She tittered. "He commissioned an artist, and I stood for a couple of hours for a few days, and then, once it was finished, I never saw it again." She angled her head and asked Richard, "Do you know if he ever hung it anywhere in Hartwell House?"

Richard's eyes widened. "That's *you*? In the painting?" When Violet gave him a blank look, he said, "There's a painting in the study. Above the fireplace mantel. A woman with white hair and a bright red gown. I... I always thought it was my mother... Arabella. Arabella Higgins. Hartwell's wife," he stammered. "She was the Earl of Greenley's daughter—quite a catch for Hartwell, I imagine, since he was a viscount. Given the style of the gown, I assumed it was painted a few years before she married my father... married Hartwell, I mean," he added.

Enjoying her soup and the conversation, Christina listened as she glanced back and forth between mother and son. Violet seemed to sober at the mention of Hartwell's wife, though, which had her asking, "Why would you think the woman in the costume was his wife?"

His brows furrowed, Richard seemed to struggle for a moment. "Because she looks just like the woman in the portrait of Hartwell and Arabella that was done in front of the Horncastle Canal, shortly after it opened in 1802," he explained.

When Christina turned her attention back to Violet, she was stunned to see there were tears streaming down the woman's face. Reaching into her pocket, she quickly pulled out her hanky and offered the square of linen to Violet. "My lady, whatever is wrong?" she asked.

Violet accepted the hanky and struggled to catch her breath. "Oh, now. I promised myself I would never cry over Hartwell," she said as she attempted to take a deep breath. "And certainly not over one of my sisters." She sniffled. "Now I understand why he never wanted to take me to Horncastle," she murmured, her gaze suggesting she was seeing something in her mind's eye. "Arabella never wanted anything to do with me, but then, I suppose I cannot blame her," she added.

"Sister?" Richard repeated in a whisper.

Christina exchanged a quick glance with Richard before

she turned her attention back on Violet. "Your father was Maxwell Higgins, The Earl of Greenley?"

"Indeed," Violet replied, her reaction indicating she was surprised Christina had come to such a conclusion. "I was born the same year he married—my mother had been his mistress—and Arabella was born the next."

Richard stared at Violet for a very long time. "You were my aunt," he murmured. "And my mother. Father never... he never *told* me about you," he added on a sigh of frustration. His eyes widened. "You have other siblings."

Violet nodded. "I do."

"Five of them," Christina remarked, remembering when she and Vivian had read about the Hartwell viscountcy in *Debrett's* just two night's prior.

"Well, four of them now, given Arabella died in the childbed," Violet acknowledged. "Max inherited the Greenley earldom when Father died in 1820. He spent several decades seeing to it in Staffordshire—he had to, given Father's penchant for gambling. He also saw to an advantageous marriage for my youngest sister, Beatrice. Barbara had already married the Earl of Bellingham—he's Devonfield's son, so she'll eventually be a marchioness," she said, brightening a bit. "And my youngest brother, Marcus, is off on some adventure in the Continent, probably digging in the dirt."

Richard shook his head. "I haven't even met half of them, and Greenley was my grandfather," he murmured in disgust. He was about to return his attention to his soup when he asked, "Did he acknowledge you?"

Having just taken a sip of wine, Violet nodded before she said, "He did. In fact, I have him to thank for all of this," she said as she waved a hand to indicate the house and the gaming establishment.

"How?" Richard asked in surprise. "I thought he was set to go into debtors' prison due to his gambling debts about the time he died."

"He was," she affirmed. "Greenley was an inveterate gambler. He lost a good deal of blunt—some of it on behalf of the Crown when he acted as a patsy for some Foreign Office scheme to hunt down missing money," she explained. "But he also won on occasion. Money, which he usually gambled away, and items of value. Jewelry. Artifacts. Deeds to properties."

Richard blinked. "Properties?" he repeated.

"Lots of properties," she replied with an arched brow. "Everything from plots of land and small cottages to hunting lodges and manor homes in the country. When he won them, he would give the deeds to his solicitor—who is also your solicitor, by the way—along with a codicil to his will."

Christina was about to ask about the codicil when the footmen reappeared, this time carrying plates with the fish course. Violet paused in her recitation to take a few bites of soup.

"I'm keeping this soup," Richard said when a footman attempted to take the bowl. "It's the best soup I've ever had," he added when he noted Christina's grin.

The footman nodded and moved on to take Christina's empty bowl. Soon, wine glasses were refilled and the servants left the room.

"And the codicil?" Richard prompted.

Violet seemed torn for a moment. "Greenley had always promised he would provide a dowry for me and allow me the use of his family name—Higgins. But I think he gambled away all those funds. Barbara didn't even have a dowry. Upon his death, all those deeds and valuables were mine to do with as I pleased," she explained.

Christina inhaled softly. "That's how you built The Queen of Hearts," she breathed.

"Indeed. I gave the hunting lodge in Staffordshire to Max, the ancient artifacts to Marcus, and the jewelry to my sisters. Then I sold off all the properties except for this house and the land on which The Queen of Hearts is located and used the funds to build it."

"I thought it was just all one property," Richard commented.

"It did not start out that way. But when it became

apparent I needed to offer a dinner service for The Queen of Hearts, I had the dining room added onto the back of the gaming establishment and the side of this house. I have direct access into that dining room at the end of that corridor out there," she explained as she waved toward the west wall.

"The one I came through last night," Richard said, realizing now how the two buildings were connected.

"I understand this is a very lucrative business for you," Christina said after she had finished her fish. "But... do you have regrets at having given up so much?"

Violet consider the query for a moment before she said, "I did at one time. Before the business. Especially when it came to Richard," she said as she indicated her son. "When Reading took him from me, I felt as if a part of me had been torn away. I believed for a very long time that I would never see him again. Or if I did, I wouldn't recognize him as mine." She paused a moment. "He did right by you, though," she said as she gazed at her son. "Raised you right. Saw to your eduction. Gave you an avocation. But I do wish there had been a mother in your life."

Richard nodded, his attention going to Christina. "That's why I want Christina to be my wife," he said. "I cannot imagine there is anyone else who would learn all of this—know the truth about me—and still remain by my side."

Dipping her head, Christina gave him a wan smile. "I am honored," she replied. "Although I will admit it will be difficult to keep all the secrets that must be kept."

"Indeed," Violet agreed. She leaned back in her chair. "Know this, young lady. Rachel and Richard are my only beneficiaries. At some point in the future, they're going to inherit this house and The Queen of Hearts, which means there will be issues to see to beyond the viscountcy."

Christina's eyes widened. "I do hope I'm allowed to help run it if that ever happens," she said with a brilliant smile.

"If you're thinking you're going to wear one of those red gowns and a white wig to do it, think again, my sweet," Richard said.

Giggling, Christina said, "It sounds as if you wouldn't even recognize me," she teased.

The footman returned with the next course, and for the rest of the evening, they spoke of Parliament and the Season's entertainments, of the wedding and the arrangements for thereafter.

Remembering he had promised to have Christina home by ten o'clock, he gave his mother a kiss on the cheek and they said their farewells.

For once in his life, Richard wished an evening wouldn't end.

CHAPTER 44

INTERRUPTING A BATH

A half-hour later, at Roth House

Cloaked in a dark mantle, Christina approached the front door of Roth House feeling as if she looked like a thief in the night. Expecting to wait for a time before the butler would appear, she was surprised when the door opened almost immediately.

The butler blinked before he waved her in.

"I know it's late, but I really need to speak with Lady Vivian," she pleaded. "It's about the wedding."

Thompkins stepped aside to allow her to enter. "Lady Vivian's whereabouts are apparently unknown, Miss Bennett-Jones."

"Unknown?" Christina repeated in disbelief.

"I believe Lady Roth was hoping she was with you." At seeing her look of shock, he added, "It's possible she is in residence, and I simply missed her arrival."

Remembering in whose company Vivian had left the garden party, Christina had half a mind to head to Weatherstone Manor. But after a quick glance at a nearby clock, she said, "I wish to see for myself."

Without waiting for a response, she hurried past the butler and up the stairs, her mantle billowing behind her as she made her way down the corridor to Vivian's bedchamber.

Not bothering to knock, she let herself in. "Vivian?" she said in a hushed voice.

"Who's there?"

Realizing the voice came from the bathing chamber, Christina moved through the darkened bedroom and into the candlelit room to the left. "There you are," she said as she regarded her best friend, seated in a bath tub and displaying more color in her cheeks than Christina had ever seen.

Nearly hidden in a mound of bubbles, Vivian had folded her body so her knees were beneath her chin. "I suppose they've noticed I wasn't at dinner," she said in a quiet voice.

"They think you're missing," Christina countered.

Scoffing, Vivian said, "I told my lady's maid to say that I wasn't feeling well."

Christina frowned. "Are you sick?"

"Hardly," Vivian replied, a prim smile appearing.

It was Christina's turn to scoff. "Where have you *been?*"

Vivian inhaled softly. "With Bash. In our apartments in Weatherstone Manor. *Alone*. And I don't regret it, Tina. I wish I could have spent the entire night with him," she said, her words growing louder. "You should see the mistress suite. Why, I can hardly wait to spend every night there."

Christina gave a start, but bit back the first thing she thought to ask. Instead, she said, "Well, good, because we're getting married Tuesday. Seven o'clock. Your future father-in-law will be announcing it during the ball, and—"

"Tuesday?" Vivian repeated. "But, my mother doesn't even know he—"

"Oh, she knows. She and my mother will be making the arrangements on Monday. I came to be sure... well..." Christina paused before she finally said, "Well, to be sure you wished to marry and to do so with me."

Vivian blinked. "I suppose that depends on who *you're* going to marry," she replied in surprise.

"Well, Lord Hartwell, of course. He proposed this afternoon. After the garden party. And for some reason I cannot quite sort, he's insisting on a quick wedding."

Vivian's eyes rounded. "You're ruined, too?"

Christina's eyes widened as much as her mouth. "Vivian!" she scolded. "Of course not."

"I don't regret it, Tina. Not one moment of it," Vivian claimed. "Well, maybe that it took so long for Bash to finally admit that he has alway intended to wed me," she murmured. "But he's well on his way to making it up to me. I'd tell you all the details, but I fear I'd get some of it wrong, and you'd think the absolute worst of me."

"Oh, Viv," Christina murmured, deciding she wasn't going to hear anything to help alleviate her fears of what would happen Tuesday night after the ball. She allowed a wan grin. "Apparently, our men have the right sorts of licenses. Given we're marrying after noontime, our service will be a civil one, I think. Not in a church. I hope that's all right with you?"

Vivian smiled. "Tuesday night?"

"Before the ball," Christina affirmed.

Giggling, Vivian disappeared beneath the bubbles for a moment before she emerged, her hair soaking wet and a cascade of suds running down her face. "I wonder if Bash knows?" she whispered in wonder.

Christina cleared her throat. "Well, if he doesn't, his mother certainly does, which means he will."

Vivian's titters turned to outright laughter. "This is turning out to be the best day ever," she said happily.

"Because Miss Pipkins has been let go?"

Giving a start, Vivian straightened in the tub. "What?"

"The footman I sent with your letter said he paid witness to your companion being sacked," Christina explained. "You did get my letter?"

Vivian's brows furrowed. "I didn't," she replied. "Which means..." She paused and rolled her eyes. *"Mother did,"* she said. "Oh, I do hope you didn't write anything untoward."

Christina angled her head. "No, but it certainly explains why it is our mothers are now planning our weddings," she replied. She regarded Vivian with a grin and then chuckled. "I really must be getting back to the coach. Father is waiting for me."

"Your Father is with you?" Vivian asked in alarm.

"Well, it wasn't as if I could leave the house unescorted at half-past ten at night," Christina countered. "I'm not married yet."

Vivian grinned. "But we will be." She once again disappeared beneath the bubbles as Christina left her bathing chamber.

*C*hristina rejoined her father in the Bostwick town coach, giving him a brief and very edited version of what she had discussed with her friend. A few minutes later, and they were back at Bostwick House.

At least, she thought it was Bostwick House.

When her father offered his arm, she stepped down from the coach and gave a start. "Where are we?"

George regarded the white stucco townhouse before them and gave an appreciative grunt. Two gas lamps illuminated the path to the front door as well as the bright blue door and the blue shutters that surrounded the windows on either side and up the front of the house. Matching flower boxes hung from the lower windows while wrought iron decorated a balcony up above. "This will be your new home starting Tuesday night," he finally said.

Christina inhaled softly. "It's beautiful," she murmured.

"And it's close," George said.

"But... why are we here tonight?"

"Because I am a sucker for young love, apparently," he replied as he lifted a hand to his chest.

"What?" she asked, just as the front door opened.

"Hartwell wanted you to see it. Thought if there was anything you didn't like, he could have the staff see to changing it before you moved in."

Christina was glad her blush couldn't be seen in the gas

light as she watched her father being greeted by a portly butler.

"He's expecting you, my lord, my lady," the servant said as he stepped aside to allow them in. He saw to Christina's mantle and George's greatcoat and hat, his manner suggesting he had been employed in his position for a long time.

About to mention she wasn't a lady, Christina realized that in only a few days, she would be.

She would be Lady Hartwell.

"Ah, I feared you might have changed your mind," Richard said from beyond the vestibule. He hurried up to them, bussing her on the back of her hand and then shaking hands with her father.

"We had another stop to make at Roth House. I do hope you don't mind that you'll be involved in some sort of double ceremony?" George asked.

Richard chuckled, his gaze on Christina. "I've already heard from Cougham with news of our shared fate," he replied with a smirk. "I wasn't sure what to think of him when I met him this afternoon, but he seems to be a level-headed sort."

"He is now that he's experienced a near-death incident," George agreed. "A few years ago, and I would have warned you away from him."

Richard grinned as he took Christina's hand. "I wished for you to see the house. If there's anything you want to have changed before you move in—"

"I'm sure it will be fine," Christina said, her gaze sweeping the front hall. Although there was a round table in the middle, it was void of decoration. A few caryatids lined the walls and featured marble busts that appeared to be of Roman and Greek origin.

"Surely there is something you'd like changed in here," Richard insisted.

Christina grinned. "I'll add a vase of flowers on the table."

"I'll have Peters order them in the morning. What are your favorites?"

Giggling, Christina shrugged. "What are yours?"

Richard blinked. "I don't know that I have one," he replied. "Roses," he said suddenly. "Red roses."

She gave him an appreciative glance.

He escorted her down the corridor, pausing so that she could peek into every room.

"I'm not sure what this is supposed to be. As you can see, Father didn't use it," he said as he motioned into a small room near the front of the house. Only a few pieces of furniture were positioned on an Axminster carpet, and despite the dark, the drapes made it apparent there were three windows.

"It will make a perfect salon. I can do my correspondence in here," Christina remarked.

"I'll order a desk for you."

She grinned. "Careful, darling. You'll spoil me," she warned.

Richard inhaled softly, his gaze darting back to where George was admiring one of the marble busts in the hall. "I like how you said that," he whispered.

"Darling?" she repeated, just as he bussed her on the cheek. "Richard!" she scolded in a whisper.

"I cannot help myself. You've gone and bewitched me, and I find I'm not at all nervous about Parliament because I have something infinitely more important to think about."

"And here I was all worried about which gown to wear to the Weatherstone ball," she countered with a giggle. "Now my wedding gown will be my ballgown."

"You'll look gorgeous in it no matter what you wear."

Christina's eyes widened upon hearing the compliment. "I like you bewitched," she teased. "I'll have to sort how to keep you that way."

He dipped his head. "Am I acting foolish?"

She shook her head. "No. I rather like that you're excited. That you're looking forward to this. Most men wouldn't, I expect."

Richard regarded her a moment as his brows furrowed. "A week ago, I might have been one of them. Marriage seemed more a necessity than a choice, but now... well, I like my decision to wed. I like my choice. My mother likes my choice. My stepmother really likes my choice, and my real father, well, I really couldn't care what he thinks."

Giggling, Christina reached up on tiptoe and kissed him on the corner of his mouth. "Thank you for taking me to dinner tonight. Your mother is to be commended for all she has accomplished, even if most ladies of the *ton* would not agree."

"Thank you for going with me. Although it was enlightening, and not necessarily in a good way, it certainly explains much."

"Well, all except for why the viscount would keep you from your real mother. And why he chose her—the sister of his first wife—as his lover."

Richard considered the comment. "Unless I find some correspondence from him hidden in a drawer somewhere, we'll never know," he replied. He glanced around the hall, noticing that Christina's father was no longer there. Deciding he must have gone into the study, Richard said, "Let me show you the breakfast parlor."

Although the small dining space was in need of brighter colored walls, Christina merely nodded and moved onto the dining room. "Well, after seeing your mother's dining room, nothing will hold a candle to it," she remarked.

"But we can have this redone," he replied. "Add a few pieces," he went on. "Do the walls in scarlet."

She grinned, and when they stepped back into the hall, Peters was there holding a valise. "Why do you have my valise?" she asked in confusion.

The butler seemed just as confused. "Lord Bostwick gave it to me. Said you would need it this evening."

"What?" Christina directed her gaze to the vestibule and found it empty. "Where's he gone?"

"Home, my lady. He said he would return for the two of you at ten o'clock in the morning, to take you to church."

Christina exchanged a quick glance with Richard, well aware her face displayed a bright pink blush.

"Where shall I take this, my lord?" Peters asked.

"Uh, the mistress suite?" he guessed.

"Yes, sir," the butler said before he headed up the stairs.

"Did you know about this?" Christina asked as she watched the servant depart.

"I did not. Although, I hope you are not... disappointed."

Christina inhaled softly. "I am not," she replied as a slow smile appeared. "Of course, I don't expect to *sleep* in the mistress suite," she said.

Richard furrowed a brow. "Well, then where?"

"The master suite, of course," she replied, giving him a look of disbelief. "With you."

It was Richard's turn to blush. He seemed about to say something before he changed his mind. He rubbed a hand over the side of his face before he finally said. "There's something you need to know," he whispered.

"*Another* secret?" she asked in a teasing voice. When she noted his expression, she quickly sobered.

He shook his head. "Not that so much. It's just... I don't really have any experience with women."

Having wondered if he had ever taken a mistress or courted in the past, Christina now realized his words in the park were true. He really hadn't been with a woman—in that way. "Well, I don't have any experience with men," she replied. "Other than the few kisses we've stolen with one another. I have seen some color plates in some books. And there was that time I paid witness to my parents making love—"

"*What?*"

"I was peeking into their bedchamber," she whispered back. "I was curious."

"Oh, well, that's a relief," he murmured.

Christina sighed and stepped closer to him. "It will be all right, Richard. We'll simply learn how to do it. Together."

He nodded. "Well, we've seen all the rooms on the ground

floor," he said. He offered his arm and they climbed to the first floor, passing Peters as he was making his way down.

"Will you require assistance undressing this evening, sir?" the butler asked.

"You won't require assistance," Christina whispered, one of her brows arching suggestively.

"I won't be requiring your assistance this evening," Richard stated. "You're dismissed for the night, but could you let the cook know there will be two of us for breakfast in the morning?"

"Of course, sir. Goodnight sir, my lady," Peters said as he gave a slight bow and continued down the stairs.

Outside the door closest to the stairs, Richard said, "This is the library, and the next one is the parlor."

Nervous and excited, Christina said, "Could I maybe look at them in the morning? When the light is better? I'd really like to see the mistress suite if I could."

"Ah, yes," Richard said as he offered his arm. They climbed the next flight of stairs and he glanced down the corridor first in one direction and then the other.

"You *do* know where the mistress suite is, do you not?" she asked.

He inhaled to respond but let out the breath in a huff. "Mayhap next to the master suite?" he guessed.

"Well, I should hope so. They should even have a connecting door," she claimed.

Richard seemed to think on it a moment before he peeked into a bedchamber whose door was slightly open. "Ah, here it is," he announced as he opened the door. Christina's valise was sitting atop the bed. "I suppose you'll want to pull out some bed clothes," he suggested.

Christina furrowed a brow. "Do you wear a nightshirt to bed?" she asked as she opened the valise and began extracting the clothes.

He blinked. "Uh, in the winter," he managed to get out, watching as she pulled out a bright primrose gown followed by two petticoats.

"But not in the spring?" she prompted as she shook out the items and draped them over the edge of the bed. She continued pulling out garments—a corset, a chemise, a pair of stockings, and a pair of slippers.

He made an odd sound in the back of his throat. "I suppose it depends on how cold it might be."

Christina made an odd sound. "Well, it seems I won't be wearing a night rail, because there isn't one," she announced brightly as she peered into the now-empty valise.

She could just imagine her lady's maid packing the bag with instructions from her mother. "This is Mother's doing, I'm quite sure."

"If... if you'd like, I'm... I'm sure I have an extra nightshirt you could borrow," he stammered.

Christina seemed to think on the offer a moment before she said, "I think it may be too warm for that, but thank you for offering."

Well aware of Richard's widened eyes, she glanced around the room, her own eyes widening with appreciation. "Why this is a gorgeous bedchamber," she said. "I've never had a japanned screen before," she added as she passed him, her gaze taking in the rose colored satins and velvets that dressed the bed and the two windows. "This is really quite elegant," she added as she moved to a corner door. "I found it," she announced. She disappeared through the door.

When Richard didn't move to follow her, she reappeared and said, "Are you coming?"

Richard cleared his throat. "Not yet, but it sounds as if I will be," he murmured. He hurried after her, surprised when they passed through his dressing room and into his bedchamber.

"Would you like help with your buttons?" she asked as she surveyed the royal blue fabrics and dark woods that dominated the room. "This is a very masculine bedchamber," she commented as she stepped in front of him and undid the buttons of his top coat. "It suits you." She pushed the garment off his shoulders and then draped it over the back of a chair.

"It does?" he asked as she turned around so her back faced him.

"Oh, indeed. Can you undo my buttons, please?"

Richard regarded the row of tiny buttons and hesitated before he began undoing them. He didn't mean to take his time, but the jets were tiny, and he struggled with pushing them through the holes. When a finger touched her bare skin, he felt her shiver and quickly pulled the finger away.

"It just tickled is all," she said, turning her head so her chin rested on her shoulder. "Are you ticklish?" she asked, a gleam in her eye.

Richard finally cracked a smile. "Truth be told, I don't know if I am." He paused and then said. "I think I got them all."

"Oh, good. Could you just pull on those bowties for my petticoats. Just... give them a good jerk and they should come loose."

His hands hovered over the loops of muslin for a moment before he found the ends. He gripped them between a thumb and forefinger and watched as the tie pulled apart with his tug. Beneath it was another, and he did the same to that one. "How many are there?" he asked as the white fabric seemed to disappear from view.

"Just two," Christina replied as she turned around. She pulled the gown's sleeves off her arms and let the garment fall to the floor as she started on his waistcoat buttons. She was aware of how he stared at her nearly bare shoulders, his breaths catching in his throat.

Her chemise, made from silk, was nearly translucent, and he reached out to touch it. "I can see through this," he murmured.

"The silk is very thin," Christina murmured as she pushed his waistcoat from his shoulders and draped it over the chair. She stepped out of the puddle of fabric at her feet and then bent to gather it into her arms. Spying an upholstered chair in the corner, she hurried to it and dropped her gown and petticoats onto it before turning around to resume undressing him.

Richard was staring at her, his gaze traveling down and then back up again, as if he had never before seen a woman in a corset and stockings. "Your limbs are... very shapely," he whispered.

Christina glanced down as she bent one leg and pointed her toe into the carpet. "You think so? I always wished they were a bit longer so that I might be taller," she replied as she moved to undo the knot of his cravat. "Do you like them?"

He blinked. "Of course. I don't think I'd want you any taller." He kicked off his shoes, which left him standing two inches shorter than he had been.

"Oh, good," she replied, standing on tiptoe to unwind the white silk from around his neck. He helped by bending forward slightly, which brought their heads close enough that the silk brushed over his face twice as it passed between them.

When she pulled the end free of his neck, she afforded him an impish grin before she kissed him. When his hands moved to her waist, as if he needed something to hold onto, she fell against him, one hand moving to his shoulder and the other wrapping around his neck.

The hunger in his kiss was unlike anything she had experienced with him before, as if she had awakened a part of him that had never before been allowed out. He kissed as if he possessed her—all of her—and she did her best to respond in kind, determined he know that she was his. That he know she would not be sharing him with anyone else.

At some point their tongues tangled, but neither pulled away in surprise or shock. It was simply the next means by which they could explore one another.

When Christina finally pulled away, breathless and aroused, she swallowed as she stared at him. "That was rather invigorating," she whispered.

He chuckled, his lips brushing over her cheeks and down her neck. "You've no idea," he murmured.

Christina was fairly sure she understood at least part of the idea. She felt the hard ridge of his arousal press into her belly, which had her hands gripping the sides of his shirt in an effort to free it from his pantaloons.

"Can you reach my corset ties?" she whispered, her frantic attempts at pulling free the fabric finally rewarded. She pushed the shirt up his torso, baring his chest, and he pulled it from his arms.

She couldn't help her inhalation of breath when the expanse of his chest was before her, so close she could touch her nose to it. Swirls of dark hair formed a broad triangle, the bottom point of which disappeared behind his pantaloons. The scent of him, a combination of musk and sandalwood, overwhelmed her senses.

No sooner had her lips begun their exploration of his chest when she felt the corset loosen. She helped with pushing it down, wiggling her hips back and forth as she did so.

"Have a care, or I shall attempt to take you standing up," he warned as his teeth captured one of her earlobes.

She inhaled softly, thinking he didn't sound like the man she had known for only two days. "Is that even possible?" she asked as she worked to undo the fly of his pantaloons.

One of his hands gripped hers, pressing it against the evidence of his arousal as he took in a breath. "I would say you're about to find out, but I'll do what I must to control myself."

"Perhaps if we were on the bed, you wouldn't have to," she suggested, surprised she could sound so reasonable when her insides were doing a series of flips, and darts of pleasure were bouncing about beneath her skin.

Her words seem to bring him out of some sort of trance. "There's an idea," he said, rather glad to see the bed linens had been turned down, at least on one side. He gripped the rest in a fist, and with a twist of his wrist, he had them billowing to the end of the bed.

"Should I remove this?" he asked as he fingered the chemise, his gaze going to the dark nipples that were silhouetted in the thin silk. "I would understand if you wish to leave it on."

He moved a thumb to brush over one of the engorged nipples, and his brows furrowed, as if he had never before seen one. When Christina inhaled, he quickly pulled his thumb away. All at once, the chemise was up and over her head and floating to the floor.

"It was in the way," she said as she stood nearly naked before him. With only a flick of a couple of fingers, the ties of her stockings were loose, and the silk tubes were sliding down her legs.

"Ah," he said, his arms hanging at his sides.

Christina took the opportunity to finish what she had started with his pantaloons, determined they come off before they got onto the bed.

"Perhaps it's best if you not..." Richard took a deep breath. "Look."

Christina stared at him. "Is it especially large?" she asked in alarm.

His eyes rounded. "Uh, no. I don't think so."

Gripping the sides of his pantaloons, Christina jerked them down, realizing too late that his arousal was caught in the fabric. When it was finally free, his member popped out, bobbing against the side of her face as she continued to push the garment to the floor.

One of his hands moved to cover it, but from her position —on bended knee with one of his hands resting on her shoulder for balance—Christina looked up at him and grinned. "You needn't be modest, darling," she said.

He stepped out of the pantaloons, his hand still on her shoulder. "I cannot cont... I did not do that... deliberately," he managed to get out, his eyes squeezed shut and his breaths labored.

"So it has a mind of its own?" she teased as she stood, her hand covering his and lifting it slightly as she pressed on it.

Hissing, Richard lowered his head to rest on hers. "Something like that," he replied.

Christina stepped out of her stockings and nudged them aside with a toe. "Do you feel tingly all over? she asked in a whisper.

"I'm not sure that's how I would describe it," he whispered.

"I do. I think I'm ready. I feel ready. Will you help me onto the bed? It's terribly tall." She let out a squeak when she was suddenly in midair and then in the middle of the bed.

Richard was atop her only a moment later, his manhood pressed against a thigh as his lips took hold of a breast and nibbled.

Giggling, Christina moved a hand behind his head and slowly sobered as his mouth made its way down her body, kissing her breasts and belly as he went.

"Where are you going?" she asked as she was forced to spread her legs and bend her knees.

"I wish to see all of you. Kiss all of you," he said, his words sounding mumbled.

"Well, that's not fair," she replied, and then she squealed when his lips took purchase on the inside of one of her thighs. "That tickles," she complained. "And your whiskers are... oh!" She inhaled sharply, and then she reached for whatever she could hold onto—a pillow and the top of his head—as the most delicious sensation she had ever experienced took her from the here and now.

She felt his chuckle vibrate the entire bed, and then he was suddenly up and over her, his mouth covering hers as his manhood slid through her quim in search of her opening. She lifted her knees to the sides of his thighs, gripping him as if she was holding on for dear life.

If there had been a maidenhead, it was soon breached, for Christina wasn't sure where she ended and he began. For all at once, he was deep within her, and a wet warmth spread through her entire abdomen.

She felt his ecstasy as much as heard it, his breath held for far too long, and his body tensed and his back arched, and his neck seemed to bend at an unnatural angle with his effort.

Then, as quickly as it had begun, it was over. He collapsed on top of her, his murmurs—and were those curses or prayers?—muffled, and his arms struggling to hold him up enough so he didn't squish her into the mattress.

Christina didn't dare move, although the hand that had somehow ended up atop his head slid over his silky hair before her fingers combed through it. The sensation of her fingernails scraping his scalp seemed to bring Richard back to life, for he groaned and then kissed her collarbone.

"Are you all right?" she asked in a whisper. She felt him chuckle again, and she grinned.

He lifted his head, although it seemed to take a Herculean effort to do so. "Well, I haven't died from embarrassment," he whispered.

It was Christina's turn to chuckle. "Whatever do *you* have to be embarrassed about?" she asked.

"You're far too arousing, my sweet," he replied. "I could not control myself. I wanted you to ... to be pleasured, and I fear I took mine far too soon." He lifted his body from hers, twisted, and landed on his back as Christina hissed.

"You were welcome to stay right where you were," she complained, immediately missing the intimacy of their coupling.

"I could not hold myself up," he replied, one arm reaching around her waist to pull her closer. "And I did not want you to suffocate."

She snuggled closer. "You're forgiven," she whispered, as one hand smoothed down his body and then over to rest atop his softened manhood.

"I must warn you that if you leave your hand as it is, then it will once again have a mind of its own," Richard warned in a whisper. "But not right away."

Christina grinned, despite seeing that his eyes were closed and his breathing was slow enough to suggest he was asleep. She leaned over and kissed him on the cheek.

After a time, she reached down for the bed linens and covered them both before returning her hand to its previous resting place, grinning when it moved slightly, as if in greeting.

She didn't mind a bit when it awakened and wanted more.

CHAPTER 45

DOUBLE THE WEDDING,
DOUBLE THE FUN

uesday night, Weatherstone Manor parlor, nearly seven o'clock in the evening

"Are you quite sure you wish to go through with this tonight?" George Bennett-Jones asked, his gaze surveying the beribboned ground floor parlor in Weatherstone Manor. Every surface in the room held a vase of flowers, and a multi-layered wedding cake covered in sugar frosting sat atop the tallest table. Off to one side of the room, the registrar, in whose office a civil service would usually be performed, was enjoying a glass of brandy as he conversed with Lady Weatherstone.

Apparently, Lord Weatherstone had some sway over the registrar. He had been able to convince the man to adopt the ground floor parlor as his temporary office for the sole purpose of performing the two ceremonies that evening.

George was fairly sure a bribe had been paid as well, but he didn't know it for a fact. All he could think was that his daughter's marriage might be remembered as the family's first Broomstick Marriage, so he was relieved to see there were no brooms in evidence.

Richard regarded his future father-in-law with a grin. "Are you having second thoughts?"

George shook his head. "Not at all. And neither is

Christina. I've never seen her as happy as she's been these past few days." He paused a moment. "But given everything that's happened to you in only a week's time, I would certainly understand if you wanted to hold off for a week or two or ten."

"Oh, no. I look forward to being a married man," Richard countered. He rolled his eyes. "I never thought I'd be saying those words so soon after my arrival in London, though."

"You're in good company," George remarked. "Given Lord Cougham is insisting on marrying Lady Vivian before you and Christina say your vows."

"I'm happy for him. Those two seem... well, perfect for each other," Richard hedged.

George chuckled. "A few years ago, I wouldn't have agreed. They were the epitome of opposites in all but their heights," he said with a grin. "But ever since his return from the Continent, Cougham has been different. His behavior is no longer notable. He doesn't drive coach-and-fours at break-neck speeds, nor is he gambling until the wee hours of the morning."

"From what you told me about Lady Vivian after dinner last week, it's apparent she is different as well," Richard remarked, remembering what Christina had told him in the park.

"Not so prim and proper," George agreed. "Which I think means they have met in the middle, so to speak."

Richard nodded. "I do hope Christina hasn't felt the need to change anything because of meeting me," he murmured.

George scoffed. "She is her mother's daughter in that regard, which means she'll..." He allowed his comment to trail off when he noticed his wife moving in his direction.

"Which means... what?" Richard prompted.

"Which means she is what she is, and she won't be changing on account of marriage," George whispered hoarsely. "It also means she'll probably expect frequent kisses and... other attentions."

"You say that as if you think I will not be wont to grant

them," Richard countered, a frown causing his brows to furrow.

George grinned as Elizabeth joined them. He leaned down and bussed her on the cheek. "You'd be wise to share them as often as you're able," he said before turning to his wife. "Hartwell hasn't changed his mind," he said.

"Of course he hasn't," she said with a brilliant smile. "And neither has Christina. She's ready, by the way."

"And what of the other couple?" George asked in a whisper.

Elizabeth inhaled slowly and said, "It seems they're not yet ready. They've asked that Christina and Richard go first."

George furrowed a brow and then remembered they were in Weatherstone Manor. Cougham had his apartment upstairs. "You don't suppose they're...?"

"Oh, I'm sure they are," Elizabeth said in delight before she hurried off to let the registrar know of the change.

A number of guests had taken seats in the parlor, including Violet Higgins. She looked stunning in a violet satin ballgown, and she held a hanky, apparently having trouble controlling her tears. Next to her were the Merriweathers, Rachel looking as if she was a cat who had eaten a canary. Next were Lord and Lady Reading, and behind them, a collection of aristocrats who insisted they wanted to pay witness to Cougham's wedding.

Apparently there were wagers on the line.

Even Christina's two brothers had come home from school for the ceremony. While Vivian's brother looked as if he wanted to be somewhere else, or at least next to the huge cake that dominated a round table at the back of the salon, he dutifully sat next to his mother as she wept into a hanky.

As the registrar moved to the front of the salon, silence fell over those in attendance.

The rest was a blur for Richard. He swore he would never forget Christina's appearance from a door that led out to the side gardens, though. In her royal blue silk de Naples ballgown, void of decoration but for the small bouquet of flowers she held, and her hair piled into a riot of curls atop her head, he thought she looked like one of Weatherstone's flowers come to life.

He offered his arm, watching as she placed a silk-gloved hand on it. "Are you nervous?"

"No. Should I be?" she countered in a whisper. Her eyes rounded. "You haven't changed your mind?"

Richard chuckled. "I have not, but there are a lot of people here."

"Oh course there are. This is what happens when my mother arranges a wedding."

Noting the registrar was moving in their direction, Richard came to attention. He knew he said some words. Repeated others. Christina said some words and repeated others. He slid a sapphire ring onto her finger, and then they were pronounced man and wife.

"That's it?" he whispered as Christina stood on tiptoe to kiss him.

"Well, it is, except for the rest of our lives," she murmured in delight.

He chuckled and bowed as those in attendance applauded, Christina curtsying and feeling as if she had played a part in the production of a play at a house party.

It was at that moment that Vivian appeared in the back of the salon, looking resplendent in a sky blue gown of satin with a gold sarcenet overdress. Her cheeks were rather rosy but devoid of a mouche.

Sebastian was suddenly behind him, and Richard turned to regard the Weatherstone heir with a smirk. "I thought you were going to wait until the library was available," he teased.

Rolling his eyes, Sebastian said, "We would be waiting all night. There's already someone in there," he groused.

At that moment, the Marquess and Marchioness of Morganfield appeared, looking rather sheepish when they realized they had missed their granddaughter's wedding.

Sebastian wasn't paying attention, though. His gaze settled on Vivian, and he made an incomprehensible sound in the back of his throat. "I should have done this years ago," he whispered as Vivian approached.

Richard led Christina to the side of the parlor, and they turned to watch as the registrar repeated the ceremony for the two people who had been destined to marry one another ever since Vivian's come-out.

Although Christina was determined to listen to every word of the short ceremony, she couldn't help but glance up at Richard. "Why did you wish to marry so quickly?" she whispered.

"To keep you for myself, of course," he replied, his attention on the other wedding. "My father—Hartwell—was a fool to take 'no' for an answer when he proposed. My mother might have gone off and accepted someone else's offer. I wasn't going to make that mistake."

Christina furrowed a brow. "But, I wasn't about to say 'no,'" she argued.

He grinned as he turned to regard her. "I didn't know that," he replied.

When applause once again erupted from those in attendance, Richard and Christina joined in. She was the second to kiss Vivian on the cheek, and accepted one from Sebastian in the fray that followed as loved ones crowded the two couples.

From his place next to Agnes, William stood holding a handkerchief to his face as tears streamed down his cheeks.

Agnes turned to stare at him in surprise. "Weatherstone, whatever is wrong?"

He shook his head. "Nothing, my sweet. Nothing at all. Everything is right as rain."

Sighing softly, Agnes took the handkerchief from him. "Give me that," she hissed, raising it to her eyes to dry her own tears.

"You never cry at weddings," William whispered.

"I've lost a wager," she replied with a watery grin.

"Over what?"

"This marriage. This wedding," she said as she sniffled.

William regarded her with a look of shock. "How much?"

"A hundred pounds."

William's eyes widened. "To whom?"

"Our son," she replied, her words interrupted by a sob.

The earl relaxed and then started to chuckle. "Oh, well played, Agnes. Well played," he said in delight.

When the faint strains of chamber music could be heard from the ballroom, the two took their leave of the salon.

The had a ball to host.

EPILOGUE

*L*ate November, 1840, Horncastle, Lincolnshire

Christina Bennett-Jones Hartwell, Viscountess Hartwell, regarded the expanse of water to her right with a happy expression. "Look at all the ships," she murmured as she pushed a perambulator along the path next to the Horncastle Canal. Her breaths came out in white puffs in the chilly autumn air. "There are more than there were last year."

"Indeed," her husband replied. "That one is off to Leeds," he said as he pointed to a barge carrying grain. "And that one is a passenger ship. A steam packet," he explained. He glanced into the perambulator. "Are you sure it's not too cold for him?" he asked, referring to his heir, Aaron Abraham Hartwell.

The one-year-old, who had already begun walking, was almost too large for the carriage. In a few months, the perambulator would be occupied by his brother or sister, and Aaron would be riding in the three-wheeled pram Richard had ordered in London prior to Parliament's adjournment.

"He's fine, darling. If I put any more blankets on him, he'll suffocate," she teased.

The boy in question kicked and squealed in delight at seeing his father's face.

"I don't recall ever being as happy as he is," Richard remarked. When Christina's expression instantly sobered, a look of hurt replacing her usual one of contentment, he quickly added, "At that age. As... as a child. I'm over the moon happy now, of course." He leaned over and bussed her on the cheek, a move he had learned would earn him quick forgiveness. "I find I adore being married, even if it means I don't spend as much time in the stables."

Christina's happy expression returned. "Do you recall why you were not happy? Did something awful happen in your youth?"

Richard considered the query a moment. "As I recall, my first father was a rather dour man back then. Very serious," he went on. "He didn't seem to want to *be* happy, at least until after I was done with university and back in Horncastle." He considered the timing. "Until he met Mother."

Christina furrowed a brow at hearing his comment. "Perhaps he feared his secret would be discovered," she said in a quiet voice. "Or revealed by your nursemaid, or someone else who knew who you really were. "

"Possibly," he agreed.

"Did you ever read all of the love letters you found in the study?" she asked then. From the way his face reddened, Christina knew he had. "Oh, now you really must share what you've learned."

He chuckled. "Well, as we suspected, he did know that Violet Higgins was my real mother..."

Christina inhaled softly.

"...but not until my twenty-fifth birthday."

Furrowing a brow, Christina considered the timing. "When you reached your majority," she said.

"Exactly. Apparently Reading kept a promise that he would share the information then. That's when my first father sought the company of Mother. He sent her an introductory letter saying he wished to meet her when he arrived in town for Parliament."

"Was there a letter in response?"

"There was," he said, chuckling as he recalled its contents. "My mother was cordial with her response. She wrote that she was not looking to take on clients but she had a couple of girls who might be able to accommodate him."

Christina's eyes rounded in delight. "Oh, dear," she murmured.

"I cannot imagine how he must have reacted," Richard remarked. "But he was persistent."

"He wrote back to her?"

"He did. He explained that he was not looking for a tumble but rather for the opportunity to introduce himself— to simply make her acquaintance. It wasn't until his third letter that he finally mentioned he had been married to her sister."

"Which your Mother must have already known," Christina argued.

"Exactly. But since Mother was never recognized by her siblings—they wanted nothing to do with her—she had no reason to make his acquaintance. Nor mine, as her supposed nephew," he explained.

"So... then what happened?"

"When he returned to London for Parliament a month later, he met her at The Queen of Hearts. Even though he wasn't a gambler, he would go there and play hazard so he would have an excuse to see her. Apparently it took almost the entire Season before she agreed to attend the theatre with him, and by then, he had won the hunting lodge from Reading along with a good deal of blunt from others."

Christina considered his words. "So, he knew that she was Arabella's sister. She knew he had a son, but thought you were her nephew."

"And because he didn't tell her otherwise, she had no reason to suspect I wasn't," Richard finished for her.

"Why do you suppose he commissioned the painting of her?"

Richard considered the query a moment. "I think because he spent half the year in Horncastle and merely wished to have an image of her that he could look upon every day," he replied. "Much like I do when I look upon the painting of you," he added with a grin.

The painting of the two of them had been done shortly after their quick wedding, the portrait painted by Laura Overby Simpson before she and her new husband, Henry, had departed London for a wedding trip. Richard and Christina hadn't taken their first trip together until Parliament adjourned in the early autumn, and then they merely relocated to Hartwell House for her confinement and the birth of Aaron.

The painting of Violet Higgins dressed as The Queen of Hearts still hung in the study above the fireplace mantel, the subject's red satin gown only slightly darkened by age.

"So why do you suppose he didn't tell her about you?"

"Ah, yes. That mystery," Richard murmured. "His plan was to tell her once she agreed to marry him. But after so much time had passed—and all those marriage proposals—my first father came to realize she would be angry he had kept the information from her. Rather than risk her wrath and a possible estrangement, he simply kept the information to himself."

"Coward," Christina said, scoffing. Her eyes rounded. "Oh, pardon. I shouldn't say such things about the dead."

Richard rolled his eyes. "I had a much worse reaction when I discovered the truth," he admitted. "But you had just told me you were with child again, and I thought it best to simply let sleeping dogs lie, so to speak."

"So... you've known a long time?" she asked in surprise as they approached their town coach. The driver hurried to help with the perambulator as she lifted Aaron from inside and into her arms.

"Just a few months," he said with a shrug. "The information was in a letter he had written to me when he was last in London. He had apparently discovered he wasn't going to live much longer—some physician told him he suffered from some sort of heart condition. He lived long enough to attend the rest of Parliament that Season and return to Horncastle. Lasted through the winter." He helped her into the coach and then followed, grinning when he saw that she had left room for him next to her.

"Where was the letter?" Christina asked as she settled Aaron onto her shoulder. The babe had fallen asleep at some point during their walk along the canal.

"I found it in a folio of documents that the solicitor in London gave to me. The same day I discovered I was Reading's son."

"Mr. Barton?"

"Junior, yes. Whilst he spoke with me and while I signed papers, I was left with the impression that he thought me... dull."

Christina chucked. "What? How can that be?"

"I was so ignorant of the truth, Tina. He actually said that there were two beneficiaries to my real mother's estate, and I didn't comprehend why he even mentioned it. And he acted as if I should have known I owned the townhouse in Park Lane. That I would inherit a hunting lodge."

Her eyes widened with understanding. "He assumed you knew everything, I suppose."

"And then, when I didn't, I suppose he thought I would simply discover it all once I read the papers in the folio." He raised his face to the ceiling and shook it. "I took that folio back to my townhouse and left it on my desk. I never even opened it. Packed it up and brought it with me when we came here last year." He shook his head. "That will teach me to read what a solicitor gives me."

Christina angled her head as she considered his words. "But... I wouldn't have found you in the park if you had stayed home and read those papers that day," she murmured.

Richard inhaled softly. "True."

"What would you have done if you *had* read those papers?"

His eyes darting about as if he knew he was about to find himself in a trap, Richard said, "I've no idea."

Christina scoffed. "Well, it's a good thing you didn't," she said with an impish grin. "However would I have fallen in love with you?"

"Oh, probably during Weatherstone's ball, during the second or third time we danced. Or maybe out in the gardens, when I kissed you senseless."

"You've become quite accomplished at kissing," she said as she giggled.

He chuckled as he leaned over and kissed her on the cheek. "I love you," he whispered.

Her grin widened. "Good. Because we're going to have a couple of guests arrive today."

"We are?"

"That steam packet you mentioned? On the canal?"

"Yes?"

"Bash and Viv are on it. They were to have arrived in Boston last night from the Mediterranean. I received a letter Viv sent from Athens with the schedule of their return trip."

Richard chuckled. "How long have you known they were arriving today?"

Christina aimed an odd look in his direction. "I've had the letter for nearly a week, and I thought I had read the whole thing, but..." She sighed. "I picked it up again this morning and only then saw their destination for today was Horncastle. Apparently they will take a traveling coach down to London in a few days."

"So, that's why you wished to walk along the canal," he accused with a grin.

"Partly," she agreed.

"We should go to the wharves," he said with some excitement. "Meet them there," he suggested as he raised his cane and knocked on the ceiling. The trap door opened and the driver's face appeared.

"Sir?"

"Take us to the wharves. To the one where the passenger ships disembark," Richard ordered.

"I hope you're not too disappointed in me," she murmured.

"Why would I be disappointed?"

"Because I didn't read the entire letter when I should have," she replied.

He kissed her again on the cheek and then on the lips. "Ah, then, we're even in that regard," he teased.

A half-hour later, Richard and Christina watched with broadening grins as Sebastian and Vivian made their way down the ramp from the steamship.

The two were not alone. A nursemaid carrying a rather large babe followed, as did a valet and a lady's maid.

"Tina!" Vivian shouted as she very nearly waddled down the ramp. "Aren't we a pair?" she added as she moved to embrace her best friend. They could barely wrap their arms around one another's shoulders given the size of their bellies, and Christina had to turn slightly in an effort to make more room.

"It looks as if you'll have your second baby much sooner than me," Christina claimed.

"Oh, I will," Vivian replied as Richard and Sebastian shook hands. "I was never this large with William," she claimed, indicating the boy who held onto his nursemaid.

"He looks as if he's already three years old," Richard remarked.

"He is tall," Sebastian replied proudly. "And this one is yours?" he asked turning to Aaron, who was sitting up in the perambulator, enjoying the excitement of the people who milled about.

"May I introduce Aaron Abraham Hartwell?" he acknowledged. "He doesn't yet know how to bow." He pointed to Sebastian's son. "William was born in Rome?" he asked.

"Indeed. We were staying in an apartment in a palace there at the behest of a duke I met the last time I was there.

The midwife who had seen to his daughter's babe delivered this one."

"So, you stayed in Rome the entire time?"

"Oh, no," Vivian said as she moved to lift Aaron from the pram. "When William was a month old, we went off to Greece. It's an excellent country in which to spend the winter, and the boat to Crete was not so bad. We were on that island for a few months." She placed a hand on her middle. "This one was conceived there," she whispered to Christina. "And then we returned to Athens."

Christina blushed. "When do expect you'll go into confinement?"

Vivian cleared her throat and seemed to consider how to respond before she said, "Oh, any day now."

"Viv!" Christina scolded, thinking her friend was teasing.

Sebastian took Aaron from Vivian and held him up above his head, giving the baby a slight shake and waving him about as he did so. Aaron giggled in delight. "Our luggage is being seen to, and if Mother is as efficient as I expect she is, there will be a traveling coach arriving for us from London on the morrow," Sebastian explained as he brought the babe down to rest in his crooked arm. "She was so happy to learn Viv had given me a boy, she and Father made the trip to Rome to meet him."

"And to see you, no doubt," Christina said as she took William from the nursemaid.

The boy stared wide-eyed at Christina and then, after giving her a tentative grin, hid his face on her shoulder. "Oh, he is a flirt," Christina said with a brilliant smile.

"Just like his father," Vivian agreed.

"I heard that," Sebastian said. He sighed. "Have you room for all this at Hartwell House?" he asked as he waved at the contingent of people and luggage that were gathered around them.

"Oh, yes, of course," Richard replied with a chuckle, taking his son from Sebastian. He had displayed a look of worry at seeing how the taller man behaved with the babe. "It will be good to have more in the house this time of the year. You're welcome to stay for as long as you'd like."

Now that the crush of passengers had cleared and the area around them wasn't so chaotic, Vivian took a moment to look around. "Careful, sir. You may find us staying until long after this babe is born," she warned, her hand going to her middle as she grimaced.

Christina gasped. "Viv, what's wrong?"

Vivian gave her a quelling glance. "Nothing's wrong. I'm just going to have a baby. Today, I think."

The Peeles stayed with the Hartwells for nearly a month, their daughter having made an appearance only a few hours after their arrival at Hartwell House. Then they set off for London, wishing to move into Weatherstone Manor before Christmas. The Hartwells would follow in late January in order to arrive in time for Parliament and the birth of their daughter, Violet.

The time together in Horncastle afforded their two boys the opportunity to play. Although neither could speak in anything other than gibberish, Christina was fairly sure they were plotting something. She could only hope it wasn't acts of derring-do or plans to drive phaetons at breakneck speeds in the middle of the night.

For the very briefest of moments, she wondered if Miss Pipkins might be available for hire.

AUTHOR'S NOTES

Mouches

From the French word for flies comes the name of artificial beauty marks that both men and women applied to their faces to cover syphilis sores or smallpox scars. They were usually made of black velvet or silk and cut into fanciful shapes such as stars, hearts and crescent moons as well as the round we tend to think of when someone mentions a beauty spot. Fashionable from the sixteenth century in France through the eighteenth century, mouches were stored in small hinged patch boxes, or *boîte à mouches* (box of flies) and kept on dressing tables.

Horncastle Canal

Horncastle, a market town for several centuries, experienced an economic boom in 1802 when the eleven-mile canal was dug and connected to the existing Tattershall Canal.

The canal was the brainchild of Sir Joseph Banks. Although he was best known as a botanist, Sir Joseph was also a patron of the sciences and an entrepreneur. Wanting to improve Lincolnshire's economy, he encouraged local landowners and businessmen to support the idea of a canal in 1786. When the Horncastle Canal was opened, the River Bain was deepened and straightened to allow 50-ton ships to navigate all the way to wharves at Horncastle, linking the town to the River Witham and the Wash.

Canal barges transported grain, coal, and wool to Leeds and Wakefield, and steam packets carried passengers to Lincoln and Boston. When the railway arrived in 1855, use of the canal waned, and it was finally closed in 1878.

The canal cuts and basins are still evident today.

Civil Marriage Licenses

The Marriage Act of 1836 re-introduced civil marriage to England and also allowed ministers of other faiths, such as Roman Catholics, Hindus, and Muslims, to act as registrars. The act was contemptuously referred to by some in the Anglican faith as the "The Broomstick Marriage Act", since they didn't believe such marriages should be recognized. They thought of them as "sham marriages," some of which involved the participants jumping over a broomstick (the plant, *common broom*, not the household sweeping tool).

The Act allowed marriages to be legally registered in buildings belonging to other religious groups. Religious groups could apply for registration for their buildings with the Registrar General, and they could subsequently conduct weddings if a Registrar and two witnesses were present. For Lord Weatherstone to arrange for his house to host a wedding meant finding a registrar willing to register it as such and perform the ceremony. Unlikely? Possibly. But an offer of money in exchange for such consideration was not out of the question.

Parliamentary Sessions

Unlike 1837-1838, when there were multiple sessions of Parliament, 1839's Parliament was in session from February 5 until August 27. Although we could have set our stories in the series to match those dates, young love works much better in the spring.

Thank you for taking the time to read The Vixen of a Viscount. *If you enjoyed it, please consider telling your friends or posting a short review. Word of mouth is an author's best friend.*

Thank you,
Linda Rae Sande

ABOUT THE AUTHOR

A self-described nerd and student of history, Linda Rae spent many years as a published technical writer specializing in 3D graphics workstations, software and 3D animation (her movie credits include SHREK and SHREK 2). Getting lost in the rabbit holes of research has resulted in historical romances set in the Regency-era as well as Ancient Greece.

A fan of action-adventure movies, she can frequently be found at the local cinema. Although she no longer has any tropical fish, she follows the San Jose Sharks and makes her home in Cody, Wyoming.

For more information:
www.lindaraesande.com
Sign up for Linda Rae's newsletter:
Regency Romance with a Twist
Follow Linda Rae's blog:
Regency Romance with a Twist